Praise for *Last Gentleman Standing*

"Traditional Regency romance reminiscent of Georgette Heyer and Sylvia Thorne. Ashford brilliantly captures the atmosphere and mores of the period with her pitch-perfect dialogue and characterizations. A delightful read for true fans of the Regency."

—*RT Book Reviews*, 4 stars

"Ashford's flawless execution of this classic plot, as well as her lively, crisply witty writing style, should prove to be catnip to readers who miss traditional Regencies."

—*Booklist*

"Jane Ashford has become synonymous with outstanding classic Regency romances and this story is proof of why."

—*Night Owl Reviews* TOP PICK

Praise for *The Duke Knows Best*

"Fans of The Duke's Sons series will want to add this conclusion to their shelves...there's plenty of wit, matchmaking, sweetness, and sensuality to keep readers highly entertained."

—*RT Book Reviews*

"With her usual flair for subtle characterization and polished writing expertly leavened with dry wit, Ashford delivers another superbly crafted addition to her Duke's Sons series...required reading for fans of cleverly conceived, smartly written Regency historical romances."

—*Booklist Online*

Also by Jane Ashford

The Duke's Sons
Heir to the Duke
What the Duke Doesn't Know
Lord Sebastian's Secret
Nothing Like a Duke
The Duke Knows Best

Once Again a Bride
Man of Honour
The Three Graces
The Marriage Wager
The Bride Insists
The Bargain
The Marchington Scandal
The Headstrong Ward
Married to a Perfect Stranger
Charmed and Dangerous
A Radical Arrangement
First Season / Bride to Be
Rivals of Fortune / The Impetuous Heiress
Last Gentleman Standing

Brave New
EARL

JANE ASHFORD

sourcebooks
casablanca

Published by Sourcebooks Casablanca, an imprint of Sourcebooks,
Inc.
P.O. Box 4410, Naperville, Illinois 60567-4410
(630) 961-3900
Fax: (630) 961-2168
sourcebooks.com

Printed and bound in the United States of America.
OPM 10 9 8 7 6 5 4 3 2 1

Prologue

As Benjamin Romilly, the fifth Earl of Furness, walked down Regent Street toward Pall Mall, tendrils of icy fog beaded on his greatcoat and brushed his face like ghostly fingertips. The rawness of the March evening matched his mood—cheerless and bleak. He couldn't wait to leave London and return to his Somerset home. He'd come up on business, annoyingly unavoidable, not for the supposed pleasures of society. His jaw tightened. Those who complained that town was empty at this time of year were idiots. Even though walkers were few in the bitter weather, he could feel the pressure of people in the buildings around him—chattering, laughing, as if there was anything funny about life. It grated like the scrape of fingernails across a child's slate.

Some invitations couldn't be refused, however, and tonight's dinner was one. His uncle Arthur was the head of his family and a greatly respected figure. Indeed, Benjamin felt a bit like an errant child being called on the carpet, though he could imagine no reason for the feeling. He didn't see his uncle often.

Well, lately he didn't see anyone unless he had to. He walked faster. He was running late. He'd had trouble dragging himself out of his hotel.

He turned onto Piccadilly and was instantly aware of several figures clustered in the recessed entry of a building on the right, as if the light from the tall windows could warm them. Ladybirds, not footpads, Benjamin recognized, even as a feminine voice called out, "Hello, dearie." One of them moved farther into the strip of illumination that stretched from the window, her appearance confirming his judgment.

Benjamin strode on. She hurried over to walk beside him. "A fine fella like you shouldn't be alone on a cold night," the woman said. "Look at the shoulders on him," she called to her colleagues. "And a leg like a regular Adonis."

"No, thank you," said Benjamin.

She ignored him. "Such a grim look for a handsome lad. Come along, and I'll put a smile on your face, dearie. You can believe I know how." She put one hand on his sleeve to slow him and gestured suggestively with the other.

"I'm not interested." Paint couldn't hide the fact that she was raddled and skinny. Gooseflesh mottled her nearly bare breasts, on display for her customers. She must be freezing, Benjamin thought. And desperate, to be out on a night like this one. He pulled out all the coins he had in his pocket. Shaking off her hand, he pushed them into it. "Here. Take this."

She quickly fingered them. "Ooh, you can get whatever you want for this, dearie. Some things you haven't even dreamed of, mayhap."

"Nothing." Benjamin waved her off and moved on. Some plights could be eased by money, he thought. There was a crumb of satisfaction in the idea. When so much misery was intractable.

"Think you're so grand," the woman screeched after him. "Shoving your leavings at me like a lord to a peasant."

Benjamin didn't bother feeling aggrieved. It was just the way of the world. Things went wrong. Good intentions got you precisely nowhere. And he didn't blame her for resenting the position she'd found herself in. He pulled his woolen scarf tighter about his neck and trudged on.

Stepping into the warmth and conviviality of White's was like moving into a different world. The rich wood paneling and golden candlelight of the gentlemen's club replaced the icy fog. There was a buzz of conversation and a clink of glasses from both sides of the entryway. Savory smells rode the air, promising a first-rate meal.

Surrendering his coat and hat to a servitor, Benjamin was directed to a private corner of the dining room, where he found his uncle standing like a society hostess receiving visitors.

Arthur Shelton, Earl of Macklin, was nearly twenty years Benjamin's senior, but he hardly looked it. The dark hair they shared showed no gray. His tall figure remained muscular and upright. His square-jawed, broad-browed face—which Benjamin's was said to echo—showed few lines, and those seemed scored by good humor. Benjamin shook his mother's brother's hand and tried to appear glad to be in his company.

"Allow me to introduce my other guests," his uncle said, turning to the table behind him.

Benjamin hadn't realized there was to be a party. If he'd known, he wouldn't have come, he thought. And then he was merely bewildered as he surveyed the three other men who comprised it. He didn't know them, and he was surprised that his uncle did. They all appeared closer to his own age than his uncle's near half-century.

"This is Daniel Frith, Viscount Whitfield," his uncle continued, indicating the fellow on the left.

Only medium height, but he looked very strong, Benjamin observed. Brown hair and eyes and a snub nose that might have been commonplace but for the energy that seemed to crackle off him.

"Roger Berwick, Marquess of Chatton," said his uncle, nodding to the man in the center of the trio.

This one was more Benjamin's height. He was thinner, however, with reddish hair and choleric blue eyes.

"And Peter Rathbone, Duke of Compton," said their host.

Clearly the youngest of them, Benjamin thought. Not much past twenty, he'd wager, and nervous looking. Compton had black hair, hazel eyes, and long fingers that tapped uneasily on his flanks.

"Gentlemen, this is my nephew Benjamin Romilly, Earl of Furness, the last of our group. And now that the proprieties are satisfied, I hope we can be much less formal."

They stood gazing at one another. Everyone but his uncle looked mystified, Benjamin thought. *He* felt as if he'd strayed into one of those dreams where you show up for an examination all unprepared.

"Sit down," said his uncle, gesturing at their waiting table. As they obeyed, he signaled for wine to be
poured. "They have a fine roast beef this evening. As
when do they not at White's? We'll begin with soup
though, on a raw night like this." The waiter returned
his nod and went off to fetch it.

The hot broth was welcome, and the wine was
good, of course. Conversation was another matter.
Whitfield commented on the vile weather, and the
rest of them agreed that it was a filthy night. Compton
praised the claret and then looked uneasy, as if he'd
been presumptuous. The rest merely nodded. After a
bit, Chatton scowled. Benjamin thought he was going
to ask what the deuce was going on—hoped someone
would, and soon—but then Chatton took more wine
instead. All their glasses were emptied and refilled
more rapidly than usual.

It wasn't simply good manners or English reti-
cence, Benjamin concluded. Uncle Arthur's innate
authority and air of command were affecting these
strangers just as they did his family. One simply
didn't demand what the hell Uncle Arthur thought
he was doing.

Steaming plates were put before them. Eating
reduced the necessity of talking. Benjamin addressed
his beef and roast potatoes with what might have
appeared to be enthusiasm. The sooner he finished,
the sooner he could excuse himself from this awkward
occasion, he thought. He was about halfway through
when his uncle spoke. "No doubt you're wondering
why I've invited you—the four of you—this evening.
When we aren't really acquainted."

Knives and forks went still. All eyes turned to the host, with varying degrees of curiosity and relief.

"You have something in common," he went on. "*We* do." He looked around the table. "Death."

Astonishment, rejection crossed the others' faces.

The older man nodded at Benjamin. "My nephew's wife died in childbirth several years ago. He mourns her still."

In one queasy instant Benjamin was flooded with rage and despair. The food roiled dangerously in his stomach. How dared his uncle speak of this before strangers? Or anyone? All Benjamin asked was that people let him be. Little enough, surely? His eyes burned into his uncle's quite similar blue-gray gaze. Benjamin saw sympathy there, and something more. Determination? He gritted his teeth and looked away. What did it matter? The pall of sadness that had enveloped him since Alice's death fell back into place. He made a dismissive gesture. No doubt his tablemates cared as little for his history as he did for theirs.

Uncle Arthur turned to the man on his left. "Frith's parents were killed in a shipwreck eight months ago on their way back from India," he continued.

The stocky viscount looked startled, then impatient. "Quite so. A dreadful accident. Storm drove them onto a reef." He looked around the table and shrugged. "What can one do? These things happen."

Benjamin dismissed him as an unfeeling clod, even as his attention was transfixed by his uncle's next bit of information.

"Chatton lost his wife to a virulent fever a year ago."

"I didn't *lose* her," this gentleman exclaimed, his

thin face reddening with anger. "She was dashed well *killed* by an incompetent physician and my neighbor who insisted they ride out into a downpour."

He looked furious. Benjamin searched for sadness in his expression and couldn't find it. Rather, he looked like a man who'd suffered an intolerable insult.

"And Compton's sister died while she was visiting a friend, just six months ago," his uncle finished.

The youngest man at the table flinched as if he'd taken a blow. "She was barely seventeen," he murmured. "My ward as well as my sister." He put his head in his hands. "I ought to have gone with her. I was invited. If only I'd gone. I wouldn't have allowed her to take that cliff path. I would have—"

"I've been widowed for ten years," interrupted their host gently. "I know what it's like to lose a beloved person quite suddenly. And I know there must be a period of adjustment afterward. People don't talk about the time it takes—different for everyone, I imagine—and how one copes." He looked around the table again. "I was aware of Benjamin's bereavement, naturally, since he is my nephew."

Benjamin cringed. He could simply rise and walk out, he thought. No one could stop him. Uncle Arthur might be offended, but he deserved it for arranging this...intolerable intrusion.

"Then, seemingly at random, I heard of your cases, and it occurred to me that I might be able to help."

Benjamin noted his companions' varying reactions— angry, puzzled, dismissive. No one, not even his formidable uncle, could make him speak if he didn't wish to, and he didn't.

"What help is there for death?" said the marquess. "And which of us asked for your aid? *I* certainly didn't." He glared around the table as if searching for someone to blame.

"Waste of time to dwell on such stuff," said Frith. "No point, eh?"

Compton sighed like a man who despaired of absolution.

"Grief is insidious, almost palpable, and as variable as humankind," said their host. "No one can understand who hasn't experienced a sudden loss. A black coat and a few platitudes are nothing."

"Are you accusing us of insincerity, sir?" demanded Chatton. He was flushed with anger, clearly a short-tempered fellow.

"Not at all. I'm offering you the fruits of experience and years of contemplation."

"Thrusting them on us, whether we will or no," replied Chatton. "Tantamount to an ambush, this so-called dinner."

"Nothing wrong with the food," said Frith, his tone placating. He earned a ferocious scowl from the choleric marquess, which he ignored. "Best claret I've had this year."

Benjamin grew conscious of a tiny, barely perceptible, desire to laugh. The impulse startled him.

"Well, well," said his uncle. "Who knows? If I've made a mistake, I'll gladly apologize. Indeed, I beg your pardon for springing my idea on you with no preparation. Will you, nonetheless, allow me to tell the story of my grieving, as I had hoped to do?"

Such was the power of his personality that none of

the younger men refused. Even Chatton merely glared at his half-eaten meal.

"And afterward, should you wish to do the same, I'll gladly hear it," said Benjamin's uncle. He smiled.

Uncle Arthur had always had the most engaging smile, Benjamin thought. He suddenly recalled a day twenty years past, when his young uncle had caught him slipping a frog between a bullying cousin's bed-sheets. That day, Uncle Arthur's grin had quirked with shared mischief. Tonight, his expression showed kind-ness and sympathy and the focus of a keen intellect. Impossible to resist, really.

In the end, Benjamin found the talk that evening surprisingly gripping. Grief had more guises than he'd realized, and there was a crumb of comfort in know-ing that other men labored under its yoke. Not that it made the least difference after the goodbyes had been said and the reality of his solitary life descended upon him once more. Reality remained, as it had these last years, bleak.

One

Benjamin rode over the last low ridge and drew rein to look down on his home. It was a vast relief to be back, far from the incessant noise of London. The mellow red brick of the house, twined with ivy, the pointed gables and ranks of leaded windows, were as familiar as his face in the mirror. Furness Hall had been the seat of his family for two hundred years, built when the first earl received his title from King James. The place was a pleasing balance of grand and comfortable, Benjamin thought. And Somerset's mild climate kept the lawn and shrubberies green all winter, though the trees were bare. Not one stray leaf marred the sweep of sod before the front door, he saw approvingly. The hedges were neat and square—a picture of tranquility. A man could be still with his thoughts here, and Benjamin longed for nothing else.

He left his horse at the stables and entered the house to a welcome hush. Everything was just as he wished it in his home, with no demands and no surprises. He'd heard a neighbor claim that Furness Hall had gone gloomy since its mistress died—when he thought

Benjamin couldn't hear. Benjamin could not have cared less about the fellow's opinion. What did he know of grief? Or anything else, for that matter? He was obviously a dolt.

A shrill shout broke the silence as Benjamin turned toward the library, followed by pounding footsteps. A small figure erupted from the back of the entry hall. "The lord's home," cried the small boy.

Benjamin cringed. Five-year-old Geoffrey was a whirlwind of disruptive energy. He never seemed to speak below a shout, and he was forever beating on pans or capering about waving sticks like a demented imp.

"The lord's home," shouted the boy again, skidding to a stop before Benjamin and staring up at him. His red-gold hair flopped over his brow. He shoved it back with a grubby hand.

Benjamin's jaw tightened. His small son's face was so like Alice's that it was uncannily painful. In a bloody terror of death and birth, he'd traded beloved female features for an erratic miniature copy. He could tell himself it wasn't Geoffrey's fault that his mother had died bringing him into the world. He *knew* it wasn't. But that didn't make it any easier to look at him.

A nursery maid came running, put her hands on Geoffrey's shoulders, and urged him away. Staring back over his shoulder, the boy went. His deep-blue eyes reproduced Alice's in color and shape, but she'd never gazed at Benjamin so pugnaciously. Of course she hadn't. She'd been all loving support and gentle approbation. But she was gone.

Benjamin headed for his library. If he had peace and

quiet, he could manage the blow that fate had dealt him. Was that so much to ask? He didn't think so.

Shutting the door behind him, he sat in his customary place before the fire. Alice's portrait looked down at him—her lush figure in a simple white gown, that glory of red-gold hair, great celestial-blue eyes, and parted lips as if she was just about to speak to him. He'd forgotten that he'd thought the portrait idealized when it was first finished. Now it was his image of paradise lost. He no longer imagined—as he had all through the first year after her death—that he heard her voice in the next room, a few tantalizing feet away, or that he would come upon her around a corner. She was gone. But he could gaze at her image and lose himself in memory. He asked for nothing more.

❧

Three days later, a post chaise pulled up before Furness Hall, uninvited and wholly unexpected. No one visited here now. One of the postilions jumped down and rapped on the front door while the other held the team. A young woman emerged from the carriage and marched up as the door opened. She slipped past the startled maid and planted herself by the stairs inside, grasping the newel post like a ship dropping anchor. "I am Jean Saunders," she said. "Alice's cousin. I'm here to see Geoffrey. At once, please."

"G-geoffrey, miss?"

The visitor gave a sharp nod. "My…relative. Alice's son."

"He's just a little lad."

"I'm well aware. Please take me to him." When the

servant hesitated, she added, "Unless you prefer that I search the house."

Goggle-eyed, the maid shook her head. "I'll have to ask his lordship."

Miss Saunders sighed and began pulling off her gloves. "I suppose you will." She untied the strings of her bonnet. "Well? Do so."

The maid hurried away. Miss Saunders removed her hat, revealing a wild tumble of glossy brown curls. Then she bit her bottom lip, looking far less sure of herself than she'd sounded, and put her hat back on. When footsteps approached from the back of the hall, she stood straighter and composed her features.

"Who the deuce are you?" asked the tall, frowning gentleman who followed the housemaid into the entryway.

Unquestionably handsome, Jean thought. He had the sort of broad-browed, square-jawed face one saw on the tombs of Crusaders. Dark hair, blue-gray eyes with darker lashes that might have been attractive if they hadn't held a hard glitter. "I am Alice's cousin," Jean repeated.

"Cousin?" He said the word as if it had no obvious meaning.

"Well, second cousin, but that hardly matters. I'm here for Geoffrey."

"*For* him? He's five years old."

"I'm well aware. As I am also aware that he is being shamefully neglected."

"I beg your pardon?" Benjamin put ice into his tone. The accusation was outrageous, as was showing up at his home, without any warning, to make it.

"I don't think I can grant it to you," his unwanted visitor replied. "You might try asking your son for forgiveness."

She spoke with contempt. The idea was ridiculous, but there was no mistaking her tone. Benjamin examined the intruder with one raking glance. She looked a bit younger than his own age of thirty. Slender, of medium height, with untidy brown hair, dark eyes, and an aquiline nose, she didn't resemble Alice in the least.

"I've come to take Geoffrey to his grandparents," she added. "Alice's parents. He deserves a proper home."

"His home is here."

"Really? A house where his dead mother's portrait is kept as some sort of macabre shrine? Where he calls his father 'the lord'? Where he is shunted aside and ignored?"

Benjamin felt as if he'd missed a step in the dark. Put that way, Geoffrey's situation did sound dire. But that wasn't the whole truth! He'd made certain the boy received the best care. "How do you know anything—"

"People have sent reports to let his grandparents know how he's treated."

"What *people*?" There could be no such people. The house had lost a servant or two in recent years, but there'd been no visitors. He didn't want visitors, particularly the repellent one who stood before him.

"I notice you don't deny that Geoffrey is mistreated," she replied.

Rage ripped through Benjamin. "My son is *treated* splendidly. He is fed and clothed and…and being taught his letters." Of course he must be learning them. Perhaps he ought to know a bit more about the details of Geoffrey's existence, Benjamin thought, but that didn't mean the boy was *mistreated*.

Two postilions entered with a valise. "Leave that on the coach," Benjamin commanded. "Miss…won't be staying." He couldn't remember the dratted girl's name.

"It doesn't matter," she said. "Take it back. I'm only here to fetch Geoffrey."

"Never in a thousand years," said Benjamin.

"What do you care? You hardly speak to him. They say you can't bear to look at him."

"They. Who the devil are *they*?"

"Those with Geoffrey's best interests at heart. And no sympathy for a cold, neglectful father."

"*Get out of my house!*" he roared.

Instead, she came closer. "No. I won't stand by and see a child harmed."

"How…how dare you? No one lays a hand on him." Benjamin was certain of that much, at least. He'd given precise orders about the level of discipline allowed in the nursery.

"Precisely," replied his infuriating visitor. "He lives a life devoid of affection or approval. It's a disgrace."

Benjamin found he was too angry to speak.

"Please go and get Geoffrey," the intruder said to the hovering maid.

"No," Benjamin managed. He found his voice again. "On no account." His hand swept the air. "Go away," he added. The maid hurried out—someone who obeyed him, at least. Though Benjamin had no doubt that word was spreading through the house and the rest of his staff was rushing to listen at keyholes.

"Would you prefer that I report you to the local magistrate?" his outrageous visitor asked. "That would be Lord Hallerton, would it not? I inquired in advance."

She scowled at him, immobile, intolerably offensive. Benjamin clenched his fists at his sides to keep from shaking her. While he was certain that any magistrate in the country would side with him over the fate of his son, he didn't care to give the neighborhood a scandal. It seemed that spiteful tongues were already wagging. Who were the blasted gossips spreading lies about him to Alice's parents? The tittle-tattle over this female's insane accusations would be even worse.

The two of them stood toe to toe, glaring at each other. Her eyes were not simply brown, Benjamin observed. There was a coppery sparkle in their depths. The top of her head was scarcely above his shoulder. He could easily scoop her up and toss her back into the post chaise. The trouble was, he didn't think she'd stay there. Or, she'd drive off to Hallerton's place and spread her ludicrous dirt.

The air crackled with tension. Benjamin could hear his unwanted guest breathing. The postilion, who had put down the valise and was observing the confrontation, eyed him. Would he wade in if Benjamin ejected his unwelcome visitor? He had a vision of an escalating brawl raging through his peaceful home. Actually, it would be a relief to punch someone.

Into the charged silence came the sound of another carriage—hoofbeats nearing, slowing; the jingle of a harness; the click of a vehicle's door opening and closing. What further hell could this be? Benjamin had long ago stopped exchanging visits with his neighbors. None would dare drop in on him.

When his uncle Arthur strolled through the still-open front door, Benjamin decided he must be dreaming. It was the only explanation. His life was a carefully orchestrated routine, hedged 'round with safeguards. This scattershot of inexplicable incidents was the stuff of nightmare. Now if he could just wake up.

His uncle stopped on the threshold and surveyed the scene with raised eyebrows. "Hello, Benjamin. And Miss…Saunders, is it not?"

"You *know* her?" Benjamin exclaimed.

"I believe we've met at the Phillipsons' house," Lord Macklin replied.

The intruder inclined her head in stiff acknowledgment.

Benjamin could believe it. His lost wife's parents were a fixture of the *haut ton*. Entertaining was their obsession. One met everyone in their lavish town house, a positive beehive of hospitality. Indeed, now he came to think of it, he was surprised they'd spared a thought for Geoffrey. Small, grubby boys had no place in their glittering lives. "And do you know why she's here?" he demanded, reminded of his grievance.

"How could I?" replied his uncle.

Too agitated to notice that this wasn't precisely an answer, Benjamin pointed at the intruder. "*She* wants to take Geoffrey away from me."

"Take him away?"

"To his grandparents," Miss Saunders said. "Where he will be loved and happy. Rather than shunted aside like an unwanted poor relation."

Benjamin choked on a surge of intense feelings too

jumbled to sort out. "I will not endure any more of these insults. Get out of my house!"

"No. *I* will not stand by and see a child hurt," she retorted.

"You have no idea what you're talking about."

"*You* have no idea—"

"Perhaps we should go into the parlor," the older man interrupted, gracefully indicating an adjoining room. "We could sit and discuss matters. Perhaps some refreshment?"

"No!" Benjamin wasn't going to offer food and drink to a harpy who accused him of neglecting his son. Nor to a seldom-seen relative who betrayed him by siding with the enemy, however illustrious he might be. "There's nothing to discuss, Uncle Arthur. I can't imagine why you suggest it. Or why you're here, in fact. I want both of you out of my home this—"

"*Yaah!*" With this bloodcurdling shriek, Geoffrey shot through the door at the back of the entry hall. Clad in only a tattered rag knotted at the waist, his small figure was smeared with red. For a horrified moment Benjamin thought the swirls were blood. Then he realized it was paint running down the length of his son's small arms and legs. Shrieking and brandishing a tomahawk, the boy ran at Miss Saunders. He grabbed her skirts with his free hand, leaving red streaks on the cloth, and made chopping motions with the weapon he held. Fending him off, she scooted backward.

In two long steps, Benjamin reached his small son, grasped his wrist, and immobilized the tomahawk— real and quite sharp. Benjamin recognized it from a display shelf upstairs.

Geoffrey jerked and twisted in his grip, his skin slippery with paint. "Let go! I'm a red Indian on the warpath." He kicked at Benjamin's shins. As his small feet were bare, it didn't hurt. His red-gold hair was clotted with paint, too, Benjamin noted. There were a couple of feathers—probably chicken—stuck in the mess.

His son began to climb, as if Benjamin was a tree or a ladder. Paint rubbed off on his breeches, his coat. Because of the tomahawk, Benjamin couldn't let go of the boy's wrist. He grabbed for him with his other hand.

Geoffrey lunged, caught the ball of Benjamin's thumb between his teeth, and bit down. "Ow!" Benjamin lost his grip. Geoffrey thudded to the floor, frighteningly close to the blade he held. But he was up at once, unscathed. The rag he was wearing fell off. Geoffrey capered about stark naked, waving the tomahawk and whooping. A drop of blood welled from Benjamin's thumb and dropped onto his waistcoat.

The immensely dignified Earl of Macklin knelt, bringing his head down to Geoffrey's level. "Which tribe do you belong to?" he asked.

The boy paused to examine Benjamin's uncle. Benjamin edged around to take his son from behind. But it was no good. Geoffrey spotted the maneuver and raised his weapon.

Benjamin's uncle Arthur waved him back. "Your ax is from the Algonquian tribe, I believe," he said to Geoffrey.

The boy blinked his celestial-blue eyes. "You know about red Indians?"

"Your grandfather was very interested in them.

He showed me his collections and told me stories he'd gathered."

Benjamin wondered when his father had had an opportunity to share his fascination with artifacts from the Americas with Uncle Arthur. He didn't remember any such sessions. Perhaps when he was away at school?

"Grandfather," repeated Geoffrey. He said the word as if he'd never heard it before. A pang of emotion went through Benjamin. Gritting his teeth, he pulled out his handkerchief and tied it around his bleeding thumb.

"Your father's father," added the earl, nodding at Benjamin.

Geoffrey turned to look. There was something unsettling in his blue gaze, Benjamin thought. Not accusation precisely; rather a speculation far beyond his years. And nothing at all like the gentle inquiry characteristic of his dead mother.

A gangling lad in worn clothing erupted from the rear doorway through which Geoffrey had come and skidded to a halt beside the boy. "You said if I reached down the paint, you'd stay in the schoolroom," the new lad said. "Where's your *clothes*?"

"No," said Geoffrey. He was holding the tomahawk down at his side as if to conceal it, Benjamin noticed.

"You gave me your word," argued the newcomer. He was a dark-haired boy of perhaps fourteen, with hands and feet that promised greater height and sleeves that exposed his wrists. Benjamin had no idea who he was.

"Didn't!" declared Geoffrey. "Never said it." The little ax came up in automatic defense.

"Where did you get that?" cried the older lad, clearly horrified.

Geoffrey laughed. He danced in a circle, waving the tomahawk.

In a move that looked well practiced, the youth stepped forward, snapped out a blanket from under his arm, threw it over Geoffrey, and quickly wrapped him up like an unwieldy package. Picking up the squirming bundle, he attempted a bow. "Beg pardon, your lordship," he said, backing toward the rear of the house. Muffled shouts of protest mixed with laughter came from the woolen folds. They faded as the door closed behind the young duo.

Silence fell over the entryway. Benjamin's uncle stood up. The postilion was staring like a spectator at a raree-show. Miss Saunders brushed at the drying paint on her skirts. She looked shaken. "You allow Geoffrey to play with…hatchets," she accused.

"That thing was on a shelf ten feet up," Benjamin said. He was pretty sure that was the spot. "In a locked room. I'm certain it's locked." Wasn't it always? "I've no notion how he got it."

"Precisely. You know nothing about your own son! Who can tell what other dangers surround him? I'm surprised he hasn't been killed."

"Nonsense."

"And was that…rustic youngster your idea of a proper caretaker?"

Unable to supply any information about this person, and aware that appreciation of his ability to truss up a wriggling miscreant would not be well received, Benjamin ground his teeth.

"I must take Geoffrey to the Phillipsons at once," his unwanted visitor added.

"Drag him into your post chaise and rattle off together?" asked Uncle Arthur amiably.

Benjamin nearly growled at him. Then he noticed Miss Saunders's expression. The prospect of sharing a carriage with his naked, paint-smeared, ax-wielding son clearly daunted her. He could almost enjoy that. Indeed, if he hadn't been defending his home from invasion, he might have laughed at the scene just past. Before taking steps to see that it never recurred, of course.

"It seems to me that we need a bit of time to consider the situation," his uncle added. "I know I would appreciate a chance to get acquainted with my great-nephew." This latter sentiment seemed perfectly sincere.

Miss Saunders muttered something. The word *savage* might have been included.

"I won't have her in my house!" Benjamin said.

"I've no wish to stay with a monster of selfishness!"

But in the end, his uncle somehow persuaded them. Benjamin was never sure, afterward, how he'd come to agree. Was it simply easier? Had he been that desperate to escape his two unwanted guests and shut himself in the library again? And why had he promised to review his son's educational program with these near-strangers? It was none of their business. And he was not afraid of what he might discover. Absolutely not. Even though he had no idea what it might be. Finally alone again, he sank into his familiar chair and put his head in his hands.

❧

Upstairs, Jean Saunders sat on the bed in her allot-
ted chamber, hands folded in her lap, jaw tight, and
contemplated a rescue mission gone seriously awry.
Her plan had been simple, efficient. She would swoop
in, collect Geoffrey, and be gone. She should be on
her way back to London by now. Her cousin Alice's
husband had been portrayed as so deeply sunk in
mourning that he didn't care what happened in his
household. Hadn't he? Where had she gotten that
notion? She'd expected to face a drooping, defeated
fellow who might welcome a relief from responsibility, not a gimlet-eyed crusader blazing with outrage.
How could people have characterized that…master-
ful man as broken by grief? His eyes had practically
burned through her. He'd pounced like a jungle cat to
restrain his rampaging son.

Jean let out a long—not entirely unappreciative—
breath at the memory. Still, the gossip about his
lordship's shameful neglect of Geoffrey was clearly on
the mark. The boy was like some sort of wild animal.
If he'd landed a blow with that hatchet… Folding her
arms across her chest, Jean realized that she'd expected
Geoffrey to be a cherubic child, like the smiling illus-
tration on top of a chocolate box. She'd envisioned
him in a little blue suit with a lace collar, dimpled
and pink, putting his arms around her neck and softly
thanking her for rescuing him. She'd thought to take
his little hand and lead him off to happiness. Nothing
could be more unlike the reality of a naked, prancing
imp painted red, shrieking, and bent on mayhem. The
maniacal glee in his eyes!

She let her arms fall to her sides and sat straighter,

gathering her tattered resolution. It wasn't Geoffrey's fault that he hadn't been taught manners—or any vestige of civilized behavior, apparently. That was the point, wasn't it? He deserved far better. He must be guided and nurtured. She'd come here to save him, and she was going to do so. Hadn't she nagged the Phillipsons half to death to make them offer refuge to their grandson? If Lord Furness found out the whole plan was her idea, and that Geoffrey's grandparents were far from enthusiastic… Well, he could hardly be angrier than he was now.

Jean gripped the coverlet with both hands. He'd been furious. Standing up to him had been like confronting a force of nature. Perhaps he cared about his child after all? She'd be glad of that, naturally. Yet he hadn't been affectionate with Geoffrey. And the boy had bitten him! What sort of bond was that?

No, Jean was all too familiar with neglectful parents. Geoffrey needed a new home. Probably her host was worried about his reputation and resented being exposed and thwarted. An old adage floated into Jean's mind. *Like father, like son.* Did Geoffrey get his wild ways from his parent? A shiver passed through her. With a grimace, she banished it. She'd vowed never to be afraid again, and one blustering earl wasn't going to cow her. Still less a five-year-old child.

The streaks of red paint on her gown caught Jean's eye. She'd had to promise the Phillipsons that she'd take care of establishing their grandson once he was in London, seeing that he had the proper attendants. They were far too busy to bother with a child. It had seemed a trivial condition at the time, with her righteous indignation in full flood. Jean's chocolate-box vision wavered into her mind again, immediately replaced by the naked, whooping reality. But Geoffrey would improve with gentle guidance and plenty of affection. Wouldn't he? Quite quickly? Jean had no brothers or sisters. Indeed, she'd never had much to do with children of any stripe. Had she made a mistake?

No. Jean pushed off the bed and stood up like a soldier reporting for duty. She knew what it was like to be a miserable child. Memories of cold, dark silence rushed over her, setting her heart pounding and making her mouth dry. With practiced determination, she shoved them away. She'd come here to do the right thing. She would fight, and she would prevail.

Two

ARTHUR SLIPPED HIS ARMS INTO THE EVENING COAT HIS valet was holding for him and waited while Clayton smoothed it over his shoulders. The mirror told him that they had achieved his customary understated elegance. "What word among the household?" he asked. "What do they say about young Geoffrey?"

Clayton looked thoughtful. The man had been with the earl for more than twenty years, and Arthur valued his canny insights as much as his personal services. "Opinions vary, my lord, depending on how close the person is to the young heir. Concerning the incident today, the general suspicion is that Master Geoffrey was playing a prank. He does not habitually run about the house clad in a tea towel, I gather."

"That tomahawk was no toy," Arthur pointed out.

Clayton nodded. "Yet he didn't actually strike anyone, I understand. Even under, er, provocation. He's said to be an intelligent child. Apparently, he can read."

"I should hope so, at five years old. Who taught him, I wonder?"

"People were reluctant to discuss the exact

arrangements of the nursery with an outsider," Clayton said. "Particularly after the housekeeper entered the kitchen."

"Hmm."

"Yes, my lord. The head gardener is of the opinion that the boy disguises what he can and can't do and is devious in bargaining for what he wants."

"At his age?" Arthur replied. "That would be precocious indeed."

"The junior kitchen maid believes he is possessed by the devil."

Arthur laughed. His valet didn't, but his eyes showed amusement. "It sounds as if he might become a son for a father to be proud of."

"Lord Furness doesn't wish to be bothered with the boy," his valet replied. "Everyone agreed on that. The servants here are expected to manage everything on their own and shoulder the blame for any upsets, while their master shuts himself up in the library. Or goes hurtling across the countryside on a demon of a horse, as the head groom put it." One who knew Clayton well, which the earl did, could hear a touch of disapproval in his tone.

"Who was that lad with the blanket this morning? The one I told you about."

Clayton nodded again. "There's something of a mystery about him, my lord. No one would say much. The cook did allow that *unconventional* people had stepped forward to keep Geoffrey out of his father's way. The housekeeper silenced her with a look."

"I see. Well, I'll find out sooner or later. Clearly, my nephew needs a bit of bothering."

"That sort of decision is not up to the servants," Clayton said.

"Of course not. So I've taken it on." Or it had taken him on, the earl thought wryly. He hadn't anticipated Miss Jean Saunders's impulsive trip to Somerset, or her demand for possession of Geoffrey. When he'd heard of her departure, and her plan, on one of his regular visits to the Phillipsons, he'd had to scramble to catch up. Fortunately, he had better horses. The young lady was more...forceful than he'd realized.

He'd meant to apply some force, Arthur admitted silently. Nothing else he'd tried had lifted Benjamin from his miasma of grief, so sad to see. However, just now, Arthur felt like a swimmer overtaken by a flash flood. His deep sympathy for the four young men he'd gathered at a table at White's was carrying him into uncharted waters. Speaking of which... "Did you send off those letters I gave you?" he asked Clayton.

"Yes, my lord."

"Good."

The valet cleared his throat. Arthur knew the sound of old. "A problem?"

"I observed a stain on Lord Furness's lapel." Clayton's fingers flexed as if he was itching to get his hands on the garment in question.

Arthur hadn't noticed, but Clayton had a gimlet eye for such things. "My nephew is looking a bit unkempt." His dress was careless, and he needed a haircut.

"Apparently, his valet left more than a year ago and has not been replaced. Lord Furness is attending himself. A groom is seeing to his boots."

Here was a situation bound to offend Clayton's exacting standards, Arthur thought. "I see."

"Something should be done, my lord."

"I can't hire staff in another man's house." He had enough on his plate already, Arthur thought.

"I thought I might offer my services. Temporarily."

"Really, Clayton?" Would Benjamin realize what a favor he was being granted?

"And be on the lookout for someone about the place I could train," the valet added.

Arthur had a sudden vision of the scene—Benjamin, the immoveable object, wishing to be left to his own untidy devices; Clayton, the irresistible force, insisting on a high degree of polish. This might be another way to jostle Benjamin out of his prolonged funk. "That's very kind of you, Clayton."

"Thank you, my lord."

తે

In a bedchamber a few doors away, Jean looked down at the only evening gown she'd brought with her, a serviceable coral muslin, now wrinkled from the valise. In this moment, it was a distinct disappointment. She would have liked to sweep downstairs looking stunning, she realized, and she was sorry she hadn't brought a prettier dress. Which was doltish. She'd packed for a daring rescue, not a country house visit. This was not an occasion for dipping necklines and flattering drapery. Even so, a scene flashed through Jean's mind—she in her amber silk, floating down the staircase, while the powerful master of this house gazed up at her, dazzled. His blue-gray eyes startled, his lips parted in astonished admiration.

A lock of brown hair sprang out over her brow, dissipating this silly vision. She pushed it back with another hairpin. Her thick, curly locks were difficult to manage. They always seemed to have a mind of their own, which did not include smoothly demure styling. Jean hadn't brought her maid on this brief journey, and she missed Sarah now. The housekeeper had been cordial but firm. She had no one to spare to help Jean dress. The kitchen maid, who had answered the door when their unexpected visitors arrived, was needed by the cook. Indeed, everyone was run off their feet. Jean had gotten the impression of a household teetering on the brink of collapse, barely held together by the housekeeper's skill and loyalty.

Jean bit her lower lip. She mustn't get distracted; the state of Furness Hall wasn't her concern. Her present hosts expected her back to help them with their extensive entertainments during the London season. She was as appreciated there as she was uninvited and unwelcome here. Also, it wasn't proper to stay without a hostess in residence. She had to fulfill her mission and depart soon.

Her stomach growled, loudly, as it was all too likely to do when she was hungry. Jean suppressed a wince. Her mother had railed at her for this unladylike trait. As if she did it on purpose! She couldn't help it if some quirk of her constitution punished her for skipping meals. She required regular, substantial fuel, and her body let her know when she didn't get it. Mama had taken it as a personal insult that Jean never grew plump on this regimen, another transgression to add to her long list.

The gurgling came again. Time to go down to dinner and press on, even if none of this journey was going as she'd intended.

Dinner was not a comfortable meal, but Benjamin didn't care. He hadn't invited his two companions, and he didn't feel obliged to act the cordial host. His uncle made some remarks about the countryside and his journey. Miss Saunders responded, and Benjamin left them to it as he brooded about his disrupted life. All he asked was to be left alone. Was that so unreasonable? Apparently these two intruders thought so.

They didn't linger at table. Benjamin led them to the library afterward, eager to get this disruption over with and be rid of his guests. They could be off first thing in the morning. Before he left his bed, preferably. As his uncle and Miss Saunders found seats, he rang the bell. His housekeeper and the nursery staff were awaiting the summons. Geoffrey would be in bed by now. Or ought to be, certainly. Had better be.

A timorous nursery maid arrived first, with Mrs. McGinnis close behind her. Benjamin stood to receive them. "Where's Nanny?" he asked.

"She retired and went to live with her sister in Devon," answered the housekeeper.

"What? When did that happen?"

"Two years ago." Mrs. McGinnis's expression was bland. "I did discuss it with you, my lord. There was the matter of her pension."

"Oh, right." Actually, Benjamin didn't remember. Two years ago had been a bad time for him. "Why didn't we hire a new nurse?"

"We did. Two. The first didn't care for the… conditions here. And you dismissed the second."

"I?" What could Mrs. McGinnis be talking about?

"The third time she tried to consult you about Master Geoffrey, you told her to get out and never come back. She did."

Was his own housekeeper trying to make him look bad, Benjamin wondered, conscious of Miss Saunders's disapproving gaze. He'd thought they got along well enough, but Mrs. McGinnis was sounding remarkably dry. He plumbed his memory. "She carped and whined, didn't she? And sniveled. She told me Geoffrey ought to be locked up." In his peripheral vision, Miss Saunders moved. Some kind of involuntary twitch, it seemed to Benjamin. "Perhaps Nanny could come back temporarily," he suggested.

"She's eighty this year," his housekeeper replied. "And not too well, I understand."

"Ah, I'm sorry to hear that." Nanny had been his mother's nurse and then his. But he hadn't realized she was quite that old. He turned to the nursery maid. "So you care for Geoffrey now?"

The girl gave a nervous nod.

"Lily took over after Christmas, when our last nursery maid left us," the housekeeper supplied.

"Said she'd rather scrub floors," the nursery maid added. "But I thought I could manage. Which I nearly didn't. And then Tom came along to help."

"Tom?" There was a charged silence. Benjamin grew even more conscious of his audience. But there was nothing for it; he couldn't hide the fact that he knew of no Tom on his household staff.

"Is that the young man with the blanket from this morning?"

The housekeeper nodded. "Yes, my lord. That was Tom."

"Tom who? What is his last name?"

Mrs. McGinnis straightened like a soldier facing enemy interrogation. "I don't know."

"You don't know?"

"He doesn't have any knowledge of his family or their name."

Benjamin wondered if his uncle was judging him. Miss Saunders undoubtedly was. He could practically feel her disapproval oozing over him. He wanted this finished in short order. "Explain Tom to me," he demanded. "At once."

His housekeeper nodded. She looked resolute but not particularly guilty. "Two months ago, Master Geoffrey ran away. We all turned out to search, of course, but we couldn't find him."

"Why was I not—"

"It was that time you were in Bath, my lord. We were just about to send for you when Tom turned up with him. He—Tom, that is—had been wandering the countryside, and he came across Geoffrey. He convinced him to return home."

From the look on the nursery maid's face, this was a significant feat.

"We found that Geoffrey would listen to young Tom as he would to no one else," Mrs. McGinnis continued. "They get along a treat. And when I saw that Tom was a cheerful, respectful lad, taking no liberties and offering no back talk, I allowed him to stay on."

"For months," Benjamin said. "When you know nothing about him?"

"I know quite a bit about him," the housekeeper answered. "But mostly I know he's a good lad. I know he watches out for Master Geoffrey like no one else has been able to do because the child won't let them."

"Allowing him to paint himself red and get hold of a tomahawk!" Benjamin pointed out.

"It's not a question of *allowing* with that little—" The nursery maid broke off, flushing.

"I did try to speak to you about this, my lord," said Mrs. McGinnis. "You directed me to manage things as I saw fit and leave you alone. Again."

Her tone was definitely critical this time, Benjamin thought. And perhaps she had a point, little as he liked hearing it. He ought to have known who was in charge of the nursery. "Let's have this Tom in and talk to him," he said.

A few minutes later, the lad came into the library, and Benjamin got a closer look at him. Tom had a homely, round face, friendly blue eyes, and prominent front teeth. Benjamin thought his appearance might improve in a few years, when he grew into his features and the large bones showing in his hands and wrists. The boy was thin, but if Benjamin knew his housekeeper, that was due to rapid growth rather than lack of food. Tom grinned, not looking at all apprehensive.

"Hello, Tom," said Benjamin.

"Milord. Was you wanting me to move on away from here? Figured you would, sooner or later." He didn't sound worried about the prospect, and his smile didn't waver.

"I wanted to find out a bit more about you," Benjamin replied. "Mrs. McGinnis says you haven't given a last name."

Tom nodded. "Don't know it. Been on my own since I was small."

"But what about your parents?" asked Miss Saunders from the sofa at the fireside.

"I don't recall them, miss. First thing I remember is the streets of Bristol, scrounging about in the garbage tips for food. I've thought I might have wandered off a ship at the docks. Or maybe I was born in the workhouse and m'mother died."

"No one looked after you?" Miss Saunders appeared horrified.

Tom shrugged, seeming not at all bothered. "It happens, miss."

"How did you live? How old are you?"

"Somewhere's about fourteen, miss, best I can reckon."

"You're not sure?"

Tom shook his head.

"And you've spent all your life alone?" She clenched her hands in her lap, her coppery eyes large with sympathy.

"Oh no, miss. Not at all. I found plenty of places, here and there, as time went on. Got taken in by an orphanage for a bit when I was small. Then I swept floors for a greengrocer. I spent a year at a dame school, doing odd jobs and seeing to the fires and all. The missus taught me to read, and my numbers, too." He was obviously proud of these accomplishments.

"Didn't you want to stay there?" Benjamin asked. "Or were you thrown out?"

"No, sir, I was not. The missus wanted me to stay, but I'd learnt all she had to teach me, see. So I went and ran the bellows for a blacksmith a bit of a while. And worked for a fellow who pickled eels. I like to know how things work, see."

"How did you end up here?" Benjamin asked. He found the lad likable, but he had some ground to make up in oversight of his household.

Tom smiled and nodded as if he was well aware of Benjamin's thoughts. "I got tired of Bristol, my lord. Seemed noisy and dirty all at once. Also, seems I've a yen to move. After a bit, I want someplace new. So one day I just set off south."

"Walking?" said Miss Saunders. "All this way?"

"Not all at once, miss. I took my time. To see what I could see." He smiled again.

Benjamin almost envied his easy attitude. "And you encountered Geoffrey."

"I did. *Hiding* in a hollow log with his feet sticking out for anyone to see. I asked him what was toward, gave him a bit of my bread and cheese, and we got to talking."

What did his son talk about, Benjamin wondered. He ought to know. "Mrs. McGinnis tells me you brought him home."

"Of course, milord."

"You might have left him and gone on. He had nothing to do with you. Or you could have taken him along on your wanderings, I suppose."

For the first time, Tom looked disturbed. "That woulda been wrong."

"Why?" Benjamin asked.

"Well." Tom frowned, seeming to grope for words. "Young Geoffrey ain't like me. He's a… regular person. Got a home and family. Belongs here."

Miss Saunders made a sound. Benjamin ignored it. "So regular that he paints himself red and threatens people with a dangerous weapon?" she asked.

"I can*not* see how he got holt of that thing," Tom complained. "He knows such stuff is not allowed. But that boy can be slippery as any eel I ever saw. He gets up in the night betimes, when you think he's sound asleep."

The nursery maid nodded confirmation of this. "I sleep right in the room, but he slips past me. I can't stay awake all night. And then when I go to dress him in the morning, his feet are black with dust. His hair full of cobwebs sometimes. When I ask how he got so dirty, he just laughs at me."

Briefly, Benjamin wished they would all just go away and let him sink back into peaceful gloom. Only yesterday, he'd enjoyed quiet solitude in this chamber, unaware of the chaos looming. But the gimlet-eyed Miss Saunders wouldn't just disappear. Nor would his interested uncle, who appeared to be stifling a laugh, damn his eyes. And clearly, something had to be done about Geoffrey.

"I can go first thing in the morning if you want, my lord." Tom was genial and respectful and apparently undaunted by the prospect of homelessness.

The housekeeper and the maid looked apprehensive. Benjamin thought his uncle's laugh would escape this time. He didn't check Miss Saunders's expression. "We'll leave things as they are for now," he said.

"While I, er, take stock." And tried to form a plan for dealing with his son.

The nursery maid slumped in relief. Mrs. McGinnis almost smiled. She touched Tom's arm and ushered the two of them out. To Benjamin's surprise, his uncle went with them. A blessed silence fell over the room.

Except... Miss Saunders sat on the sofa, hands still folded in her lap, and a comprehensive critique of his character on her tongue, no doubt. She certainly looked disapproving, and primed to speak, and...really rather pretty. A curl of brown hair had escaped its pins and fallen over her brow, as if to point out the fine bones of her face. Her eyes crackled with intelligence and conviction, that coppery sparkle very much in evidence. If her lips hadn't been pressed together—to hold back disparaging remarks, no doubt—they would have been beguilingly full, a lovely rose pink.

A vagrant spark illuminated Benjamin's inner gloom. He found himself moving and then sitting beside her. "Well, have at it," he said.

"What?"

"Tell me what a dreadful person I am."

Jean had been thinking something like that, but his urging and his expression gave her pause. The melancholy cast of his handsome face reminded her of an image of Sir Galahad she'd seen in a stained-glass window. Dark lashes made his blue-gray eyes startlingly vivid. It was disconcerting to have him so close. From inches away, there was no denying the power of his presence. But nothing excused his cavalier treatment of his son. "Well, it's even worse than I expected," she said.

"It?"

Briefly she was lost in the intensity of his gaze. "Geoffrey." She must stay focused; she had a mission. "Your son, Geoffrey. Who is growing up completely unsupervised, apparently, except by a vagabond."

"That seems a harsh description for young Tom," he replied.

To herself, Jean admitted that the boy had been likable—and oddly reassuring somehow. As if he could definitely be trusted. But that didn't excuse the situation. "He isn't a proper teacher. Geoffrey needs to learn responsibility and the skills to fulfill his future position in life. What if he decided follow Tom's example and wander off across the country?"

"Like a 'red Indian'?" asked her host. He smiled.

A tremor ran through Jean. A simple change in expression should *not* be able to alter a man so completely. That wasn't credible. Or fair. Lord Furness wasn't warm or sympathetic. She'd seen how he was, how he treated his child. But his smile was like a sudden burst of sunshine through that stained-glass window she'd pictured. He was illuminated, and the result left her breathless.

At a loss, she fell back on stored outrage. "You find that prospect amusing?"

"No. Of course not."

His smile died. Jean dismissed her sharp pang of regret.

"You are unmarried," he said.

He had no right to examine her in that searching way. *She* had no reason to feel flustered. "Obviously. As I told you, I am *Miss* Saunders."

"A spinster, in short. What do you know about rearing children?"

"I know what everyone knows. That they require love and *attention*." The chocolate-box boy drifted through her mind again. Those truisms would have sufficed for him. Would they for the untamed Geoffrey?

"Because you're a woman, you know this?"

Jean was immediately conscious of being a woman in the close company of a very attractive man. His arm lay across the back of the sofa. One muscular leg was crossed over the other. He was bent a little toward her, satirically attentive, and he seemed to fill her mind as well as her vision. What did she know? Anything? She hadn't questioned her mission before meeting Geoffrey, or really planned for afterward, except in the vaguest way. "I know that your child would benefit from a father's firm but kind guiding hand," she managed.

"Do you? How fortunate for you. My father never provided such a service. Perhaps yours was a paragon?"

Jean felt herself flush. She would *not* talk about this. Or think of her late father and his string of mistresses. She barely remembered what he'd looked like.

"Did he guide you in this exemplary way?" her companion asked.

"He lived in London."

"And you did not?"

"No." Jean braced to repel any further intrusive questions. This was none of his business. And who was he to judge fathers—or daughters, for that matter?

"So he was absent in reality. Rather than in the next room and oblivious. Which seems worse somehow."

Jean stared and saw her surprise mirrored in his expression. He hadn't meant to say that, obviously.

"My father spent most of his time right here in this room," Lord Furness added. He looked around as if seeing the library with new eyes. The view appeared to unsettle him. "I was brought in occasionally to be... viewed."

"Scolded, you mean?" Jean wondered.

"No. My mother and Nanny took care of that, when necessary. Just to affirm my existence, I think. As the son and heir." He looked perplexed.

She gazed at him. His face was forbidding again. That smile seemed like a dream.

"I am *not* sending Geoffrey away," he said fiercely, surprising her. "If you think you can force me to do so, you are delusional."

Jean's righteous indignation came flooding back. "If you think I'll leave him in his present state, you do not know me!"

"A lack for which I can only be grateful."

She sprang to her feet, more hurt than she wished to admit. Why had she stayed here alone with him? He was impossible. And it wasn't proper. Jaw tight, Jean stalked out, heading for her bedchamber.

Benjamin sat on, solitary, as he liked to be, in his usual refuge. His pulse, which had accelerated, gradually slowed. He told himself that he welcomed the silence. Hadn't he been wishing for it? Solitude was solace. He'd have to find a way to be rid of Miss Saunders—and his uncle, too—tomorrow. Why had he allowed them to stay this long?

He had a sense of being watched. He looked up at the portrait of Alice, meeting its serene blue eyes. He could find no resemblance to her irritating cousin in those perfect features. Alice had been quiet not disruptive, gentle not argumentative. "What do you think of our son?" he asked.

Of course, there was no answer, and never would be. Alice wouldn't see Geoffrey listen to reason and give up his ferocious behavior. Grow tall, go to school, whatever else the future might bring. She was gone.

Gloom rolled over Benjamin, submerging all else. He slumped, resting his head on the back of the sofa. He was so very tired.

Three

Arthur Shelton lingered at the breakfast table the following morning, wondering when the other denizens of Furness Hall would appear. It felt rather like waiting for the curtain to rise on a new play—one where he was both audience and…accidental instigator. There was a neat phrase. Now if he could just ensure that the action of this drama benefited all the players. In a life that had been full of responsibility, this was a new sort. He buttered a second excellent scone. His nephew's staff had a number of deficiencies, but the cook was outstanding.

Miss Saunders came in as he ate. She wore the same dress she'd arrived in, still showing signs of the red paint Geoffrey had smeared on it, suggesting she hadn't packed a great variety of clothing. "Good morning," Arthur said. "I hope you slept well."

"Not terribly well." She sat down opposite him.

"I am sorry."

"Did you hear a sort of…screech in the middle of the night?" asked Miss Saunders as she filled her cup from the teapot.

"A screech?"

She frowned. "That's not the right word. The noise was high-pitched, but it also had a whispering quality. I don't know what to compare it to."

"I heard nothing. Are you worried the house is haunted?"

Miss Saunders looked surprised. "I thought it might be an owl outside my window. Or Geoffrey playing a prank, since they said he gets up at night."

She was an eminently sensible young lady, Arthur noted. Pleasant and intelligent, if a bit more forceful than he'd realized when he met her at the Phillipsons'. She'd impressed him before he'd learned of her connection to Alice and her strong views on children. She was pretty, too, which Benjamin was bound to appreciate. And the way her hair tended to spring from its pins, as if making a bid for freedom, added a piquancy to her character.

"It's so odd that you're here," she went on, helping herself to a scone. "I came because of a rather unusual conversation we had at the Phillipsons'."

This called for a diversion. Arthur was aware that his actions skirted very close to interference. Or to be honest—which he always tried to be, at least in his mind—they fell right into that category, a place he'd never thought to find himself. But he couldn't sit by and watch Benjamin grieve his life away. "Didn't we discuss how our families are related?" he said.

"Well, yes, but—"

"My sister was married to Benjamin's father, you know." He'd noticed her interest in his deceased brother-in-law yesterday.

"So you were friends with the previous Lord Furness."

"I'm not sure I could call him a friend. My visits were too few, and he never came to London. Ralph and I were acquainted certainly."

"What sort of man was he?"

Arthur was mildly puzzled by the question. But he was happy to talk of this rather than explain the hints he'd let drop at the Phillipsons' about neglected children. "He was scholarly. That's the best way to describe him. He was happiest delving into a new book or scientific paper, adding to his extensive stock of knowledge. He might have been better suited to a university post than the position he was born into. He did his duty by the estate, but he much preferred his studies. His chief area of interest was the native peoples of North America."

"Red Indians," said Miss Saunders.

"I wonder where Geoffrey picked up that name? Ralph thought it stupidly inaccurate. He was fond of telling people—on the rare occasions when the matter came up in conversation—that they are neither red nor Indian."

She looked puzzled.

"It's a pity he's not here," Arthur went on. "Ralph would be only too glad to explain that the explorers who first encountered the native tribes were looking for a sea route to India. They called them Indians because they thought they'd succeeded. At first."

Miss Saunders appeared to consider this and file it away. "So he was more interested in his studies than his family?"

Arthur nodded. "He cared for my sister. I have

no doubt about that. But otherwise…that seems a fair statement."

"It's a legacy that just goes on, isn't it?" She sounded bitter. "Some people should not be allowed to be parents!"

Here was the fire that had caught Arthur's attention in the beginning. "Such a ban would be difficult to enforce."

Rather than reply, Miss Saunders bit into her scone and chewed in an oddly vengeful way.

"I thought we might speak with Geoffrey this morning," Arthur said.

She cocked her head.

"If there is to be a change in his living arrangements—"

"As there must be!"

"We should find out what he would like," he concluded.

Miss Saunders looked startled, then thoughtful. "You'd ask him?"

Arthur nodded. "He's allowed an opinion. Or an inclination, shall we say, at his age. He won't have everything his own way, of course. He is a small child."

She had put down her scone and was examining him closely. "You are an unusual man," she said.

This was not a line of thought he wished to encourage. It might lead to questions about how the current situation at Furness Hall had come to be. The earl rose. "I'll fetch Benjamin."

Miss Saunders didn't object. She simply watched him go. Intelligent indeed, Arthur thought. It would be best to keep her mind busy with topics other than himself. He'd line up a list of subjects. An idea occurred to him. This young lady might offer a canny female perspective on his other projects.

Arthur found his nephew still in his bedchamber, engaged in a battle of wills with Clayton. Benjamin could not know—yet—the futility of opposition. "Good morning," Arthur offered.

"It might be, if I was allowed to dress in peace," growled Benjamin. He reached for a coat hung on the bedpost.

"Not that one, my lord," said the valet.

"One coat is as good as another," Benjamin replied impatiently.

Clayton's impassivity wavered momentarily at this heresy. "There is a small stain on that one, which I will be happy to—"

"No, there isn't."

The valet silently indicated the stain. It was hardly noticeable, Arthur thought. Until one's attention was drawn to it.

Benjamin sighed. "Very well." He tossed the coat on the bed and turned toward the wardrobe. Clayton was there before him, opening the doors. "Don't get in there," protested Arthur's nephew. "Ah, you are in."

After a rapid, expert inventory, Clayton chose a coat from those in the wardrobe and brought it over to help Benjamin put it on. "If you will let me have your boots this evening, I'll see what I can do." He averted his eyes from Benjamin's footgear as if the sight pained him.

"Isn't that rather beneath your touch?" Benjamin asked.

Arthur was glad to hear amusement in his tone this time. A feud between his nephew and his valet would be awkward. "Clayton has a special formula for top boots," he said. "Mine are the envy of the fashionable world."

Clayton didn't show satisfaction, though Arthur knew he felt it. His expression stiffened when Benjamin glanced at Arthur's boots and said, "Nice gloss."

"I would also be happy to cut your hair, my lord." The valet got his own back through a dry, critical tone.

Benjamin ran his hand through his undeniably shaggy locks. "Deuce take it. I hate haircuts."

The earl had rarely seen Clayton at a loss, but this pronouncement clearly astonished him. "Hate them, my lord?"

"All that fussing about my head. With sharp blades." Benjamin made a throwaway gesture. "You'll have to content yourself with my boots."

Gathering up the stained coat, Clayton bowed himself out, dissatisfaction in every line of his immaculate form.

"Your valet is a petty tyrant," Benjamin said when he was gone.

"There's nothing petty about Clayton," Arthur replied.

Benjamin turned from the cheval glass, gathering his floating thoughts. They'd been dominated by a pair of sparkling brown eyes for the last little while. Some earlier musings returned to his mind, centering on the nature of coincidence. "Tell me again how you became acquainted with Miss Saunders."

"It was at a rout party, I believe. We were talking of our families and discovered they were connected. I came to see if you're ready to talk to Geoffrey."

An uncomfortable combination of annoyance and guilt distracted Benjamin. "He is my son. I require no *readiness*."

"Precisely. Shall we go and find him?"

He went out before Benjamin could reply, much less object. And by the time he caught up, he found Miss Saunders with his uncle, the two of them waiting at the foot of the stairs like sentinels. He walked between them, without wishing his other self-invited houseguest good morning, and started up. "Let's get this over with."

The nursery at Furness Hall lay in a wing that jutted from the back of the main block, putting it quite a distance from the public rooms. A large space on the third floor, painted a faded blue, it was an irregular chamber of peaked ceilings and dormer window nooks. When Benjamin entered, the books on the shelves, the long table with mismatched chairs at one end, the slightly shabby cushions, and boxes of toys were instantly familiar. The cone-shaped tent made of draped blankets was new, as was the clutter of dry branches, leather scraps, and pebbles on the floor nearby.

The nursery maid sitting by the fire jumped to her feet when they entered, dropping her mending. She appeared to be alone. "Where is Geoffrey?" asked Benjamin.

The makeshift tent shuddered. Tom crawled through a flap and stood. Geoffrey emerged behind him. At least he was dressed this time and clean, Benjamin thought. "Ah, there you are."

"Have you made a blanket castle to play in?" asked Miss Saunders. Her tone was all sweetness, nothing like the way she habitually spoke to Benjamin.

"It's a tepee," replied Geoffrey, his tone and expression contemptuous.

"A…" She looked bewildered.

Benjamin hadn't spent sixteen years around his father for nothing. "A type of dwelling used by the native tribes on the prairies of North America," he supplied. "And you shouldn't answer so rudely, Geoffrey."

His small son simply looked at him. Those blue eyes might be shaped and colored like Alice's, but she'd never given him such a stony look, Benjamin thought.

"We've come to ask you what sort of things you might like to do," his uncle said. Benjamin felt a spurt of annoyance at the interference.

Geoffrey's response was immediate. "I want to go to the gorge at Cheddar."

"Nonsense," declared Benjamin, just as quickly. "That's no place for a child."

"Geoffrey should be allowed to choose," said Miss Saunders.

She seemed to delight in contradicting him, Benjamin thought. If he said the sky was blue, she'd probably argue the point.

"Is it something to do with cheese?" she asked. "I like cheddar very much." She smiled at Geoffrey, who ignored her as effectively as a haughty grande dame might any toadeater.

Benjamin didn't entirely blame him. Miss Saunders had no idea what she was talking about.

"I've heard there's a warm spell coming up," said his uncle. "Your head gardener, who's said to be a weather oracle, reckons a taste of spring is on the way. Perhaps we could put together a picnic."

"At the gorge," said Geoffrey.

Tom, who had stood silently by till now, said, "I could chase after him, my lord. Make certain he don't get into trouble. He's been wanting to see that place for ages." From his expression, it appeared that young Tom was curious about the gorge as well. "I told him nothing doing, of course. Not without permission."

Everyone looked at Benjamin, even the nursery maid whose name he'd forgotten—all of them primed to cast him as the villain of the piece. Well, he wouldn't be. And on their heads be it. "Fine. A picnic. In March. What could go wrong?"

Geoffrey leaped into the air, waving his arms and shouting in triumph. Miss Saunders started visibly at the noise.

"Let's go and consult the housekeeper about arrangements," said Benjamin's uncle. "What is her name?"

"Mrs. McGinnis," said Geoffrey. His small face turned sly. "She'll make Cook give us muffins, if *you* ask her."

"Splendid."

Benjamin wasn't quite sure how it happened, but the earl swept Geoffrey, Tom, and the maid along in his wake, leaving him alone with Miss Saunders. He was making a habit of this, Benjamin thought. It was beginning to seem suspicious.

"So generous of you to grant a little boy a small treat," his remaining companion said.

"Small? The gorge at Cheddar is a steep, dangerous place, full of caves to lure in curious children and lose them. We'll have to watch Geoffrey every minute to make certain he stays safe."

Miss Saunders looked daunted; Benjamin enjoyed her expression. "I didn't know. You might have said so."

"Yes, and be the sole voice forbidding, as you say, his treat. I didn't care for the role. But please don't encourage my son to think he can always get his own way."

"As opposed to never getting it?"

Could this admittedly very pretty female have any idea how annoying she was? "Are you trying to turn Geoffrey against me? Is that your game? I won't allow it."

"I would never do such a vile thing!" exclaimed Miss Saunders.

"So you draw the line at kidnapping?"

"I do not... I wouldn't—"

"You came here meaning to take him from me. If you'd managed to bundle him into your carriage, would you have waited for my permission?"

He watched her face, a pleasure in itself. And even more so as her irritation faded into doubt. "This inflammatory language is not helping our situation," she said.

"Inflamm—" Benjamin surprised himself by laughing. "Our? In what sense is anything *ours*? There is no *our*. We're speaking of *my* son, in *my* house. You really have no business here, Miss Saunders."

It was unfair that his smile should be so distracting, Jean thought. He turned it on her like a secret weapon. And it very nearly worked. "I meant that such provocation is not a way to reach agreement."

"Agreement on what?"

Why did the word fluster her when he said it? She'd had a point, hadn't she? "Surely there are things we can agree on?" she managed.

"You think so?" He smiled again, as if he found her amusing.

Jean's temper flared; she refused to be laughed at. "Geoffrey needs a sensible routine. No one could argue with that."

"Do you always speak in absolutes?" He met her eyes as if trying to see what lay behind them. "But I won't dispute this one. He does."

"And you must pay more attention to him."

"Again a *must*. I might quibble over the phrasing, but I will allow it."

Weary of his superior tone, Jean said, "Now you."

"I? What?"

"You suggest something we can agree on."

"Why should I? This is your game. You're the cause of this whole uproar."

"I'm not sorry!" She might be beset by doubts over methods, but the central fact remained. "Geoffrey deserves better than what he has received up to now."

Briefly, the earl was silent, his handsome face unreadable. He didn't appear angry, but certainly not contrite either. "I believe we can agree that the weather in March is a chancy thing," he said.

"That isn't fair."

"How so?"

"It's too true."

"Can a thing be *too* true?"

"Stop repeating words back to me like some sort of…parrot. You know what I mean."

"Very well." He hesitated, then reached over with one finger and flipped a curl that had, typically, sprung free of her hairpins. "Perhaps we can agree that your hair is marvelously…active."

Startled, Jean didn't move. His gesture had felt like a caress, though he hadn't touched her. She'd never heard his voice gently playful till now, or seen his eyes dance. "It is excessively curly," she replied, breathless at this glimpse of a different person.

"Would you say excessive? That seems harsh. Of course, I haven't seen your tresses set free in all their glory."

He smiled at her, warmly this time. Jean's pulse accelerated. Was he imagining her hair wild and loose? Would he bury his hands in it? And what then?

The nursery door banged open, hitting the wall so hard it bounced back. Geoffrey burst into the room like a miniature whirlwind. "Bradford says I can't ride a horse." The boy skidded to a halt in front of Benjamin and stared resentfully up at him. "You'll say I can't go now."

Tom hurried in, looking like a foxhound whose quarry had slipped by him through trickery.

Benjamin set aside his resentment at the interruption. "Can you ride, Tom?"

"Yes, my lord. Pretty well. I learned when I worked for the blacksmith and had to get accustomed to the horses."

Benjamin turned back to his scowling son. "You'll ride with Tom. The two of you won't be a great burden."

"I want to ride *myself*," Geoffrey declared, his little fists clenched.

"Well, you can't. You're too small to control a mount. You'd fall and hurt yourself."

"I wouldn't!"

"You will ride with Tom, or we won't go."

Geoffrey's face reddened. His little jaw set; his eyes narrowed. Startled, Benjamin recognized a resemblance to his own father in the cast of his son's features. He almost expected an explosion of irritation—the kind of scolding he'd received when he interrupted his father's studies. But Geoffrey was silent, blue eyes burning. He was braced for a lecture, Benjamin realized. The shoe was on the other foot.

"You should learn to ride, however," Benjamin said. "I'll make inquiries about a pony."

Geoffrey froze for a long, incredulous moment. Then delight swept his face, and immediately died away. "You'll forget," he said.

"No, I won't. Why do you say so?" He'd expected a bit of gratitude at least, Benjamin thought. Did Geoffrey know the word *thanks*?

"You always forget. You forgot the cricket bat and the top."

Benjamin, in fact, had no recollection of these things. Had they been discussed at some point? Surely he would know. And he would have said that Geoffrey was small to handle a cricket bat. He did not believe promises had been made. Still, Benjamin was assailed by an uncomfortable mixture of shame and resentment and impatience. He couldn't entirely dismiss the reproach in his son's gaze. "I give you my word that I will look for a pony," he said. "I can't guarantee I'll find a suitable animal at once, mind."

Geoffrey put his hands on his diminutive hips and stared up at him. After a moment, he pursed his lips and nodded like a much older child. And thus he was judged, Benjamin thought, amusement taking over. A strange gurgle at his back made him turn to Miss Saunders. "Is something wrong?"

"I…I have no riding habit with me," she replied.

"Ask Mrs. McGinnis. I'm sure she can find you something."

"I'll take you," said Geoffrey, clearly eager to remove any impediments to the promised expedition. He grabbed Miss Saunders's hand and tugged. She allowed him to pull her along, but Benjamin thought she looked apprehensive as they went out. He smiled. One of the few pleasures of the intrusion that had turned his peaceful life upside down was watching his pretty houseguest cope with his unruly son. Miss Saunders had obviously expected quite a different sort of child. And didn't it serve her right!

Only then did Benjamin realize that it had been hours since he'd thought of Alice.

Four

"I'VE FOUND YOU A HABIT THAT'LL FIT WELL ENOUGH, I think," said Mrs. McGinnis the following morning. She spread a swath of crimson cloth on Jean's bed and set a tricorn hat atop it.

"Was it Alice's?" Jean asked. She didn't want to wear her dead cousin's clothing, for a variety of reasons.

"No, miss. Her ladyship's clothes were given away. This belonged to Lord Furness's mother when she was young. We got it from a trunk in the attic. It's been brushed and aired, and it was stored away clean, of course."

Jean fingered the skirt; the cloth was very fine. "Did you work for her as well?"

Mrs. McGinnis nodded. "I came along with Lady Evelina when she married. Several of us did. There wasn't much staff here at the time. Rather like now. My lord's father didn't pay much heed to his household, so long as he had candles to read by and a fire in the library." The housekeeper paused, then added, "She was the daughter of an earl, you know."

"Lord Macklin's sister."

"Yes, miss." She sounded proud and fond.

"I don't know much about her. I'm related to Alice's side of the family, you know."

Mrs. McGinnis nodded.

"Did she meet Lord Furness, the previous Lord Furness, in London?"

"No, miss. He wasn't one for society. They met in Oxford. He was working in a college library, and my lady was visiting her brother. He was a student there."

"Lord Macklin was a friend of Lord Furness?" Hadn't he said he didn't know him well?

"I don't think so, miss." Mrs. McGinnis looked uncertain.

"So they met in a library?" Jean prompted, getting back to her chief interest.

This brought a smile. "My lady used to laugh about it. She was looking over the shelves and saw a book she wanted right up at the top. She turned to a gentleman at one of the desks and asked him to reach it down for her. He growled at her—that was the word she always used—and told her to take herself off. That she had no business in such a place." The housekeeper's smile broadened. "That was not a thing to say to Lady Evelina."

"What did she do?" Jean asked.

"She marched over and picked up the papers he'd been working on, read out a few bits, and showed him a mistake he'd made. I can't remember what it was, though she told me. Something complicated. She said he gaped at her as if he'd been poleaxed."

Jean laughed.

The housekeeper nodded. "My lady wasn't

beautiful. Called herself right homely, she did. But she had the quickest wits."

"And Lord Furness appreciated that."

"He did." Mrs. McGinnis smiled sadly. "The old lord wasn't an easy man. He didn't care much for people, in general. New maids went in terror of him until they became accustomed to his ways. He loved my lady though. Eleven years older, he was, and irascible, but he never raised his voice to her." Her expression suggested that she would have had something to say about it if he had.

"I'm sorry I never met her. It sounds as if I'd have liked her very much."

The older woman looked gratified. "Everyone did, miss. If she was still here, the house wouldn't have got so—" She pressed her lips together as if to keep the rest of this sentence inside.

"When did she die?" Jean asked.

"Six years ago, of the influenza. Only forty-eight, she was. Never saw her son married or her grandson born." Mrs. McGinnis shook her head sadly. "I hope the habit'll do," she added in the tone of a woman with a list of tasks on her mind.

"Very well, thank you," Jean replied.

The housekeeper went out with a cordial nod. Jean sat on the bed and fingered the military-looking frogging on the jacket of the riding habit. Her host had suffered a series of losses, she thought. His father when he was young, his mother a few years ago, and then Alice a little after that. Did it seem as if the house had emptied around him? She remembered the feeling of a pervasive presence suddenly removed—like taking a step in the dark and finding the floor missing. Even when one's chief emotion was relief.

Jean shook her head. There was one great difference between her case and her host's. He had a child. When the man and boy had faced off this morning over the hope of a pony, the sight might have wrung her heart if she had allowed such a distraction from her mission—to see to it that Geoffrey had a childhood nothing like her own.

At eight o'clock the following morning, Jean stood before the mirror in her bedchamber and assessed her appearance. The borrowed riding habit was a bit loose on her, but not enough to matter. Its full red skirts fell to her ankles; the matching jacket had a small skirt of its own, which flared over her hips, and long, tight sleeves. A white stock and bow tie, white gauntlets, and the tricorn hat compiled the ensemble, old-fashioned but quite serviceable above her own sturdy traveling boots. The latter weren't ideal for riding, but she could manage.

Jean settled the hat more firmly on her wayward hair, which was already threatening to escape its pins. She missed Sarah, her maid and sartorial magician. Wild curls didn't plague her when Sarah had dressed them. Jean sighed and went downstairs to join the others.

Her entry into the breakfast room caused a minor sensation. Lord Macklin and Lord Furness both stopped eating and stared at her. "I remember that habit," said the older man. "It was a favorite of Evelina's. She insisted on the red, even though our mother thought it garish."

"She told me that," his nephew replied with one of his beguiling smiles. "Mama said her face gave her the right to any color she wanted. I never understood what she meant by that."

"Evelina had this conviction that she was plain," Lord Macklin said. "I once watched her stand at a mirror and inventory her supposedly *too small* eyes and *lumpy* nose and *undernourished* lips. In a dismissive tone she wouldn't have used about anyone else in the world. She never grasped that charm is in the life of a face more than its shape."

Lord Furness gave him an approving look. "Precisely."

They turned back to Jean, who had been absorbed in this interesting exchange. She felt self-conscious under their combined gazes, like a display model at a modiste's shop. "Mrs. McGinnis got it out for me," she said.

"I like seeing it again," said Lord Macklin. "Evelina loved to ride."

"She taught me horsemanship in that habit," said his nephew. "Mama was so patient. She led my pony 'round and 'round a paddock while I learned how to manage him."

"So *you* had a pony," said Jean.

He frowned at her, a spark of anger in his blue-gray eyes, and Jean was almost glad. When he smiled at her, it was too easy to forget all else.

A shout resounded from the front hall, followed by the patter of footsteps and then Geoffrey, dressed for the outdoors. "When are we going to *go*?" He danced from foot to foot with impatience.

"Miss Saunders has not had her breakfast," said his

father. "We cannot leave until she has eaten. She is our guest."

Jean started to object—anything to keep Geoffrey from throwing a tantrum. But in fact she was quite hungry. She didn't relish the thought of a morning's ride on an empty and almost certainly growling stomach.

To the manifest surprise of every adult in the room, Geoffrey quieted at once. He gazed first at his father, and then at Jean, as if consulting some inner reference. "We never have any guests," he said.

"Well, now we do." Lord Furness seemed displeased by his own words. "For a short while."

The boy cocked his head like a wild creature catching an unfamiliar scent. He had the face of her chocolate-box phantasm, Jean thought, but his inner workings were a mystery. "Can I have a muffin with her?" Geoffrey asked in an ingratiating tone.

His father snorted. "You *may* have one."

Geoffrey walked over to Jean. "There's blackberry jam." He smiled up at her.

Even though she'd seen him painted red and chopping at her with a hatchet, Jean's heart nearly melted. She prepared a muffin to his specifications before filling a plate for herself.

With the gentlemen looking on, Jean didn't linger over her food but ate as fast as good manners would allow. She was surprised to see Geoffrey savor rather than bolt his muffin and jam. They finished at the same time, and the group headed for the stables together.

Half an hour later, Benjamin paused to consult his memory of the route. He felt as if he was guiding a caravan. His uncle and Miss Saunders rode on either side of him. Tom and Geoffrey, on a sturdy gelding, were a little ahead, at Geoffrey's impatient urging. Further back, the nursery maid rode pillion behind a young groom; she looked nervous at her sideways perch. The fellow, Jack his name was, led a packhorse with the supplies for their picnic. As Benjamin's apparently infallible gardener had predicted, it was a sunny day, warmer than it had been for some time.

"Are we going to those hills?" asked Miss Saunders.

She looked at ease in his mother's old saddle. As she closed her eyes and turned her face up to the sun, a twist of brown hair sprang from beneath the tricorn hat and curled down her temple. Benjamin was startled by an intense desire to reach over and tuck it back into place. And then, perhaps, to trail his fingertips along the glowing skin of her cheek. He blinked and turned away. "Yes, the gorge cuts through them."

"The Mendips," said Benjamin's uncle. "A curious word. Your father told me that no one is sure where it comes from."

Geoffrey was flapping his elbows and kicking at his horse's sides to urge him on, an ineffectual gesture because his feet didn't reach the stirrups. Tom the wanderer had a steadying arm around him.

Benjamin wondered how he had ended up out of his house, with this oddly mixed party, on such a quixotic expedition.

They rode on, reaching the small village of Cheddar after an hour in the saddle and passing through it into a long, winding gash in the hills. Stony gray cliffs rose vertically on either side of the trail, enclosing them in towering walls. The gorge looked far too deep to have been cut by the stream flowing through it, but Benjamin understood this was its origin. Trees grew where they could find purchase, giving way to grass on the steeper parts. The place wasn't as verdant as it would be in the summer, but there was no wind here at the bottom. When the sun reached its zenith and the shadows drew back, the temperature would be pleasant.

The horses picked their way along the flowing water, avoiding fallen boulders and ruts. Their riders exclaimed over the dramatic scenery. Rounding a sharp bend, they came to a wider place in the gorge. A swerve in the cliff formed a space like a lawn, with the stream running along one side. "This looks like a good spot for our picnic," Benjamin declared, pulling up.

"I want to ride all the way to the end," protested Geoffrey.

"That's too far," Benjamin replied. "A good five miles. And the road is rough. The gorge looks the same all the way along."

"But there are caves!"

And Benjamin had chosen this place precisely because the caves were not here. Young Tom seemed quick and trustworthy, but confronted with a cave, Geoffrey was all too likely to plunge in and lose himself.

"I could ride a bit further," said Miss Saunders.

"Must you always say the most unhelpful thing," Benjamin muttered.

She heard him. He hadn't meant her to, or…he didn't *think* he had. She looked surprisingly mortified. He could never set a foot right with this young woman. "This is where we picnic," he declared. "Or, we can turn around and go home again."

Geoffrey looked mutinous.

"You wanted to come to the gorge, Geoffrey. This is the gorge. Perhaps a little gratitude is in order." Benjamin frowned at his son.

"Come along," said Tom. He jumped down and lifted his small charge off the horse. "Let's look about." He gave Benjamin a wink.

The two servants unloaded the packhorse. Benjamin and his uncle unsaddled and tethered their mounts while Jack began to collect wood for a fire.

Helping Lily the nursery maid spread blankets on the grass and set out hampers, Jean watched her host move about the area. His tall, athletic figure drew the eye. No one observing their small party would fail to see that he was in charge.

"Heigh-ho," came a shrill cry. "Look at me!"

Everyone turned, and searched, and discovered Geoffrey clinging to the face of the cliff many feet above their heads. He appeared to be standing on a narrow ledge, a tiny figure against the towering wall of rock. As Jean stared, he let go with one hand and waved to them. Appalled, she ran over to stand just below the boy. Lord Furness came up beside her, his face pale and set. His uncle, on his other side, looked equally concerned.

Tom had his hand on the cliff. "I turned away for one minute, and he swarmed up there like a monkey," he said. "I'll climb up and fetch him." A flake of rock came off under his fingers and rattled to the ground.

"I don't think this stone will hold your weight," said Lord Furness. He pulled at a small outcropping; it came free and fell. "And how would you carry him down?" He examined the cliff and murmured, "How the deuce did he get up there?" He raised his eyes, let out a breath, and spoke more softly. "An amazing feat, Geoffrey. Can you come back down now, please?"

Geoffrey grinned with pride. "You can't get me."

"No. You've outdone us all. Truly astonishing. But come down now."

"All right." The boy lifted a foot and felt about as if trying to find to place to put it. Lord Furness reached up futilely, then waited with spread arms. Geoffrey found no purchase. He frowned. "I can't," he said in a much more subdued tone.

"I'll go up," repeated Tom. "I was supposed to be watching him."

"That won't work," Lord Furness replied.

Words burst from Jean. "You can't leave him up there!"

She received a searing look in response and a turned back.

After a moment, Lord Furness gave a nod and said, "All right." He strode away. "Jack, help me saddle Blaze. Quickly." The servant jumped to aid him.

"My arms are tired," said Geoffrey.

In a few moments, Lord Furness sprang onto his horse and guided it over to the cliff beneath his son. He still couldn't reach him. Jean didn't see what he'd accomplished by mounting up. "Tom, get up behind me," he said. "And then climb onto my shoulders."

The youngster grinned. "Yes, my lord." He leapt onto the horse's withers and then drew up his feet. Carefully, he stood. Lord Furness controlled the nervous horse as Tom maneuvered onto his shoulders.

Seated there, his ankles hooked in the other man's armpits, Tom reached upward. His fingers brushed the heels of Geoffrey's boots. "You'll have to let go," he said to the boy. "And I'll catch you."

"No," said Geoffrey. He was clinging to the cliff now, and he looked like a scared little boy rather than a triumphant scamp.

"I'm right here," said Tom. "I can almost reach you. I won't let you fall."

"No." Geoffrey's voice trembled.

"Geoffrey," said Lord Furness.

The boy twisted his head around to peer down at him.

"Look how bravely you climbed up." His voice was soothing, encouraging. Startlingly so, Jean thought. "Now you must be brave again and help yourself down," he added. "We've done all we can."

"Just let go and lean a little," said Tom. "Easy. No jumping."

Briefly, it seemed he wouldn't. Then Geoffrey tipped back and away from the ledge, falling into Tom's waiting arms. Jean cried out as the human ladder wobbled with the impact. But Lord Furness kept them steady. "Hand him down to me," he said.

Tom lowered the boy into his father's grasp. Controlling his mount with his knees, Lord Furness took him. "Now you climb down."

Tom eased himself off his perch and onto the ground. Benjamin held his son to his chest. His small frame—fragile as a bird's, it seemed—was trembling. His hands clutched Benjamin's coat; his face was buried in his shoulder. A visceral reaction shuddered through Benjamin, as strong as anything he'd ever felt. Fear and relief, protective ferocity and tenderness muddled together until they choked him.

"Shall I take him, my lord?" asked the nursery maid at his stirrup.

Benjamin didn't want to let him go. But Geoffrey's trembling had eased. He raised his head and noticed his audience. "I didn't cry," he declared. "I wasn't scared." He wriggled in his father's grip, eager now to be free.

Torn between laughter and exasperation, Benjamin let the maid help the boy down. "I should take you home and confine you to your room for that little trick," he said.

The flash of apprehension in his son's eyes, along with a hint of resignation, shook Benjamin. His intrepid, reckless child looked braced for disappointment. Was he really so accustomed to it? That was a curiously lowering reflection. Yet Geoffrey did need to learn obedience.

"I've got a better idea," said young Tom. He'd gone over to the pack saddle, and now he returned with a length of rope. "We'll leash you, ya mad imp, so you can't get up to any more mischief."

Geoffrey eyed the rope. "Like a guard dog?"

"More like a sheep that won't stop straying." Tom made a comical face.

The boy laughed and submitted. Indeed, he surveyed the rope as if imagining the opportunities for mayhem it might provide. Benjamin started to object that they couldn't throttle his son, then watched with interest as Tom looped the tether over the back of Geoffrey's neck, around under his arms, crossed on

his back and then his belly, only to knot it unreach-
ably behind. He fastened the loose end to his own
wrist. Once again Tom was unexpectedly ingenious.
Benjamin looked up, encountered Miss Saunders's
equally fascinated gaze, and nodded.

Geoffrey tested the limits of his bonds with a flying
leap. When he was brought up short, he laughed,
spreading his arms and swinging from side to side like
a pendulum. "You could hang me down into a cave,"
he cried. "Like a bat." He flapped his arms.

Benjamin tensed at the picture, calculating the
distance to the nearest cavern in his mind.

"Or I could tie you to a tree," Tom replied.
"And leave you there to watch us eat the feast Cook
packed up."

Miss Saunders jerked as if someone had pushed her,
though she stood quite alone. The look on her face
puzzled Benjamin.

"You wouldn't do that," said Geoffrey.

"Not unless you drive me to it with your daft
starts," Tom replied. "Hang you down a cavern
indeed! Nasty creatures, bats."

To Benjamin's surprise, Geoffrey took this in good
part. "I'm hungry now!"

"You're always hungry."

"So are you!"

Tom acknowledged the hit with a grin.

"It seems we should eat," said Benjamin. He herded
his party over to the spread blankets. The two servants
began to lay out the contents of the hampers—a crisp
roast chicken, bread, a block of cheddar cheese, a jar of
pickles, bottles of cider, an array of small cakes. When

his son dived for the latter, Benjamin said, "You can help serve our guests, Geoffrey."

The boy's hand halted in midair. He met Benjamin's eyes, blinked, and drew it back.

Benjamin carved the chicken and set a portion on one of the plates from the stack wrapped in a napkin. He handed it to Geoffrey.

With his leash played out to a greater length, Geoffrey carried it to Miss Saunders. Someone had taught him a few manners, Benjamin thought. He ought to know who, but he didn't. Geoffrey took the next serving to his great uncle, and so on down the line. When everyone had chicken, he trotted about offering the other dishes. Everyone was served before he glanced at his father, received his smile and nod, and sat down before his own food. Geoffrey snatched up a chicken leg and took an enormous bite. He chewed the hunk of meat with some difficulty, his small cheeks distended.

"Geoffrey!" said Benjamin.

His son struggled on, jaws working mightily, and finally managed to swallow. Tom handed him a napkin, and he wiped his greasy lips and hands on the cloth. Under his father's frown, Geoffrey then raised the drumstick in careful fingers and took a dainty bite. He smiled angelically at the watching adults.

It was as if Alice suddenly sat in their circle. The bright hair, the piquant face with precisely that slant of brow, the cerulean-blue eyes, even the hint of a dimple that appeared when she smiled in just that way. Memory and regret sank their claws into Benjamin. Bitterness rose in his throat. He wanted to rail at the unfairness of life. Then Geoffrey bent to tear off a bit of bread, and the resemblance wavered—as if the portrait in the library had moved, realigned, and revealed another person entirely.

Shaken, Benjamin took up his plate. He would have given a great deal to be magically transported to that library, and to be alone. But reality was cruel and offered no escape. He sat in the place his uncle had left him, next to Miss Saunders.

"You *wouldn't* have let Tom tie him to a tree," she said.

The quaver of fear in her voice grated on feelings rubbed raw. A bolt of rage slammed through Benjamin, cleaving his gloom and resentment and confusion. "Why not?" he hissed with quiet venom. "According to you, I neglect and torment my son. What should stop me from staking him out like a sacrificial goat?"

She flinched as if he'd hit her. Her plate fell from shaking fingers, spilling chicken, pickles, and the rest over the crimson folds of his mother's riding habit. Runnels of grease and brine trickled onto the blanket. "Oh!" cried Miss Saunders, and burst into tears.

The picnic erupted. The nursery maid surged forward with a handful of napkins to sop up the spill. Benjamin's uncle pulled out his handkerchief and leaned over to offer it to Miss Saunders. Geoffrey moved to retrieve the dropped plate, was brought up short by his leash, and flailed in the center of the blanket. Jack stepped in to tidy the mess. Tom poured a glass of cider and set it near Miss Saunders's side.

Through it all, Benjamin sat still, feeling beleaguered.

He'd been rude—granted. He admitted it. Very rude. He shouldn't have growled at her. But he'd said harsh things to the woman before without provoking such an extreme reaction. Worse things, and she hadn't dissolved into a watering pot. There was no excuse for such a display: wailing and snuffling and making him look like a brute. She'd invaded *his* house after all. No one had asked her to come here and turn his life upside down. He hadn't meant to overset her, of course, but *why* did she keep on crying?

"Let's walk a little farther into the gorge," his uncle Arthur said. He picked up Geoffrey, leash and all, and walked toward the winding lane. Tom followed perforce, pulled by the rope. At his uncle's gesture, the servants went along. And just like that, Benjamin was left alone with a sniffling, hiccupping…mess. When his uncle threw an enigmatic look over his shoulder, Benjamin vowed to have a serious discussion with his august relative at the earliest opportunity, right before he sent him packing.

"I beg your pardon," snuffled his companion.

"I think I am supposed to be begging yours," Benjamin replied. "I'm sorry you're distressed."

"You don't sound sorry." She sniffed. "You sound annoyed."

"Can you blame me? You've subjected all of us to a bout of inexplicable waterworks."

Jean felt herself flush, even more mortified, if that was possible. She was *not* a weeper. She couldn't remember when she'd cried this way, made such an absolute fool of herself. Something about that phrase—sacrificial goat—and the way he'd said it had set her off. Coming after the look on his face when he'd held his son close. The two together, or one after the other, or something, had cut too close to the bone.

"I *am* sorry I made you cry," he said in a kinder tone. "I'm not sure how I did, really." He looked rueful. "I was no ruder than on a couple of previous occasions. Of course, it has been a trying morning."

Something between a choke and a gurgle escaped Jean's throat. "An understatement."

Lord Furness nodded. "Geoffrey did his best to stop my heart with that climb. He appears to have a positive genius for mischief."

"It seems I'm no good with children." The words burst from Jean, as uncontrollable as the tears. "I didn't know. I had no brothers or sisters. I never associated with any other children."

"None?"

"No." Jean bit off the word. She wasn't going to blather on anymore. She was going to think before she spoke.

"Well, I did," he replied. "A gaggle of neighborhood boys. And at school. I can't say these experiences are helping. Geoffrey appears to be unique. Due to my...inattention, I suppose."

"You're better with him." She hadn't meant it to sound like an accusation. "Geoffrey obeys you."

"Intermittently. And for his own purposes, I suspect. I had no notion a five-year-old child could be so devious."

Jean was grateful for his honesty. She offered a bit in return. "I had a wrongheaded idea of what would happen when I came here."

He looked at her. It felt to Jean as if his gaze had weight, like a brush of fur passing over her skin. His expression suggested that he was really seeing her for the first time. Which was a ridiculous thought. He'd seen all too much of her; he'd made that clear.

"I should go back to London," she said. She'd never been more conscious of the fact that she had no real home. Not that she was going to tell him that. "Now that Geoffrey's situation has been brought to your attention." She'd accomplished her mission. This man was obviously not going to neglect his son any longer. She ought to feel glad and proud, not...empty.

Offered exactly what he'd been requesting, Benjamin found, ironically, that he no longer wanted it. Not immediately. Miss Jean Saunders was too interesting. "I don't know exactly what should be done about Geoffrey, however. I don't suppose I can send him off to school."

"He's too young!"

Benjamin admired the flash in her dark eyes, the swell of her bosom as her spine stiffened. She'd risen to his bait like a striking trout, and the return of her indignation was curiously stimulating. "I could hunt up a tutor to start him on Latin," he continued. "And ancient Greek."

"Are you mad? Greek?"

"He seems unusually intelligent. Perhaps he's a prodigy. Mozart's father used to show him off in the courts of Europe at about his age."

"Like an organ grinder's monkey?"

She practically gave off sparks when she was outraged, Benjamin thought. Pushing her into that state was…fun. He couldn't remember when he'd last had fun. "You're very quick to criticize," he said. "What are your ideas?"

"Geoffrey needs time to be a little boy," she declared. "He needs freedom, with safety. Encouragement, with guidance. He needs love and joy!"

The passionate emotion in her voice moved him beyond amusement. "A tall order," Benjamin said. "I don't see how anyone could guarantee all that. Perhaps you should stay a bit longer and…advise."

Her eyes flickered unreadably. "I suppose I could."

"Two heads are better than one."

"Indeed."

"We could do with a woman's touch."

She flushed at the thoughts this phrase evoked.

Lord Furness held out his hand. She looked at it. "A joint project," he said. "Agreed?"

Miss Saunders hesitated, then finally nodded. Slowly, she extended her hand. He shook it, to her obvious surprise. Benjamin wouldn't have minded keeping hold of her fingers, but she pulled away at once.

Five

THE DREAM BACK CAME THAT NIGHT. IT HAD BEEN quite a while since it had tormented her. Long enough for Jean to imagine that the nightmare was gone, at long last. But no. Here she was, curled tiny in the stifling darkness. The air pressed down on her. The silence intensified her isolation. She knew it was no use moving, except to squeeze her own flesh and prove she still existed. She'd learned very early that there was no recourse, and no escape, no matter how she clawed and cried. The blackness would crush her until it was lifted on a whim—after minutes or hours, no telling how long. Then she would be yanked into the light like a captured mole, blinking and cringing under a stream of acid mockery. Or perhaps a bewildering shower of caresses and regrets. There was no way to predict which it would be.

Jean jerked awake in her dim bedchamber, heart pounding. She'd left the draperies open, as she always did, and a pale wash of starlight came through the windows. She sat up, put her arms around her knees, and shivered for a little while, facing the crushing disappointment of the dream's return. Then she lit the candle waiting on the bedside table, as it always was. The darkness retreated to the corners. She reached for the book carefully placed beside the candlestick—part of her hated, necessary routine. She opened it and settled to read and wait for dawn. Sleep wouldn't return to her in the dark after that dream. Part of her would fight it; part of her would dredge up unwelcome memories. But she could divert her mind with stories, as long as her book was good enough.

This one was. Jean read. The minutes ticked by. When the sky finally began to brighten, she set the volume aside, snuffed the candle, and drifted back to sleep.

⌘

Benjamin encountered his uncle Arthur in the breakfast room. A few days ago, this would have irritated him; he would have consigned his uninvited relative to perdition. But he was in a surprisingly mellow mood today. "Good morning, sir."

The older man nodded amiably across the table.

"Is your plot going well, do you think?"

"My plot?" He raised his eyebrows.

"Come, Uncle. I may be slow, but I'm not stupid. Do you deny that you aimed Miss Saunders in my direction? Fired her off, in fact, like a cannon barrage?" Benjamin liked the comparison; it fit his spirited guest.

"An interesting young lady, isn't she?"

"Why?"

"Her upbringing, I suppose. I don't know a great deal about her early youth."

"No, Uncle Arthur. Why did you send her here?"

"I didn't do that." The older man shook his head.

The smile that had been tugging at Benjamin's lips emerged. "Oh, come. You arrive on her heels for an unheralded—and unprecedented—visit. And then you lurk around the edges of our company, saying little, looking more, continually slipping out to leave us alone. Quite unlike your usual, convivial self."

Lord Macklin sipped his coffee. An answering smile escaped him. "What a picture you paint. I promise you, I had no idea Miss Saunders meant to come here. It was her own idea entirely. Quite unexpected. I only followed when I discovered she'd gone."

"Because?"

"Because it seemed I *had* set her off somehow. Through our conversations about you."

"Have you turned matchmaker, Uncle?" Benjamin didn't appreciate that notion.

"No indeed. Nothing so pedestrian. I only wanted to shake you up a bit."

"Because?" Benjamin repeated, his temper stirred.

His uncle regarded him gravely. "There has been talk about your retreat from the world, Benjamin. More with each passing month. And about Geoffrey as well."

He hated this idea as much as ever. "But instead of simply talking to me, you hatched this scheme."

"I tried talking. Several times. After our dinner in London, I concluded that talking had little effect."

Benjamin gazed at his older relative. He'd nearly forgotten that strange gathering. More precisely, he'd put it from his mind when he returned to his shuttered routine.

"And then I came across Miss Saunders," his uncle continued. "And it seemed to me that she was particularly suited for…shaking."

"How so?" Curiosity overcame Benjamin's irritation.

"I'm not certain. Her quickness, her responses in conversation. Call it an instinct."

"You've become remarkably cryptic, Uncle Arthur."

"There's a trick I've seen," his august relative replied, gazing out the window at the garden. "Perhaps you have too. If you drag a magnet beneath a sheet of paper holding bits of iron, it pulls them into patterns. Without actually touching them at all."

"What?"

His uncle laughed. "Don't look as if I've gone daft. I promise I haven't."

Benjamin waited for him to go on. When he didn't, Benjamin thought of pressing, but in the end, his uncle's philosophical musings didn't really matter. Miss Saunders was here, and he wasn't…entirely sorry. "I've conceded that Geoffrey requires more care," he said instead. "Miss Saunders and I have agreed to… consult about that. So if you have other business to attend to—"

"Nothing pressing," his uncle interrupted cheerfully. Before Benjamin could reply, he added, "And I am a sort of chaperone, you know."

This brought Benjamin up short.

"Not the usual type. By rights, we should find an older female to lend her countenance."

"No more guests!" Benjamin declared.

"Well, we are all family members, in an extended sense. It should be all right while I'm here."

Benjamin couldn't call it blackmail when his uncle had such a good point.

"I wonder if she's written to the Phillipsons. Or if I should do so, as I've spirited away their very useful guest. However accidentally. They're good friends of mine. I wouldn't want them upset. Perhaps I should."

Benjamin's mind went back to earlier confrontations. Suddenly, he feared he'd made a mistake. "Are they in this with you? If they think they can take Geoffrey from me, they will find themselves in a fight."

His uncle shook his head. "They'll be glad—relieved—to hear that your son will remain in his proper home. I promise you."

Benjamin eyed him suspiciously. "Then why upset?"

"The word is too strong. They expect Miss Saunders to help organize their entertainments and will be mildly annoyed by her absence."

"Is she a poor relation?" This was a new view of her, one that surprised him. She had none of the diffidence he'd observed in such dependents.

"I don't think so. The friendship doesn't have that... feel. But I'm not aware of her exact circumstances."

Benjamin stood up. "What are you aware of, Uncle?"

"That I've overstepped, and you're angry. I understand that. Also, that you're more animated than I've seen you in months. Years, perhaps. And that I've never given you any reason not to trust me." The older man regarded him steadily.

Only partly convinced, Benjamin turned away. "I'm going out. I promised Geoffrey I'd search for a pony."

"You should take Miss Saunders with you. As part of your *consultations*."

Torn between anger and amusement, Benjamin nearly growled. "Don't push me too far, Uncle Arthur." And yet, as he walked down the corridor toward the back door, the idea grew on him.

❧

Leaving her bedchamber rather later than usual, heavy-eyed from her broken night, Jean nearly bumped into Lord Macklin's valet. Briefly, it seemed the man would drop the pile of freshly laundered neckcloths he was carrying, but he recovered with an adroit side step. "I beg your pardon, miss," he said.

"My fault," replied Jean.

The man gave her a small bow, and all at once Jean felt grubby and unkempt. There was no visible reason for this mortification. The valet—Clayton, she remembered—was an unassuming figure in middle age, with a round face that was pleasant rather than handsome and mild brown eyes. He was perfectly polite, without a hint of emotion in his tone. But he seemed to…exude criticism.

Jean was suddenly conscious of the wrinkles in her gown—the same one she'd worn for several days now—and of her only partially tamed hair. Alone, she fought a long, losing battle with her wild curls. If she was staying on at Furness Hall, and it seemed that she was, she needed her things. She needed her lady's maid, Sarah. Sarah was every bit as competent as Clayton. She'd put Jean to rights and depress the valet's pretensions in short order.

"Excuse me," said Jean. She stepped back into her room to compose a message asking Sarah to pack her clothes and bring them here as soon as could be managed.

Five minutes later, Jean made her way downstairs. There was no tray for letters in the front hall, as there would have been in a London town house, and no one about to ask how to post items. From what she'd seen of this household, Jean doubted that they had any such system. Could she pay a groom to take it? London was a long way off.

"There you are." Benjamin was glad to have found her at last. He hadn't been able to catch a maidservant to go knocking on his female guest's door. His staff had been so well schooled to avoid him in recent years that they scurried away as soon as he appeared. Perhaps Mrs. McGinnis's pleas for changes had some merit. "I missed you at breakfast."

"I'm a bit later than usual this morning," Miss Saunders said. Her stomach growled quite audibly. She flushed.

Benjamin gallantly ignored the sound. He didn't even smile. "Is that a letter?"

"Oh." She looked down as if she'd forgotten the folded paper in her hand. "Yes. I need more of my things. And my maid. If that's all right."

Oddly enough, it was, even though it meant another stranger in his house. "Shall I frank it for you? And make sure it goes on its way?"

"Thank you." She handed over the letter.

A dark curl came loose at her temple, unfurling like a silky ribbon. Her stomach growled again. Benjamin spoke before Miss Saunders could flee, as she was clearly about to do. "Would you care to accompany me on another expedition?"

"An—"

"I'm going in search of a pony, as promised. That should form part of our *consultations*, should it not?" Benjamin borrowed his uncle's phrase.

"Oh yes. All right."

"*After* your breakfast."

Miss Saunders's flush deepened. A hand strayed to her midsection and immediately dropped. He did enjoy flustering her, Benjamin thought. Her unease was such a contrast to her usual forthright—not to say abrasive—manner. "I'll send someone with your letter," he added.

"I should like it to go quickly."

Not totally flustered then. Benjamin bowed. "Your wish is my command."

She made a sound rather like a snort. But it was drowned out by another signal from her stomach, demanding breakfast at once. With a hasty thanks, Miss Saunders hurried away.

Benjamin realized that he was smiling. He'd smiled more in the last few days than in previous months. Once, this might have seemed a betrayal of his bereaved state. But today it didn't. He decided not to probe the reasons for this change. He would simply enjoy it, he decided as he went off to do his guest's bidding.

❧

Mrs. McGinnis's limited staff had done wonders with the riding habit, Jean thought as she and Lord Furness rode out of the stable yard and into the drive. It had been magically sponged clean of food stains. If only her fatigue could be as easily removed. Wisps of the nightmare hovered in the back of her mind. "Where are we going?" she asked.

"There's a farm nearby that breeds horses," replied Lord Furness. "Mrs. Fry also takes in all sorts of stray animals. We'll see if she has any ponies on hand at present. With expert help." He indicated the groom who rode behind them.

"So you can keep your word to Geoffrey," Jean said. The thought made her happy.

"Did you doubt that I would?"

Was he going to be prickly again? She'd thought they were getting on better, that he'd given up challenging every remark she made.

"There may not be any suitable animal," he added.

They rode on. Although Jean was stiff from yesterday's expedition, as she seldom rode, she enjoyed the crisp air and the early signs of spring. Leaves were beginning to unfold in the hedges on either side of the road. Tiny flowers peeked from under them, while birds called from the shelter of their branches.

At a break in the bushes, they turned down a lane, which soon opened out into a farmyard. A two-story house on one side faced a barn and sheds on the other. The buildings were neat and well kept, but Jean's first impression was of a wealth of animals. A trio of dogs ran up to assess them, their barking informative rather than threatening, and she could see cows and sheep in one set of fields, horses in another, and pigs rooting in a fenced pen beside the barn. When she dismounted, she spied a cat curled around her litter beside the front door. Jean stopped to bend over her.

"I hope you're not going to coo over the kittens," Lord Furness said, knocking on the door.

"Of course I am," Jean replied. "For quite some

time, in a sickening way. There's nothing on Earth as charming as a kitten, and if you don't know that, you may go and grumble elsewhere."

The door was opened by a large, red-faced woman. The sleeves of her gown were rolled up over muscular arms, and her apron had a dusting of flour.

"Good morning, Mrs. Fry," said Lord Furness. "I hope you're well."

"My lord." She seemed quite surprised to see him. Turning toward the barn, she called, "Len!" Her voice was so loud that Jean started. When a lad who resembled Mrs. Fry appeared, she added, "Help his lordship's groom with the horses."

He hurried out to do so, and they led all three mounts into the barn.

"Come in, my lord and miss," said Mrs. Fry. "It's baking day, and we have scones just out of the oven."

"Thank you, but I don't want to interrupt your work for too long. I've come to see if you might have a pony that would do for my son. He's five years old."

"And so he is. How time flies, eh?" Their hostess untied her apron and hung it on a hook inside the door. "I've two ponies about the place just now. Come along, and I'll show you." She didn't bother with a wrap but took them through the yard, around the barn, where the Furness groom joined them, and into a fenced enclosure.

There were several horses cropping the grass on the far side. When one of them moved, Jean saw the smaller figures of the ponies beyond them. They stood head to hocks, swishing flies off each other with their tails. One was brown with a pale mane and tail, the other patterned in black and white.

Mrs. Fry led her party across the field and put a hand on the black-and-white pony's shoulder. "Molly here is fifteen," she said. "But she has good years in her yet. She's gentle and even-tempered."

"And the other?" asked Lord Furness. "He looks younger. And smaller would be better, I think."

"Aye, Fergus is just eight. A gelding. He's a fine animal. Had it a bit rough where he was when we came upon him. Near starved he was, which is why he's undersized." For a moment Mrs. Fry looked fierce. "But he's splendid now, aren't you, lad?" She ruffled the pony's pale mane, and he whickered. "Particularly since he's found a friend in Molly."

"I don't want a chancy mount for Geoffrey," said Lord Furness.

"Nothing chancy about Fergus," the farmer replied. "He's steady and strong, far more patient than I'd be, after what he endured."

"You should take them both," said Jean, moved by what she'd heard. "Tom could ride Molly."

"I have plenty of mounts for Tom to use. He's tall enough for a horse."

"Yes, but see how they like to be together." The ponies clearly knew they were being discussed, Jean thought. They were examining the strangers with wary interest. She could almost believe they realized their future was being settled.

"This pony is a means of transport and education," said Lord Furness. "My decision will not be based on sentiment."

"Of course not." Jean searched for a logical reason, and found one. "But I'm sure Geoffrey would like

Tom to be on his own level as he learns. Who likes to be loomed over? It might make him quite cross to be looked down on from horseback."

Lord Furness gazed at her. His blue-gray eyes seemed skeptical, but a half smile tugged at his lips. Quite a charming half smile. Jean blinked and looked away as he said, "Check them both over, Bradford."

The groom came forward and murmured to the ponies as he ran his hands over their legs, examined their teeth, and felt along their torsos. When he finished, he gave a nod of approval. Molly pushed at the man in a friendly way and then rested her head on Fergus's back.

"Oh, very well," said Lord Furness. "Both. What will you take for them, Mrs. Fry?"

"I'll give you a good price for the two." She gave Jean a sly wink as they started back.

An amount was agreed upon. Scones and tea were duly consumed. Afterward, Mrs. Fry sent Len out to the field with halters for the ponies. He brought them back and handed them over to the groom, ready to be led to the Furness stables, then turned to the barn to fetch the visitors' horses.

About to mount up, Jean paused by the basket of kittens again. They tumbled over their mother, an adorable profusion. "That cat looks right smug, don't she?" said Mrs. Fry from the doorway. "She came in from the road three months ago, dead of winter it was, took a look around the farm, rubbed up against my ankles, and settled herself down. A week later, she produced six little ones." Resignation and fondness showed in the woman's face. "Knew what she was doing, I reckon."

Benjamin watched Miss Saunders gaze down at the kittens. As if pulled, she bent and picked one up, a gray striped tabby. It cuddled against her neck. Which looked like a rather pleasant thing to do, he found himself thinking. "Geoffrey would probably like a kitten," she said.

"He'd train it to pounce on us from high places," said Benjamin.

"Ah, cats have the advantage of being quite untrainable." She held up the small creature and gazed into its green eyes. "You wouldn't join in his pranks, would you? You'd teach him his utter insignificance."

Benjamin laughed. "If you want a kitten, don't use my son as an excuse. Just have one."

Mrs. Fry nodded amiably. "They're ready to leave their mother. I'm looking for homes for them."

"*Mew*," said the kitten.

With a slight shake of her head, Miss Saunders set it back among its littermates. "I have no place to keep a cat."

For an instant, Benjamin thought he glimpsed desolation in her face. Surely not, over such a trivial issue? But he was nevertheless moved to say, "Take it. It can live at Furness Hall."

"Really?"

"What's one more cat?" He pretended carelessness, despite the amazing way she'd lit up at the offer. "We have them all about the stables, don't we, Bradford?"

"Yes, my lord," said the groom.

"I'll get a basket for you to carry him home in," said Mrs. Fry, clearly glad to have settled one of her charges. She disappeared inside briefly, returned with a small covered basket, scooped up the tabby, and closed him into it.

Thus, some while later, Benjamin and Miss Saunders walked through the front door of Furness Hall with a mewing package. Geoffrey popped out of the door at the back of the hall as soon as the door closed. He must have been lurking there. Was no one watching him? Didn't he have lessons?

"What's that?" he asked.

"Miss Saunders has acquired a kitten."

"Can I see?" She opened the basket, and they peered together at the small creature. Looking envious, Geoffrey reached in to stroke it. "When the stable cat had kittens, I wanted one, but Cook hates cats."

"She does?" asked Miss Saunders uneasily.

"She said they're sneak thieves, and that I wouldn't take care of it. But I *would* have." He pouted at Benjamin. "How come *she* can have a kitten, and I—"

"Why worry about kittens," Benjamin interrupted, "when you have a pony?"

Geoffrey froze. He stared up at his father as if afraid to move. "A pony?" he whispered.

"Bradford has taken it—them—around to the stables. We will—"

But Geoffrey was gone, with only the pounding echo of small feet to show he'd ever been in the front hall.

In the past hour he'd granted two people their wishes, Benjamin thought. Rather minor wishes, he'd have said. Particularly the kitten. And yet the effects had been rather stunning.

"I didn't know Tab would upset your cook," said Miss Saunders, closing the basket.

"Tab?"

She flushed. "I thought I'd name him Tab. He's a tabby."

His accidental houseguest was adorable when she was embarrassed. "Ah. I'm sure the cook will manage."

"I can keep him in my room, out of her way. I'll set up a sand box for him and feed him there. He's really not old enough to wander about anyway. Unless... you don't think he'll feel *imprisoned*?"

Her voice vibrated with emotion far beyond what the situation warranted, Benjamin thought. "I'm sure he'll be happy to have a home." It seemed the wrong thing to say, because she winced.

"He can stay when I go," she replied. "You said so. Geoffrey will take care of him. Obviously, he'll be glad to."

She hurried up the stairs with the basket before Benjamin could respond to this series of emphatic remarks, which had left him quite bewildered.

Six

JEAN ESTABLISHED TAB IN HER ROOM WITHOUT difficulties. She was adept at making friends with the staff in houses where she stayed, and those in Furness Hall supplied the kitten's needs without much complaint. Cook grumbled quietly when asked for a dish of chopped meat, but relented when assured Tab would live in Jean's room. For his part, Tab seemed content. After a thorough exploration of all the chamber's corners and his meal, he curled up in the window seat and went to sleep.

Watching the rise and fall of his tiny rib cage, Jean wondered if she might take him along when she left here. A cat wasn't much trouble. Many people liked them. And many didn't, she had to admit. The latter tended to have very strong opinions. She shook her head. No, a polite visitor didn't arrive with a pet. She came prepared to socialize and entertain. Even when she didn't feel like either.

Jean turned at a brisk knock on her door, glad for the interruption. She'd come very close to moping. Which was unacceptable. She hadn't even changed out of her borrowed riding habit.

Lord Macklin stood in the corridor outside. "I was just going down," he said. "I thought you'd want to see Geoffrey's first riding lesson."

"I do indeed." Jean came out, making certain the latch caught to keep Tab safe. She walked downstairs at the older man's side.

"I had a surprising encounter this morning," he said.

"I hope it didn't involve Geoffrey and his hatchet."

Lord Macklin smiled. "The tomahawk is securely locked away, I understand. No, I went walking, and I met an old friend in the village. The last person I would have expected to see in the country. I'd have said that she is an absolute fixture in London."

"Did you lure her here with tales of some wrong that must be righted?"

The older man looked down at her. He and Lord Furness shared fathomless blue-gray eyes, Jean observed, and a disarming smile. "We may have spoken of the beauties of this part of Somerset. No more. Are you twitting me, Miss Saunders?"

He was years older and greatly respected, but Jean couldn't quite let it go. "You *are* behind my presence here. Those conversations we had at the Phillipsons'... You steered them."

"No." The word was emphatic. "They evolved. Things you said, or almost said, turned my thoughts in a particular direction. I merely...continued along the path they laid out for me."

Jean didn't like the idea that she'd revealed things she was unaware of. What had he seen in her, or thought he'd seen?

"And I must say that the decision to come down

to Furness Hall was wholly your own. Your…sudden initiative startled me."

"And so you came after me."

Lord Macklin gave her a half bow as they walked. "You are a most astute young lady. I did feel in some way responsible."

"Aha."

He laughed. "So what will you do now that you've extracted my confession?"

Jean wasn't ready to be charmed. "Do you make a practice of interference? Even in the affairs of strangers?"

The older man shook his head as he opened the front door of the house for her. They stepped out onto the grass together. "I never have. Before. I beg your pardon if it seems that way to you, Miss Saunders. I was very concerned about my nephew. I felt I had to do something for him."

"And your great-nephew," said Jean.

"And Geoffrey, of course."

She doubted this, though she believed he cared about Geoffrey now that he'd met him. Just as Lord Furness was recognizing his neglect. She'd accomplished that much. But there was another important point in what Lord Macklin had said. "You *were* concerned about Lord Furness?"

"I was."

"Not *am*?"

"Thanks to you."

Although this idea gratified Jean, she had to object. Lord Macklin's expression wasn't quite patronizing. He was too kind for that. But she detected a hint of complacency over his quite wrongheaded notion. "I don't much care for being the *something you had to do*," she said. "I'm not, in fact, a chess piece for you to move around the board."

"Of course not."

"Nor am I a helpless female who requires *herding*."

"I can see that."

"So no more *evolving* conversations. With me or about me."

"I give you my word." Lord Macklin shrugged. "In my own defense, I must tell you that I have four nieces, and I'm often called upon to make arrangements for them. To anticipate what might be needed to save time and trouble."

"Their wishes being irrelevant to the process."

"Of course not." He looked chagrined. "They always seemed quite pleased with my plans."

"Or resigned to their fate."

"I really think not. I suppose I'd better ask," he added ruefully.

"I'm not your niece," Jean pointed out.

"Not at present."

"What?"

"Ah, here is the famous pony." With a few long steps, Lord Macklin left her behind. It was a moment before Jean followed.

Geoffrey bounced like a maddened hare on the cobbles of the yard, begging to mount up. Benjamin was glad to see that Fergus the pony took this enthusiasm equably. He didn't shy or offer to nip at the wild little figure dancing around him, though he did follow the boy's movements with a wary eye. There was no need for him—or Tom, who held the pony's bridle—to intervene.

At last, Bradford appeared with the saddle Benjamin had used as a child. They'd had to hunt it up and clean it. "All right," said Benjamin. "Geoffrey, watch how the straps work. A good rider knows everything about his mount."

His son jerked to a stop and stared intently as the chief groom saddled Fergus, then stood aside. Benjamin reached for his son. "Now I will lift you—"

"I want to get up on my *own*," Geoffrey declared

Looking down at the militant, ruddy-haired figure, Benjamin found the words "you're too small" dying on his lips. His son *was* too small to reach the saddle, but he obviously wouldn't be told so.

"You can use the mounting block," said Miss Saunders. "I often do."

With a glance at Benjamin for permission, Tom led the pony over to the two stone steps in the middle of the yard. Geoffrey sprang onto the top and poised to leap.

"Set your hand on the front of the saddle," said Benjamin. "And then throw your right leg over it."

Geoffrey exhibited a moment's confusion about which leg he meant, then obeyed. In the next instant he sat atop Fergus. The grin that lit his face was like nothing Benjamin had seen before. A critical inner voice suggested that he ought to be more familiar with the boy's infectious delight.

Benjamin let him enjoy the sensation for a bit, then said, "Put your feet in the stirrups." These had been shortened as much as possible on the child's saddle and still barely sufficed. "Tom will lead you about at first to accustom you to Fergus's gait."

Tom clucked at the pony and started him off in a circle around the yard. Bradford observed from one side, Benjamin's uncle from the other.

Geoffrey turned out to be a natural rider. Soon he'd taken the reins and was urging the pony along on his own. "I want to gallop," he declared not long after that. "I bet I could race the dogs and beat them!"

"You must take things slowly," Benjamin replied. "For Fergus's sake." He enjoyed the shift in his son's expression as a budding rebellion died. "He needs to learn to trust you," he added, cementing the idea. "You make friends with your mount first, and then he will do whatever you ask of him. Even very hard things, which are difficult for him. That's a great responsibility. Do you understand what I mean by that?"

Geoffrey nodded. "How do I make friends?" he said in a subdued tone.

A small noise from Miss Saunders at his back made Benjamin wonder if she, like him, was daunted by the idea that Geoffrey had no friends. "You'll groom him," he answered. "And talk to him, bring him an apple now and then. But not too many treats, for fear of upsetting his stomach. Ask Bradford first. You'll learn what makes a pony feel safe and what he can and cannot do."

As Geoffrey nodded again, emphatically, Miss Saunders let out an audible sigh.

"And then, after a while, you can ride about the estate with Tom and Molly and the grooms," Benjamin finished.

His son looked like a boy who'd glimpsed a heavenly vision. "I'll work hard," he said. "I'll learn fast."

"I'm sure you will."

They watched for a while longer. Bradford offered Geoffrey some pointers about the way he sat in the saddle, and Geoffrey adjusted immediately. It was a pleasure to see, and yet a strain as well. As Geoffrey moved, frowned in concentration, and laughed, it was as if Alice appeared before Benjamin's eyes, vanished, then reappeared. Over and over, like a flickering phantasm, forcing Benjamin to wonder, for the thousandth time, at the cruelty of fate, which had decreed that the boy would so resemble his dead mother. Trusting the groom to end the session if the pony tired, he said, "I must go in. You're doing very well."

Turning, he nearly bumped into Miss Saunders, who had moved at the same moment. There was something odd about her face "Are you crying?"

"No. Of course not." She swallowed. "Why would I be?"

Benjamin had no idea. And he'd reached the limit of what he could endure. He strode away, feeling his uncle's eyes on his back. There were times when sympathy felt as onerous as judgment. He would retreat to his library refuge, Benjamin thought, and this time he would lock the door.

When she returned to her room after the riding lesson, Jean discovered that Tab had attacked the pile of writing paper on the desk, leaving tiny fang punctures on every page. At first she feared that this was a sign of displeasure at being shut up. But he seemed proud of his achievement, joining her to add a few more holes as she looked over the damage. On the positive side, the kitten had used the sand box for its designated purpose.

Jean tidied up the desk, changed out of the riding habit, and sat down by the window. Immediately, the scene in the stable yard rose in her mind. Geoffrey had looked so happy on his pony. His father's expression, by turns fond and pained, had brought tears to her eyes. Whatever their difficulties, they were a family. They belonged in a way she didn't. Any more than she belonged at the Phillipsons—or anywhere, really. Yet she had to be somewhere.

Whatever Lord Macklin imagined he'd learned about her, he didn't comprehend her system of living. She depended on hospitality, going from house to house on an established yearly round. In the five years since her mother had died, she'd made herself a welcome guest, and she couldn't afford to annoy her various hosts or cause gossip. It wasn't, as many people must think, a question of money. Far otherwise. She had plenty of money. But as a young lady of independent means, one's choices were actually quite limited if one didn't wish to be alone. Jean swallowed. A person could be competent and confident and yet not wish to be all alone.

Tab batted at the quill pen on the desk, trying to bite the feather. When Jean lifted it out of reach, he jumped, missed his footing, and tumbled into her lap. Laughing at his indignant expression, Jean got hold of herself. She had a system for her life; it worked quite well. The important thing was to preserve it. She should write the Phillipsons, in the guise of a report on their grandson perhaps. Their relief at hearing that Geoffrey wasn't coming to live with them would outweigh any other concerns.

The letter took a while to draft. Tab wished to add toothmarks to the fresh paper, or at the least chew on the quill, and the simplest words came slowly. The task left Jean curiously fatigued.

∝

"That went well," Arthur said to young Tom as they walked back to the house together. Geoffrey had stayed on in the stables, brushing his pony under the groom's supervision.

"Love at first sight, I'd say," replied Tom with a grin that lit his homely face.

"You're happy for Geoffrey." Arthur was interested in Tom. He hadn't come across anyone just like him before.

"'Course I am."

"Why?"

"Beg pardon, milord?"

"You haven't known him long."

"It don't take time to like seeing people happy. Most folks do, unless they're bad 'uns."

"I'm surprised to hear you say so, with the life you've led."

Tom looked over at him as they walked. "It ain't been that bad, milord."

"Many would disagree with you. Don't you grieve for your parents, for example?" Grief had been on Arthur's mind recently.

"I never knew them." Tom shrugged. "I don't think a person grieves over what they can't remember."

"Even though their loss was quite unfortunate for you, and unfair?"

"That's not the same, is it, milord?" The lad's plain face creased in thought. "I might feel aggrieved, if I was that way inclined, which I ain't. Because what's the use? But that wouldn't be grieving."

"No?"

Tom shook his head. "Grief is more like… Say I had a meat pie, and I took a bite, and I found it was the finest pie I'd ever et. A little taste of heaven, y'see? Everything about it just perfect. And then say, right then and there, I dropped that pie in a river. After just that one bite. And there wasn't another such pie to be had, for any money. Then I'd grieve."

"Because you knew what you'd lost."

"That's it, milord." Tom nodded, satisfied he'd made his point.

"'Grief' seems a strong word to use over a meat pie," Arthur replied. He was finding Tom a surprisingly stimulating conversationalist. "Not much like losing a person you care about."

"I 'spect that's a deal harder. I wouldn't know." The lad thought for a moment. "I've left some people behind. Mrs. Dunn who ran the dame school was right sad when I went. But I had to move on."

Was he shallow or cold? "You weren't sorry to make her sad?"

"I was, milord. But you know, she was sad over every single kiddie who left for more schooling or a 'prenticeship. So it weren't just me. And I promised

I'd go back and visit her. Which I did. And will whenever I get back to Bristol."

The path divided before them, one branch heading for the front door of Furness Hall, the other for the back. "Was there anything else you wanted, milord?" Tom asked. Arthur shook his head, and the lad gave him a little bow before taking the latter route.

He should do something for Tom, Arthur thought as he walked on. He wasn't sure what as yet, but the lad was full of possibilities. Was this more of the interference that Miss Saunders had deplored? Surely helping people was a good thing? Arthur smiled as he heard Miss Saunders's voice suggesting that he might want to consult Tom before defining the specifics of this *help*.

The meal Jean shared with Lord Furness and his uncle that evening was stiff and formal. They'd had easy conversations over the last two days, but on this night their exchanges died away after a response or two. Their host seemed morose, his uncle distracted. Jean's spirits sank as she searched for remarks to break the silence. She was glad to rise from the table and go back upstairs.

Some hours later, she woke from a bad dream and lit her candle. She took deep breaths to push the dark away. Reaching for her book, she looked also for Tab. He'd curled up on the coverlet when she got into bed, a purring comfort, but he wasn't there now. "Tab?" she said.

He had a habit of mewing when she spoke to him, but there was no response. Jean held up the candlestick and looked about the room. He wasn't on the window seat or the armchair or the hearthrug. She couldn't see him anywhere. "Tab?"

Silence. Jean got out of bed and carried her light about the room, illuminating the dark corners. She looked under the bed, inside the wardrobe, behind the open draperies. There was no sign of the kitten. She checked the windows. They were securely closed against the raw March night. Tab couldn't have gotten out, yet he wasn't there. "Tab?"

Concerned, she looked everywhere again. There was no sign, no sound. She set down the candlestick and put on her dressing gown and slippers. Holding her meager light, she slipped out into the corridor. It ended on her left, and Tab wasn't in it. Jean turned right and walked toward the center of the house, searching. She knew there was little chance of finding one small kitten in this great, dim house, but she couldn't help but try.

At the stairs, she could only go down. The servants' quarters above were reached by another stair. Jean searched the parlors on either side of front hall, calling softly and beginning to feel foolish. This was obviously a futile quest. She had given up and turned back when she noticed a line of light under the library door. She went in, finding the chamber still warm, the coals of a fire still glowing. "Tab?" she said.

"I beg your pardon?"

Jean started so violently that a drop of hot wax splattered from the candle to the back of her hand. The pain made her breath catch.

Lord Furness rose from the chair by the hearth. "What are you doing here?" she asked. "With no lights?" In her fright, she sounded accusing.

"I don't sleep well," he replied. "I often come down. And you?"

"I was looking for the kitten."

"Got out, did he?" Still half in his broken reverie, Benjamin eyed his guest. The lines of her body were beautifully revealed by her thin wool dressing gown and gossamer nightdress. Her hair had been braided down her back, but soft tendrils had escaped all around her face. He imagined what that hair would look like loose—what a wild riot of curls.

"I don't see how," she said, her tone oddly defensive. "But he's not in my room." The candle wavered in her hand. "Oh, what if he's in the kitchen when your cook gets up?"

"The cook will cope." Miss Saunders's unexpected appearance was like a dream, yet so different from the ones that usually disturbed his nights.

"Why must everything I do go wrong? I had this one small creature to care for—"

"And tomorrow we will find him," Benjamin interrupted. "There's no sense looking in the dark. Too easy for him to hide. We'll turn out the staff in the morning. By then, he'll be hungry and come looking for food."

"Yes." Miss Saunders startled suddenly, setting the light of her candle dancing over the walls. "The portrait seemed to move."

Benjamin looked up at Alice's likeness above the mantel. "Yes, when it's dim like this, she does. Seem to."

"You loved her very much," said Miss Saunders softly.

"We met at a ball in London, fell in love, married, and were parted by death all in a year. Such a short time to encompass so much."

"A life sliced in half," she replied. Her tone was contemplative and…bitter?

"Yes." Benjamin sank back into his chair. "You understand that?"

"Oh yes." Absently, she sat down opposite, putting her candle on the low table by the fireplace.

"A love you lost?"

She shook her head, setting the errant curls bobbing. "Say rather…a person who defined my existence."

It was a striking phrase. He waited a moment. When she didn't go on, he asked, "Who?"

Miss Saunders hesitated before answering, "My mother."

"Ah. That can be a deep bond."

"Yes."

The single word dropped between them like a rock tossed into a well. The echoes were odd, Benjamin thought. Not sadness, not regret. "You miss her a great deal."

Miss Saunders laughed without humor. "How I wish I did. She haunts my dreams."

Benjamin felt as if some mighty hand had reached deep inside him and struck a chord. His whole being resounded with it. He leaned forward and took her hand. It was trembling.

As his strong fingers closed over hers, Jean couldn't look away. Under his dressing gown, his nightshirt was open at the neck. The strong column of his throat rose above a muscular chest. She'd never been more intensely aware of another person, much less a man.

"The past keeps its claws in us," he said.

The phrase was so exactly right. "It feels like

talons," she said. "Sunk right in. No matter how you fight, they won't come loose."

"A mouse carried off by a hawk," he said.

Lips parted in amazement at his understanding, Jean nodded. Lord Furness leaned nearer. She'd moved toward him as well, she realized, irresistibly. For a moment, a kiss seemed inevitable. They grew closer, closer. She could feel a hint of his breath on her skin.

Then, all at once, he seemed to become aware of their proximity, their laced hands. He let go, drew back. In a welter of emotion, Jean did the same. Color flickered in the corner of her eye; the image of her cousin Alice looked down on them from above the mantel.

Lord Furness cleared his throat. "So, you see." He took a breath. "Previous…events make it more difficult with Geoffrey. For me. Despite what I might wish."

Jean gazed at him.

"The resemblance." He indicated the portrait with a gesture. "It…flashes out at me. There and then gone. He looks just like his mother, and then he doesn't. If it was one or the other, I'm sure I'd grow accustomed. But I find it hard to take the…sudden blow."

She nodded. Her dreams were like that. Some memories as well.

"I'm very glad you're here to help," he added.

"You are?"

"Yes."

"I'd thought you seemed to be doing well. With the pony and all. Perhaps I wasn't needed."

He sat straighter. "We agreed to work together, for Geoffrey's sake."

"But I'm not sure what I can do." She wanted

to help him, Jean realized. She wanted a number of things she hadn't recognized until tonight.

Lord Furness turned away. "I ran today," he said in a harsh tone. "I had to get away from him. My own son. I hid in this room as I've been doing for far too long. I wanted never to come out."

"But you did."

"And I was a bear at dinner. Surly and curt." He turned back to her. "Do you see that hiding is easier?"

Jean couldn't look away from those blue-gray eyes. They were mirrors and temptations and beckoning abysses. "Yes," she whispered.

He blinked. Jean felt as if she'd tripped on a missed step. She felt Alice staring down at her. In a confusion of emotion, she stood. "I…I should go up."

He didn't argue. Was he finding it just as difficult to speak? Shaken, Jean took her candle and went.

When she entered her room—minutes, eons, later—Tab was sitting on her bed. He gazed at her in seeming reproach and mewed. "Where were you?" cried Jean. "I looked everywhere."

"*Mew*," said Tab. He kneaded the damask coverlet, pulling a thread of the pattern loose.

"Don't. Oh, I'll have to ask for a plain bedcover." She put the candlestick on the bedside table and ran a hand over the kitten's silky fur. He flopped over and offered his pale belly, tiny paws waving in the air. Jean laughed and petted him.

Seven

WHEN BENJAMIN ROSE THE NEXT MORNING, AFTER A restless night, he discovered that someone had slipped a scrap of paper under his bedchamber door. He picked it up and read the unfamiliar handwriting:

Kitten found.

The terse message made him smile, and then frown. She'd really been there in the library—last night. With her unruly hair and clinging dressing gown and haunted eyes. He might have thought it a dream, but here was proof. And so she'd also heard him say things he never said to anyone. She'd struck a sympathetic chord, at that late hour, in those shifting shadows, and he'd succumbed. Of course he regretted it now, as one did a reckless indulgence. Miss Saunders would look at him differently today. She'd imagine she understood him, and perhaps pity him. Benjamin gritted his teeth. He dressed quickly and headed out to get some air.

A soft mist drifted over the lawns of Furness Hall and, with it, a hush. He could hear the soft drip of dew from leaf and branch. The damp air brushed his cheek as he walked through the gardens, where daffodils poked from the earth. The sky would clear later, he judged, and the day would be warm. The lure of a good gallop drew him around to the back of the house. Physical exertion always improved his mood.

Benjamin strode into the stables and was about to call for a groom when he heard a high, light voice say, "We'll go everywhere." There was no one in sight, but he knew the voice. It was Geoffrey, in conversation with someone. "To the stream," the boy continued. "And the woods. Tom says there's a fox den on the other side of the hills."

Geoffrey was in the loose box with his pony, Benjamin realized. The other new arrival, Molly, looked on from the next stall.

"He wouldn't take me to see it, because he didn't have *permission*."

Geoffrey said the final word as if it was a curse.

"We'll find it. And watch the kits play. I won't let them hurt you!"

Benjamin smiled at the picture.

"When I'm bigger, we'll go to the gorge. *Ourselves*. And stay as long as we want. I'll show you the caves."

The boy's tone implied that he was intimately familiar with these caverns.

"You can't go inside though," Geoffrey continued. "Because you might get lost and fall into a...a pit. There's lots of pits."

He'd been told exactly this on their picnic, Benjamin remembered. He could tell Geoffrey had no idea what a mine pit was really like.

"I wouldn't let you though. You don't have to worry. I'll never let anything bad happen to you."

On the echoes of that fierce little voice, it came to Benjamin that Geoffrey possessed a personality all his own. Startlingly intelligent for his age and defiant, he wasn't the least like Alice. His looks were a distraction, in a way a deception. He was…developing into himself.

"I'll be like the lord," his son continued. "*He* can go riding whenever he wants. Wherever he wants."

Moving without thought, Benjamin stepped forward. "Don't call me *the lord*," he said.

Geoffrey had been tucked into the back corner of the stall on a pile of dry straw. He jumped up.

"You should call me Papa," Benjamin added.

His son eyed him with Alice's blue eyes but his own stubborn jaw. His expression was an odd mixture of shyness and doubt. Benjamin had the uncomfortable feeling that his appearance had spoiled the boy's fun. Only then did it occur to him that someone ought to be watching him. "Where is Lily?" he asked.

It was precisely the wrong thing to say. Geoffrey scowled. "Asleep. I can go down to the kitchen and ask for breakfast if I wake up at the *crack of dawn*." A sideways flick of his gaze seemed to acknowledge that this was not the kitchen. Going on the offensive, he added, "Fergus is *my* pony. Isn't he?"

A long tug-of-war over what was and was not permitted unfolded in Benjamin's mind. Yet in the face of his son's vibrating longing, he had to say, "Yes, he is."

There was that grin again, blazing on Geoffrey's small face. The air of the stables seemed to lighten with it. Benjamin's heart stirred. And again, he made a misstep. "But Lily, or someone, should always know where you are," he said.

Geoffrey scowled again. "When I'm grown up, I'll do what I want!"

"You won't, actually," replied Benjamin. "It may look that way to you now, but life isn't like that." Why had he said that? He'd sounded like his own gruff father, with his discouraging philosophizing. Benjamin tried to make amends. "Have you had your breakfast?"

But Geoffrey took this as a dismissal. Scowl deepening, his son pushed off the side of the stall, scrambled over the rail, and stomped out of the stables.

Benjamin watched him go with a mixture of perplexity and regret. When the sound of Geoffrey's footsteps had died away, Benjamin turned toward the box where his own horse was kept and discovered Miss Saunders, standing by the open door at the other end of the stable aisle. Their eyes met. Benjamin felt his cheeks warm. How much of that conversation had she heard?

She should have moved on earlier, Jean thought. But she'd been transfixed by the scene. When Lord Furness told Geoffrey to call him Papa, and the boy wouldn't, she'd felt so mournful. And now, facing this tall, masterful figure, she was shaken. He had the looks and bearing of an autocratic nobleman, yet his commands meant nothing to a stubborn little boy.

She'd come here to save Geoffrey from neglect, Jean thought, and she wasn't sorry, no matter what anyone thought. But she'd been wrong about the method. Man and boy should be brought together, not separated.

The idea bloomed in her mind like a rose opening, revealing petal after petal. She imagined Geoffrey truly finding a father. She saw Lord Furness joyful over his son, instead of always melancholy. Yes. It only remained to see how she could bring this about. She had no notion, but she was filled with the determination to try.

The silence had stretched into awkwardness. "I came out for a walk," she said, very aware that she'd just thrown on a cloak. She hadn't even bothered with a bonnet.

"What?"

She'd spoken too softly. "I was out for a walk," she repeated. "And I heard voices."

He moved toward her. "I did the same. Geoffrey was talking to his pony."

"Yes." Jean glanced at Fergus and Molly, who gazed out from their stalls with ears swiveled toward them. "And he seemed to listen."

Lord Furness turned to follow her eyes. "I hadn't noticed. They appear attentive, don't they?"

"Well, horses must know how to listen. Or else no one could train them."

"They merely react to gestures and a firm tone of voice."

He stopped beside her. She kept forgetting how large he was, Jean thought. Until he stood right next to her and practically...oozed attraction. "You don't think they care for their riders?"

"Care?" he replied in a distracted tone.

"Horses. Even love them and want to please them?"

"Ascribing such feelings to an animal is sheer sentimentality."

"But you told Geoffrey to make friends with Fergus," Jean pointed out. "You said the pony would do whatever he asked once he trusted him."

"Have you never heard, Miss Saunders, that it is annoying to quote a man's words back to him?"

"Not from people who stand by what they say."

A corner of his mouth twitched, from amusement, or perhaps irritation. "I was teaching Geoffrey caution. I said what was necessary."

"So you don't believe that true bonds are based in trust?"

Lord Furness looked down at her. "The damp causes your hair to curl even more, doesn't it? What must it look like, free of all those pins?"

"A mare's nest," replied Jean, well aware that this was a distraction. Which was working.

"Harsh," he said. Gazing at her head, he walked around her.

Jean could feel his eyes on her back. She resisted an impulse to tuck back wayward tendrils of hair. Her hair did expand in wet weather, making it even harder to control. There weren't enough hairpins in the world.

"You had it in a braid last night. Partly. It does keep coming loose, doesn't it?" He came around her other side and faced her again. His blue-gray eyes were definitely amused now. In another moment he would reach out and flick a wayward curl.

He was trying to make her self-conscious. And succeeding. Jean started walking back toward the house.

Lord Furness fell into step beside her. "I'm glad your kitten was found. Where was he?"

She'd scurried like a thief to slip a note under his door this morning, Jean remembered. "He was in my room when I got back. Apparently, he was there all the time. Though I looked *everywhere*."

"There are those who say cats can walk through walls."

She glanced at him. He smiled. Purposefully. Meltingly. With a clear intent to charm. Jean had no doubt he wanted to fluster her, to render her speechless. Because he didn't want to answer her question about trust? Or couldn't? There was an interesting thought. She also noted that he and Geoffrey had this trait in common. Their smiles transformed their faces, and they knew it. "I'll keep an eye on Tab," she said. "And learn how he does it."

Jean was gratified to see that her tone seemed to startle him considerably.

Gazing out the window of the breakfast room, Arthur watched his nephew and Miss Saunders approach the house—side by side, together and yet clearly not. What had taken them out so early? They were coming from the direction of the stables, but there was no sign they'd gone riding.

Friction makes heat, he thought. Whether that was a good thing or a bad thing depended on circumstances. It seemed to him that these two might do very well together, but that wasn't for him to say. As both of these young people had pointed out.

Miss Saunders said something that made his nephew laugh, and Arthur smiled in sympathy. And with just a trace of envy, remembering the joys of companionship. He'd filled the decade since his wife died with

familial responsibilities, needed and appreciated by
nieces and nephews and cousins of all sorts. But the
generation below him was grown up now. He was
welcome in their homes; affectionate bonds remained.
Their main attention had turned elsewhere, however.
Arthur was no longer required. Except perhaps by
Benjamin and others like him. He thought of the
other young men who'd attended his London dinner.
They deserved to laugh again as well.

He turned from the window and addressed his meal.
Arthur was a student, almost a connoisseur, of grief. He'd
grappled long and hard with loss—the sudden absence
of a beloved partner. He'd faced down the void that
opened when the person who'd shared a dozen daily
anecdotes, and listened to his similar stories, was gone.
He'd felt existence constrict around him like a nar-
rowing tunnel, and he'd come out the other side intact.
Contented even. He wanted the same for Benjamin.
Even more perhaps, as his nephew was young, with
most of life before him. So although Arthur had a lively
circle of friends and an active social round, which he
missed, he was glad he'd come to Furness Hall.

He sipped his cooling coffee. There was also
Geoffrey. Arthur was ashamed that his great-nephew
hadn't figured in his plans until he met him and
discovered a bright, troubled spirit. He ought to
have considered what grief had done to the boy;
Jean Saunders had shown him that. He wanted to see
Geoffrey carefree and laughing, too.

"I cannot agree," said Miss Saunders as she entered
the breakfast room. She stopped in the doorway. "Oh,
good morning, Lord Macklin."

"Miss Saunders," Arthur replied. "You're out early this morning." She'd taken off her cloak. Her cheeks glowed from the outdoors, and her hair had reacted to the floating mist. It wasn't appropriate to compare the result to Medusa. For many reasons. Yet the dark strands did seem to have a life of their own.

"I felt like a walk," she replied. She moved forward, and Benjamin came in behind her.

An atmosphere entered with them. It was interesting, Arthur thought, how an almost visible connection could vibrate between two people even when their conversation was perfectly ordinary. And others— married couples too—gave no such impression even when they embraced.

A hairpin fell from Miss Saunders's rebellious locks to the floor. The ping as it landed seemed disproportionately loud. Benjamin bent, picked it up, and offered it to her like a bouquet. Miss Saunders flushed, took the pin, and shoved it back into her hair.

"Do you often lose pins?" Benjamin asked with a clear intent to provoke. "You must have a great many."

Miss Saunders gave him a flashing look. She proceeded with dignity to get her breakfast. "I was thinking," she said when seated. "We should ask Tom about Geoffrey. He's been watching over him for a while and must have a good notion what he's like. His character, I mean. How we might best approach him. Beyond the pony, which Geoffrey obviously adores."

"That's a good idea," said Arthur. He'd been impressed by Tom's common sense.

"I don't know," said Benjamin. "Tom's little more than a boy himself."

Arthur wondered if his nephew liked to argue, or just couldn't resist teasing Miss Saunders. Catching the glint in Benjamin's eyes, he suspected the latter.

"A youth," said Miss Saunders, refusing the bait, "whose life has made him older than his years."

"Let's talk to him," said Arthur. He was interested in what Tom might have to say, regardless of its practical uses.

Tom was sent for and offered a chair in the library, to which the group had adjourned. He appeared in the same clothes as before, with the same cheerful air. They ought to see about finding him another coat, Arthur thought. And a shirt or two. The lad was rapidly outgrowing the ones he had. His own clothes would be too large, as would Benjamin's, but surely the household could come up with something suitable.

"We wanted to talk to you about Geoffrey," Miss Saunders said.

Tom nodded. His round face and prominent front teeth gave him the look of a friendly squirrel. His expression was sharply intelligent, however. And he didn't look the least bit anxious. That was remarkable in itself, Arthur thought, for a youngster in his position.

"What would you say about his character?" Miss Saunders asked.

"He's hardly old enough to have one," objected Benjamin.

"I'da said he was older than he is," Tom replied. "If it weren't for his size and all. He's that quick. If he hears a word once, he knows it. Better than me, half the time." He grinned, unconcerned by the comparison.

"Very intelligent," said Arthur. He'd marked it himself.

"He's got a cartload of opinions too," added Tom. "More than you'd credit. Mrs. McGinnis said he's like one of them—what was it?—barristers. The ones who stand up in court. Geoffrey don't easily change his mind."

"That is to say, stubborn," said Benjamin. "I've noticed."

Tom nodded. "Though he *will* listen, if a thing is laid out for him in a way he can understand."

"I would have said he was too young to be swayed by reason," Benjamin replied.

"He can see a fact when it's in his face. Little as he may like it."

There was a short silence as the adults contemplated the facts that had governed Geoffrey's life so far. At least, Arthur did. And he thought the others did as well.

"He's curious as a cat, but he don't always stick with things," Tom went on. "See now, he's finished with the red Indians since that he got the pony. I'd think the two would go together. Don't those Indians ride about marauding?"

"Do *not* suggest it to him," Benjamin said.

Tom grinned again. "No, my lord. Anyhow, the cook thinks Geoffrey's a sneak, 'cause he nicks the odd muffin, but she's wrong."

"You sound quite certain of that," said Arthur. Tom was an interesting character.

"I am, my lord. Geoffrey's always on the lookout for ways to get what he wants. Well, who of us ain't? He don't lie or cheat for 'em though. He does tell stories—and a pure wonder some of 'em are. But he knows the difference between a tale and an untruth."

"Which is?" asked Miss Saunders curiously.

Tom blinked, considered the question. "A story's fun, yeh? You might learn summat or have a laugh, but no more than that. A lie gets you something that mebbe you have no right to, or covers up your sins, like."

"Where did you learn such wisdom?" Arthur wondered.

"Wisdom?" Tom looked abashed. "I don't claim nothing like that. I've been watching people all my life, that's all. On the streets, you have to figure who's all right and who's dangerous."

"My son has not been a homeless wanderer," said Benjamin, his voice harsh with reproach. Was it directed at Tom or himself, Arthur wondered?

Miss Saunders looked distressed. "He didn't mean—"

"'Course he hasn't," said Tom. "Beg pardon if I offended, my lord."

"No, no. I understand you didn't mean that." Benjamin's expression remained stiff.

Tom nodded. "Anyhow, Geoffrey's merry as a grig now you've gotten him the pony. You should hear him tell Lily and the others all about Fergus. Seems that animal was on a whole raft of adventures before he came here." Tom laughed. He had the secret of joy, Arthur thought. Somehow, despite his rough life, he'd discovered or retained it.

"That could be useful," Benjamin said. "We might ration access to the pony to make sure Geoffrey does as he's told."

A look of horror crossed Miss Saunders's face.

There was no other word for it, Arthur thought. She jumped up. "You cannot threaten to take his pony!"

"I didn't say 'take,'" Benjamin began.

"That would cruel, inhuman. Do you want to make him bitter?"

"I did not say—" Benjamin tried again.

Miss Saunders wouldn't let him speak. "He already loves Fergus. Anyone can see that. And he expects that the things he loves will be taken away from him. You can't have missed seeing that."

"If you will allow me to—"

"Punishment is never the answer! A child learns nothing being shut away and ignored. Nothing but fear. And despair."

Benjamin rose, holding out a hand. "Miss Saunders, please. You're twisting my words all out of recognition."

She stood for a moment as if frozen, then burst into tears and ran from the room. The three males remained behind, variously bewildered, uncomfortable, and appalled.

Eight

THE ATTIC OF FURNESS HALL WAS A HUGE PEAKED space, topping the entire length of the building. Sunlight streamed through round windows at the gable ends, but the illumination barely reached the middle. Jean carried an oil lamp to guard against her engrained hatred of dark spaces.

Her stated purpose was to search for old games and toys that Geoffrey might like. In fact, she was hiding. Since her humiliating outburst about Geoffrey's pony, her lordly housemates looked at her sidelong, with wariness or sympathy. She didn't try to figure out which. It was too annoying.

In the last five years, Jean had become herself—a sociable, reliable person whom hostesses were glad to see and companions were happy to include in any outing. She did *not* cause discomfort or awkwardness, much less enact scenes from Cheltenham tragedies. As far as anyone knew, would *ever* know, she had no reason to do so. That carefully nurtured persona would not break down now. She simply wouldn't let it. A little time, some stern self-control, and all would be as before. And so, though she didn't care for solitude in poorly lit spaces, she'd withdrawn to this large, silent attic to regroup.

Under the slanting rafters, dust motes drifted on dim brown air. Rough floorboards stretched away, littered with discarded bits of furniture, boxes, and trunks. Jean walked among them, holding up her lamp.

As she passed, she bent to open any container that looked interesting. She found tattered books, frayed linens, periodicals from the last century. Boring. Not enough to make her forget her lapse, until she raised the lid of a wooden case and confronted a garishly painted face screwed up into a wild grimace. Jean dropped the lid and jumped back, only just managing not to shriek.

The lamp wavered dangerously in her hand, making the shadows dance. Jean put it down on a small, battered table, making certain the top didn't wobble before letting go. Then she waited for her heart to stop pounding. "Idiot," she said. She opened the case again and looked more closely. The menacing face was a carved mask. Red, yellow, and black paint outlined a ferocious frown. A tuft of tattered feathers stood in for hair at the top. Lord Furness's father had been interested in North American tribes, she remembered. No doubt this was an artifact he'd collected.

When she'd proved to herself that she wasn't afraid of the thing, she retrieved the lamp and moved on.

Toward the far end of the attic, Jean came upon a row of leather trunks bound in brass. Resettling her lamp securely, she opened the first. The scent of camphor wafted out at her. Pushing aside a layer of tissue paper, she unearthed a swath of satin brocade in an exquisite shade of peach.

Jean pulled the cloth out. It proved to be a sumptuous gown with a square bodice, elbow-length sleeves trimmed with ribbons and rows of lace, and a skirt as broad as a tent. Exquisite embroidery adorned the neckline, glinting with tiny jewels. Although the fashion of another era, it was one of the loveliest gowns she'd ever seen.

Under more layers of tissue, she found other, similar garments. A second trunk contained still more. A third held gentlemen's clothing from the same epoch—long full coats in bright hues and laced with gold—and a fourth had a variety of other clothes. Jean examined them all with admiration. Wealthy people had strutted about like peacocks fifty years ago.

She was drawn back to the first dress, running her fingers over the gorgeous brocade. It was so lovely. There was no one around, and she was so tired of the few outfits she had with her. She couldn't resist. She slipped off her much plainer gown, placing it out of the dust on a sheet of tissue, and slithered her way into the peach creation.

The dress was a bit large on her. Fortunately, it laced up the side so she could reach to pull it tighter, but the shoulders still threatened to slip off. Her shift and stays showed above the low neckline, and without the elaborate underpinnings such a garment required, the skirt sagged around her in heavy folds. Even so, she felt very grand.

There was a broken cheval glass farther down the huge room. Jean held up the dragging skirts and went over to stand before it. Though her image was fragmented by two long cracks in the mirror, she wielded an imaginary fan as she thought a lady at the court of Louis XV might have done.

"Very elegant," said an appreciative male voice.

Jean whirled and nearly lost the dress. She frowned at Lord Furness, who stood near the head of the attic stair, as she pushed the shoulders back into place. "What are you doing here?"

"This is my house."

"Yes, but you went riding."

"And I returned." Benjamin strolled toward his disheveled houseguest. In his ancestress's gown, Miss Saunders was an unsettling combination of little girl playing dress-up and lush courtesan, with her clothes falling off and her curling hair making a determined break for freedom.

She gathered the heavy skirts and retreated to a rank of trunks a little distance away. "I was just... I'll put on my own gown."

Benjamin walked a bit closer.

"If you will go *away*."

"But I came up to help you look for toys for Geoffrey." It was an increasing delight to tease her. There was something so charming about the look she got, which said she knew precisely what he was up to and refused to stoop to acknowledge it. And yet she couldn't help but react.

"I haven't found any."

"Only a hoard of finery." Benjamin walked along the row of trunks and glanced inside them. He rummaged through one at the end and pulled out a child's tunic and breeches in deep-blue velvet. "What about this?"

"Just like a chocolate box," said Miss Saunders.

"What?"

She half shrugged, which had a tantalizing effect on her gown. "Geoffrey would never wear that."

"Perhaps if I told him it was an ancient horseman's garb."

"I don't think he'd believe you. And if he did, he'd be bound to spoil the velvet."

"I suppose you're right." Benjamin replaced the small garments and picked up a satin coat. "I think I remember my grandfather wearing something like this, with lots of lace at his shirtfront. Perhaps it was this very coat." He held it up and looked closer. "I'm not sure. He died when I was around Geoffrey's age." He smiled at his disheveled companion. "Grandpapa didn't care much for change at the last. Or for what people thought of his appearance. He wore what he liked." Geoffrey would have appreciated that attitude, Benjamin thought. "He had a dueling scar across his cheek." His hand went to his own face to demonstrate. "A bit puckered and quite frightening, as I recall. They don't seem to go together—all this frippery and bloody sword work."

"I imagine gentlemen took off their coats when dueling," replied Miss Saunders.

Benjamin laughed.

"You should try it on," she added in an odd tone.

He looked at her, hands clutching the brocade bodice to keep it from sliding off, a beam of sunlight shining through the uninhibited glory of her hair.

Holding her gaze, Benjamin slowly took off his coat. "No wigs," he said. "I draw the line there."

"I haven't found any," she answered breathily.

He donned the bright satin garment. It fit well enough, only a little tight in the shoulders. It felt strange to have wide skirts around his legs. He made an elaborate bow. "Pon rep, my lady, I am so pleased to see you. I hope I find you in better health?"

"What do you mean, better?"

Benjamin straightened. "I've been concerned about you since—"

"I'm fine," she interrupted. "My…outburst in the library was quite uncharacteristic, I assure you. It won't happen again."

"No apology is necessary."

"I wasn't apologizing." Coppery glints snapped in the depths of her eyes. "Only informing you that all is well."

He didn't believe her, though he couldn't have said why. Her bearing and expression were calm, her manner quelling. Clearly, she didn't want to talk about the bout of weeping, and he had no right to press her. Why should he wish to? "I don't know how ladies moved about in those gowns." He indicated the sweep of peach brocade trailing over the floorboards.

"With stately elegance," she replied.

"That is to say, very slowly. Have you seen the sort of shoes they wore? Teetering along on four-inch heels must have made it hard to run away."

"From what?" she asked with a quizzical glance.

"Anything." Benjamin had spoken randomly. All his attention was on her, leaving his tongue unsupervised. "Bears."

"Bears?" She laughed.

It was a delightful sound. Benjamin realized he hadn't heard it nearly often enough. Irresistibly drawn, he stepped closer. "Or impertinent admirers."

"The gentlemen wore heels, too," Miss Saunders said. "So it would have been an equal race, mincing along the cobblestones in a satin-draped procession."

She looked up at him, still smiling. Her eyes were suffused with warmth now, her lips a little parted, and Benjamin couldn't help himself. He moved closer still and kissed her.

Just a brush of his mouth on hers, an errant impulse. He pulled back at once.

She leaned forward and returned the favor, as if purely in the spirit of experiment. Benjamin felt a startling shudder of desire.

In the next moment, she'd twined her arms around his neck, and they were kissing as if their lives depended on it. He buried his fingers in her hair, as he'd been longing to do for days. It sprang free and tumbled over his hands, a glorious profusion of curls. Hairpins rained onto the attic floor.

She kissed with sheer inexperienced enthusiasm. One of the open trunks pressed against the back of Benjamin's legs, and he nearly lost his balance and fell in. Her borrowed dress fell off one shoulder, revealing more of her underclothes. He was so tempted to help it along to the floor.

Then she pulled back and blinked at him, her eyes wide, dark pools. Her arms dropped to her sides. She took a step away, and another. "Oh."

The small sound was a breath, a worry, an

astonishment. Benjamin struggled with his arousal, glad now of the long, concealing coat.

Miss Saunders put her hands to her wild crown of hair. The lovely lines of her body were outlined in peach brocade and sunlight. "Oh dear."

"I could help pin it up, if you like." Benjamin bent and gathered a handful of hairpins.

"No, you couldn't."

He gave her the pins. "I have a deft hand," he said.

"My hair is beyond deftness. It has to be wrestled into submission."

He nearly lost his careful control at the phrase and the thoughts it elicited. "I have strong fingers."

Miss Saunders flushed from her cheeks, down her neck, and across her half covered bosom.

She was delectable, Benjamin thought, so very alluring. She was also an unprotected young lady and a guest in his house. He'd very nearly crossed the line here, and he wanted to, desperately, still. He had to leave before he did. He reached for his coat. Miss Saunders moved when he did. Not a flinch, he decided, but a demonstration of uncertainty.

Benjamin snagged his coat. Rapidly, he shed the antique satin garment and resumed his own. He turned, reluctantly, and spotted a small white face peering from behind a broken cabinet near the stairway. "Geoffrey?"

His son darted from hiding and scurried down the stairs. Benjamin knew there was no catching him.

"He looked angry," said Miss Saunders, her tone subdued.

"Only curious, I think." In fact, Benjamin couldn't

have defined his son's expression, seen so fleetingly. The boy had surely witnessed the kissing. There was nothing to be done about that, and nothing useful to say just now. Was he required to explain it to him? Benjamin found he couldn't imagine that conversation.

As he walked to the steps and down into the inhabited parts of the house, he realized that he'd never spoken to his son about his deceased mother. Not one word. He had no idea what Geoffrey thought about Alice. Or knew about her, beyond the portrait in the library.

Part of him argued that this was best. He hadn't burdened a child with the weight of his grief. Should Geoffrey have heard him rail against the cruelty of fate? Seen him pound the desk drunkenly and weep?

But another part wondered how he'd let his life grind to a halt. And so many responsibilities lapse.

When she was certain she was alone again, Jean's knees gave way, and she sank onto one of the closed trunks in a welter of peach brocade. One sleeve of the gown fell off her shoulder. She didn't notice. She simply reverberated, body and mind, with the aftermath of those kisses. She'd never felt anything like *that*.

She wasn't a complete novice. She'd been kissed before. More than once, actually. Gentlemen would flirt and seize their chances, and she'd allowed a few of them to take minor liberties. When she felt curious, or temporarily beguiled. But she'd never been tempted beyond a fumbling embrace or two—those empty bits of nothing compared to what had just occurred. Jean put her hands to her blazing cheeks.

Everyone expected her to marry, of course. Her

birth was genteel, and she had a tidy little fortune. But marriage meant putting her person, and her money, under another's power. Jean couldn't contemplate such a step without a shudder.

And so she moved from hostess to hostess, shedding complications with the changing scenes. The next time an importunate gentleman looked for her, she was gone. By the time they met again, the incident was long past, its lack of consequence obvious. None of these beaus had followed her about the country to press their suits. None had made her head spin. How could fingers running through her hair turn her weak with desire?

But Geoffrey had seen! She'd come here to save him, not dally with his father. What had the boy thought of their embrace? He'd certainly scowled. Hadn't he? She couldn't be certain now.

Jean's hands shook as she changed into her own gown and tidied up the trunks. Alone in the dim, cavernous space, she could admit that she would very much like to kiss Lord Furness again. Even though that was probably a very bad idea.

She returned to her bedchamber, expecting every minute to see Geoffrey peering reproachfully around a corner. She reached safety without encountering anyone, however. "Tab?" she called as she closed the door behind her. A kitten seemed just the thing right now.

There was no response, and no sign of the little animal.

"Have you disappeared into your mysterious hiding place again?" She sighed and let it go. He'd emerge eventually to use the sand box and eat the food still in his bowl.

But he didn't.

The day passed. Not ready to face Lord Furness, Jean wrote several letters and read for a while. When Tab didn't reappear, she searched the room again, with no more success than the last time. Finally, when dinnertime loomed, she went downstairs to inquire.

"He was there when I made up the room this morning," said a young housemaid. She smiled. "He likes to pounce on the sheets when I shake them out."

"You're sure he didn't get out when you left?" asked Jean.

"No, miss. I was careful."

Jean continued along the lower corridor to the kitchen, busy with preparations for the meal. Everyone there disavowed any knowledge of Tab. Overhearing, Mrs. McGinnis came out of her room and said the same. The cook, impatient at the interruption of her work, sniffed. "I'd look to young Master Geoffrey. When things go missing in this house, it's usually him."

Jean took this as prejudice. She walked through the lower floors of the house, calling softly for Tab, but got no response. Finally, she climbed the stairs to the nursery and asked her question there.

"I haven't seen him, miss," said Lily the nursery maid, who sat at a worktable with a pile of mending. "Have you seen Miss Saunders's kitten, Geoffrey?"

The boy, making a tower with wooden blocks on the floor before the fire, didn't look up.

A sound escaped the blanket tepee. It sounded remarkably like a *mew*.

"What was that?" asked Jean.

It came again, muffled but unmistakable. Jean walked

over to the improvised tepee and pulled back a flap. A closed basket sat inside, the source of the mewing. One of Tab's paws poked through a narrow opening in the fibers. Quickly, Jean bent, opened the basket, and lifted Tab out. She straightened with the kitten in her arms.

Geoffrey hit out at his construction, knocking the blocks helter-skelter over the floor. One hit the fire screen and bounced back to strike his knee. He showed no reaction.

Lily sprang up. "Lord a' mercy, what have you been up to?"

"I wanted to play with him," mumbled Geoffrey sullenly.

"But you weren't playing with him," Jean said. She couldn't keep the emotion out of her voice. "You shut him up in a prison and left him."

Geoffrey stuck out his tongue at her.

"Geoffrey!" Lily came to stand over him, hands on hips. She didn't present a particularly authoritative figure. "Beg pardon at once. You told a lie, too. You know what Tom said about—"

"Didn't! Didn't speak!" The boy jumped up. "This is *my* house. The kitten was born near here. It should belong to *me*, not her." He ran from the room.

Lily sighed. She looked quite dispirited. "Sorry, miss."

"I spoke too sharply to him." The kitten clawed at Jean's hand. "I'm going to take Tab back to my room." She carried the squirming animal downstairs, feeling remorseful. She should have moderated her tone with Geoffrey; he was very young. But the truth was, she would never react well to the thought of creatures shut in small spaces.

Tab visited his sand box, dug into his food bowl with gusto, and retired to the window seat for a thorough wash. When Jean went down to dinner soon after, she used the key that had been lying on the mantelpiece and locked her bedchamber door.

Word of Tab's kidnapping and retrieval had reached her companions. "I'm glad your kitten has been found," said Lord Macklin as they sat down to dinner.

"And sorry that Geoffrey took him," said Lord Furness. "He is confined to quarters and will apologize to you tomorrow."

"That's not necessary."

"It is. He'd been told the cat was yours."

"Perhaps, you know, after he saw us in the attic…" Jean faltered under his uncle's interested gaze.

Lord Furness spoke self-consciously. "There was nothing wrong with that. From Geoffrey's point of view."

"Nor from mine," said Jean.

Their eyes met. The look was nearly as intimate as the kiss.

"And what of yours, Benjamin?" said Lord Macklin.

Their host blinked, turned to the older man. "My…?"

"Your point of view. We've heard about Geoffrey's. And Miss Saunders's. What about yours?"

For a moment, Jean thought he knew about the kiss. Then she saw he was only teasing, from the hints he'd picked up.

"I agree with Miss Saunders," said Lord Furness, gazing at her again.

"You share her opinion that there was nothing

wrong with…it?" his uncle replied. He appeared to be enjoying himself.

"Wholeheartedly."

"And should *it* recur?"

Lord Furness's eyes, which remained fixed on Jean, glinted with amusement and something more. "I shall live in hope," he said.

Jean couldn't stop the flush that warmed her cheeks, or the thrill that went with it. She could, however, change the subject. "Have you seen any more of your friend, Lord Macklin?"

"My friend?"

"The one you were surprised to meet in the village. Who's such a creature of London."

"Ah." The older man accepted her diversion with a smile. "I have, in fact. She's settled here for some weeks. For a rest."

"From the rigors of society?" Jean asked. "The season hasn't even started."

Lord Macklin shook his head. "She has taxing… work."

"What sort of work?" asked Jean, intrigued by this unusual piece of information. Ladies from London who were friends with an earl didn't usually have employment.

"Who is this?" asked Lord Furness at the same moment.

"A friend I was surprised to see in Somerset, as Miss Saunders said."

"I hope she doesn't expect formal calls," said their host, reverting to his earliest crusty manner. "Or entertainment."

Something about the last word appeared to amuse

his uncle very much. "She does not. She's known for a charming lack of formality. And she's here quite privately, on a repairing lease. She doesn't want attention."

"Surely we could exchange visits," Jean said, even more interested in this mysterious figure.

"No," said Lord Furness. "The neighborhood would take it as a signal that their society is welcome here and…erupt into a flurry of calls and invitations."

"Like a volcano?" Jean found the image, and his uncharacteristic agitation, amusing.

His uncle calmed him with a gesture. "As I said, she's here for a rest. She doesn't want to see you either."

Lord Furness blinked, nonplussed. Jean laughed.

Through the rest of dinner, she tried to discover more, but Lord Macklin was an old hand at evading questions he didn't wish to answer. He revealed nothing significant.

❦

When Benjamin sent for Geoffrey the next morning, to discuss his transgression and arrange for the official apology, the boy was nowhere to be found. He'd apparently sneaked out of his bedroom in the night, after Lily was asleep. As no doors or windows had been unbolted, he had to be in the house, but a search turned up no sign of him. Even Tom couldn't find him, which he thought odd. "Reckoned I knew all his hidey-holes," the lad said.

Benjamin organized a more systematic sweep of the house, beginning at the bottom and working up, but the dearth of staff made this a slow process. By noon, he'd begun to worry. *Had* Geoffrey gotten outside?

Standing in the empty front hall, Benjamin reviewed the possibilities. No, not without leaving the exit he'd used open. Benjamin had been an inquisitive child here himself; there were no secret passages or escape tunnels at Furness Hall.

Miss Saunders came through the doors to the reception room. "Still no sign?"

Benjamin shook his head.

"I shouldn't have scolded him," she said, practically wringing her hands.

She reviewed the story of Tab's release, as she'd done more than once, despite Benjamin's reassurances. She was overly concerned about a sharp remark, as he was just a bit weary of telling her. Benjamin headed for the stairs. He felt better when he kept moving.

He walked an upper corridor, wondering what to do next. There was nowhere else to look. Every box and trunk in the attic had been opened and examined under his supervision. They'd peered under beds and behind sofas. They'd shaken each drapery and ransacked every cabinet. Perhaps his son, like cats, could walk through walls.

Struck by a sudden impulse, Benjamin went over and opened a door he never opened. The bedchamber beyond was barren—with the requisite furniture and draperies, but no ornament. He'd had Alice's room cleared out a week after she died. The sight of her clothes and trinkets—the mere knowledge that they existed—had lacerated him beyond bearing. He hadn't thought that Geoffrey might want some of them. He hadn't thought at all, actually. "Did I do wrong, Alice?" he said aloud.

A small sound, a seeming response, startled him. Had he really heard it? And was he in the presence of a ghost? For months after his wife died, he'd half hoped for a visitation. Futilely, of course. Was he to receive one now? Preposterous. But he couldn't help saying, "Alice?"

The soft, slithery sound came again, and this time he traced it to the cupboard at the top of the wardrobe. Which he knew to be locked; the key was in his jewelry case with his cuff links.

Benjamin went over and pulled at the cupboard door. Locked indeed. But a sudden flurry of movement from inside was not the least ghostlike. He knocked sharply. "Geoffrey?"

"Go away!" came the muffled reply.

Not bothering to argue, Benjamin went to fetch the key. He was not astonished to find it gone. Back at the wardrobe, he said, "Come out of there at once."

"Won't!"

"Then I shall have to break the door. That would be a shame."

There was a short silence. Then the key turned in the lock. One of the cupboard doors opened, and Geoffrey peered down at him.

Benjamin opened the other, revealing a chamber pot sitting next to his son. He didn't care to imagine using it in such a confined space. There was a clutter of stuff in the back of the cupboard as well. "Come down," he said, holding out his arms.

Geoffrey didn't jump into them. He climbed down, using carvings on the wood of the lower doors as handholds. "I fell asleep. I'm hungry."

"You've no one to blame but yourself for that."

The boy scowled. "This is my mama's room."

"It was. How do you know that?"

"Cook told me."

The cook was a testy creature and often impatient with Geoffrey, though an artist with viands. Not the best source of information, Benjamin thought. He should have realized that the servants would talk about Alice, even if he didn't. He should have realized a number of things.

"She died in here," Geoffrey added.

Benjamin braced himself for questions, reproach, tears. What should he say? Geoffrey's expression was bland, uninformative. "Yes," Benjamin said. He'd hated this room for so many months. Now, it seemed just empty.

"The old lord died in your room. His wife died in the one across the hall from here."

Startled, Benjamin gazed down at him. "Are you keeping a list?"

"I 'spect people have died all over this house. It's old." Geoffrey said this with a certain relish.

"Yes."

"The lord with the long curls in the picture gallery broke his neck on a hunt. Over a regular rasper. Bradford said so."

"It's true. You're, er, interested in death, are you?" What a foolish thing to say to a small child, Benjamin thought. Was this fascination related to Alice? Could it be when it appeared so...clinical?

"Tom doesn't know where his family died," Geoffrey answered with no sign of distress. "'Cept maybe Bristol."

"Yes."

"But I do." This knowledge seemed to gratify him.

"Indeed," said Benjamin. "I'm still alive, of course."

Geoffrey gave him one of the measuring looks that always made the boy seem older than his years. Benjamin wondered if he ought to say something comforting about Alice. He couldn't say she'd loved her son, because she'd died without even seeing him. She *would* have loved him of course, but was that a consolation? "You look just like your mother," he said. And then nearly cursed. Had the servants talked about his reaction to this fact?

The boy still seemed unaffected. "I know. She's in the library."

Did he believe Alice was actually there? Had Benjamin's brooding over the portrait taught him that? Benjamin felt all at sea and just a bit aggrieved. Gentlemen of his acquaintance were not required to grapple with such questions. Women took care of the children. Didn't they? Finally, he said, "Her picture is there, yes."

Geoffrey stared up at him. Benjamin had rarely felt at such a loss for words in his life. Before he found any, his son shrugged and turned away. "I'm hungry," he said again. He started to walk away.

"Wait a moment." He'd been searching for a miscreant before they veered into this exploration of mortality, Benjamin remembered. "We have certain matters to discuss. Concerning Miss Saunders's kitten."

Geoffrey's expression grew sullen.

Benjamin pressed on. "You shouldn't have taken it from her room. You understand that was wrong?"

"I would've put him back," his son replied impatiently.

"And Lily says you lied about having it."

"I did not! I didn't speak!"

"A lie isn't always spoken aloud. Not admitting what you'd done was a lie."

Geoffrey scowled. He was quite good at that, Benjamin noted.

"Did you take Miss Saunders's kitten because of... anything you saw in the attic?"

The boy looked less, not more, self-conscious. His celestial blue eyes, Alice's eyes, fixed on Benjamin. Then he let out a sigh and spoke like someone wishing to conclude an irritating bit of business. "What's the punishment?"

"Eh?"

"That's the rule. There's always a punishment. Lily gives really stupid ones."

He appeared to see this as an annoying game. Misbehave, receive a silly punishment, and forget the matter. "An honorable gentleman makes things right," Benjamin said. "When he sees that he has made a mistake, he takes steps to correct it."

Geoffrey's face showed apprehension for the first time. Or perhaps it was just confusion?

"What do you think the punishment should be?"

His son blinked, astonished.

Briefly, Benjamin enjoyed seeing the boy as bewildered as he was coming to feel much of the time. Then, Geoffrey's cerulean eyes flamed. "I won't give up Fergus!" he declared. He stood straight and fierce, his little hands closed into fists. "If you try to take him away, I'll...I'll—"

"No." Benjamin knelt and started to put his arm around the small, rigid figure. But Geoffrey stepped away before he could touch him. Benjamin put his reaction to this aside. "No, that's too much." And it was too much to ask the boy to choose his own punishment, he realized. "You will apologize to Miss Saunders. And you will leave her kitten alone unless you have her permission to play with it. Also, you will have no cakes for…a week."

Geoffrey's glare gradually eased. His chest still rose and fell rapidly. "Muffins?" he asked.

"No muffins. Or jam. In fact, no sweets of any kind."

"Not even cocoa?" The wheedle of negotiation had entered his tone.

"Not even." Feeling a little foolish on his knees, Benjamin rose. "So that's settled then." His son shrugged and turned toward the door. "You shouldn't have taken that key from my room," Benjamin added.

Geoffrey's hand went to his shirtfront and clutched at something beneath the cloth. Did he have the key on a string around his neck? "It's mine!"

Benjamin glanced into the still-open cupboard. He could just see a mass of white crumpled at the back. From a spray of lace along the edge, he thought he recognized one of Alice's nightgowns. With a pang of muddled emotion, he let the subject drop.

Twenty minutes later, Geoffrey stood before Miss Saunders and apologized. Not exactly sullenly, Benjamin judged—more like a workman ticking off an irksome task.

"I'm sorry I took your kitten," he said. "I won't do it again."

Miss Saunders nodded and smiled at the boy.

"I'm sorry I shut him up in the basket, too."

The tone of this second part was different. Insinuating? But that was ridiculous, Benjamin thought. Still, some odd emotion seemed to travel between the other two, palpable but mysterious. Unless he was imagining it; surely he was.

"That's good," said Miss Saunders, no longer smiling.

Geoffrey looked at Benjamin, waited for a nod to signal that his duties were complete, and left the library.

The room was very quiet in his wake.

Benjamin wouldn't have minded a compliment. He wanted to feel he'd done well, fulfilled some of his responsibilities as a father. On the other hand, he wasn't certain the apology had gone well. For some reason. "I don't recall things being so complicated when I was a child," he said. "None of this trouble."

"You were the *child*," replied Miss Saunders.

He shook his head. "My mother was just better at it," he said, trying not to sound aggrieved. "Everyone knows women are more suited to caring for children."

"Everyone?" Her voice vibrated with some new outrage. "Does *everyone*?"

"It is a generally accepted—"

"So you've never encountered a bad mother? Not that you would have noticed, since women are simply designed by nature to care for their children. As *everyone* knows. And so, whatever they do must be right."

He took offense at her contemptuous tone. "I didn't say that."

"No, you repeated platitudes. You have no idea what you're talking about."

"How the deuce have I offended you this time?"

"Women can be as cruel as men," she replied bewilderingly. "More so!" Her dark eyes burned into him, as if to etch her point onto his brain. Then she walked out.

"Damn it all!" exclaimed Benjamin. He kicked at an ottoman. "What the devil was that about? What the hell is wrong with the woman?"

His gaze caught on the portrait of Alice above the fireplace. "*You* never spoke to me that way. *You* thought my ideas very astute, as I recall. Yes, and admirable, too."

And now, instead of Alice, he had a female who exploded like a defective cannon at the least excuse—indeed with no excuse whatsoever, as far as he could see. Who complained and argued. Who…set him afire when she kissed him.

Benjamin stood very still in the middle of the library. Why had he thought *instead of Alice*? He wasn't going to put Miss Saunders in his wife's place. Certainly not. He'd never know what to expect from one day to the next. Which was not—emphatically *not*—a curiously attractive notion.

Nine

THE FOLLOWING DAY, JEAN WAS SURPRISED TO HEAR the clatter of a carriage coming up the drive of Furness Hall. No one else had visited since she arrived, and curiosity drew her downstairs to see who this might be. She found her host and his uncle already at the front door, outside in the sunny afternoon. The arrival must be an oddity indeed to have brought them there. "Were you expecting someone?" she asked.

"No," replied Lord Furness. "It's a post chaise," he added. "Not one of the neighbors." The carriage pulled up, and a lady stepped out. "Now I am experiencing déjà vu," he went on. "Chaise, unknown female, trunks. Is this your doing, Uncle? Not your friend from the village, I hope?"

"No, of course not. Looks nothing like her. And why would she be in a chaise?"

Jean rushed past them onto the drive. "Sarah?"

"Yes, miss."

"Hmm," Jean heard Lord Furness say behind her. "Rather the look of a superior lady's maid."

"I believe she is," replied Lord Macklin. "I seem to recall seeing her at the Phillipsons'."

"You were quicker than I expected," Jean said. She was so glad to see Sarah.

"It seemed you wanted me to hurry."

"Yes, I did." Jean gazed at the two large trunks tied on the back of the chaise. "You've brought so much."

"It was Mrs. Phillipson's opinion that I should pack all your things."

"*All* my things?" Jean was heartily sick of the clothes she had with her, but she hadn't meant to abandon the Phillipson house altogether.

"*All* her things?" Lord Furness echoed from the doorway.

Sarah handed Jean a note. She broke the wax seal, read it, and crumpled it in her hand. "What did you say to Mrs. Phillipson?" she asked Sarah. "She bids me farewell, sorry that my visit was so brief."

"I said nothing about that, miss. Your letter put me in a flurry. I was packing when she came to speak to me. She said something about her grandson and then directed me to take everything. I did think that perhaps she'd heard from someone else down here."

"Who?"

Sarah merely shook her head.

Jean marched back to the doorway. "Did you write to the Phillipsons?" she asked, including both noblemen in the question.

"I did," said Lord Macklin. "As I would to any of my friends. The blandest of letters. I said nothing that would get you thrown out."

"I haven't been *thrown out*!" Though in a beneficent

way, perhaps she had been; she couldn't easily return to the Phillipsons this spring. "I've been…inconvenienced, because you inserted yourself into my affairs." She didn't intend to share the rest of Mrs. Phillipson's message, or to reveal the history of their negotiations over Geoffrey. "I wish you'd left well enough alone." Jean was aware of Sarah's curious, amused observation. And, even more, of Lord Furness's steady gaze.

"I cannot believe that anything in my letter had this effect," the older man replied.

Miss Saunders was pure delight when that fiery spirit was directed at someone else, Benjamin thought. Particularly someone like his uncle, whose assumption of omniscience was slightly inflated. In his opinion. How forceful she was! As well as extraordinarily pretty when her eyes snapped with indignation.

"If there is any question of propriety," Uncle Arthur began, "I would be happy to write again."

"No!"

He should have offered a simple apology, Benjamin thought. It was easy to see the wiser course when Miss Saunders's ire was not directed at him.

"There is *no* such question," she informed him. "And you promised you wouldn't interfere again."

"Again?" asked Benjamin. This was better than a play.

"I certainly won't. But if I can set right any misunderstanding…"

She walked up to the older man. She might be inches shorter, Benjamin thought, but she made him draw back. "*I* will do any setting right that takes place," she said. "Is that clear?"

"Perfectly."

Silently, Benjamin urged his uncle to add an apology. Or more than one. Repetition was not unwelcome in such cases, he'd found. But Uncle Arthur only nodded. Miss Saunders looked at the waiting postilions. "Yes, all right, bring the trunks in," she said.

At this order, Benjamin was struck by a mixture of excitement and apprehension. "Do you have nowhere to go?"

She went very still. The contrast between her previous animation and this sudden quiet was striking. "I have any number of places to go. Do you want the trunks left on the chaise? Shall I go to one of them?"

Easy to see what others ought to say, Benjamin thought. And impossible to apply the same good sense to oneself—or to escape the reaction to remarks better left unsaid. "No. I was only concerned about your welfare."

"My welfare is…quite well, thank you." She marched inside, followed by her maid and then the postilions carrying a trunk. Benjamin stifled a laugh when the maid's hand reached out, seemingly involuntarily, to her mistress's untamable hair.

In her bedchamber, Jean waited until the postilions had put down their burden and departed for the second trunk. Then she flattened out the crumpled note and read it again. "Do you know what Mrs. Phillipson wrote?" she asked Sarah.

"No, miss."

"She commends me for my cleverness in becoming *so close* to Lord Furness. She thinks he would make a fine husband for me, and I a consoling wife for him. *Consoling!* She says I mustn't imagine they would have any objections. In fact, they would be very pleased at the match." Jean gritted her teeth. She hated the notion of a bridge burned by somebody else.

"Well, it is only her opinion," replied Sarah calmly. She took a key from her reticule and unlocked the trunk.

"Yes, but it makes it awkward—impossible, really—to go back there. And I'd planned to spend the season at the Phillipsons'."

"As you'd said, miss. Yet you've stayed here a goodly while and sent no word about returning to London."

The appearance of the postilions with her second trunk spared Jean the necessity of replying to this irrefutable fact.

And so Jean said nothing as she watched Sarah deal efficiently with the luggage. She'd hired Sarah herself, after her mother's death, and gotten just the attendant she wanted—a skilled, calm, older woman, who knew nothing about her family history. Sarah was nearly forty and very good at her work. She didn't stand on ceremony like some superior lady's maids, and yet had more dignity than many, Jean thought. She was also an acute observer of society. They'd formed a cordial bond in the last few years, and Jean was glad to have her here despite her uncomfortably sharp observations a moment ago.

The kitten emerged from under the bed to survey the additions to his realm.

"You've gotten a cat," said Sarah.

"Yes, his name is Tab. I hope you like cats."

"I'm very fond of them, miss." Sarah held out a hand. Tab went closer, sniffed, and accepted a pat on the head.

"Why do I have so many things?" Jean asked. The

trunks took up a large portion of the bedchamber's floor. Their contents would never fit into the wardrobe. This was a disadvantage of having no settled home. She carried much of her life with her.

"I'll unpack what you're likely to need here in the country," said Sarah. "They'll store the rest in the box room, as usual. But first, if you wouldn't mind." She eyed Jean. "May I do something about your hair, miss?"

"Oh yes, please." Jean sighed with sheepish relief. "It's gone quite…feral without you."

Her curls set to rights by Sarah's skillful fingers, Jean put on her bonnet and shawl and headed outside. Geoffrey could be found at the stables every afternoon at this time. Probably other times as well, given his delight in his pony, but his official riding lesson would be in progress now. Jean had felt on a poor footing with the boy since his stilted apology. She wanted to be… *Reconciled* seemed an odd word, but it was the one that occurred to her. She was determined to show him she wasn't an ogre.

Also, Lord Furness might be observing the lesson, and she wanted to speak to him. She could still hear him asking if she had nowhere to go. There might, perhaps, have been pity in his voice, which she *would not* have. Her departure also gave Sarah room to arrange things as she liked. Her bedchamber was a small space for two people, two trunks, and a lively kitten.

Sarah managed the unpacking with practiced ease. When she finished, she went downstairs to find someone to take the trunks away, which was more difficult than one might have expected in a nobleman's country residence. It seemed there were no footmen at all.

She introduced herself to the housekeeper and the cook and was offered a cup of tea and a chat at the servants' dining table. Mrs. McGinnis presented various lower servants as they came in and out in the course of their work, and Sarah busily gathered impressions. She was interested to find that there was no butler at Furness Hall, and that Lord Furness kept no valet. The latter omission was the subject of some mild levity. Sarah gathered that Lord Macklin's valet was attempting to set the master of the house to rights, against his inclination, if not his will. Lord Furness's evasive actions amused his staff, particularly over the matter of an unwanted haircut. There was no malice in the laughter, however. What servants there were seemed to like the place well enough.

By the time Sarah headed back upstairs, she'd concluded that although Mrs. McGinnis was competent, this was a haphazard house with a master who paid no heed to the necessaries. It needed attention, a mistress who cared about everyone's welfare as well as the state of the carpets. Sarah gave no sign of this opinion, of course.

Due to her employer's style of living, Sarah was adept at creating a place for herself in different kinds of households. The process had its disadvantages. Unlike some other lady's maids of her acquaintance, she had no settled community, with friends made over years and a settled hierarchy. However, there were advantages to being a guest. She had no stake in long-standing rivalries, and she offered the allure of new stories to tell, a fresh voice in a group that might be bored with one another.

Fortunately, Sarah enjoyed seeing new places and

meeting new people. She wouldn't have stayed on in her position if she didn't. Her efforts to please added to her own comfort and that of her employer, which gratified Sarah. Over the five years of their association she'd come to admire Miss Saunders's determination to make a life on her own terms. She'd also observed a deeply hidden vulnerability in the younger woman—some legacy of her early history, Sarah concluded. She'd learned, from snippets of talk gleaned here and there, that Miss Saunders's parents had lived apart. Some said they'd hated each other. These hints had brought out what Sarah supposed were her maternal instincts. She enjoyed smoothing the way for her charge—a step beyond keeping her luxuriant hair in check. Walking along the corridor on the upper floor, Sarah allowed herself a small smile.

At a turn in the hall, she encountered a stocky, black-haired man carrying a small pile of laundry.

"Good day," he said. "I'm Henry Clayton, Lord Macklin's valet."

Of the disputed haircut, Sarah thought. But she said only, "How do you do, Mr. Clayton. My name is Sarah Dennison. Miss Saunders's lady's maid."

"Pleased to make your acquaintance, Miss Dennison."

He paused to look her over, and Sarah returned the favor. Mr. Clayton seemed about her own age, so he probably had more than twenty years of service under his belt, as she did. He had a round face, with wide cheeks and a snub nose. His brown eyes were as sharp as Sarah knew her blue ones to be.

He would be finding her angular and buttoned up, Sarah knew, an impression she'd cultivated for years.

Since her youth, when she'd been middling attractive and noticed that a beautiful lady's maid was not a long-lived creature. Mr. Clayton was very well turned out, as he should be. Nobody wanted a slipshod valet. Except for one small oddity beside his left lapel. "Do you always carry a pair of scissors?" she asked.

Mr. Clayton so far forgot himself as to glance down at the pointed blades peeking out of his upper pocket. He looked up at once, meeting her gaze. A wealth of information silently passed between them. "Have you heard about that already?" he asked.

"There's talk of a haircut in the kitchen. Or rather, of a haircut that never happens."

"I'm well aware." He sounded rueful. "So perhaps you understand why I keep scissors at the ready, in case I should ever be allowed to use them."

"His lordship would benefit from your skill, I'm sure."

"Did you see him? He looks positively shaggy!"

Sarah didn't reply to this intemperate comment, which Mr. Clayton appeared to regret as soon as it was made. Instead she offered a sort of admission of her own. "Hair can be a challenge."

They indulged in another wordless exchange.

"Your young lady must be very glad to have you here," said Mr. Clayton.

He was her counterpart, a personal servant who was not part of the household, making a place within it. They were rather like two foreign agents coming face-to-face on the same mission, Sarah thought, amusing herself. Mr. Clayton would add interest to this visit. She gave him a small smile. He returned it with a little bow and went on his way.

❧

It was impossible to sleep with an important task undone, Jean thought some hours later, sitting up in bed and lighting her candle. On the other side of the bed, Tab raised his head and gave her an inquiring look.

The thing preyed on one's mind, Jean thought, and loomed larger—larger than it should, perhaps. If she'd just been able to speak to Lord Furness for a few minutes. But his uncle had come out to watch Geoffrey ride and then walked back to the house with them. He'd been present at dinner, of course, and afterward had challenged Lord Furness to a game of billiards. With no interest in being a passive observer, Jean had left them to it and gone to bed early. Lord Macklin was an admirable gentleman, she thought. His presence lent an air of propriety to her visit, but it also put a damper on private conversation.

And so she was left with a distasteful idea growing in her mind—that Lord Furness now saw her as some pitiable poor relation. A sad spinster-auntish sort of female. A woman no one wanted, pushed along from house to house. What man would want to kiss such a person? Again.

Jean wrapped her arms around her ribs. Those kisses had gone through her like a flame through tinder, like an unexpected introduction to desire. Her body had sprung to attention as if to say, "Ah, so *this* is the thing I've heard so much about. How do you do?" She wanted to further that acquaintance. She wanted to see her host's blue-gray eyes burning just for her once again. To imagine pity there instead—the idea was unbearable. She had to set him right!

The house had grown quiet. It was nearly midnight, but Jean knew that Lord Furness stayed up late. She threw back the coverlet and rose, putting on her dressing gown and covering it with a lacy cashmere shawl. Ignoring Tab's interrogative *mew*, she picked up her candlestick and slipped into the corridor.

Like last time, the house was dim and silent. Jean kept a sharp eye out for Geoffrey, said to wander the halls at night. But she saw no one as she made her way down to the library.

Lord Furness was there, sitting on the sofa beneath his dead wife's likeness and sipping a brandy. He rose when Jean came in, startled. "Is something wrong?"

"I have plenty of places to go," Jean blurted out. "In London and the country. I'm welcome in great houses all over England. Indeed, I've been told I grace any occasion. By some high sticklers, I might add."

Benjamin had had more than one brandy, as he occasionally did when the night deepened and regrets rose, and he didn't expect to see anyone until the following day. He wasn't drunk. Not nearly. But his mind was somewhat…slowed. Its first response to these remarks concerned how delicious she looked in her dressing gown and shawl. "Who could doubt it?" he managed.

"I wanted to make that clear. It would be…distressing if you had the wrong impression. And thought me some half-tolerated hanger-on."

"I would hate to distress you."

"Thank you."

She gathered the shawl closer. The frothy fabric

clung to the lines of her body. She looked soft and lithe and delectably embraceable. Benjamin decided to sit down. "But I have no idea what you're talking about," he added.

She sank onto the other end of the sofa. "You asked me. If I had nowhere to go. When Sarah arrived."

Who was Sarah? Ah, must be her maid. "I didn't mean anything distressing."

"If you imagine that I'm to be pitied, you couldn't be more wrong," she declared.

She leaned toward him, a creature of earth and fire, with that coppery spark in her dark eyes. He'd been alone a long time, Benjamin acknowledged. Shut in his morose little world. Until she'd burst in, shaking him up, trailing desire in her wake. "I don't pity you," he said. "I'm grateful." Her lips parted in surprise. "You mustn't do that."

"What?"

"Look irresistible. I'm less able than usual to resist tonight."

She leaned closer and kissed him. Softly, with exploratory sweetness. Benjamin simply responded at first. Then he caught the kiss like a tossed cricket ball and took it deeper. His arms reached for her, drew her close. She embraced him. Her body, unlaced under the wool of her dressing gown, fitted against him as her shawl fell to the floor. One of his hands found the fastening of the braid down her back and pulled it off, freeing her matchless curls. The other hand drifted up her side, caressing.

Here was delight, Jean thought. Here was amazement. She'd swum in the sea once, long ago—pushing at the waves and being swept along by them. These kisses were like that. Give and take, offer and float away. She wanted more. He pressed her against the sofa back, becoming more urgent. One of his knees slipped between hers.

And her mother's shrill voice went off like a claxon in her mind—feeling, as it had always been, an inch from her ear. "Lose your virtue, lose everything. Do you hear me!" As if Jean could have helped hearing. "One slip, and you're stuck alone in the middle of nowhere with the *results*." Her mother had spit that final word with such venom. For as long as she could remember, Jean had known it meant her. She was the perpetrator of disaster, the rightful target of reproach. And after that came the stifling darkness. Jean jerked away from that old mental lash.

Benjamin released her at once. What the hell was he doing, seducing a young lady, a guest under his roof, on the library sofa? The door wasn't even locked. Which was irrelevant because he was going to stop right now. Breathless and aching, he drew back. Miss Saunders looked as if she might cry, which filled him with remorse. Then her expression hardened into… anger? "I'm sorry," he said to cover both.

"It isn't *your* fault," she replied.

Her emphasis confused him. Did she mean it was hers? There was no one else here. She did sound angry. He considered taking her hand, but when she looked up, he understood she was *furious*.

"No," she said.

"I stepped over the line," Benjamin replied. "It won't happen again."

She put her hands over her ears. "Stop!"

This was a bit much, particularly when his body was trying to take the reins from his slightly befuddled mind. She'd kissed *him*, after all. "I have," he said. "I did."

Miss Saunders retrieved her shawl and stood up, so Benjamin did, too. He wished he hadn't had the brandy. She pulled the wrap on and held it close around her neck. Her dark hair foamed about her shoulders. "I must go," she said.

"You're not going to walk out of here without telling me what's wrong."

"It's obvious. I behaved too freely. I came down to correct a wrong impression, and now I have given you another. I hope you will forget it."

There was something wrong with her tone. She spoke like a student repeating a rote lesson. "It's more than that," he said.

"I don't owe you explanations."

"I think you do, after what has passed between us."

He'd put some righteous indignation into his voice and managed to surprise her, which brought life back into her eyes. She seemed truly aware of him again. She hesitated, then said, "I *won't* be ruled by the past."

Feeling out of his depth, Benjamin settled for "That seems sensible."

"How would you know?" she snapped back. "You've been wallowing in your grief for years."

"I beg your pardon?" The words came out cold, but Benjamin couldn't care. Did she *want* to offend him?

Oddly, Miss Saunders nodded. He had no idea what the gesture signified. "This has nothing to do with you," she said. "Now and then, the past rears up and tries to…squash me. And I refuse." She looked grim.

"Nothing to do with me." That phrase had outweighed the others for him. "You were in my arms. Happily, as I judged. Do you say I was mistaken?"

"No," she answered quietly.

"Whatever I did wrong—"

"Not you."

"There's no one else present, Miss…Jean. Just you and me." Benjamin was suddenly conscious of Alice's portrait above them. But she *wasn't* here. She was gone forever.

"If only that were true." She had to go. Her mother's remembered voice was still shrieking in her mind. Once those memories rose, they had to be fought down. She knew how to do that—all the necessary steps. First, banish the crushing disappointment that they hadn't gone for good.

Before Lord Furness could speak again, Jean hurried from the library. She almost ran to her room, locking the door behind her. She added fuel to the coals of the fire and sat before it, hands folded, staring into the flames.

After her mother's death, Jean had vowed to live the life she wanted, free of all sorts of prisons. Even the one her mother had tried to leave lurking inside her. And she'd managed to do just that. The struggle grew easier with time. Tonight though, the past had roared back with a vengeance. Literally vengeance, Jean thought. Her mother always wanted to see someone pay.

Why tonight?

She'd never let herself go so far before, Jean

thought. She'd never opened herself to pleasure, embraced desire. She'd never encountered a man like Benjamin, or felt that heady combination of tenderness and passion. It was as if her mother had set a trap, and Jean had sprung it.

She pushed back her hair, which fell around her shoulders and curled over her cheeks. Her father's hair, as had been continually pointed out to her through her childhood. Profligate, stubborn, uncaring hair. Jean had been blamed for things she couldn't help before she understood what the words meant.

Her hands tightened. "Lies," she whispered. Finally, painfully, after long struggles, she'd understood that her mother lied. That the shrieking and the darkness weren't her fault. She'd vowed that the past wouldn't rule her future. And so it hadn't, and wouldn't. Tonight was *not* a setback, simply another step.

At a touch on her leg, she jumped. But it was only Tab, pawing at the end of her shawl, wondering why she was awake in the middle of the night. Jean picked up the kitten and put him on her lap. His soft purr began, remarkably soothing. *Her cat*, Jean thought fiercely. She was allowed comfort now. She would take it. Along with any other pleasures she might desire. She wouldn't be oppressed again! But other parts of her were only too aware that it wasn't that easy.

Ten

WHEN BENJAMIN AT LAST FELL ASLEEP THAT NIGHT, very late, he dreamed about Alice. She stood beside him, looking just as she did in her portrait—more perfect than life, red-gold hair gleaming, blue eyes gazing out at nothing. He held her hand, but she didn't seem to notice. He knew it was no good speaking to her. She wouldn't answer. He tried anyway, and was proved right.

Then, with a dream's sudden shift, he saw a mail coach bearing down on them—sixteen pounding hooves, a shouting, gesticulating driver. The big vehicle was going so fast that it careened from side to side. There was no chance it could stop before running them down. They had to move, to dive out of the way. But Alice was immovable. He tried to pull her, lift her, but her slender form might have been made of stone. She was rooted to the road. Benjamin pushed with all his strength, shouted in her ear. No response. The coach came closer and closer, until he could feel the thunder of its passage in his bones. He could escape if he abandoned her where she stood, but

of course there was no question of that. And then the
vehicle hit them with an apocalyptic slam.

Benjamin jerked awake. His pulse was pounding,
his head thick. He panted, and the roar of the dream
lingered in his ears. He put his hands over them.
"Could I do no better than that?" he said aloud.
The significance of the scene was ridiculously obvious. He had to leave the past behind or risk disaster.
"Oversimplified," he told whatever part of him composed dreams.

He threw back the coverlet and rose, going to the
window that overlooked the gardens and parting the
draperies. The sun was just rising. Shafts of golden
light made dewdrops sparkle; trees threw long fingers
of shadow. This place was beautiful. His family and
people who depended on them had made it so over
centuries, Benjamin thought. The house, the land felt
like part of him, or vice versa. He loved it.

Did Geoffrey feel anything like this? Sadness
descended on Benjamin. This place was meant to
be a home, with a family, and he'd been living here
alone. He'd insisted upon it. He'd even, now and
then, gloried in it. Worse, he'd forced isolation on his
son. He didn't need to be hit by a mail coach to see
his mistake.

His bare feet grew cold. Still in his nightshirt,
Benjamin made up the fire. Following his standing
orders, no one would enter his room until he left it.
He dressed and headed for the stables. He knew from
too much experience that a hard ride could alter a
morose mood.

As he galloped along a lane between blooming

hedges, Benjamin realized that he hadn't given any thought to scandal. Had anyone walked into the library last night—his uncle, a servant—there would have been an uproar. Many young ladies, most he supposed, would be expecting a proposal today. He was fairly certain Miss Saunders wasn't. Indeed, he doubted she wanted one. Not because she was scandalous, but because she was unlike any woman he'd ever known. Her concerns seemed more mysterious and darker than gossip. A man would have to fathom them before he offered for her.

Not that he was actually considering an offer. He was merely…considering. She was such a heady mixture of independence and allure. Recalling various incidents of her visit lifted his spirits and made him smile. She'd taken a tomahawk in stride—cliffs, a kidnapped kitten. Between one bout of kissing and the next, she'd wakened him. And now? What lay behind her behavior last night? He needed to know.

Back at Furness Hall, Benjamin found his uncle at the breakfast table, which seemed to have become a central exchange for information since his unexpected guests arrived. Benjamin wished him good morning, poured coffee, and sat where he could observe the entry. "Tell me all you know about Miss Saunders's family," he said then.

The older man raised an inquiring brow.

"From a remark she made, I believe there's something odd about it."

"And if there is, it's our affair because?"

"Because I've grown interested in her."

"Interested? As in *interested*?"

"More and more as time goes by."

Meeting his nephew's eyes, Arthur rose from the table. "Shall we take a turn in the garden, where we won't be overheard?"

"Is your information that ominous?" Benjamin frowned at him.

"It is private," Arthur replied.

Looking uneasy, his nephew followed him outside.

They walked along a path bordered by nodding daffodils. "I have made some inquiries," said Arthur then. "I understand that Miss Saunders's father was forced into the marriage. The young daughter of a country neighbor found herself with child, and he was undoubtedly the culprit." He had heard the girl in question called a dreadful creature, but Arthur took that with a grain of salt, considering the source. "Mr. Saunders was not pleased. Having ample resources, and control of them at a young age, he moved to London soon after the wedding, and he remained there until his death several years ago. From overindulgence, if gossip was correct."

"He abandoned his family?"

Arthur nodded. "Essentially. He provided an allowance." His female source had called this income *sufficient*. Arthur translated this as miserly.

"He lived a solitary life?"

"Hardly that. He kept a string of mistresses."

"So he scarcely knew his own daughter?" Benjamin sounded thoughtful.

"I'd say he didn't know her at all."

"But what about his property, his responsibilities?"

"I gather there was no large estate to manage. Naturally, I don't have financial details."

Benjamin nodded. "And her mother? There's something important about her."

Arthur waited, but his nephew provided no clarification. "She was the daughter of a country squire, quite young when she married. That's as much as I know."

"Unhappy, I imagine. Married to a man who didn't want to see her."

"That seems very likely."

"So I suppose she wasn't a…jolly parent."

"She may have found solace in her child."

"I don't think so."

Once again Arthur waited for more. But Benjamin was silent.

They continued along the path for some time, each occupied with his own thoughts.

❦

Sarah spent half an hour combing out Jean's hair that morning. "It came loose from the braid in the night," Jean told her.

"Did you have a nightmare?" the maid asked as she dealt with the tangle of curls.

Jean winced. It was difficult to hide her bad dreams from the person who shared her room at inns when they traveled. "A kind of nightmare, yes," Jean said. In the mirror, her eyes had a steely glint, which she was pleased to see. She'd wrestled that strident inner voice into silence once more. As she *always* would.

Downstairs, Jean stopped in the library, first peering around the doorframe to make sure the chamber was empty. She searched the shelves until she found what she was looking for and went on to breakfast.

Blessedly, that room was vacant, too. But when she came out after her meal, she encountered Lord Furness and Lord Macklin returning from a walk. She spoke before either of them could. "I was thinking I could read to Geoffrey. I always liked being read to as a child. I suppose you did as well."

"No," said Lord Furness.

"You don't wish me to read to him?" Jean felt a spurt of indignation. "Why not?" She wanted to make a more personal connection to Geoffrey. She also wanted to divert attention—her host's attention—from last night's debacle.

He regarded her steadily. Not diverted, Jean thought. Not even a little. "No, I didn't like being read to," he said.

"Really?" Stories had been a rare solace of Jean's childhood. They took you somewhere else entirely, and she'd often wanted to be somewhere else.

"I preferred being outside on my own." Lord Furness gestured at the book she held. "What have you got?"

She showed him. "The enjoyment often depends on the reader."

He scanned the cover. "*Goody Two-Shoes*? Are you serious? That sounds dreadful."

"I found it in the library," Jean replied. "There weren't many books for children. I thought perhaps this had been read to you when you were young."

"No." Lord Furness eyed the book. "Does that girl keep a menagerie?"

The image included two birds, a sheep, and a dog. "I don't know," said Jean. "One reads books to discover what they're about."

"Is it so indeed?" He pretended to be amazed.

"I've heard of that book," said Lord Macklin. "Rather well known, isn't it?"

"Did *you* like being read to as a child?" Jean asked him.

"Never was, much. Were you?"

It seemed to Jean that both men were overly interested in her answer, which made her more reluctant to give it. Her mother had been a marvelous reader, or rather performer, of books. When in the mood to entertain, she'd used different voices and swept about the room, miming the action as she held the volume up before her. Even when Jean didn't understand the story, as was often the case with the sort of book her mother enjoyed, she'd been enthralled. And her mother had reveled in the applause and admiration she offered. Reading had brought some of their rare moments of harmony. "Yes." Jean turned away. "I'm going to try it on Geoffrey."

Both men moved to follow her.

"It's not necessary for you to come," she said. Better if they didn't. Lord Furness was a…disturbance. He loomed in her consciousness. She'd meant to avoid him this morning. Hence the book.

And so of course he said, "Oh, I have to see this."

"I admit I'm curious," added his uncle.

As she couldn't prevent them from coming, Jean turned and marched off. They trailed her upstairs to the nursery, where they found Geoffrey and Tom sitting on the floor in front of the blanket tepee. A spread of wooden blocks before them seemed part of a counting game. Geoffrey sprang up at once. "Can we go to the stable early?"

"No," said his father. "Miss Saunders has come to read to you."

"Read?"

"From a book."

The boy shot him a suspicious glance. "Why would she?"

"For your amusement. And edification."

"What's 'ed-i-fi-cation'?"

Geoffrey had only a little trouble repeating the word, which was impressive at his age, Jean thought. She didn't want him to hear a definition, however. That would put a damper on things. "For *fun*," she said. "Let's sit on the sofa, shall we?"

She led the way to that shabby piece of furniture under a row of windows. Tom and Lily the nursemaid found perches nearby, both looking interested. The two men took chairs opposite, and naturally Lord Furness chose to face her directly. She'd be unable to raise her eyes without meeting his. Well, she simply wouldn't look up from this no-doubt fascinating volume.

Jean patted the cushion beside her, and Geoffrey slowly climbed onto it. He examined the cover of the book as if he'd never seen such a thing before. He didn't look rebellious, however. Perhaps this could be a chocolate-box moment, Jean thought.

She opened it and read the first words of *The History of Little Goody Two-Shoes*. "'Care and discontent shortened the days of Little Margery's father. He was forced from his family and seized with a violent fever in a place where Dr. James's Powder was not to be had, and where he died miserably.'" She stopped. This wasn't what she'd expected.

"Died miserably," repeated Geoffrey. He didn't sound distressed. He seemed, in fact, to relish the phrase. "You thrash about when you have a fever. Bob fell right off his bed. Hit the floor with a great thud and wr…writhed."

Jean looked down at him. His angelic blue eyes were bright.

"Geoffrey keeps a tally of local deaths," said Lord Furness dryly. His gaze turned to Lily. "He should not be allowed in sickrooms, however. Bob's or any others."

The maid winced. "He's slippery as an eel."

"Bob?" asked Lord Macklin.

"He's the gardener's boy, my lord," said Lily.

"Ah."

"I wasn't in. Jack told me about it," said Geoffrey. "What comes next? Does somebody else die?"

"Yes, *do* read on," said Lord Furness.

Jean looked down the page. "'Margery's poor mother survived the loss of her husband but a few days, and died of a broken heart, leaving Margery and her little brother to the wide world.'" She closed the book. "Clearly, this isn't suitable."

"That must be worse than a broken leg," Geoffrey said. "Mr. Foster's leg is all right now. He didn't die." He leaned over to examine the book with more interest than he'd shown before. "Is it all about people dying?"

Jean had had the impression, from hearing the title mentioned, that it was a sweet, poignant story. Quite suitable for her mythical chocolate-box child. She ought to have looked it over before she started this. But she'd been too eager for a diversion.

"That would be an original approach to narrative,"

said Lord Furness. He smiled at her as if he knew precisely what was going through her mind. Which he did *not*!

"Perhaps Margery dies next," said Geoffrey.

"Not likely so soon," put in Tom. "She must be the one on the cover, with the sheep." He pointed at them. "Mebbe her little brother."

"Eaten by a wolf," Geoffrey suggested.

"In sheep's clothing," replied his father. "Don't keep us in suspense." He gestured at the book, annoyingly amused.

"Very well." Jean wouldn't be embarrassed. If he wanted his son to hear this, then he would. She found her place and read on. "'It would both have excited your pity, and have done your heart good, to have seen how fond these two little ones were of each other, and how, hand in hand, they trotted about. They were both very ragged, and Tommy had two Shoes, but Margery had but one.'"

"Shouldn't the book be called *Goody Three-Shoes* then?" asked Lord Furness.

"Perhaps she catches cold without a shoe," said Geoffrey. "And dies."

"Or develops chilblains, at the least," said Lord Macklin, apparently entering into his great-nephew's point of view.

"Ye get a limp after a while, walking with only one shoe," said Tom. "It ain't good for you."

Lord Furness laughed.

Jean felt a tremor of amusement in her throat. She resisted it and read on. "'They had nothing, poor things, to support them but what they picked from the hedges, or got from the poor people, and they lay every night in a barn.'"

"They got to live in a barn?" exclaimed Geoffrey. "I'd like to live in our barn, with Fergus."

"But with both your shoes," replied his father.

"Acourse."

"And all four of his."

A laugh escaped Jean. Lord Macklin joined in. Tom grinned, and Lily giggled. Geoffrey looked confused, but ready to be amused.

In a more satirical tone, Jean continued. "'Their relations took no notice of them; no, they were rich, and ashamed to own such a poor little ragged girl as Margery, and such a dirty little curl-pated boy as Tommy.'" She frowned. "What do curls have to do with it?"

"Clearly a sign of ungovernable temper, are they not?" said Lord Furness.

"No!" Jean exclaimed. She caught the gleam in his eye. "Very funny." She read on. "'But such wicked folks, who love nothing but money, and are proud and despise the poor, never come to any good in the end, as we shall see by and by.'"

"I sniff a moral coming up," said Lord Macklin.

"Inescapable in such sickly stuff," replied Lord Furness.

Geoffrey squirmed.

Jean leafed through the book to see what was ahead. "Margery gets shoes. She is a paragon of virtue." She paged farther. "She starts giving spelling lessons to other children, and then lessons about life in general."

"Oh, we must hear those," said Lord Furness.

Geoffrey sighed audibly.

Jean read, "'He that will thrive, must rise by five.

He that hath thriv'n, may lie till seven. Truth may be blam'd, but cannot be sham'd. Tell me with whom you go, and I'll tell what you do. A friend in your need is a friend indeed. They ne'er can be wise who good counsel despise.'"

Geoffrey squirmed some more.

Jean flipped more pages. "These go on for quite a while."

"I think we've heard enough to get the gist," replied Lord Furness. "Platitudes."

"But what about the sheep and the birds in the picture?" asked Tom.

"Margery makes friends with animals," said Jean, scanning quickly through the book. "She does many good deeds, is a model of perfection, and makes a success of her life." There was a chapter about a funeral, she noticed, and a dead dormouse, and a dead husband near the end. The author seemed as enamored of death as Geoffrey. In fact—she read out the end. "'Her life was the greatest blessing, and her death the greatest calamity that ever was felt in the neighborhood. A monument, but without inscription, was erected to her memory in the churchyard, over which the poor as they pass weep continually, so that the stone is ever bathed in tears.'" Jean closed the book. "Mawkish."

"No inscription," said Lord Furness. "Odd."

"Because she was a woman, she must remain nameless, I suppose," said Jean.

"What did she die of?" asked Geoffrey.

"It doesn't say. Old age."

"How old?"

"I don't know, Geoffrey." Jean set the book aside.

"No wonder no one read to you," she said to Lord Furness. "If this is a sample of your library."

"You ought to see some of my father's volumes about the American tribes."

"And his collections," added Lord Macklin. "Didn't he have a scalp?" Then he pressed his lips together and glanced at Geoffrey.

"Old Jacob told me a better story," said the boy. "It was about the ancient days. When the Black Death came, and nearly everybody died." He gazed up at Jean like a bloodthirsty cherub. "They swelled up until they burst. Even their eyeballs." The idea seemed to fill him with unholy glee.

"Who is Old Jacob?" asked Lord Furness.

"I told you not to talk to that dirty, old hermit," Lily said to Geoffrey.

"Hermit?" said Lord Furness.

"He moved into a broken-down woodcutter's hut," added the maid apologetically. "He used to come begging to the kitchen sometimes. He's gone now."

"He died," said Geoffrey. "Bradford found him, all stiff and cold."

Lord Furness contemplated his son. "We really must do something about your obsession with mortality," he said.

Geoffrey gazed back at him. If Jean had had to label the boy's expression, she would have called it smug.

"The Duke of Hamilton hired a hermit for his estate," said Lord Macklin.

"Hired?" repeated Jean.

"He said it was quite a difficult position to fill. He had to advertise."

"You don't say he paid somebody to act the hermit?" Tom asked.

The older man smiled. "How to separate the acting from reality in this case? The fellow was required to lurk in a stone grotto in ragged clothes and keep a long beard. I suppose the acting came in when he was exhibited to visitors."

"Did he have to rave at them?" Tom asked. "That'd be a hard sort of job."

"Do you think so?" answered Lord Macklin, looking both interested and amused.

Tom nodded. "What would you say, raving? What sort of…topics, like? The feller couldn't just go on about the weather and such, could he? Likely this duke would expect somethin' more entertaining."

"A good point." Lord Macklin shook his head. "I wish I knew the details of his…role, but I don't."

Geoffrey opened his mouth to speak.

"No, he did not die," said Lord Macklin. "At least not so far as I am aware. Eventually, of course—" He let this sentence trail off.

Jean rose. "*Goody Two-Shoes* goes back to the library."

Lord Furness rose with her. When Lord Macklin stood, he went over to examine the wooden blocks and asked about the counting game the lads had been playing. They came to show him its intricacies. Jean waited a moment, but the older man showed no signs of departing. She was left to her host's company once again.

"Well, that did not go well," said Jean as she passed through the nursery door. She would talk about the book until she could escape him.

Benjamin walked beside her. He'd never been so

acutely conscious of another person. The tiniest tilt of her head called out to him. He was entranced by the soft swish of her skirts. The feel of her was branded on his body. "Geoffrey seemed to enjoy himself," he said.

"Do you call it that? I should have looked for a book about the plague," she added acerbically. "But how was I to know that? How could anyone?"

He laughed.

Miss Saunders frowned. "You're not worried that Geoffrey keeps talking about death?"

"Not really. He seems more curious than uneasy about it."

"You don't…" She hesitated, then said, "What if he's thinking of his mother?"

It was like one of those moments in the boxing ring when a smashing blow slips past your ear, Benjamin thought. The pain—so crushing, so often felt—brushed by him this time, leaving just a whisper of an echo in its wake. "I don't think he is," he answered.

"Why?"

"Because he speaks with such gusto."

She stopped on the stairs and looked at him. Benjamin took the full force of her challenging gaze. He wanted to kiss her. He wanted to be able to kiss her whenever he liked, and to follow the kisses with much more. After last night, what man wouldn't? A dry inner voice countered that question with others. A man who didn't care for high drama? One who had enough on his plate already?

"He does," she said slowly. "And he seems to enjoy shocking us, too. But can he really? He's so young."

"I know very little about children in general,"

Benjamin replied. Miss Saunders shrugged in wry agreement. "I have to judge Geoffrey by his own yardstick. And I see nothing mournful in his words or manner."

She considered this, biting her lower lip in a way that made Benjamin long to pull her close. "I agree." She started moving again. "Very observant of you."

He fell into step beside her. "You sound surprised."

"After the state of things when I arrived? Of course I am." She walked faster. "I'm not going to read him grisly accounts of epidemics. Reading at all was a bad idea, I suppose."

She sounded dejected, and Benjamin found he wanted to cheer her up. "What about something like *Waverley*?"

"Scott is far too old for him."

"But we've agreed that Geoffrey is one of a kind. I expect he'd like the battles."

"But shouldn't we be trying to discourage such impulses? Do you want him flying at visitors with a lance instead of a tomahawk? Mounted on Fergus, no doubt, and armored cap-a-pie."

"At least he'd be clothed," said Benjamin.

Miss Saunders stared at him for a blank moment, and then she began to laugh. The sound was musical, infectious. He joined her. She laughed more heartily. Their eyes met, shining with humor. His spirits rose. He tried to remember when joy had last rung through his hallways. Too long ago.

Then they reached the library door. And stopped—walking and laughing. The wooden panels loomed. Miss Saunders seemed to share his feeling that another world lay beyond that portal.

She held out the book. "There's no need for both of us. You can put it back."

"I don't know where it goes," he said, opening the door and not quite chivying her through.

She strode to the shelves, slipping the copy of *Goody Two-Shoes* between two narrow volumes. "There. Done." It was as if their laughter had never been. In another moment she would go.

"We should speak about last night," he said.

"No, we should simply erase it from our minds."

"Memory can't be so easily expunged."

"Yes it can!" she said, her expression fierce.

Benjamin felt a pang of regret. "And this is what you want? That we should pretend you never kissed me? That I never held you?"

"What else?" She stood like a soldier on inspection, the antithesis of the pliant, ardent woman he'd embraced in this room.

It was a good question. Benjamin wasn't prepared at this moment to give the conventional answer—an offer of marriage. And he had no others ready. Yet this...void she proposed was deeply unsatisfying. "I don't want you to be uneasy," he began.

"I'm perfectly well," she said. "There is no need to worry about *me*."

And with that, she slipped past him and away, leaving Benjamin to wonder at her emphasis. Who or what was he supposed to worry about? Geoffrey, he supposed. Or himself?

Eleven

"I THINK WE'LL BE MOVING ON FROM HERE SOON," Arthur said to his valet the following morning.

"Indeed, my lord." Clayton helped the earl into his coat.

"I have a feeling matters will be resolved satisfactorily." He couldn't suppress a trace of smugness. He'd wanted to rouse his nephew from his grief, and he'd done so with a vengeance. Or, rather, Miss Saunders had. Arthur gave credit where it was due. That young lady had turned out to be a much larger personality than he'd realized when he met her in a London drawing room. There'd been moments when he felt like a man whose cat had grown into a tiger. Arthur smiled into the mirror as he adjusted his neckcloth. A most inappropriate comparison. Miss Saunders's eyes would snap at him if she heard it. He'd keep it to himself. "There are several other visits I'm eager to make," he added.

"Because of the letters you received, my lord?"

"Yes. There've been some interesting developments." Arthur went over to the small writing desk and unfolded a recent missive to look at it again.

"What would you do, Clayton, if you found that a total stranger had received a large legacy in your parents' will?" His valet would know, of course, that Arthur wasn't referring to the elder Claytons, who'd kept a tiny village shop and had little to leave anyone. He would instead consider a hypothetical situation. Over the years, Arthur had discovered a sharp mind and a deep well of common sense in his servitor. Clayton had become a valuable sounding board when he was working out a course of action. Arthur reasoned better by talking aloud than through introspection.

"Perhaps this would be a distant relative, my lord?"

"No. No familial connection whatsoever apparently. A complete stranger."

"I would wonder," Clayton said.

"As who would not?"

"I would inquire, investigate why this came about, and who this person was."

Arthur nodded.

"The clerk who wrote the will might have information."

The earl flicked the letter with one finger. "Instructed to reveal nothing. Part of the terms of the will. Viscount Whitfield is…perplexed."

Clayton considered this piece of news. "The viscount was at the dinner you held at White's." He didn't specify *which* dinner. There was only one they referred to in this tone.

"He was." Arthur folded up the letter and tucked it away. "How would you feel about this mysterious heir, Clayton, if it was your parents' will?"

"Suspicious," replied the valet at once. "Resentful, I imagine, depending on the details."

"Precisely." The earl ran his fingers over other letters lined up in a cubbyhole of the desk. "How far are we to blame for others' actions, do you think?"

Clayton took a moment to digest the change of subject. "Not far," he said then. "In most circumstances."

"If your sister—assuming you had a sister, Clayton—behaved very foolishly and suffered for it, would you feel responsible?"

"I don't think I would, my lord. Unless I had told her to do the foolish thing. Or made her do it somehow."

Arthur shook his head. "Not the case here. And yet people do blame themselves."

"Claiming responsibility," Clayton said slowly. "If a thing is your fault, that would mean you are, or might have been, in control."

"Rather than the victim of a malign fate. A telling point, Clayton. You are as incisive as ever."

"Thank you, my lord."

"You ought to have been a barrister or a member of parliament. You know my offer to help you into another profession still stands."

"I'm very happy where I am, my lord."

"Are you?" The earl examined his valet's round face. Clayton's nod gave him the air of an equal rather than a servant.

Arthur accepted it in a similar spirit. "All the better for me. I'd be lost without you." He picked up two letters he'd written and moved away from the desk. "What do you think of young Tom?" he added.

"Intelligent," answered the valet at once. He

appeared to be prepared for this question. "Enterprising. Never impudent even though he's always…outspoken. And—what one notices most, I think—remarkably cheerful despite a hard life."

"Well put. I agree." Arthur considered the lad. "He talks of resuming his travels soon. Apparently he doesn't wish to stay at Furness Hall, though I think he'd be welcome. I've thought of offering him a position."

"What sort of position, my lord?"

"That's the question. I don't know. It just seems wasteful to allow him to wander off. Well, we shall see." Arthur handed the letters to Clayton. "Send those off, would you?"

"Certainly, my lord." Clayton took them and left the room. In the corridor, he encountered Sarah Dennison. She was carrying a small canvas bag, held well away from her skirts. The smell suggested that it held the contents of a feline sandbox. "Are you cleaning up after the cat? That's not your job." He felt offended on her behalf.

"No." She looked rueful. "But who's to do it? There's no bootboy or footman. The housemaid is run off her feet as it is. And I—and my mistress—have to be in the room where the cat *is*."

Clayton nodded his understanding. "The staff's not what I'm used to on a country house visit."

"Well meaning, but overwhelmed," agreed the lady's maid.

They exchanged a commiserating glance. "Still carrying those scissors, I see," said Miss Dennison.

He couldn't restrain a sigh. "I do hate to see a nobleman—closely related to his lordship, too—so ill-kempt. But Lord Furness absolutely refuses my services."

Sarah Dennison shook her head. "Even though he can see—as we all do in Lord Macklin's turn-out—that you're a master."

"Thank you. Miss Saunders's coiffure is immaculate since you arrived."

They took a moment to bask in mutual approbation.

"I might have an idea," said the lady's maid then.

"Really?" Clayton didn't see what she could do.

"You might try telling Lord Furness that my young lady is very particular about hair, considering the trials she has with her own. And that she appreciates a neat appearance."

"You think that might change his opinion?"

"I think there's a good chance of it."

Clayton absorbed the implications of her suggestion. "Is that the way things are trending then?"

Miss Dennison shrugged. "It's not my place to say anything about that."

He thought some more. "You like Somerset?"

"I don't mind it."

"Furness Hall offers a good bit of…scope, considering the state of the household."

"I expect it might." She sounded just a bit complacent.

"And the earl's…family would most likely spend some time in London each year as well."

"The nobility is fond of the season."

Clayton didn't smile, but his expression showed appreciation. Here was a sharp wit who could carry on an oblique conversation. He'd missed that at Furness Hall. "Thank you for your advice."

"Happy to be of service, Mr. Clayton. I must get

on now and be rid of this." She held the odiferous bag well away from her person.

Clayton watched her go. If her idea proved useful, he'd owe her a favor, in the intangible currency of belowstairs. He didn't mind. Indeed, he was pleased to add her to his long roster of connections in the households of Lord Macklin's far-flung family.

❧

Geoffrey's first expedition on Fergus was allowed that day, due to his incessant requests and because he'd taken to riding as if horseback was his natural element. The boy, wildly excited, had argued for going back to the gorge, but his father had ordered a much shorter circuit around the neighborhood.

The party set off at midmorning to make a turn about the nearby lanes. Geoffrey took the lead with Tom at his side on Molly; the others followed, keeping to the pace of his pony.

"That boy might be half centaur," said Lord Macklin as they watched Geoffrey chatter to Tom as he rode.

"He seems bound to be a fine rider," their host agreed.

Jean, silent in her crimson riding habit, tried to keep her mind off kisses. Despite the turmoil this man's touch had roused, the thrill of them came back to her all too often, as they were doing right now when she and Lord Furness rode side by side. She gave him a sidelong glance. She wanted more, even as she shied away from the tumultuous results. And so she was frozen, suspended between desire and apprehension. "When will you hire a new nanny for Geoffrey?" she asked. The question dropped into the conversation like a stone tossed into a still pond. "Lily is a sweet girl, but he doesn't listen to her."

"Would he to anyone?"

"He would if it was my old nurse," said Lord Macklin. "She was born to be a master sergeant, I think. She had a certain tone of voice that made any child within range spring to attention and obey. Even if they'd never met her before."

"I don't suppose she's available," joked his nephew.

The older man smiled. "Long gone, I'm afraid."

"There are agencies in London, I believe," said Jean. Again, she sounded stilted. She tried to soften her tone. "Perhaps in Bristol as well?"

"I could write to my daughter," said the earl. "She might know of someone."

Lord Furness accepted both ideas with a nod. "We need just the right sort of person. Someone Geoffrey can like and respect."

How his tone had changed since she arrived, Jean thought. That was good. She'd accomplished that much.

"He couldn't go to school in his present state," their host added. "He needs a bit of…polish first. Fortunately, there's time."

"Polish," echoed Lord Macklin, his smile widening. "A curious way of putting it. A touch of town bronze for the nursery set?"

"Smoothing a few rough edges," his nephew answered.

Geoffrey shouted "Heigh-ho!" and kicked Fergus's sides. The amiable animal responded with a quick trot and then, with more urging, a gallop. The others hastened to catch up, their larger mounts well able to close the gap. Geoffrey leaned over his pony's neck, eyes shining, whooping with delight, perfectly in control even at speed. They pounded over the turf like the field at Newmarket in the heat of a race, the adults holding back so that Geoffrey could lead.

Like a wave of marauders, they rounded a small copse and came face-to-face with another riding party traveling at a far more sedate pace.

Disaster loomed. Collision seemed inevitable. With an eye on her companions, Jean managed to swerve to the left. Tom came with her. The two men went right, and they flowed around the new group in two surging streams. Geoffrey, on the other hand, pulled Fergus to a halt right under the new horses' noses. One of them shied; another tossed his head and sidled. The strangers struggled to maintain control.

It took a few minutes for everyone to get sorted out. They backed and milled and finally gathered in one larger group next to the copse.

They'd nearly run down two gentlemen and a young lady, Jean saw. She judged that they were neighboring gentry, a father and his offspring, most likely. All three had pale hair and slender frames, with blue eyes and the easy seats of people at home on horseback. The woman wore a habit far more fashionable than Jean's.

"Furness?" said the older man. He seemed surprised.

"Hello, Wandrell. How are you?"

"Very well. Good to see you out in company."

Lord Furness hunched a shoulder. "Allow me to introduce my uncle Macklin and Miss Jean Saunders, who are visiting, as well as my son, Geoffrey, of course."

Geoffrey received curious looks.

"My nearest neighbors," Lord Furness continued. "Mr. Theodore Wandrell, his son, Teddy, and his daughter, Anna."

The parties exchanged mounted bows. The younger Theodore Wandrell looked about her age, Jean thought, his sister a bit younger. The latter was eyeing her, maneuvering her horse closer. "You're staying at Furness Hall?" she said when she was nearer.

"Yes."

"How funny. We've heard that no one visits there anymore." Miss Wandrell's gaze was sharp, running over Jean's antiquated dress and tricorn hat. Her hair was straining at its bounds, Jean thought, eager to spring out and embarrass her; an escaped curl twining down her temple. "You're here with your mother?" Miss Wandrell added.

Jean suppressed a start. What had her mother to do with it? "My mother? No, she's dead."

"Oh! I'm so sorry." Her interrogator sounded more inquisitive than regretful. She awaited further information. Jean gave her none. Rather, she turned to the gentlemen.

"Yes, Geoffrey is trying out his new pony," Lord Macklin was saying.

"Got away from him, did it?" replied the elder Mr. Wandrell. His tone was patronizing. "Best to keep youngsters inside fences at his age, I always found."

"Geoffrey was doing splendidly," said Lord Furness.

"He nearly barreled into us," replied his neighbor.

"And yet, he did not."

"Are we going on soon?" Geoffrey asked.

The adults looked down from their taller mounts. Geoffrey should have seemed dwarfed in their midst, Benjamin thought. But somehow he didn't. The Wandrells clearly didn't approve of his complaint, however.

"Come over here," said Tom, putting a hand on Fergus's bridle. They moved to the edge of the trees. Tom set Geoffrey practicing his mounted turns.

"Mama will be *so* glad to know you're receiving visitors again," said Anna Wandrell in a caressing tone. She spoke to Benjamin, but she had her eyes on Miss Saunders.

All of the Wandrells awaited Benjamin's answer, another sign of the speculation his long period of mourning had roused in the neighborhood. A flood of intrusions loomed. "Not really," he said. "Family only."

This made Miss Wandrell frown. Questions showed in her expression.

"We should move along," Benjamin added, signaling his horse with his knees. He bowed from the saddle and smiled as if all was well. He also got away as quickly as possible, turning back toward home. His party followed along, while the neighbors sat still, watching them ride away.

Alice hadn't particularly liked the Wandrell family, Benjamin remembered. She'd remarked on Mrs. Wandrell's malicious tongue and more than once said that Anna bid fair to be just like her mother. He had no doubt that they'd make inquiries about Miss Saunders and soon discover that their relationship was vanishingly distant—no excuse to dispense with chaperones. The isolation he'd thrown over his household was broken.

The Wandrells habitually went up to London for

the season, where they could question many more
people and spread whatever story they concocted
even farther. And tongues would wag more furiously
because he'd made himself such an object of curiosity.
Benjamin felt a flash of rage. They had no right to
target Miss Saunders.

Her voice drifted into his thoughts. "No, I never
had a pony when I was small."

Benjamin turned to look. His houseguest and his
son rode in tandem on his right.

"How did you learn to ride?" said Geoffrey. "You
do very well," he added with the air of a connoisseur.

"Thank you," said Miss Saunders gravely. "Our
head groom taught me, on a barrel."

Geoffrey gazed up at her, his interest definitely
caught. "A barrel?"

Her head was far above his son's, but her tone wasn't
the least patronizing, Benjamin thought. Nothing like
Wandrell's condescension.

"We didn't have many horses," she answered. "None
I was allowed to use. But Matthew thought I should
know how to ride. So when I was a little older than you,
he fastened a small cask to a rail fence, with reins tied
to the post. He showed me how to sit and hang on."

Benjamin was touched by the picture this presented. The implications were more concerning. Why
hadn't she been allowed to use the horses?

"That's smart," commented Geoffrey. "Were you
very poor?"

Miss Saunders looked nonplussed.

"Tom said he had no horses when he was young
because he was poor."

"Ah. We weren't poor like Tom. We were"—she groped for a word—"careful."

Geoffrey looked confused.

"We had to practice economies," Miss Saunders added.

Her flat tone gave Benjamin the notion that most of these economies had involved her.

"What's 'econ-omies'?" Geoffrey asked. "Are they hard to practice? Lily says practice makes perfect."

"It means deciding which things you can afford to have, and which you can't."

The boy thought about this. "You deciding? Or somebody else?"

"Somebody else," Miss Saunders answered tonelessly.

Geoffrey nodded. Benjamin watched the two of them exchange a look of perfect understanding. A simple glance, conveying worlds.

Benjamin felt something twist in the region of his heart. Suddenly, in a moment of absolute clarity, he knew exactly what he should do.

The riding party reached Furness Hall a few minutes later. Geoffrey stayed with Fergus in the stable to help with the pony's grooming, and young Tom joined him. The three adults walked up to the house together. Jean was eager to change out of her riding habit and to be alone for a bit. She couldn't quite absorb the fact that she'd never felt so thoroughly understood as in the recent exchange she'd shared with a five-year-old boy.

Lord Furness said, "May I speak to you in the library, Miss Saunders?"

"In the library?" She stopped. "Why not right here?"

Instead of replying, he put a hand on her back. Warmth seemed to spread from that light touch through Jean's entire body. It made her want to nestle into the curve of his arm. Lord Macklin walked on as if nothing was happening, and Jean let herself be guided into the book-lined room where the portrait of her cousin Alice presided. "Sit down," Lord Furness said with a gesture.

Jean moved a few steps away from him. She didn't care to be commanded. "No, thank you."

"It's not always necessary to argue, you know."

But quite often it was, Jean thought. That or be trampled by other people's whims. Not arguing had been the bane of her early life. "What is it?"

Lord Furness looked aggrieved. He came closer and reached for her hand. "I could do this much better if you would sit," he said.

Jean's pulse stuttered and began to race.

"But I see that you won't. Very well. I shan't kneel then. I shall simply ask you to be my wife."

"Ask?" His tone suggested a fait accompli rather than a request. Jean felt as if the eyes in Alice's portrait were drilling into her back.

"It's the obvious answer. Since you…erupted into my life, I've come to see many things differently. I need a change. This household needs a change. And Geoffrey requires a mother."

"He needs a parent. He has one in you." Jean's lips felt stiff, as if she'd been out in the cold for hours, though the weather was clement. She pulled her hand from his.

"You could be another. Isn't that what you wanted? You came here to take him from me."

"To his grandparents' house."

Lord Furness smiled skeptically. "My uncle tells me the Phillipsons were never going to take charge of a little boy. He said Geoffrey's care would have fallen on you."

Jean shifted uncomfortably. That plan had never been well thought out. She was glad to be able to abandon it.

"As my wife, you can make sure he's cared for as you think best." He said it as if presenting an irresistible inducement.

Jean felt as if a heavy weight had descended on her spirit. "I don't intend to marry. Marriage is a wretched state."

"That was not my experience."

The picture of Alice loomed even larger in Jean's mind. His great love; his lost ideal. Alice had taken everything. There was nothing left. "You were fortunate. My views are very different." Jean gathered the long skirts of her riding habit and turned to go.

"Geoffrey isn't the only reason for my offer."

Something sadly like hope fluttered her pulse. Jean stood still. If he kissed her now, she might waver. Even give in. Which made her want to go and to stay in equal measure.

"The Wandrells, the family we met on our ride today, will probably call here tomorrow," he went on. "I can evade the visit. But that will just make them more likely to poke and pry and gossip about your presence here, unchaperoned."

Jean was glad she had her back to him, because humiliating tears flooded her eyes. She blinked them back. "So you think we must marry in order to satisfy the proprieties?" It was the very reason her parents had been forced into marriage—yoked together in misery for the rest of their lives. She would rather give up society and live as the Duke of Hamilton's hermit than settle for such a thing, Jean thought fiercely.

"We have rather crossed the line," Lord Furness added. "More than once. But I didn't want to frighten you with expressions of passion."

Jean turned to stare at him. "Frighten me?"

"As I did the other night."

She gritted her teeth. "I wasn't frightened of you. I'm not frightened of anything! I told you it had nothing to do with that."

"I wasn't quite clear on what you were telling me."

"You might try listening instead of making pronouncements."

"I don't think that's quite—"

"The point is, I've seen the wretched results of a forced marriage," she interrupted. "And I'd rather beg in the street." She turned away again. "I'll leave for London as soon as I can arrange for a chaise."

"Miss Saunders, wait."

She didn't.

"Of course I also feel regard for you."

Jean stood rigid, her hand on the doorknob. *Regard.* Was there a more pallid word in the English language? She stalked out. She did not, of course, slam the door. Such pettiness was beneath her.

Benjamin stood, stricken, under the portrait of his…first wife. He hadn't thought of Alice in those terms before. Not until a young lady with stubborn curls and an indomitable spirit had shown him a new side of his son, and of himself. She couldn't go. How could he keep her?

With that thought came the realization of just how badly he'd botched his proposal. He'd rushed in on a surge of emotion, roused by the look she and Geoffrey had exchanged. He'd been wild to cherish and protect. But the words that came out of his mouth had suggested a cold bargain instead. He was an idiot!

He sank down on the sofa and put his head in his hands.

She'd kissed him with such innocent fire. It made him wild to remember those kisses. And if she'd pulled away with more than a maiden's concern, well, Benjamin understood the weight of the past. Didn't he? Not enough to make his case, it seemed.

He sprang up, suddenly desperate. He needed time. He needed help.

Twelve

"I'D THOUGHT MATTERS WERE ALL BUT SETTLED," SAID Benjamin's uncle half an hour later, after Benjamin had poured out his troubles in one great rush. "This is unfortunate."

Benjamin gritted his teeth. He hadn't felt so clumsy since he was fifteen.

"How can I help you?"

"Urge her to stay?" A spark of hope penetrated his general gloom. Miss Saunders seemed to like his uncle. Perhaps she'd listen to him.

"And tell her you want her for your wife," said his uncle.

"I…believe I do."

"If you're not certain, we should disband this house party at once." Lord Macklin's tone and expression were stern.

And then he would never see Jean again, Benjamin thought. At least, he might encounter her in society, but nothing would be the same. "I do want her," he said emphatically.

"Then you will have to woo her."

His uncle spoke as if this made all clear, but it didn't. Benjamin required specifics. He said as much.

"You got a wife once before."

"I know, but that was...easy."

His uncle looked at him with raised brows.

"Not the right word," Benjamin went on. "Say rather that the process with Alice was obvious. We met at a ball during the season. We liked each other. After that, the steps were all set out before me. Ask her to dance more than once, call and take her driving, send bouquets. If one received encouragement—which I did from her and her mother—then make an offer." He nodded. "Her mother left us in the drawing room together at a crucial moment. I didn't realize till now, but I expect they arranged it between them. I spoke. Alice accepted. And that was that. I knew where I was all the time."

"And now you don't?"

"I've strayed off the map into uncharted territory," said Benjamin. "No waltzes, no drives in the park." He met the older man's eyes. "Wooing. Is that what you did? Before you married?"

His uncle looked thoughtful. "Well, my courtship was rather like yours with Alice. Only more so. Your aunt's mother was a formidable woman."

"Miss Saunders has no mother to smooth the way," Benjamin replied, and from what he'd heard about Mrs. Saunders, that was for the best.

The two men looked at each other. "I don't think bouquets will have much effect in this case," Benjamin said. There were flowers from the gardens all over the house.

"You must do things to please her," Lord Macklin said.

The pleasures that leaped to Benjamin's mind were surely not what he meant.

"Think of what she enjoys, or needs, and provide it." His uncle brightened. "Like knights of old, performing tasks set by their ladies in order to win their favor."

Benjamin was surprised to discover a streak of fantasy in his uncle. And yet the idea had a curious appeal. "Tasks."

"Acts of chivalry. Think of Raleigh, spreading his cloak over a mud puddle to allow the queen to pass."

"I always found that tale doltishly theatrical," replied Benjamin.

"He sacrificed for her comfort."

"He made a load of work for his washerwomen, more like."

"You're missing the spirit of this, Benjamin. The point is to put her before you or do something she would like."

"Yes, I know. But I'm rather short of dragons to slay." A thought struck him. "Clayton mentioned something."

"Yes?" His uncle came alert. "I've always found Clayton's views very helpful."

"Perhaps I'll do it then," Benjamin said. He'd suffer far more than a minor irritation for Jean. And that was the point, wasn't it?

His uncle waited. Benjamin let him. He didn't intend to explain; the thing was foolish enough without talking it to death. After a short silence, the older man nodded. "Meanwhile, I'll take steps to help Miss Saunders feel more comfortable at Furness Hall," he said. "Do your servants tattle?"

"What?"

"Do they gossip in the neighborhood?"

"No," replied Benjamin, mystified. "The ones who were so inclined left over these last years while I was playing the hermit."

"Splendid." His uncle rose. "May I borrow a carriage? I'll be back in an hour or less."

"Where are you going?"

"To explore a possibility."

"What sort of possibility?"

"Let's see how I do before I explain."

Benjamin had to be content with this unsatisfying reply, because in the next moment his uncle was gone.

⟡

Jean took a gown from the wardrobe, folded it, and put it on her bed. She hadn't summoned Sarah to pack for her because the physical movement was a relief after the scene she'd just endured. Also, Sarah would notice that she was ridiculously upset. So she hadn't ordered her trunk to be brought either. Yet. "Regard," Jean muttered, pulling out another dress. "'Of course I feel *regard* for you.' Really? As one does for a distant acquaintance? Or perhaps a doddering old retainer?"

Tab, dozing on the window seat, raised his head from his paws and looked at her.

"Even you expect something more than *regard*," Jean said to him. "And you are a cat."

A knock on the door silenced her. Briefly. If Lord Furness had come to offer more insulting arguments and tepid sentiments, she'd be glad to give him a piece of her mind. She'd thought of several cutting remarks that she really ought to have delivered in the library. Jean flung the panels open.

Geoffrey flinched on the threshold. He stood there all alone, small and a bit grubby. "Geoffrey," said Jean, surprised. He'd never approached her so directly before.

"I brought you this." The boy held up a little figure made of twigs and an acorn and bits of moss. "I made it myself," he added, then ducked his head. "Well, Tom helped me stick some of the bits together, but I thought of it. It's a forest fairy, like in the storybooks."

"It's wonderful," said Jean, taking the gift carefully. The figure was sturdier than she'd expected.

"You like books."

"I do."

Geoffrey nodded like a boy whose theories have been confirmed. He regarded his offering with similar satisfaction. "If you make things out of stuff you find, no one can say you can't have them," he added. "'Cause they're yours."

"Very true." She remembered a tiny village she'd created out of similar materials in a secret corner of her childhood garden. No one had taken it from her because no one ever found it.

The boy's gaze moved past her to the bed and the folded garments resting there. "Are you going away?"

Jean hesitated as Geoffrey took a step backward.

The emotion she'd glimpsed on his face—sadness, resignation?—was quickly masked.

"Everybody leaves here." He shrugged and turned away, head bent, as if disappointment was his native habitat.

The slump, the abandonment of hope, was hauntingly familiar to Jean. She knew, viscerally, how it felt in body and soul. She knew that despondence could become engrained. It was odd but undeniable that she'd rarely felt more akin to anyone than to this little boy. She couldn't walk away from Geoffrey, even though he had the most infuriating father in the world. "No, I was just looking over my dresses. To…to see which needed pressing."

He looked back. His expression could not have been called hopeful.

"I can't go." Jean held up the figure he'd made for her. "Now that I have a new friend."

The cat padded over to investigate, his eyes on the gift. "See, Tab thinks so, too," said Jean, though she feared he saw the little figure as a new chew toy.

Geoffrey did not smile. But he gave a small nod before walking away.

When he turned the corner of the corridor and disappeared, Jean shut the door. She placed the wood fairy on a bit of carving above the mantelshelf, well out of Tab's reach, she hoped. Its tiny painted eyes glinted at her. As much as she wanted to flee Furness Hall, she also wanted to stay, Jean admitted. For Geoffrey's sake, and other reasons. Which she did not intend to explain just now, even to herself.

She began to return her dresses to the wardrobe.

❦

Lord Macklin returned in less than an hour. Hearing the sound of carriage wheels, Benjamin went to look out the window and saw his uncle emerge from the vehicle, then turn to hand down a lady in her middle years. The newcomer was beautifully dressed and carried herself with immense dignity. When he went downstairs to investigate, he found the pair in his front hall.

"Ah, Benjamin," said his uncle. "Mrs. Thorpe has agreed to come and stay with us for a while, lending her countenance to our household."

He gave no hint as to who she was or where he'd found her. Benjamin was quite familiar with his near neighbors; she wasn't one of them. A grande dame such as this would have been a force in local society.

"She is well known to me. I need not say that she is perfectly respectable."

Benjamin didn't understand the sidelong glance the woman threw his uncle. He only knew that he wouldn't want to be the target of her disapproval.

"Unless you object, of course," his uncle finished.

"No." A proper chaperone solved one of his problems—the Wandrells. Not the most worrisome perhaps, but important nonetheless. "You are most welcome, Mrs. Thorpe."

"Thank you." Her voice was musical, with a note of command as impressive as her appearance.

"I'll take her to meet Miss Saunders," said his uncle. He offered his arm, and they swept up the staircase as if they, rather than Benjamin, owned the place.

"Need not say I am perfectly respectable?"

murmured Mrs. Thorpe when they reached the upper corridor.

Lord Macklin acknowledged the reproof in her voice with a nod. "I mustn't indulge in sleight of word."

"Sleight of—" She laughed, a charming sound. "This may very well not work, Macklin. You're taking a chance."

"Which I haven't done often enough in my life."

"But it's not your life at the center of this. We'll see what the young lady thinks. I've told you this is her decision."

"How could she help but like you?"

"Liking isn't the issue," Mrs. Thorpe answered dryly as he knocked on a bedchamber door.

"Miss Saunders," said Lord Macklin when the door opened. "May I present Mrs. Thorpe to you?"

With a graceful bow, he launched the older woman in Jean's direction. Jean stepped back. Mrs. Thorpe came in, closing the door behind her, and Jean found herself alone in her room with a stranger.

The older woman smiled. There was something so warm and engaging in the expression that it was impossible to take offense as Mrs. Thorpe sat in one armchair before the fireplace and directed Jean to the other. Jean felt rather as if the queen had dropped by for a chat. One didn't raise objections in such a case. "I told Lord Macklin that you had to be in on our scheme," Mrs. Thorpe said. "And in fact that the whole is up to you. I won't go on without your approval."

Jean grew even more curious. She examined the poised figure sitting opposite. Mrs. Thorpe's black hair was immaculately dressed. Her clothes obviously came from a fashionable modiste. Her face was a bit pale, but nothing could detract from its classic bone structure. Her blue eyes gleamed with sharp intelligence. "Scheme?" Jean asked.

"For me to serve as your chaperone."

"Oh."

"I'm happy to play the role. I've grown rather bored with rusticating. But only if you approve."

"*You* are the mysterious friend in the village," Jean said, making the connection.

"It's no great mystery that I'm staying there."

"But there is some mystery? A reason I shouldn't approve?"

Mrs. Thorpe smiled again. Jean couldn't help smiling back. Her visitor's charm was palpable. She was rapidly becoming fascinated, Jean thought.

"I'm an actress," said Mrs. Thorpe. "Down from London on a repairing lease. My husband declared I'd been running too hard and sent me off for a rest." She made a comical face. "He said I'd never get any in town or with him about, and he was right. He generally is. Such an annoying trait in a man."

Mrs. Thorpe's voice made you want to listen to whatever she cared to say, Jean thought.

"I'd heard of the beauties of the village here, so I took a cottage for a few months. I've been keeping to myself. With just my maid to do for me. None of the neighboring gentry has noticed me. That's important."

"To the scheme," Jean replied.

"Oh good. You're not stupid."

Jean laughed. "I hope I'm not."

"So do I, my dear. For your own sake, mostly." The older woman nodded.

"Lord Macklin is a friend of yours." Was he more than that? Jean wondered. Her father's history made that idea all too plausible.

"Of my husband's."

"He is?" Jean wouldn't have expected the very proper earl to know the husband of an actress. Even a superior one, as Mrs. Thorpe clearly was. Who was Mr. Thorpe?

"Yes." Her companion's eyes glowed with understanding. "He really is. And so today when he called and asked if I'd consider being your chaperone, I thought, why not? I feel excessively rested. I don't have enough to do. If *you* would like it. I *am* a respectable married lady, despite what some may think of my profession."

Jean remembered Anna Wandrell's sharp examination. That girl and her family were on the lookout for improprieties. And then she imagined this formidable lady at her side when she faced that scrutiny again. She could use a polished ally, and she would need one soon if she wasn't mistaken. But was Mrs. Thorpe a good choice? Not that she had any others. If she was found to be alone here, neighborhood tongues would wag.

Tab strolled across the room to survey their visitor. He took his time, seeming to catalog every detail. Then he jumped into Mrs. Thorpe's lap, turned around twice, and lay down, purring. The lady smiled down at him, running a gentle hand over his fur. "Hello, young sir," she said.

She looked good-humored and wise as well as formidable. "No one knows you here?"

"Only Lord Macklin. I haven't spoken with anyone else."

It wouldn't be for long, Jean thought. It couldn't be. The thought filled her with a kind of reckless melancholy. "All right," she said. "Yes, why not?"

"Good." Mrs. Thorpe tossed her head. "Hardly a demanding role, but it holds some potential for amusement."

The clearly characteristic gesture sparked Jean's memory. "I've seen you onstage! I never would have recognized you if you hadn't told me."

"I'm an *actress*. And a good one."

"But surely your name was different?"

"Thorpe is my married name. I kept the one I started out with for the stage." She smiled impishly. "Mr. Thorpe prefers it; he's a rather important banker."

"Lady Macbeth." Jean's recollections expanded. "Oh my. You gave me chills."

Mrs. Thorpe accepted the praise with a pleased nod. "So we're agreed then. We will embark on a small, harmless deception. I'm a perfectly competent chaperone, I assure you. I don't intend to let you get into mischief."

"I don't plan any."

"Really?" The older woman's brows rose in a perfect picture of skepticism. "None at all?"

Perhaps a few more stolen kisses? But she wouldn't be kissing Lord Furness again, because he was an idiot. She'd forgotten for a moment.

Mrs. Thorpe's expression suggested that she could read Jean's mind. "It will be our secret. You, me, and Lord Macklin. And Lord Furness, of course."

"He doesn't know?"

"Not yet. I insisted that you be allowed to decide the matter first."

Jean appreciated that.

"This is his home," continued her companion. "He has a right to know. But young men can be intemperate. I don't know him. What do you think?"

"Let's wait a bit. I'll tell him." She imagined his surprise and recognized that she'd enjoy it.

"Just as you say, my dear." Mrs. Thorpe looked amused. "Now we should get acquainted. You must tell me about the household and what I would be expected to know about the people here."

But they'd barely begun when a servant arrived to announce that the Wandrells were downstairs.

"Lord Macklin thought there might be an immediate need. I'll go down." Mrs. Thorpe rose and surveyed Jean. "Your gown is very well. Your hair—"

"Has escaped its bounds as usual, no doubt. My maid, Sarah, can subdue it."

"Have her do so, and then join us. I'll keep our guests occupied till then."

Jean enjoyed the relish in her tone. She hadn't appreciated Miss Wandrell's prying questions.

❧

Benjamin leaned back in his chair and watched his new houseguest chat with Mrs. Wandrell and her daughter, Anna. He'd once seen an exhibition in Spain where men evaded charging bulls with the grace of lethal dancers. He hadn't much cared for the outcome there, but in Mrs. Thorpe's case, he could fully appreciate an expert at work. She seemed to answer every probe his nosy neighbors threw out. And yet she gave them no real information at all. Smiling, gracious, she didn't appear to notice the resulting frowns.

It was relaxing, Benjamin thought, to watch Mrs. Thorpe at work. Whoever she was, she had the manner of a princess. Even Mrs. Wandrell, so sour and satirical, was clearly impressed. Alice had never managed them so deftly.

The drawing room door opened, and Miss Saunders came in. The sudden sight of her made Benjamin's heart skip a beat. He hid his reaction, or hoped he did, by rising and offering her his chair. This allowed him to move a bit farther from the center of the action.

It wasn't just her beauty, he thought. After a while, the impact of beauty lessened. A man became accustomed to it, in a way. But he'd learned that Jean Saunders was so much more than pretty.

She didn't look at him. He felt a pang of disappointment. He'd wanted to glimpse that coppery sparkle in her brown eyes and know that she appreciated the scene before him as much as he did.

"Mrs. Wandrell, allow me to introduce my charge to you," said Mrs. Thorpe. "This is Miss Jean Saunders."

Miss Saunders dropped a curtsy. She might have been any demure young lady in the care of a chaperone. Even her glossy brown curls had been smoothed and tamed—rather a shame, Benjamin thought. However, he knew that whatever thoughts were going through her head, they were not those of the ingénue she was playing.

Miss Saunders sat down. So did Benjamin.

The ladies were a marked contrast, he thought. The Wandrells, with their pale hair and eyes, their ferret-like manner, seemed one sort of creature. Opposite them, Mrs. Thorpe and Miss Saunders were all warmth and restraint. Benjamin met his uncle's eyes across the room and saw that he'd noticed it, too. A small secret smile danced in his gaze, Benjamin noted.

"How are you related to Miss Saunders?" Mrs. Wandrell asked, going for the blunt question this time. She'd tried to get information about Mrs. Thorpe's antecedents in several ways so far, and failed.

"I think of her as an honorary niece."

"Honorary?" The caller examined them.

"It is indeed an honor," said Miss Saunders, effortlessly falling in with Mrs. Thorpe's ploy. "I have no aunts of my own. Have you, Miss Wandrell?"

Their younger visitor blinked. "Yes. Two."

"How fortunate. Do they live nearby?"

"No."

"But how did you become *honorary*?" asked Mrs. Wandrell, curiosity driving her to the edge of rudeness.

Mrs. Thorpe gave her a look. Benjamin admired the nuance layered into it—surprise, reproof, indulgence. The lady shrugged with consummate grace. "What are the usual ways?" she replied. "Long acquaintance, similar interests, warm regard."

"I am an orphan," said Miss Saunders, her timing perfect.

"But a member of Lord Furness's family?" said Mrs. Wandrell. "I believe he told my daughter so."

"Alice was my cousin."

Second cousin, or third, or something of the sort,

Benjamin recalled from an earlier conversation. The clock on the mantel chimed the half hour. Benjamin suppressed a smile. Alice had placed the timepiece there to admonish callers who lingered too long. Mrs. Thorpe responded with a subtle change in posture that nearly caused Benjamin to rise and depart. The lady was that forceful.

Mrs. Wandrell stood. As did her daughter.

"So kind of you to call," Mrs. Thorpe murmured as they took their leave. She then gathered up Miss Saunders and swept away, leaving the two men alone in the drawing room.

"What a splendid woman," said Benjamin.

"Mrs. Thorpe is a…temporary solution," his uncle replied. "You'd better get about your wooing."

"I have a plan."

"Good."

Upstairs, the two ladies sat down to continue their earlier conversation. "You were just splendid," said Jean.

Mrs. Thorpe smiled and shrugged. "Society rests on conventions, you know…a set of expectations about how people will behave. If you act like a duchess, others see you as superior and defer."

Jean considered. "You make it sound easy. But people are often mocked for their pretentions."

"Ah." The older woman held up a finger. "First, you must *act*. That is, you must really become that person. Believe it. Embody it. And second, you must behave like a real duchess, not the vulgar crowd's idea of what one is like."

"Do you know many duchesses?" Jean asked. "Not that you shouldn't. It's just… I don't."

"I am a keen observer of human nature," replied Mrs. Thorpe with another smile. "Now tell me more about the household."

Jean did so.

"So you're here at Furness Hall because of the boy," said her companion when she was finished.

"I came because I had heard Geoffrey was being neglected, yes." Jean gave a sharp nod. "And he was."

"But no longer?"

"The situation has improved. It is not...fully resolved."

Mrs. Thorpe nodded. "You've made extraordinary efforts for the child."

"Alice was a cousin."

"Even so. You must care a great deal about children."

"Doesn't everyone?"

"Alas, no." Mrs. Thorpe paused for a noticeable moment, and then added. "I knew your father."

Jean had been full of admiration for her new chaperone. Now she felt as if she'd tripped on an unlighted stairway and fallen into the dark.

"I thought I should say so. When Lord Macklin told me your name, I recognized it."

Jean's stomach roiled. Papa had had a penchant for actresses. Had Mrs. Thorpe been one of his mistresses?

"We were not good friends," the older woman went on, as if reading Jean's mind. "But he was often around the theater."

"I believe he was a connoisseur of opera dancers," replied Jean. "So the gossips say, at least. I wouldn't know."

"Not a proper topic for his daughter," said Mrs. Thorpe.

"Daughter!" The word came out bitter. "By blood, yes. But in no other way. I saw him perhaps three times in my life. We did not converse on any of those occasions."

The older woman nodded. She didn't look shocked. "Some men appear to have no interest in family," she said. "They see it as a female realm and leave such matters to their wives and mothers."

"Except for their sons, I suppose." Jean had always known her father would have cared about her if she'd been a boy. Her mother had said so. She breathed more deeply to regain control of her emotions. She didn't intend to expose any more of her history.

"And then others, like Lord Macklin, are devoted to family interests," said Mrs. Thorpe.

"Indeed." Jean stood, ready for this conversation to be over.

"I expect their attitudes depend on how they were taught and treated as children," the other woman went on. She appeared not to notice Jean's impatience. Or she merely refused to acknowledge it.

"Perhaps. If one wishes to make excuses." She did not. People could overcome their upbringing. She had.

"So I see why you were so concerned about young Geoffrey," continued Mrs. Thorpe. "You mean to make good fathers of them both."

"Both?"

"Lord Furness, and then Geoffrey, in his turn."

Jean stared at her. She'd never put it that way. But the idea grew in her mind.

"The same goes for mothers, I suppose. Though they do say that's more of a natural instinct."

A snort escaped Jean. "You have children?"

"I do not," replied the older woman. "I would have liked them. But it never happened for me. It seems I'm barren." Her tone was melancholy but even. "Still, one can be *motherly*. I'm always ready to comfort and advise youngsters in the theater."

Jean didn't know if this was an offer or a simple comment, but it didn't matter. She didn't want or need any maternal impulses. She wanted to end this conversation. "You should come and meet Geoffrey," she said. "And Tom. You'll like Tom." She went to the door and opened it, standing ready to depart.

Even Mrs. Thorpe couldn't ignore such an obvious signal. She rose, and they walked together up to the nursery.

Thirteen

THE NOISE WAS OBVIOUS EVEN BEFORE THEY ENTERED the nursery a few minutes later. Jean opened the door to find Geoffrey racing around the perimeter of the large room, yelling at the top of his lungs and waving a stick with a tuft of feathers fastened to the end. His high-pitched shrieks bounced off the peaked ceiling; his small feet pounded on the wooden floor.

Tom lay in wait at the far side of the chamber, ready to grab the child when he passed by, while Lily the nursery maid tried to remove breakable or hazardous objects from his path. Geoffrey skipped and leapt. Just before he reached Tom, he veered one way, then the other, causing Tom to stumble into the cone-shaped tent. It collapsed around the older lad, tangling him in folds of cloth.

Geoffrey laughed. He put the stick in his teeth and swarmed up the draperies on one tall window like a maddened cat. He swayed at the top, leering down at them with a mouthful of feathers. With his red-gold hair and celestial-blue eyes, he looked like a cherub gone wrong.

"I can't get up there," said Tom, beating back the encroaching tent and rising. "I'm too heavy. The curtains will come down, and Geoffrey with them."

Geoffrey opened his mouth to say, "Ha!" The momentarily forgotten stick clattered to the floor. "I'm a mighty chief!" the boy declared. "You can't catch me."

"He likes to climb," said Jean, remembering the incident at Cheddar Gorge. "He's…a very lively child."

"My dear, I work in the theater," said Mrs. Thorpe. "This is nothing." She stepped over to pick up the stick and examine the feathers. "This looks quite old."

"The label on the shelf said it was Mohawk," answered Tom. "I don't know what that means. It's part of the old lord's collections, which we just went in to *look at*. I told Geoffrey to leave it alone." Unusually, he sounded a bit weary.

Jean introduced them, then looked back up. "Geoffrey, this is Mrs. Thorpe. Now that she's here, I can stay longer."

The boy looked puzzled.

How was she to explain a chaperone to a five-year-old?

"A duenna," said Tom. "I heard that word in Bristol. She's like a…a nursery maid for young ladies."

Mrs. Thorpe laughed.

"Come down and say how do you do," Jean added as if this was a normal introduction. "You are one of her hosts, you know."

Geoffrey cocked his head, surveying the group below him with solemn doubt. Then he smiled—a sweet, charming smile that reminded Jean of his father while being all his own—and slid down the drapery to alight at their feet. "Hello," he said. His polite little bow was all a high stickler could ask. "*Are* you her nursery maid?"

"More a companion," the older woman replied. She cast a shrewd eye over the group. "Like you and Tom, perhaps."

"Oh." Geoffrey nodded. "Where did you come from?"

"I've been staying in the village for a little while."

The boy looked her over more closely. "Are you the mystery lady?"

The two women exchanged a surprised glance.

"They talk about her in the kitchen," Geoffrey went on. "Because the other lord said he met her on his walks. Cook thinks she's a French spy. Only Bradford said that's daft because the war's over. And anyway, what would she spy on here? Lily reckons she's run away from a tie-rannical husband."

Jean and Mrs. Thorpe looked at Lily, who flushed.

"*I* think Clayton knows," Geoffrey added. "He looks like he does. But he won't tell."

"I was staying in a cottage for a bit of rest," said Mrs. Thorpe. "Not hiding. Or spying."

Geoffrey looked disappointed.

"I did meet a French spy once though."

"You did?"

Mrs. Thorpe nodded. "Shall I tell you the story?"

An affirmative chorus encouraged her.

"Come and sit." Mrs. Thorpe settled on a battered sofa. Her audience found seats around her, Geoffrey right at her side.

"The young man in question—his name was Etienne—joined a London theater company as a cover."

"What's a cover?" asked Geoffrey.

"He pretended to be an actor. Do you know what an actor is?"

The boy looked wary, as if he didn't want to admit ignorance and yet wished for information.

"It's like when you're Robin Hood and I'm the sheriff," said Tom. "That's playacting. Only actors do it inside a big building in front of a load of people."

"Like a barn?"

Tom shook his head. "A fancy building with velvet draperies and chairs. The actors have special clothes to wear. Sometimes there's dancing." Seeing that the others were looking at him, he added, "I saw a play once—part of one—in Bristol."

"So the spy was pretending to pretend," Geoffrey said.

He really was an exceptionally quick child, Jean thought as Mrs. Thorpe nodded. "But after a while, Etienne found that he enjoyed acting more than spying," said the older woman.

"Why would he?" Geoffrey wrinkled his nose. "Didn't he want to sneak around and find secrets? And fight with swords?"

"Well, I'm afraid he wasn't very good at any of those things. And he was rather a good actor. Audiences loved him."

Jean caught the twinkle in Mrs. Thorpe's eyes. She wondered how well the lady had known this young Frenchman.

"So he just stopped being a spy?" Geoffrey asked with disgust.

"He might have, but someone, er, tattled on him.

One of the other actors told the Home Office he was a spy. It seemed he would be arrested."

"So *then* he had to fight."

Mrs. Thorpe looked rueful, clearly aware that her tale wasn't going over well with her smallest listener. "Etienne decided to go back to France," she continued. "We, some people I know, dressed him as a young lady so that he could slip away to a ship."

Geoffrey gazed up at her. "He ran away? Dressed as a girl?"

"Yes. It was his most challenging role, and he did it superbly. He made it home, too. After a while, he went to work in a theater in Paris, and he's still there. He specializes in playing oafish Englishmen."

"Really?" asked Jean.

"All quite true," said Mrs. Thorpe with a graceful gesture. "You might say we shouldn't have helped him, but he had no important information, and we couldn't see him hanged."

"That's not a very good story," Geoffrey said.

"Not much action was there? I'll do better next time."

The boy shrugged.

The door of the nursery opened, and Lord Furness walked in. At once, the room felt smaller to Jean; the air seemed to crackle with energy. He fixed her with a penetrating stare, as if no one else was present, and said, "Ah, there you are. It's a lovely day. I thought we might take a walk in the garden."

Geoffrey climbed down from the sofa and walked toward him. "There's frogs in the pond," he said. "I could show you."

Benjamin tore his gaze from his lovely, baffling

houseguest and looked down. His son looked back at him, blue eyes clear, though a little wary. Benjamin saw the problem at once. The nursery was Geoffrey's territory. It was logical to conclude that anyone coming here was looking for him. In fact, Benjamin had searched several other parts of the house first. "Frogs," he repeated.

"There's baby ones, too," Geoffrey replied. "They're called tadpoles. Tom told me." He made a wriggling motion with his hand.

Benjamin hesitated. He saw doubt begin to creep into his son's face, quickly replaced by a stoic blankness. He couldn't tell the boy he'd misunderstood the invitation. "I must have a look at those," he said. "Have you ever seen a tadpole, Miss Saunders?"

"No."

"You must come as well then." Benjamin edged around to cut woman and boy out of the herd filling the nursery.

"I suppose that's quite all right since Geoffrey is accompanying you," said Mrs. Thorpe.

He'd thought only of the advantages of her presence when the Wandrells called. Now Benjamin realized there were a number of disadvantages as well. Mrs. Thorpe was another barrier between him and Jean Saunders. His new houseguest smiled at him as if she knew precisely what he was thinking.

"I should fetch my bonnet and—"

"No need. It's quite warm. We'll go as we are. You don't care about a hat, do you, Geoffrey?"

"'Course not."

No more than he would have as a child, Benjamin

thought. Hats were good for nothing but falling off at inopportune moments and earning one a scolding for careless destruction of haberdashery. "Lead on," he told the boy. He thought of offering Miss Saunders his arm, but settled for chivying her gently toward the stairs. She didn't seem reluctant. Bemused, yes. That was all right.

It was a beautiful spring day. The sun was warm, punctuated by a few floating clouds. Flowers were in bloom, scenting the air all over the gardens. Bees hummed around them, and birdsong trilled. His grounds held several romantically secluded spots. Benjamin went over them in his mind, plotting various routes.

"The pond's this way," Geoffrey said to Miss Saunders.

That was one of them, Benjamin thought. There was a bench. But Geoffrey would be more interested in the muddy verge, he suspected.

A few minutes later, the boy squatted there, water lapping at the toes of his little boots. "There," he said, pointing. "Tadpoles." He looked over his shoulder and up at them, triumphant.

Miss Saunders bent beside him. "The things that are all head and tail?"

"That's it," said Benjamin. "Frogs start out that way. They develop legs later."

"There are so many. You'll be up to your ears in frogs soon."

"No," said Geoffrey. "Birds eat 'em. They pick 'em out of the water and swallow them down." He lifted his chin and made a gulping noise. "They've gotten a lot already."

Miss Saunders nodded.

"Must feel funny in their throats," Geoffrey added. "Wriggling like that. They die in the bird's stomach, I reckon." He looked to his father for confirmation.

"I suppose they do." Not an image to beguile a young lady. He would take her to the bluebell wood next time, Benjamin decided.

"I wanted to put some in a fishbowl and watch 'em," Geoffrey went on. "But Tom said they'd likely die." He glanced up again, as if hoping for a different answer.

"Very true," said Benjamin. He had no idea whether it was or not, but he knew he didn't want his house filled with newly mobile frogs.

"Fish are surprisingly fragile," said Miss Saunders. "I had two goldfish. Not at the same time. They both died." When her companions gazed at her, she turned her head away.

"Did you have a fish funeral?" Geoffrey asked.

"No. The servants just disposed of them."

"I'd've had a funeral," he declared. "Look!"

On the opposite side of the pond, a flash of color. In the next instant, a bird flew off with a tadpole in its beak.

"That's a kingfisher," Geoffrey said. "Tom told me." He stood up to watch it disappear. "They're kings because they're the best of all the fishers."

"Lovely," said Miss Saunders.

She was lovely, Benjamin thought. He needed to speak to her, to hold her again. "Shall we walk?" he asked.

As he'd hoped, Geoffrey ran ahead of them. He found a sturdy stick and waved it about like a sword, beheading random bits of vegetation with great panache.

"You should get him a dog," Miss Saunders said.

"You seem determined to populate my home with animals."

She laughed. "It just seems natural that Geoffrey would have a dog. Look at him run and jump."

"Did you have a dog? Along with your fish?"

"No." She bit off the word.

Benjamin took the hint and didn't ask further. "We had three when I was a boy," he said instead. "Shadrach, Meshach, and Abednego."

"What?"

He acknowledged the oddity of the names with a nod. "My mother found them as tiny puppies in a shed that had caught fire."

"A fiery furnace?"

"Not quite so bad, but it made her think of the Biblical story. They were her dogs. Papa had no interest in pets. We ended up calling them Shad, Mesh, and Ben, of course."

"Animals weren't allowed in my home. Mama thought dogs dirty and noisy, cats sly and cold."

The more Benjamin heard about her mother the less he liked her. "Parrots? Rabbits? Hedgehogs?"

As he'd hoped, she smiled. "I never heard her opinion of those."

"Heigh-ho!" shouted Geoffrey. He'd leapt onto a large, flat rock at the side of the path and was fencing with an encroaching thistle.

The stone, and the trees behind it, sparked Benjamin's memory. "Ah," he said. He went to a certain spot in the thicket, pushed aside one large leafy branch, and then another. A narrow, twisting path, just barely visible in the leaf litter, was revealed.

"Hey!" shouted Geoffrey.

"What is it?" Jean asked.

"Come and see."

His smile was so impish that Jean went, even though the opening was dark and close. Slivers of sunlight did filter down through the tangled branches.

Lord Furness bent his tall figure and stepped inside.

"Hey," called Geoffrey again. He pushed past Jean and plunged into the thicket. The opening fit him much better than the adults.

The path bent around great clumps of roots. Jean had to duck under swathes of bramble. At one point she was so hunched over, she was nearly crawling. Her chest tightened in the constricted space.

And then the way opened out into a strange half hut in the middle of the thicket.

Four posts held a roof of old planks inches over Jean's head. There were no walls, only the thick vegetation. A scatter of flat stones covered the ground. It would be dry here in the rain.

"How did you know about this place?" Geoffrey demanded. Hands on hips, he confronted his father, looking outraged. "It's mine! I didn't even show Tom."

"I made it," replied Lord Furness. He had to stoop to stand in the odd little building. "When I was ten years old. It was my secret hideout."

The boy stared up at him, his face shadowed. "It's *my* secret hideout." His voice held astonishment as well as resentment.

"I'm amazed you found it."

"I'm an explorer," declared Geoffrey. "I know every place in the gardens."

"So did I. Still do, I suppose." The man looked about as if remembering many happy days in this place. "Did you find the treasure?"

Geoffrey gazed up at him, startled. "What treasure?"

"Come and see." He led the boy to the back edge of the little shelter. Kneeling, Lord Furness worked his fingertips under a flat rock that lay half in and half out of the cleared area. He pulled until it came free of the earth, then turned it over like the lid of a container and set it aside. "Help me dig," he said to Geoffrey. "You can use your stick to loosen the soil."

After another moment of hesitation, the boy fell to his knees beside his father.

They dug together, with rising enthusiasm. Jean watched them while fighting her need to run. This space wasn't closed in, she told herself. It had no walls. She could leave whenever she wanted.

The task took several minutes. Father and son had grubby hands by the time they uncovered a small metal box and pulled it from the hole they'd made. "I buried this years ago," Lord Furness said. "I'd almost forgotten."

He set it down between them. Man and boy looked at each other, eyes gleaming in the dimness. Geoffrey looked like his mother, Jean thought, but he also resembled his father in more subtle ways. Their faces showed identical glee at the result of the treasure hunt.

Lord Furness pushed the box toward Geoffrey. "It's yours now."

The boy's lips parted. He blinked, then set his

small hand on the lid as if it was an emperor's hoard. "What's in it?" he whispered.

"You know, I don't quite recall. Things I cherished, years ago."

Geoffrey started to open the box.

"No," said his father.

The boy snatched his hand away from the lid. His face went carefully blank.

"Open it when you're alone." Lord Furness added, "Don't let anyone else see. Whatever's in there, it's your secret now."

Their eyes met. Jean watched them share a moment of perfect kinship, perhaps the first they'd ever experienced. For this brief time, at least, they understood each other completely and agreed. Her throat grew tight, and tears stung. She blinked them back.

Geoffrey gave a small nod. He picked up the metal box and held it to his chest. His father smiled.

Jean wanted to savor their reconciliation, but the oppression she'd felt since entering this low space was increasing. She knew the walls of bramble and the low ceiling weren't closing in on her. And yet it seemed as if they were. She had to get out into the open air. Turning, she looked for the path. A dizzying flash of panic suggested it was gone. Then she spotted the narrow opening and plunged through, snagging her hair on a spray of thorns as she hurried along. She ignored the pain as a few strands pulled out and rushed on. Her skirts tangled with more briars. She yanked them free and shoved at the final screen of branches.

The relief when she broke out of the thicket was immense. The light and air and space opened around her like a benediction. She stepped away from the thicket and drank in the garden vista. She took deep breaths to control her frightened panting and fought the terror that she hated so much. She would win; always, she would win.

Lord Furness emerged from the trees. "Are you all right?"

"Perfectly." Jean refused to admit her weakness. She twisted the bits of her hair that had pulled loose back into place. Her fingers did *not* tremble. As ever, the strands resisted her efforts. No doubt she looked as if she'd been pulled through a thicket backward, as her mother used to say. At least this time she actually had been.

"Geoffrey is reburying the box in a new place that no one else will ever know." He smiled, asking her to appreciate this.

"Good." She looked at open sky, the far horizon. She was free to go wherever she wished.

"Funny the things one forgets," he added. He bent to clean his hands on a tuft of damp grass.

Forgetting was not the problem, Jean thought. There was so much she would be delighted to forget.

"I hadn't thought of that hideaway in years. I'm glad Geoffrey found it."

Jean nodded. She began to walk. Movement was helpful in these instances, a sign from her body to her mind that she was unfettered.

Lord Furness fell into step beside her. Blessedly, he said no more. They walked in silence for a bit. Birds sang. Jean's ruffled spirits settled. They passed a bench under a leafy arbor.

"Would you care to sit?"

They did. Bees hummed in the flowers above their heads. A sweet scent drifted down. After a while, Jean realized that she felt peaceful, which was surprising under the circumstances. Of course, this man also disturbed her peace. Was he going to talk of marriage again? She wanted him to, and yet she didn't.

"I must thank you for returning Geoffrey to me," said Lord Furness.

"What?" This wasn't what she'd expected.

"If you hadn't come to kidnap him, well, who knows how things would have gone between us."

"I did not come to kidnap him!"

"I seem to recall a swoop down out of nowhere to do exactly that," he replied with a sidelong smile.

He was teasing her. And, unexpectedly, she rather liked it.

"Whatever we call it, you restored him to me," he continued.

"You did that yourself," Jean answered. "You saw that a change was needed, and you made it." Which was a rare gift, she thought.

"I never would have done so without your... instigation." Benjamin liked this word that had come to him. It was exactly right. Miss Jean Saunders was a lovely, lively, occasionally maddening instigator. She'd hurtled into his closed world and shaken him. Shaken him to depths he hadn't known he possessed.

Her lips were just a little parted. He ached to kiss her. Did she want that as much as he did? He leaned closer, exploratory.

She moved at the same moment, more quickly, and their mouths met with an awkward bump. Benjamin steadied them into a kiss. One searching, tender kiss before he made himself draw back as he ought.

She moved with him, plunging them into another, fiercer kiss. Her body pressed against his. Her arms slid under his coat, and he felt her fingertips on his ribs as if his shirt didn't exist. Did she have any idea how thoroughly she roused him?

The question was submerged by a deluge of kisses. Rational thought sank out of sight, unregretted. Benjamin's hands found the curves beneath her clothes. She murmured lusciously at his touch. He wanted to hear more of that—much more. To make this woman cry out with pleasure would be as satisfying as sating the desire that thundered in his veins. If only they could be rid of all these blasted garments.

"Hoorah!" Geoffrey came running up to them. He was astride his stick now, using it like a hobbyhorse rather than to execute innocent vegetation. "It's time for a ride," he cried. "Let's go to the stables."

Miss Saunders pulled back. Benjamin did the same as he wrestled with a mixture of thwarted desire and anger and chagrin. "You go ahead." He waved his son away. "I'll come along in a while."

"Now," declared Geoffrey. He pushed the end of the stick between them, jostling as if it really was a restive mount. "Fergus wants to see you."

"He'll see me later," Benjamin replied. He struggled to get his surging emotions under control.

"But it's *time*."

Miss Saunders rose. "I should go in." She sounded a bit breathless.

He stood beside her. "No, you should *not*. Go on

to the stables, Geoffrey." Benjamin was aware that his sharp tone was a step backward with his son. But it was the best he could do.

The boy—hands and knees grubby from his excavations, mouth turned down and sullen—gazed at them for a moment, then curbed a revolt from his imaginary mount and ran away. They watched him go.

"He'll be all right," Benjamin said as much to himself as to his companion.

"You should go and watch his ride."

"I will watch Geoffrey ride on many future occasions. But not just now." He sounded annoyed. He *was* annoyed at the interruption, but he mustn't be. "I'll speak to him later. He's a child; he'll forget." Benjamin made himself take a deep breath. Miss Saunders was a guest in his house. He couldn't ravish her in his garden arbor, or anywhere else. With that thought, a number of other tantalizing locations occurred to him.

"We can't go on this way," she said as if reading his mind.

"What way shall we go on?" popped out of his mouth. "Sorry. What I meant was, you should marry me."

"Should."

"Yes." He struggled with impatience. To pull her back to him now would be a mistake. The spark in her eyes told him that. "It simply makes sense."

"Does it?"

"Yes, Jean. It does. We enjoy each other's company and have much in common. You care about Geoffrey. You like kissing me."

She started to speak.

"You cannot honestly deny that. Not after the last few minutes."

She looked away, but not before he saw agreement on her face.

"You could be happy here," Benjamin continued, belatedly recalling that he was supposed to be wooing her. He didn't need his uncle's advice to know that ordering her to marry him was not wooing. "We could."

She shook her head, more as if to clear it than in contradiction.

"What else do you intend to do?" he asked, irritation surfacing again.

"I have plenty to do!"

"Living the nomadic life you described to me? Wandering from house to house like a society gypsy. Will you still be doing that when you're forty? Fifty?"

She turned away from him. Benjamin hoped it was because he'd made a telling point. "I don't know what to do," she said.

She sounded almost anguished. Which was better than indifferent, but far from what Benjamin desired. She'd been ardent and willing in his arms. Once out of them, she became someone else. He had to find a way to make her eager there, too. But would he have an opportunity to do so? She looked on the verge of running away again. Plans he'd made earlier in the day came back to him. "I need your help," he said before she could speak again.

Blessedly, she turned back to him.

"Clayton wants to cut my hair," Benjamin went on. "What do you think?"

Her dark eyes widened. She blinked at him in wordless astonishment.

"My uncle's valet, you know. Clayton."

"I know who he is."

"My unfashionable locks fill him with despair. He's after me to cut them." Had he actually said *unfashionable locks*? Benjamin gritted his teeth. Desire had scrambled his brain.

"You want my help in getting a haircut?" she asked as if she couldn't believe what she was saying.

"You're something of an expert on hair." Clayton had made this point. It had sounded reasonable when *he* said it. Benjamin couldn't imagine why just now.

Miss Saunders put a hand to her luxuriant curls. She gazed at him as if she didn't know whether to be offended or concerned.

"But that wasn't it." Why had he listened to such an idiotic idea? Clearly, she thought it was daft. As it was. He needed something far better. "What I wanted help with. That's something else."

"What then?"

What? He had to come up with something sensible. Quickly. And then, in a flash, Benjamin saw the answer. This would sway her. And the best part was, his request was perfectly sincere. "Finding Geoffrey a new attendant," he said. He nodded, agreeing with himself. "He needs someone more responsible than Lily until he's old enough to go to school. Of course, Tom is welcome to stay if he wishes."

"You should do something for him," she said.

"I intend to. But Geoffrey needs a proper nanny. And she will have to be a rather special person, I think."

Miss Saunders considered. Benjamin thanked Providence that she looked interested now, not bewildered. "Active, not old," she said.

"Kind, but firm," he said.

"Intelligent and curious, to keep up with Geoffrey's precocious mind."

"Tolerant," said Benjamin. "I want him guided, not stifled."

"With a strong sense of humor," his companion put in.

"An ability to laugh is indispensable," he agreed.

She smiled. "I'm not sure where you'll find such a paragon."

He might have said that she was standing right in front of him, but he refrained. He didn't want this delectable woman as his son's *nanny*. "Will you help me find her?" he asked instead.

"I'm not sure how I can."

"By giving me your opinion on the candidates," he replied promptly. "And on how Geoffrey seems to like them as well. You notice all sorts of things that I do not."

She looked flattered, which was good, though the compliment was honest. "I learned careful observation very young," she answered.

The sadness that never seemed far from her reappeared in her face. He needed to know the full story behind that expression, Benjamin realized. Things wouldn't be right until he did. But this was not the moment to press her.

"All right." She nodded. "I'll help you search for this marvelous creature. I'm glad to help."

Benjamin felt an unexpected rush of joy. She wasn't leaving! When he met her eyes, he thought he saw a similar emotion there. Or perhaps he only hoped so.

Fourteen

AS SARAH BRUSHED OUT JEAN'S OBDURATE HAIR THAT night, wrestling it into a braid for sleep, Jean couldn't keep her mind from drifting back to kisses. She'd felt so utterly…marvelous when Benjamin was kissing her—marvelous through her whole body in a quite unprecedented way. She wanted to be back in his arms, this minute and every minute. She would gladly have offered more than kisses there in the arbor, in full view of anyone who passed by. Propriety be damned.

With a profound shock, Jean realized that she could almost understand her mother's disastrous slip those many years ago. If Mama had felt like this… But she couldn't have, because she'd never cared for Papa, had scarcely known him, in fact, at the time of their indiscretion. Later, she'd positively hated him. Jean's thoughts came to an abrupt halt. Did she care for Lord Furness then?

"Are you all right, miss?" asked Sarah. She fastened the end of the braid with a bit of ribbon.

"Yes. Of course."

"You looked so worried for a moment there." The maid placed a hand on Jean's shoulder.

"I'm fine." All right, perhaps she did care for him, Jean thought. Somewhat. In a way. She would still do just as she pleased.

"Is there anything else?"

"No, thank you, Sarah. Good night."

"Good night, miss." Taking garments for the laundry, the maid went out.

Did she care, or did she simply *want*, Jean wondered. Strong sensations—delirious kisses—seemed to overwhelm reason. How was she to know the difference?

She rose from the dressing table and went over to climb into bed. Tab jumped up to curl on his customary corner of the coverlet. People made such a mystery of physical passion, Jean thought. For young ladies, at least. Based on her parents' lives, Jean had assumed that it was crude and perilous. Rutting like one saw in the barnyard. But Benjamin's kisses suggested something far sweeter. She wanted to know more, wanted it very, very much.

And why not? Jean sat straight up as the astonishing idea expanded in her consciousness. Why not indulge these dizzying new desires? Hadn't she vowed to make her own decisions for the rest of her life, and never to be *shut in* by anything ever again? And didn't that include the bonds of convention?

Her mother's shrill protests tried to rise in her mind—deriding, threatening catastrophe. Jean fought them down, a struggle she'd mastered with so much effort and pain. She'd do as she wished, and she'd manage the consequences on her own terms. She wasn't seventeen and under the sway of a tyrannical father. No one could make her marry. No one could make her do anything. That was the point of her life now. And if she indulged—Jean shivered at the luscious word—Lord Furness wouldn't tell what she'd done. He was an honorable man.

A beguiling man, a dizzyingly attractive man. He valued her opinion and abilities; he'd said so. Marriage might even be possible. *Probably not*, declared an immediate inner commentator. *Most likely not.* Marriage still seemed like a trap, and Jean would never be trapped again. She would evade all traps.

Tab was sitting up, tail curled around his front paws, staring at her.

"I'll be clever as a fox, wily as…can be," Jean told him. She'd arrange matters just as she wished, find the perfect place and time for secret passion. And then she would know many delicious, important things. After that, well, she would see. She lay down again, head full of the memory of kisses and imaginings of more.

Jean went downstairs a little later than usual the next morning, with her lips curving in a secret smile. Sarah had commented on the expression as she did her hair. Keeping her plans from her maid was going to be one of the greatest challenges, Jean thought. Sarah's omniscience, usually welcome, was an obstacle. Yet the difficulties in getting what she wanted added another kind of zest to her efforts.

At the foot of the stairs, Jean's path was blocked by two servants carrying a large picture frame. When she stepped aside to let them pass upward, she saw that it was Alice's portrait from the library. Jean stood still as her second cousin's image moved slowly past her. Alice looked outward with serene unconsciousness.

How odd to encounter her just at this moment, when Jean was so intent on her husband.

"I'm simply moving it to the gallery with the other family pictures," said a familiar resonant voice, sending a thrill through her. Lord Furness emerged from the archway that led to the library. His uncle followed him. "It was always meant to hang there."

"Why just now?" asked Lord Macklin.

"It's past time." In fact, Benjamin was tired of being overlooked by his dead wife. He knew that a few months ago he would have raged at the idea of *removing* her. But much had changed since then. "You accused me of being stuck in the past," he added.

"I?" said his uncle.

Benjamin stopped short as the servants moved on, revealing Miss Saunders pressed against the wall. He realized that *she* had thrown that taunt at him, not his uncle. So much had come to revolve around her.

And now she was looking at him in a way that sent a wild crackle of energy down his spine. What *was* that look? He couldn't think of anything but how fiercely he wanted her.

"Good morning," she said.

Why he should be reminded of a cat crouched over a mousehole, Benjamin did not know.

"Good morning," said his uncle. "I trust you slept well."

"Wonderfully."

A throaty overtone in that single word shivered through him. She looked fresh and lovely in sprigged muslin. Not a single curl escaped her hairpins. That was too bad.

"Benjamin is making a change," the older man observed. He watched the servants move up the stairs with their burden.

People seemed to be ripe with implication this morning, Benjamin thought. It only needed Mrs. Thorpe to join them with some suggestive remark. "I'm sending Alice's portrait to the family gallery. Where she…it belongs. It's no great matter." Although he knew it was.

"What will Geoffrey think?" asked Miss Saunders. She never shied away from the hard questions. She never would, Benjamin thought, and for some reason that only increased her allure. "He'll be delighted. He can go and see her…her picture whenever he likes. No need to ask permission to enter the library." At their expressions, he added, "It's my workroom."

"Were you keeping him—" began Miss Saunders.

"Did you tell him—" said his uncle at the same time.

"He's five years old," replied Benjamin. "I don't have to explain every move I make to a child of that age."

And then there the boy was, standing at the back of the hall like a sudden apparition. He had an uncanny ability to arrive just when one hoped he wouldn't. Geoffrey's celestial-blue eyes caught Benjamin's gaze; then he looked up to follow the progress of his mother's image.

Alice seemed to be floating around the curve of the staircase, looking down on them, being no help whatsoever. They might have carried the canvas the other way about, Benjamin thought, feeling slightly beleaguered. His son might make a sound or two when he moved about the house. "The portrait is going back to the gallery," he said. Again. And sounded pompous this time. Geoffrey looked at him, and Benjamin realized that *back* meant nothing to the boy in this context. The picture had hung in the library all his short life.

"Am I going there, too?" his son asked.

"Where?"

"The gallery."

"You may whenever you like," Benjamin said. "You must tell someone first," he added quickly.

"Everything else is just the same," said Miss Saunders. She smiled at the boy, making Benjamin's pulse accelerate even though the smile wasn't directed at him.

Geoffrey gave her a sidelong glance. Benjamin was vividly reminded of the incident with the tomahawk in this very spot. He spoke before his son could say something rude. "It's an honor to have a portrait in the gallery. Your mother will take her place alongside past ladies of the household. She'll always be in her proper position there."

"Respected," said Miss Saunders.

"Remembered," said Benjamin's uncle.

It was gratifying to be surrounded by intelligent people, Benjamin thought. Or was it irritating to be surrounded by people who thought he required assistance? "We should have your picture painted, Geoffrey."

The boy put his reassuringly empty hands behind his back. "Would I have to die afterward?"

"My likeness hangs in the gallery, and I am not dead." Why did he have to keep reminding his son of this fact? "Nor do I plan to be anytime soon. It is not a requirement."

Geoffrey shrugged. Silent and supple as an eel, he

slipped around them and up the stairs. In the next instant he was gone. Heading to the gallery to watch them mount Alice's portrait, Benjamin had no doubt.

"With his mother moved out of the center of the household, he feels as if he has been, too," said Lord Macklin.

"Insofar as he's ever been in it," replied Miss Saunders.

Benjamin felt a flash of anger. "You're making a great to-do out of nothing. Next to nothing." The change was significant, but for him, not his small son. "Geoffrey isn't capable of such complicated thoughts. I'd wager anything you like he's up there begging to climb the ladder and try out the hammer as they hang the painting." Which was paint on canvas and nothing more, he thought. They should *all* remember that!

His companions considered. "You're probably right," said his uncle.

"I am. It happens now and then."

"Geoffrey will grow accustomed," said Miss Saunders. She nodded. "You should have his portrait made."

"I shall. Though I pity the artist who tries to make him sit still."

They all smiled.

"Tom could do it," said his uncle. When the others turned in surprise, he added, "A pencil sketch anyway. He has great natural ability. I don't know that he's ever had real paints though."

"Perhaps we should get him some," said Miss Saunders.

"Perhaps we shall," answered Benjamin.

❧

Furness Hall was positively packed with people, Jean thought later that day. She hadn't noticed how crowded the place was until she thought of arranging a clandestine encounter. Mrs. Thorpe was everywhere, eager to offer her companionship and conversation, charming but inconvenient. Jean saw the irony—that she'd acquired a chaperone just when she particularly didn't want one. Lord Macklin roamed about the estate like the kindly uncle he was, with no set routine. Geoffrey was liable to pop up anywhere, at any time. And then Tom, with or without Lily the nursery maid, would show up to find the boy. There was the whole staff of servants, of course. This group had seemed paltry when one was trying to get fresh tea at breakfast. Now they appeared to be everywhere. In particular, Sarah came in and out of Jean's bedchamber at unpredictable hours.

Finally, her target had his own tasks and whims, not easy to pin down. She might have enlisted Lord Furness's help, of course, and simplified matters considerably. But she wasn't going to. This was her idea and her decision. She didn't *think* she would change her mind, but she might. So she would figure things out herself. Clearly seducers had to be quite clever, she thought as she pondered the details. Or perhaps cunning was a better word.

Where wasn't a difficult question. The public rooms were obviously unsuitable, as were the gardens, as well as possibly inclement. Her bedchamber was haunted by Sarah, and also Jean would have to herd him there and then out again afterward. She wasn't certain how that could be managed. No, it would have to be his room, late at night when the household slept, she concluded. She'd visit him there. He'd be at her disposal. She felt a delicious little thrill at the idea, even as a part of her was shocked and another a bit anxious.

Was she really going to do this? After a period of lively inner debate, she made up her mind. She was.

And so, that night, at an hour when everyone was settled for sleep, Jean put on her dressing gown over her nightdress and slipped out of her room under Tab's questioning gaze. She took a candle but did not light it. The glow would advertise her presence, should anyone be about.

Instead, she crept slowly in the dark, trailing her left hand along the corridor wall, counting doors. She'd made triply certain that she knew which room belonged to Lord Furness. What a fiasco if she walked in on Mrs. Thorpe or Lord Macklin! But she wouldn't. This one was right. On a deep breath, Jean opened the door and went inside.

The bedchamber was less dark than the corridor. The day had been chilly and rainy; the coals of a fire cut the dimness. Jean could see a great four-poster bed. Indeed, the pale linens were like a kind of beacon. She took off her wrapper and slippers, leaving them with her candle by the door, where she could easily find them again, and moved toward the bed in only her thin nightgown.

She felt like a thief or a spy. And then she tripped over a stray shoe, stumbled into a small table, and knocked something to the floor. It clattered.

"Who's there?" asked her host's deep, resonant voice, seeming loud in the darkness.

Jean faced a moment of truth. She could still flee. He might suspect, but he'd never know her identity for sure. Surprisingly, she hadn't the least inclination to run. "Jean Saunders," she said clearly.

"What are you doing here? Is something wrong?" He threw back the covers, poised to rise.

In for a penny, in for a pound, Jean thought. She rushed forward and climbed in with him.

"What are you doing?" he repeated.

"Coming to bed with you."

There was a short, charged silence.

"It seemed an obvious thing to do, after all that kissing," Jean added.

"Obvious!"

"Well a…possible way to go on," she said, echoing their earlier conversation. "So I decided."

"Do I have anything to say about it?"

"No."

Sitting on the other side of the bed, he was outlined by firelight. His head moved interrogatively.

"I mean, you don't have to say anything." Jean had been taught that men were always eager for physical passion. A young lady was trained to discourage them, never to allow them the least opening because they would immediately take advantage. Had her mother been wrong about this, too? "Unless you don't want to?" she added. Humiliation threatened to engulf her.

"Oh, I want to." His voice was throaty, thrilling. "It's you I'm worried about."

"We're not going to worry," Jean replied. "Or argue. We're going to indulge."

That final word, and the way she said it, roused

Benjamin to a state where it was difficult to think. "But have you considered…"

"Could you just keep quiet?" she interrupted.

He could, but should he? Taut with desire, amused, and just slightly offended, Benjamin didn't know. Before he could decide, Jean lunged across the bed-clothes, pushed him flat, and kissed him. Her aim was a bit off, but she soon remedied that. Her skills had benefitted from their previous kisses. Her body was a soft, sensuous pressure on his.

Benjamin's objections went up in flames. He sank into the kiss. He let his hands go where they'd been wanting to for days—up along her ribs, over her breasts, down the lovely curve of her back. He made it a tanta-lizing game, getting her to gasp and moan. She wriggled atop him as if to get closer. Her knees slid down on either side of his hips, and he moaned himself.

He eased her nightgown up her thighs. She straightened above him, grasped the hem with both hands, and pulled it off, throwing the filmy garment across the bed toward the door. Benjamin laughed. She really was the most astonishing creature.

He stopped laughing when she began to unbutton his nightshirt, from the neck down over his chest and the muscles of his torso. Her fingers were quick and deft. She had to rise on her knees to get the last few buttons, a process that set him groaning again. She pushed the cloth away, leaving only his arms covered, and bent to kiss him again. Her skin was hot against his. They were burning each other up. He ran his hands up and down her body.

His sleeves were an annoyance. Holding her against

him, Benjamin turned over and ripped off the night-shirt. He looked down at Jean. Her eyes were pools of darkness, her skin pale as moonbeams. She reached for him, and he willingly went. Indulging indeed in kisses and touches and excited murmurs. He made certain that his caresses carried her over the peak of desire before he entered her to find his own delicious relief.

Afterward, they lay curled together, panting, while heartbeats and breathing slowed. A tide of tenderness washed over Benjamin.

"That was rather good," she said. Her tone was contemplative.

"Rather?" he replied. "Good?" He was amused but piqued as well.

"All in all."

"I beg your pardon?"

"Parts of it were quite wonderful," she went on. "Most of them really."

"And the other…parts?" Benjamin tried not to feel criticized.

"I didn't mean to offend you."

"I'm not the least offended." He wasn't. Not offended. He was just a little irked. She'd certainly seemed to be enjoying herself. "Merely curious."

"Well, there were a few awkward bits," Jean said. "I'm sure they were my fault."

"If I hurt you—" He hated the idea.

"Not really. And it's nearly obligatory, I understand."

"Obligatory?" Had there ever been such a marvelous woman?

"And only the first time, I believe."

"Practice makes perfect. I'll be only too happy to

demonstrate the truth of that adage. You'll see when we're married."

She moved away from him. "We're not talking of marriage."

"I am. I have, several times."

"And I said no."

He rose on one elbow to look down at her. "And then you came to my bed."

"The two things have nothing to do with each other."

"Nothing!" Benjamin sat up in one lithe movement, startling her into a gasp. He found the tinderbox and lit his bedside candle. He had to see her expression.

But he found no clue on her face. She looked the same as ever as she gazed up at him from the pillows. Her hair had escaped its bonds and curled wildly over the white linen. She was delectable, and incomprehensible. "Really, Jean, what more do you want? Why won't you marry me?" he asked plaintively.

"I don't have to!"

"That's not the issue. We are discussing wanting to. Why don't you *want to*?"

She was silent briefly. Then she said, "There's no going back from marriage. You give your word of honor. You're trapped for life."

"Or bonded, mated, even loved." He dared the word.

She moved farther away from him. He hated it. "Tell me why you're this way," he said.

"What *way*?"

"Stubborn and adorable and prickly and so very… stimulating. Tell me."

She pulled the coverlet higher on her chest.

Benjamin leaned back against the headboard like the most patient of men and waited.

She'd vowed never to tell anyone, Jean thought. The very idea was dreadful. The past couldn't be mended. What could anyone offer her but pity and contempt? Which she rejected with every fiber of her being!

He was looking at her. She could feel his gaze even though she didn't meet it. She'd been closer to this man tonight than she'd ever come to anyone. She hadn't imagined such tenderness. Her spirit trembled at the memory. If there was to be any future with him…which there probably wasn't, a quick inner voice declared. The idea was very unlikely. But if there was to be any chance, she had to admit that the past sometimes hovered over her like a vengeful ghost. Perhaps there was a softer way to tell it.

But even as she searched for gentler words, the truth tumbled from her mouth. "I ruined my mother's life," she said. "She could have been happy, if not for me."

"Happy how?"

He didn't argue that she was mistaken, which somehow made it easier to speak. "Free," Jean replied. "Able to go about in society and enjoy herself. Married, eventually, to someone who adored her. Unlike my father, who never cared a whit for either of us." The last came out bitter; she couldn't help it.

"An ideal existence, in short."

Was that sarcasm? Beset by turbulent memories, Jean wasn't sure. She pushed on. "So of course she got angry. Having lost all that."

"At you?" There was no doubt this time; he sounded judgmental.

Heart sinking, Jean considered stopping. But the story was rising in her now, jostling to get out. "She didn't wish to beat me. She always said that. Over and over. She hated violence in all its forms. So she locked me away until she felt better."

"Away? Where?"

"There was a cupboard." A childish tone had crept into her voice on that hateful word, Jean realized. "A small, dark place, waiting for me as long as I can remember. And even before that, I think."

"When you were an infant?" He sounded outraged. Jean cringed a little at the anger in his tone.

"I suppose she started putting me there from the very beginning."

"Jean." He reached for her hand, but she couldn't let him have it right now.

"The door was so tight, no light got in at all. And it was deathly quiet. Sometimes I wondered if I was dead. Especially when she forgot about me."

"Forgot?" He seemed to choke it out.

"Mama never stayed angry long. Her temper was like a…a lightning storm. Flashes of fury and then gone. She hardly knew what she did, sometimes. When it passed, she'd go off, here and there. And then she'd recall. After a…while."

"She left you—a small child—locked up in a cupboard for long periods of time?"

"If it was long, she'd be so sorry when she remembered." Jean almost smiled. Not quite. "She'd run to fetch me and cry and order cakes and new hair ribbons. She could be terribly charming."

"Terribly indeed." He captured her hand and held

it, strong and steady. "This is outrageous. No one helped you? How could that be?"

"The servants didn't want to cross her. She shrieked so. And threw things. Our staff wasn't very good, because we couldn't pay them well."

"Someone should have stopped it."

Jean set her jaw. "Someone did. Me. Eventually, I learned to recognize her rages coming on and to disappear." She tried to make a joke of it. "Not into the cupboard, of course. I had much pleasanter hiding places."

He let go of her hand, but only long enough to pull her up and nestle her close against his side. His skin was hot against hers. Even under the coverlet she'd gotten chilled. "It's a pity she's dead," he said. "I missed the chance to tell her off properly."

A spurt of manic laughter escaped Jean. "She'd been forced into a life she didn't want, you see. And that made her…"

"Cruel? Tyrannical? Heartless? No, she allowed herself to be those things."

"But I was…"

"Blameless. You do know that, don't you?" He looked down, his eyes boring into hers.

"I can be annoying," Jean said in a small voice. "You've said so."

His arm tightened around her. "Do you equate me with your horrible mother?"

"No, of course not. It's just that…"

"Just nothing. You were a child, her child. You deserved her love and care. And to be shielded from her unhappiness. My God, who knows that better than you? Didn't you teach me that very lesson with Geoffrey?"

Tears welled up. Jean tried to stop them. Crying had always brought reprisals in her childhood.

Benjamin simply pulled her closer and wrapped his other arm around her. "I could weep with you for such a childhood," he said.

Jean choked on a sob. He held her tighter. She couldn't hold back then; she leaned on him and cried.

It was like a tempest blowing through her. Her body shook. Her breath came in gasps. The tears seemed never-ending. Each time she thought she could stop, another sob rose in her throat. The small, frantic inner voice insisting this was forbidden went unheeded. She was swept away, shattered.

When, at long last, the weeping tapered off, Jean felt not better but...emptied. As if all those tears had hollowed her out. She drew back and took stock of her situation. She'd confessed her shameful secret. She'd turned a romantic interlude into a melodrama. But she had no emotion left for embarrassment. What was done was done. No choice but to go on. She cleared her throat and took control of her voice. "Your shoulder is wet."

"So is your face," Benjamin replied. He pulled up a corner of the sheet and dried both.

When it came to her running nose, Jean revolted. "Not on the bed linens!"

"I have no handkerchief at hand."

"It doesn't matter." She tried to snuffle discreetly, then had to stifle a soft protest when he let her go and got up.

Benjamin walked across the room, naked in the wavering candlelight, and fetched a handkerchief from the wardrobe. Turning, he brought it back.

"How beautiful you are," Jean said when he handed her the square of cloth.

"Isn't that my line?" He climbed back into bed and settled at her side once more.

"I have no objection to you saying it." Emptiness was lighter, Jean noticed. A bit like floating. She blew her nose.

The ache of physical passion was familiar, Benjamin thought. But this desperate desire to make her happy again was new to him. "You *are* beautiful," he said. "Far more than I realized."

His tone made her tremble. She tried for a light response. "Without my clothes, you mean?"

"When seen in your…entirety." He ran a hand along her arm. He wanted to make love to her with boundless tenderness and wild abandon. But only a few minutes ago, she'd been sobbing. This might not be the moment.

She answered him by casting her arms around his neck and pulling him down onto the pillows. In the ensuing enthusiasm, the handkerchief was lost.

Some while later, the candle guttered, an unwelcome reminder of the passage of time. Jean sat up. "I should back go to my room," she said. "I can't stay all night."

"More's the pity." He'd like to wake beside her and greet the new day with embraces, Benjamin thought. He still hoped to. But this wasn't the time to bring up marriage again. He was in too good a mood.

She left his bed, found her nightgown on the floor, and slipped it on. Benjamin saw that she'd arranged her wrapper, slippers, and a candlestick in a little pile next to the door. This sign of forethought made him smile as he retrieved his nightshirt. "I'll go with you."

"No, you won't. No one must see us together like this." She indicated her nightclothes with a gesture.

"I feel that I should escort you 'home.'" He acknowledged the silliness of this with a shrug.

"Don't be ridiculous."

He was never going to tire of her. He carried the dying candle over to the door. "Here, light yours from this before it goes out."

"I'll creep along without a light."

"Nonsense."

"But someone might see me."

"At this hour? They're all sound asleep. And if someone should happen to, tell them you were sleepwalking."

She giggled. Benjamin thought he'd never enjoyed a sound more. "In my slippers, with a light?" she asked. Her smile as she slipped out of his room buoyed his spirits even more.

Jean walked quickly down the corridor, mind and body full of the past few hours. She was only a few feet from her bedchamber door when a hint of movement in the dark made her jump.

A small, pale figure hovered in the blackness beyond her candle flame. Was Furness Hall haunted? The phantom shifted again. "Geoffrey?"

After a lengthy pause, the boy came into the light.

"You scared me out of my wits. What are you doing out of bed at this hour?" Had he seen her leaving his father's room? Jean wondered.

"What are you?" he replied.

"I couldn't sleep." For reasons he was not to know. "I often read when I'm wakeful. There are so many books in the library." None of that was lies, Jean told herself. She could be excused a bit of indirection.

Geoffrey looked at her empty hands.

"But so hard to find one you actually want to read. Remember *Goody Two-Shoes*." She shouldn't have offered an explanation. She didn't really owe him one. "You ought to stay in bed at night," she added.

"You can't tell me what to do."

Jean had a sudden vivid memory of being small and at the mercy of any adult who wished to criticize one's behavior. She'd hated that!

"This is *my* house," Geoffrey added. "I can go wherever I want."

She didn't want to argue with him, though this was not quite true. "You should return to your room now. I'll take you." She held up the candle to light more of the hallway.

Geoffrey whirled and scampered away. In moments, his small figure was lost in the darkness. There was no sense chasing him, Jean thought. He was faster. He knew the house far better than she did. And he would fit into a hundred little hiding places. With a sigh, she turned and went into her bedchamber.

Fifteen

"COME AND SEE," SAID THE MASTER OF FURNESS HALL the following afternoon as he entered the parlor where Jean was sitting with Mrs. Thorpe.

"See what?" Jean asked. A tremor went through her. She hadn't seen him since she left his bed.

"Just come."

He looked amused, almost mischievous. When he beckoned, they both rose and followed him upstairs.

Benjamin—Jean couldn't think of him as *Lord Furness* any longer—opened the door of the nursery like a showman pulling back a curtain. Inside, Tom stood before a tall easel, pencil poised over a canvas. Geoffrey posed before him, feet apart, one hand raised.

The boy turned when they entered. He gave Jean a sidelong glance, and she wondered if he was going to mention their nighttime encounter. He said nothing, however.

"The subject of a portrait must stand very still," Benjamin told his son.

"I did! For ages."

"It makes no matter," said Tom. "I'll draw him as he is."

"A blur of motion?" asked Benjamin.

Tom smiled amid general laughter. Geoffrey glowered. "No, but catch as catch can," said Tom. "May as well. I'm not a real artist."

"I wouldn't say that," said Jean. He seemed to be capturing Geoffrey's lively spirit in his sketch, which was not an easy task. "You're doing very well."

"I like showing what I see with some lines on a page." Tom gestured with his pencil. "It's magical, like."

"When you're good at it, which you certainly are," said Mrs. Thorpe.

Beginning to look embarrassed, Tom shook his head. "I never had one of these canvas things before. Only bits of paper. And I'm not sure how I'll do with the paints, milord. I've only tried them twice in my life."

"You'll do your best. It seems you always do."

Tom flushed.

"He's going to put Fergus in it," said Geoffrey, as if this was the far more important point and justified the entire effort. Resuming his pose, the boy wiggled his raised hand. "Tom'll paint the reins in just as if I was holding them. And then Fergus next to me. He'll be part of my picture forever."

They all agreed this was a splendid idea. "We'll leave you to it," Benjamin said then. "I know I hate being overlooked when I'm trying to concentrate on a task."

Jean thought Tom looked grateful as they filed out. And then she forgot all else when Benjamin met her eyes. His gaze was intimate as a caress.

"That lad is a treasure," said Mrs. Thorpe as they descended the stairs.

Benjamin agreed with a nod. "I don't know where we'd be without him."

"I wonder if Tom would like to study painting," Jean said, having caught her breath. "It seems a shame not to develop his talents."

"I could find him a place to do that in London," said Mrs. Thorpe. "I know several painters."

"He seems determined to wander," Benjamin replied. "We've asked him what he would like. Offered him a place here or more schooling. But he intends to move on. More than that, he will not say."

"We?" Jean asked.

"My uncle is full of admiration for the lad and wants to help him."

"As soon as you can agree on what *help* means to him," said Mrs. Thorpe.

"Precisely. And before Tom heads off on his own. Because I think he will. The nursery will soon have a new ruler. The applicants for the position are coming tomorrow. I had a note confirming my arrangements this morning."

"They're coming here?" Jean was surprised.

"From Bristol. I'm sending a carriage. Much more efficient to interview them all in one day, I thought."

"That should be an interesting journey," said Mrs. Thorpe dryly. "Do they know they're rivals for the same position?"

Benjamin blinked. "I suppose they'll find out."

"I suppose they will," the older woman replied, hiding a smile.

"How many are there?" Jean asked.

"Four." He frowned. "Do you think we should have gone up to Bristol instead?"

"We?" Mrs. Thorpe looked from him to Jean and back again. Jean could practically see the wheels turning in her mind.

"Miss Saunders has agreed to help me evaluate them."

"How kind of her."

"You could help as well," said Jean as a diversion.

"Oh, I'll leave it to you...two. I'm sure you'll do a fine job. Shall we return to our sewing, Jean?"

Life at Furness Hall had been simpler without a chaperone, Jean thought as she followed Mrs. Thorpe back to the parlor. But even then she couldn't have dragged Benjamin off to his bedchamber for a repetition of last night. It was broad day; they'd be missed immediately. Catching Mrs. Thorpe's eye as they sat, Jean felt as if her improper thoughts were written all over her face. She flushed, and with that came echoes of the venomous inner voice that had plagued her youth. Had she gone mad? Her mother's sneering face flitted through her memory. Was she so stupid that she'd risk her freedom and her future? Grimly, Jean fought the voice down.

"Are you all right?" asked Mrs. Thorpe.

"Of course."

"Not feeling ill? For a moment, you looked queasy."

That was a good word for it, Jean thought. But she wasn't going to think of Mama, or let her revenant intrude. "Sewing makes me bilious," she joked.

"Ah. The rise and fall of the needle?" Mrs. Thorpe's hand created waves in the air. Her eyes twinkled.

"Like a ship's deck in a storm."

The older woman laughed.

&

The carriage full of prospective nannies arrived at eleven the following morning, pulling up before Furness Hall with a clatter of hooves. From an upper window, Benjamin observed the four women who emerged. They all appeared to be in their thirties; he'd stipulated youth with some years of experience. All four wore plain, sensible gowns and bonnets. Their hair and gloves were immaculate. One was rather tall. One quite short. The other two were of medium height. He could tell little else from this distance. If the journey together had disturbed their composure, none showed any signs.

He didn't hurry downstairs. His housekeeper was primed to welcome the candidates and offer them respite and refreshment. In due time, he would speak with each of them in the library. He went to join Jean Saunders instead.

He knew exactly where she was. These days, he always seemed to. Her presence throbbed in him like a second pulse. If he let it, the bond took him to her. Indeed, it was becoming more and more difficult to stay away.

And there she was, striding along the corridor toward him. Did she feel the same pull? He dared hope so.

"They've arrived," she said.

"I saw."

"They don't look very…jolly." Her expression was dubious.

"I don't believe that's a requirement for the position."

"Little boys should have fun!"

"How much more of Geoffrey's *fun* can this household afford?" Benjamin joked.

"Mischief isn't fun."

"Really?" He enjoyed making her blush. He admitted it. He delighted in making her think of the pleasures they'd shared. It seemed only fair. He thought of them all the time.

She wanted him all the time, Jean thought. Desire was the new lodestone of her life. Which set off every danger signal she possessed.

"Shall we go down to the library?"

Where they'd kissed, more than once. So many commonplace words now seemed suggestive. Jean gathered her dignity with a nod and walked toward the stairs. She knew he was smiling as he followed. His smiles were as palpable as a fingertip running down her spine.

A triangle of armchairs had been placed near the glass doors that led to the garden, an arrangement Jean had thought better than the desk. "I thought we would proceed in alphabetical order," he said. He took a sheet of paper from his pocket and consulted it.

"As good a system as any," Jean replied. It was both soothing and unsettling to be here with the portrait of Alice gone. A bucolic landscape had replaced it over the fireplace.

Benjamin rang the bell. "Miss Carter," he told the maid who answered it. The girl bobbed a curtsy and went out. She returned at once with the first of the applicants, a tall, thin woman with dark hair and pale skin. "How do you do," Benjamin said. "I am Lord Furness.

This is Miss Saunders. Shall we sit?" He indicated the chairs. They sat. "Tell us about your previous position."

As Miss Carter began to describe her place in a wealthy Bristol household, caring for twin boys who had now gone off to school, Jean surveyed her. The woman had deep-brown eyes and a no-nonsense manner, which didn't mean she wasn't kind. "What is your educational philosophy?" Jean asked.

"My what?" Miss Carter appeared puzzled but not irritated, which was good.

"By which principles do you regulate a nursery?" Jean said.

"Oh." She gave a decisive nod. "I set great store by a daily schedule. It is best to learn discipline at an early age. Then, I believe that children, particularly boys, require ample outdoor exercise."

As she continued, Miss Carter's gaze kept straying beyond them, as if irresistibly drawn away. Jean finally turned to see what was distracting her.

Geoffrey stood just outside the glass doors. He wore only a grubby tea towel tied around his waist. His face and bare torso were streaked with paint, as they had been when Jean first encountered him, a seeming life-time ago. He brandished a fat stick and made horrific faces. Jean clamped her jaw on a...laugh?

Benjamin swiveled to see what was diverting them. "Ah," he said as Geoffrey stuck out his tongue, waggled it at them, and pranced about. "My son."

"Indeed, my lord. I suspected as much."

Miss Carter's tone was dry but not horrified, as far as Jean could tell. She *had* looked after twin boys. The thought of two Geoffreys momentarily boggled Jean.

"Have you brought references?" Benjamin added.

Wordlessly, the woman took a folded sheaf of paper from her reticule. Benjamin took it, read, and passed it to Jean. Miss Carter's former employers were full of glowing praise. Jean returned the pages to be tucked away again.

"Thank you for making the journey," Benjamin said.

Miss Carter took her cue and rose to go. "Thank you, my lord, miss." She departed without looking back at the window.

Jean looked. Geoffrey was gone. Hiding somewhere in the garden, no doubt. "I'll get Tom to go and catch him," she said.

She was surprised when Benjamin shook his head. "Let him be. I think Geoffrey is an important part of our interviews."

"But they'll…" Jean paused. "They'll see what he's like," she went on in a different tone.

"Precisely."

"Which would be best, I suppose."

He nodded. "I should have thought of this myself."

"Thought of having Geoffrey smear himself with paint—oh dear, Tom's new oils I suppose—and bare his teeth at them?" Her smile escaped.

He smiled warmly back at her. "In broad strokes, if not in every detail, yes."

"Because their reaction will be revealing," Jean went on thoughtfully.

"Definitive, I would say. If they can't deal with a bit of…performance…"

"They can't deal with Geoffrey," they said in unison.

"Precisely," he said again. Their shared smile

became tender. Benjamin reached for her hand, then drew back and reluctantly rose to ring the bell. "Miss Enderby," he told the maid.

They went through the same set of questions with each of the other three applicants—their experience, their philosophy, their references. Geoffrey performed his grimacing war dance every time, disappearing between interviews so that he couldn't be scolded. By the fourth iteration, the boy was looking quizzical and a little tired. Jean thought he was glad to run off at the end, toward the back door rather than the bushes this time.

"So what do you think?" Benjamin asked after they had interviewed all four.

"Which one do you like best?"

"I prefer that we work the matter out between us."

He seemed to really care for her opinion. The look in his eyes thrilled Jean to the tips of her toes. "All of them appeared to know their way around a nursery," she said.

"And their references were splendid."

"Mrs. Phillipson says that all references are good—because if they aren't, you never see them."

"Ah."

"Miss Carter had a quiet dignity," Jean said.

"Geoffrey could certainly use a bit of that. But could she keep up with him? Hah, we should have sent each of them out to catch him. To test their gait and wind."

"You could stage a footrace before they go," replied Jean dryly.

He acknowledged her tone with a smile. "It isn't a terrible idea. Chasing Geoffrey is a large part of the position."

"Until their fabled *discipline* takes hold." Every applicant had used that word with careful reverence.

"Indeed. The way one of them said that made me shudder."

"Which?" asked Jean.

"Which do you think?"

She knew the answer, but this game was beguiling. She wanted to prolong it. "Not Miss Enderby. She was very sweet."

"But she's only looked after an *angelic* little girl." Benjamin made a cherubic face.

"Still, she took Geoffrey's antics in stride."

"If that's what you call sitting like a stone with dread in her eyes. I predict that she will remove herself from the running."

Jean smiled in agreement. "Miss Phipps wasn't bothered. She scowled."

"At one point, I thought she was going to lunge for him and drag him into the library."

"I didn't like her remarks on caning."

"Which came *after* she saw Geoffrey."

"She was the one who made you shudder," Jean concluded.

"She was." Benjamin took a stub of pencil from his pocket. "Do we agree that she is unsuitable?" When Jean nodded, he made a mark on his list. "One applicant eliminated. Two, really. Because I don't think Miss Enderby will do. She seemed no more capable than Lily."

"Lily has done very well," Jean said. "She's young."

"And so we want to hire someone she will like, who will help her along. What did you think of Miss Warren?"

"She seemed the saddest at losing her previous charges."

"Two boys sent off to school together," he said.

"Even though the younger was scarcely ready," Jean added, echoing Miss Warren's description.

"But it will be good for them to have each other's company in a strange place," said Benjamin, doing the same.

Jean nodded to show she recognized the phrases. "When she saw Geoffrey, I thought at first she wanted to laugh."

"But she didn't, of course, because that wouldn't have been right for a proper nanny. Her eyes danced, however."

"I think we have come to the same conclusion," Jean said.

"Miss Warren."

"Yes."

"We have a similar way of thinking. I like that." His gaze was warm on her again.

Jean's cheeks flushed in response. "Or simple good judgment. Common sense."

"Not so common." He reached for her hand. "The house requires more staff, I'm told. We must do this again soon."

"I'm sure your housekeeper would be better at finding them." Must she always argue? Jean wondered. *Yes*, replied that militant inner voice. She had to hold her own.

"Perhaps. But this was so stimulating."

It had been. Jean was about to admit it when her stomach growled. One of the lengthy, gurgling sounds it could produce when she was hungry. Almost always when she really didn't want it to, of course. She flushed. The interviews had stretched on long past midday.

One side of Benjamin's mouth quirked up. He rose. "Stay here," he said.

"I should just—" How to say that her stomach required placating?

"You should just promise to stay here," he said.

"But we're finished with our task."

He pointed at her. "Here."

"Oh, very well," Jean said, a little irritated.

He went out. Jean's stomach growled again. At least this time she was alone. She'd go to the kitchen in a few minutes and ask for tea and bread and butter. That would have to hold her until dinner. Why had he made her wait? she wondered.

In a remarkably short time, considering his burden, Benjamin returned carrying a tray. It held appetizing slices of cold roast beef and cheese, a round of bread, a bottle of local cider, and a dish of early strawberries, whose fragrance immediately filled the room. Jean's stomach voiced its approval of the scent with unusual vigor.

"I beg your pardon," she said, uncertain whether she was more embarrassed about the sound or grateful for the bounty he brought.

"For what?"

Her stubborn stomach provided the answer with a particularly artistic gurgle. "I've always been like this. Mama said—"

"Don't tell me. It's bound to be something idiotic."

Jean gazed at him. He wasn't laughing at her. And he looked quite unembarrassed.

"It's perfectly natural that a fiery spirit requires regular fuel," he went on. "How else could it burn so bright?"

Sudden tears filled her eyes. She blinked them back and swallowed. "Is that cheddar?"

He laughed. "It is indeed."

Heart full, but stomach empty, Jean reached for a slice. Benjamin held up a hand. "Allow me."

Rapidly, he sliced bread, added ham and the cheese. There was butter, too, Jean saw. He offered her the resulting hearty sandwich with a flourish and gestured for her to go ahead as he repeated the process for himself. She bit into what seemed like the best meal she'd ever eaten.

They munched in silence for a while. When the sandwiches were gone and glasses of cider consumed, Benjamin picked up a strawberry and held it out as if he meant her to eat from his fingers. Like a baby, Jean thought, or a little girl who could never be sure whether her mother would give her the treat or pull it away with a trill of mocking laughter. She reached out and took the berry from him. "I prefer to feed myself."

"As you wish."

"I don't mean to seem—"

"You seem yourself, which is exactly as it should be." He popped a strawberry into his mouth. "Marriage could be, would be, like this," he added before she could reply. "Pulling in tandem. Deciding on the course of our lives together."

He didn't run roughshod over her as all men

yearned to do, according to her mother. But she hadn't vowed at the altar to obey him either. Even though she didn't want to, Jean could clearly hear her mother spitting out the word *husband*, explaining how they treated you like the dirt under their feet once you were shackled to them. Of course her mother had been wrong about nearly everything. Yet…to surrender her freedom… How could she do it? "Was your marriage like that? With Alice?"

Benjamin hesitated. Jean wondered if he would lie. But he shook his head. "No. But I'm a different man now."

It was true. She'd seen him change before her eyes. She wanted to agree. But she couldn't, quite. "I'll think about it."

Benjamin exulted silently. This was more than he'd gotten from her before. He wanted to sweep her into his arms and cover her with kisses. Which would not be wise. He'd seen her pull away before she answered. "I'll go and tell the applicants our decision," he said instead.

"Tell them you'll write and let them know," Jean replied.

"Are we not decided?"

"Yes, but they have to ride all the way back to Bristol together."

"Ah. You're wonderfully acute."

"You would have thought of it."

"Perhaps. Probably after we saw them off. You've spared me that regret. Thank you."

She flushed. He liked it when she did that.

Her brain felt overstuffed, Jean thought when he'd gone—as if a great crowd of ideas was jostling to push through a narrow passage. She retreated to her room, where Tab immediately pounced on her toes. She picked up the cat and carried him to a chair. But Tab had no interest in lap sitting at the moment. He squirmed from her grasp and jumped down. "Very well," said Jean. She found his ball of yarn and dangled the end before him. He snatched it with every appearance of delight.

"My mother hated cats, you know, Tab."

The cat leaped, captured the ball of yarn with his front claws, and then curled around it, back feet pumping to disembowel his woolen prey.

"If a dog fawned over her, she enjoyed it. As long as it didn't paw at her."

Rolling on the floor, Tab bit at the yarn.

"Neighbor dogs," Jean added. "She wouldn't have one in the house. 'Too dirty and smelly,' she said. I expect you'd agree."

He released the ball, struck it, then batted it across the floor. It unrolled, leaving a trail of yarn in its wake.

How did she know that about the neighbor dogs? Jean wondered. Her mother or one of the servants must have mentioned them. "Mama was acquainted with our neighbors," she continued, working out the idea as she spoke. "She'd grown up in the area. Why did I never think of that? She went visiting. She wasn't left all alone."

Tab harried the diminishing ball of yarn around the floor.

"She never took me along on her calls or allowed me to meet them. I was… I…" She faltered, trying to put half-formed thoughts into words. "I became the fate she complained about."

"*Meow*," said her cat.

"Confusing, yes. What I mean is, the plight Mama bemoaned over and over—being alone, having nothing. That wasn't really true for her. She made that *my* life." Jean was shaken by a mixture of anger and sadness.

Tab growled around a mouthful of yarn.

"Of course, we couldn't afford much of anything. Papa gave us a *pittance* to live on." Jean could hear her mother's voice repeating these phrases, a truism of her childhood. "That was the word she always used, a pittance. With such venom, you can't imagine. I don't know how much it was really. And she kept no records. None that made sense anyway." Jean had had to deal with her mother's tangled affairs when she died. She'd left most of it to a helpful solicitor, and by the time he'd sorted everything out, her father's fortune had come to her by law a year later. Jean had spent her time learning to manage her new income, rather than dwelling on the past.

"*Meow.*"

"But I'm just realizing, Tab, that if she wanted a new gown or trinket, she always got it." There'd been no talk of hardship when such things arrived. Jean remembered bouts of wild gaiety, dancing through corridors, until her mother's discontent descended again. "Why did I never see this before?"

She'd pushed away her memories in the years since her mother died, Jean realized. She'd been so eager to put her early life behind her, and to establish herself on her own terms. Now, with some distance, the picture looked different. "Mama hardly ever told the truth," she said meditatively.

"*Meow*," declared Tab.

"Or, she had a distorted picture of life." Jean nodded, better pleased with this phrase. "So why would I believe her about anything? Including the nature of husbands. She was probably—almost certainly—wrong. I should ignore her dreadful advice. I will!"

"*Meow!*" said the cat more emphatically.

The trouble was, there were ideas and resolutions, and then there was how she felt, Jean thought. You could be in a dark cupboard even when you weren't.

A scrabbling, scraping sound made her turn. Tab was thoroughly entangled in the yarn he'd unraveled, like a parcel of cat tied up with woolen bonds.

"Oh dear." Jean went to kneel beside him and undo the snarl. "Stay still while I get it off."

He did not, of course, but tried to hurry the process along with teeth and claws. Jean avoided these hazards as she accepted the lesson circumstance had offered. Freedom sometimes required time and patience. The slowness and setbacks could be irritating, but it didn't do to give up.

Sixteen

"MISS WARREN WILL BE JOINING THE HOUSEHOLD IN A week," Benjamin told his son. He'd decided to give Geoffrey this news during a riding...session. One could hardly call them lessons at this point. In truth, despite his small stature, Geoffrey was now capable of handling his pony at any gait. He took a daily ride with Tom and a groom in tow, and he always seemed happiest at these times. Benjamin often joined in and asked Jean along as well, as he had today. He wanted her everywhere he was. His uncle came less frequently; he seemed preoccupied with matters of business, if the number of letters he wrote and received was any measure.

"Is she the one with the horrid eyebrows?" Geoffrey asked.

Benjamin had no recollection of such a feature on any of the hopefuls. Was this a trap? "No."

"The scared one?" the boy asked slyly.

"And why would any of them have been scared?" They hadn't discussed Geoffrey's performance outside the library. Benjamin had decided to leave this issue to the new nanny, telling himself it was a good test of her skills. But if Geoffrey chose to bring it up, he wouldn't shy away.

"Bugs," said his son promptly. "Or maybe rats."

All of them looked at him. He grinned as if he knew very well he was being absurd. "Miss Warren was the last one we talked with," Benjamin said.

"Oh, the one who almost…" Geoffrey paused, then said, "She was the best."

"Who almost what?" asked Jean Saunders.

She looked as curious as Benjamin felt. How had he been graced with such a precocious son? Though he didn't undervalue his own intellect, Benjamin was certain he'd never been as sharp as Geoffrey at this age.

"Did you help choose?" Geoffrey asked her instead of replying.

Jean nodded. "I hope you'll be kind to her."

"Me?" The boy turned to stare at her, angelic blue eyes wide. "What about her? She might beat me!"

"She won't be allowed to do so," Jean replied at once. Benjamin watched her expression shift from militancy to a rueful consciousness of having been goaded. He would never tire of reading the emotions on that face, he thought.

"Nor would she wish to," Jean added. "Miss Warren is coming to a new household where she hopes to be a…success. We should try to make it pleasant for her."

Benjamin liked the use of *we*. It hinted of permanence and buoyed his spirits.

"What about me?" Geoffrey asked.

"Pleasant for you, too," Jean answered. "Kindness does that."

"How?"

Benjamin watched her puzzle over an answer, watched Geoffrey wait for one. He wanted to observe this process for the rest of his life, he realized.

"You could think of it like throwing a ball back and forth," she said. "Having fun together."

"But I could throw it really hard and break somebody's nose."

Jean snorted adorably. "That would certainly not be kindness. Let us say that it's more like riding Fergus then. You want to command him. Perhaps you'd like to kick him to make him gallop. But you want him to enjoy the ride, too, and feel happy. So you're kind to him. And he learns affection for you."

Geoffrey looked down at his pony. The boy actually seemed impressed. A real achievement, Benjamin thought. Oddly, he felt proud of them both.

Their group rounded a stand of trees and continued along the base of a low hill. Catching movement in the corner of his eye, Benjamin looked up to find Teddy and Anna Wandrell riding down the slope toward them.

It was absurd to think the two young neighbors had been lying in wait here near the border between their two estates, but this sort of *accidental* encounter had happened before.

The newcomers naturally joined them. It would have been churlish to protest, but Benjamin evaded Anna by falling back between Geoffrey and Tom. Anna always ignored the youngsters, as much as she did the groom, focusing all her attention on Benjamin. She looked disgruntled as she settled for riding beside Jean instead.

They moved on, chatting. And so his entertainment was reduced from fascinating sparring to polite nothings, Benjamin thought. He wondered how soon he could be rid of the newcomers.

Teddy Wandrell gradually brought his horse closer, finally inserting himself between Benjamin and Geoffrey. He swerved, forcing Benjamin to slow and allowing the boys to draw ahead. "I should like to say something to you," he said.

Benjamin waited, not particularly interested. He thought of the young man as an amiable dolt.

"Perhaps I shouldn't, but…well, I should like to."

What was Anna telling Jean? Benjamin wondered. Neither woman looked pleased by their conversation. Quite the opposite.

"It's my mother, you see."

Jean was frowning. Should he ride to her rescue? But what could he do, actually? It would be the height of rudeness to gather her up and gallop away.

"She's going a bit beyond the line," said his young companion.

"Your sister?"

"My *mother*," replied Teddy. He looked at Benjamin like an aggrieved sheep.

"Your mother is going beyond the line?" He repeated the lad's words because Mrs. Wandrell was the very definition of conventional.

"Don't like to mention it." Teddy practically squirmed in his saddle. "But we should stay on good terms, you and me. When I take over from Papa— years from now, God willing—we'll be neighbors. Have to work together on boundaries and the like.

Well, for the rest of our lives, eh? Could be a long stretch of time."

"God willing," Benjamin replied, beginning to be fascinated.

Teddy nodded. "Don't want any bad feelings hanging about."

"That would be unfortunate."

"Exactly." The younger man seemed relieved, as if he'd actually communicated some important bit of news.

Benjamin waited for him to continue. He didn't. "Er, bad feelings about what?"

"Oh." Teddy grimaced. "I didn't say. It's rather difficult." He took a breath to fortify himself. "The thing is, Mama's got this notion that you're Anna's rightful property."

"I beg your pardon?"

Teddy nodded. "You see? Beyond the line."

You couldn't expect clarity from a sheep, Benjamin thought. "I don't understand what you mean by *property*."

"Oh, right." Teddy nodded like a man who often didn't understand conversations and could sympathize. "The way Mama sees it, you're a widowed neighbor in need of a wife. And Anna looks rather like the dead…previous one. So it only makes sense that you'll offer for Anna. Eventually. Or that's what she thinks, at any rate."

Nonplussed, Benjamin glanced at the fellow's sister. Anna Wandrell was blond like Alice, slender and delicate, but otherwise nothing like her.

"Only now she's angry that you've a young lady

staying at Furness Hall," his companion continued. His words spilled out faster. "Seems to see it as poaching on Anna's territory. Mama says she has to put an end to that, however she can. She took against your chaperone, too. Mrs. Thorpe, isn't it? Mama's asking questions about her, making a great mystery out of nothing. As she tends to do." He frowned. "Mama ought to go on up to London. All those theaters, there, plenty of dramas without creating your own."

Perhaps Teddy Wandrell wasn't stupid, Benjamin thought, feeling a breath of concern waft over him. Perhaps the lad was careful. "You might tell your mother—" he began.

"I can't tell her anything," Teddy interrupted. "She won't listen to me, and anyhow, I don't want to rouse a fuss. Telling *you* instead." He gave a half shrug. "You aren't likely to rail at me."

"You think not?" A bit of shouting might have relieved Benjamin's feelings. Just when his wooing was going well, this complication had to arise.

"Ride away if you did," Teddy said. "Can't ride away from Mama."

"No."

The younger man let out a long breath. "Said my piece. That's it." He kicked his horse's flanks and moved off to join the ladies.

Benjamin let him go, striving to be grateful for the warning. Teddy had nothing to do with this problem, and Benjamin had far more important things to consider. How to watch over his household, for example. And how to preserve the future he hoped, trusted, was unfolding.

❧

Sitting in the drawing room with Mrs. Thorpe later that day, Jean held a book from the library—a biography that Lord Macklin had recommended. But rather than the words on the page, her mind's eye was full of Benjamin. Most particularly the image of him walking across his bedchamber with a handkerchief, clothed only in flickering candlelight. She hugged the memory to her, a secret joy.

She could go to his room again tonight, Jean thought. There was nothing to stop her. He'd welcome her with open arms. And then all she could think of was his arms around her again, his kisses, the feel of his body as they came together. Words like *propriety* and *scandal* were puny in comparison.

"Whatever you're considering, I hope you will weigh the consequences carefully," said Mrs. Thorpe, as if reading Jean's mind.

"What?" Was her face so transparent? Her new chaperone couldn't know what she'd done. Unless Geoffrey had let something slip? But she didn't think he had. That boy was good with secrets.

"I'm happy to look out for you this little while," said the older woman. "But we've scarcely met and don't really know each other at all. So you must look out for yourself, too."

"I *do* look out for myself." She'd been doing that since the moment she was able. She would never stop, whatever her future held.

"The thing of it is, it's difficult to see clearly when you're in love."

"I'm not in love!"

"My dear." The older woman looked at her with skeptical kindness.

"I don't even know what that silly phrase means." Her mother had despised it more than any other.

"Are you asking me to define love? I'm not sure even the great poets have managed to do that."

"I'm not asking you anything." The strident inner voice that haunted Jean rose up in fury. Jean pushed it back, but she couldn't resist trying some of its phrases on Mrs. Thorpe. "'In love' is what seducers say, and then forget about as soon as they've gotten what they wanted."

"Sometimes it is," agreed her chaperone, unshaken.

"'In love' is just another way of saying 'insane.'" Her mother had been fond of that pronouncement, as if it was a clever bon mot. She'd repeated it over and over, especially when she'd a glass of wine, or three.

"I can't agree with you there."

"It's a fairy tale," Jean interrupted, carried along by the past. Her mother had been so eloquent on this subject, and the memories were beginning to shake her as a terrier does a rat. "You might as well talk of unicorns. 'In love' is a delusion."

"No."

The contrast between Mrs. Thorpe's brief serene reply and the chaos inside her head brought Jean up short.

"The state is quite real," continued the older woman. "I know this myself. I fell in love with my husband in only a week, and I'm still in love with him after fifteen years."

Words popped out before Jean could think. "You're

here without him. He's in London doing whatever he likes. You don't know what he might be getting up to."

"Missing me," answered Mrs. Thorpe.

Jean struggled with the scorn that tried to well up in her. "Is that what he says?" Mrs. Thorpe received letters nearly every day. "And you *believe* it?"

"He does say it. My friends remark upon it. And years of experience and observation assure me it's true." Mrs. Thorpe gazed at Jean, seeming puzzled rather than offended by the barrage of questions. "I know how he feels since I am missing him just as much."

Her mother hadn't *missed* her father, Jean thought. Her flights of fancy about a different sort of life had never included being with him. He was the obstacle, the enemy to be vanquished. As for Papa, he'd been too busy with his mistresses to miss anyone.

"When you fall in love, the other person fills your mind and your senses," Mrs. Thorpe went on. "You think of them all the time. You enjoy their company and see yourself enjoyed in turn. That's important. You respect and, of course, desire them." She pursed her lips. "You do *not* conclude that this person is perfect in every way. That would be infatuation, not love. I'm very clear on *that*. Quite a different thing and not to be wished for. Heavens, how philosophical I'm growing."

Although Jean scarcely moved, the book slid from her lap to the floor. She sat there stunned and faced the fact that every point Mrs. Thorpe had made applied to her. She was—was she?—in love with Benjamin.

Her hateful inner voice went mad. This was disaster, catastrophe, it shrilled. She'd done the precise thing that her mother had warned against. She'd been a stupid, heedless chit and wrecked her life. Now, she was doomed. Misery was her only prospect.

As a tempest of despair threatened to crush Jean, something rose up against it. A strong support that had been established in the last five years, when she'd had charge of her own life and grown more solid during this time at Furness Hall. A bulwark of new confidence reared up to sustain her. What had her mother known about anything? Jean asked herself. Mama had never loved anyone in her life.

This painful truth pierced her through and through. It was rather like lancing a boil, Jean thought. A distasteful comparison but apt. The process hurt. The results were unpleasant. But it had to be done if one was ever to heal.

Her mother had claimed boundless love for Jean when she was in alt, fawning and cooing over her. And her every action had shown this was a lie. She'd been cruel and selfish. Anything Mama had said about love was simply nonsense.

"Jean?" asked Mrs. Thorpe. "Are you all right? I'm very sorry if I've upset you."

"I'm all right." There was more pain than relief so far, Jean thought. But she understood that this was the final step. She'd begun to actively oppose her mother at ten, rebelling against the dreadful cupboard. She'd taken the reins when her mother died and carved out a kind of life. Satisfying, but limited. She'd come to Furness Hall to save a child, and she'd rescued two—Geoffrey and her browbeaten younger self.

Jean half rose on a wave of elation. She had to go

and find Benjamin. He deserved to know she loved him, and she *wanted* to tell him.

"Jean?" said Mrs. Thorpe again. She sounded worried.

She sank back into her chair. Now was not the time. She'd speak to him later. Meeting her chaperone's concerned gaze, Jean smiled. The world was full of all kinds of love, she thought, just waiting to be appreciated. In that moment she loved Mrs. Thorpe, who'd been more of a mother during this one conversation than she'd ever had in all the years before. "I was just thinking over what you said," she replied. "It was very helpful. Thank you!"

"You will take care."

"I will." Jean nodded. "I will take care, and I will nurture and cherish it."

The older woman looked quizzical. "If I hadn't been sitting here with you this whole time, I'd wonder if you'd been into the brandy."

Jean laughed.

❧

He was in love, Benjamin thought at dinner that evening. He hadn't put it that way before, but tonight the fact was clear. On his left, Jean Saunders sparkled brighter than the diamonds in her earlobes as she chatted with his uncle and Mrs. Thorpe.

How fortunate he was, Benjamin thought. He'd loved Alice, and he would always cherish her memory. And now he loved Jean—in the same way, and yet differently. Because he was different with the passage of years, and she was unique. Love was expansive, he thought. Jean had shown him that as she'd swept into his life like a whirlwind and thrown open his closed mind, his muffled spirit. Now how was he going to get her to himself so he could tell her this?

He had to plow through the meal first. And in fact, he was hungry. The pork was done just as he liked it. The roasted potatoes had a savory crunch, and there were slender spears of new asparagus from the garden. He'd spent the last few years hardly tasting his food. He could regret that, or he could plunge in and enjoy the bounty before him as much as he had the pickup meal with Jean in the library. An easy choice, Benjamin thought, digging in.

"The Roman emperor Augustus loved asparagus," said his uncle, holding up half a spear on his fork. "He had a phrase for decisive action—*velocius quam asparagi coquantur*, quicker than cooking asparagus." He popped the vegetable into his mouth and chewed.

"How in the world do you know that?" asked Mrs. Thorpe. "Have you made a study of culinary history?"

The earl shook his head. "I know a good deal about Augustus. I developed an interest in him when I was in school. All that Latin, you know."

"Why?" asked Jean. "I mean, what interested you particularly?" Benjamin admired the intelligence in her expression as much as the lovely line of her figure. She glanced his way, and a shiver of desire ran through him. From the way her eyes darkened, he was sure she felt it, too, and he reveled in the knowledge.

"He was a rather benevolent autocrat," replied his uncle. "I say 'rather,' because of course he had lapses. Absolute power, et cetera. But he led the Roman Empire into a long era of peace. Who among us, given such scope, would have the ability and use it in that way?"

"Wouldn't most people want to bring peace?" Jean asked.

"A great many would be too busy getting revenge on their enemies and enriching their family and friends," said Mrs. Thorpe.

"And Augustus did those things," said the earl. "But not *only* those."

The table fell into a game of what would you decree if you were emperor, which grew sillier as dinner progressed. It continued into the drawing room afterward, but Benjamin was beginning to have hopes of getting Jean away from the others when, to his vast frustration, he heard a carriage pulling up outside.

They all paused to listen. "Who could be arriving at this hour?" Mrs. Thorpe asked.

"The days are getting longer," said Lord Macklin. "Some people drive out in the evening to look at the moon."

They might, Benjamin thought. But they didn't pay calls during such expeditions. No, something was up. He frowned when Mrs. Wandrell and her two offspring entered, trailed by an anxious servant.

"We are such good neighbors," said Mrs. Wandrell. "I told your maid there was no need to stand on ceremony and announce us." Her smile was steely.

Tomorrow, he would begin a search for a fearsome butler who could repel unwanted guests, Benjamin thought.

"We were passing by after a small party at the

Hendricks' and thought we simply must stop in," added Mrs. Wandrell. She made an imperious gesture.

As if launched, Anna Wandrell made a beeline for Benjamin. She smiled and took his arm and more or less forced him to sit down beside her. Her evening dress was cut daringly low in front, and from the way she leaned forward to speak to him, Benjamin was certain she had instructions to make him notice this fact. She was practically offering herself on a platter. Yet the effort was curiously cool. Benjamin couldn't tell how she felt about this assignment. Although she smiled and laughed, she showed as little real feeling as Teddy, who was carefully ignoring everyone.

Jean, watching from across the room, wasn't jealous. Anyone could see that Benjamin had no romantic interest in Anna. She'd been thrust upon him, just as Jean had been pulled as far from them as the chamber allowed by Mrs. Wandrell. Still, it was hard to look away from such a blatant flirtation.

"I've been hearing such mysterious things about you," said Mrs. Wandrell to Mrs. Thorpe, who sat on her other side.

"You surprise me," Jean's chaperone replied in a tone that implied just the opposite.

"I won't rest until I know *absolutely everything*." Their visitor's voice had an edge, even as she pretended to tease.

"Then I fear you will grow very tired," said Mrs. Thorpe. Her expression was serene, but her eyes were acute.

"Oh, I spare no effort when it is a question of my daughter's happiness."

This might have caught Jean's full attention, but just then Benjamin looked at her. And then she could think of nothing but being alone with him again. If only all these people would go away.

"We were talking about the Emperor Augustus earlier," said Mrs. Thorpe.

Their visitor blinked at her, confused.

"The Roman emperor," Mrs. Thorpe went on. "And the uses of power. Or misuses. Far more common, sadly."

"Do you imagine you're being witty?" asked Mrs. Wandrell. "Because you're quite mistaken if you do. And pathetic. Wordplay won't stop me."

"Some clouds blowing up," said Teddy Wandrell. Stationed by a window, he'd pulled the drapery back to look out.

"No they aren't," replied his mother without turning her head.

Lord Macklin went to stand beside Teddy, pulling back the other curtain. "Clouds," he agreed, with a calm authority that couldn't be ignored. "Not long before they cut off the moonlight."

"Jed Coachman said the weather was changing," Teddy added. He let go of the drapery and stepped forward. "We should be on our way home."

Benjamin stood. "That sounds sensible. We wouldn't want you caught in a storm."

Mrs. Wandrell couldn't argue with such a united masculine front. She looked mad as fire, however, as Benjamin escorted them out.

"What a tedious woman," their host said when he returned. "She seems to believe she will discover some

shameful secret that will *show me how mistaken I am.*
She would have stood in the darkness beside her coach
and explained just how and why and what steps I am
to take, if I had allowed her to do so. She belongs in a
Cheltenham tragedy."

"Melodrama can be quite effective," said Mrs. Thorpe.

Benjamin resumed his seat on the sofa. He sighed.
"I suppose I'll have to make some calls in the neighborhood and receive more visitors to show everyone
how ridiculous she's being." He knew it was past time
for him to rejoin local society. He rather liked the idea
of introducing Jean to his circle of acquaintances. He
hoped to present her as his promised wife, of course.

"I don't know," said Mrs. Thorpe.

"It won't be such a penance. My other neighbors
aren't at all like Mrs. Wandrell. You'll like them."

"It's not that. I don't know whether our scheme
will hold up with a large number of people." Mrs.
Thorpe looked at his uncle. "I understood it was to
be rather private."

"Scheme?" Benjamin asked.

His two older guests turned to look at Jean. "I
forgot to tell him," she said.

"Tell me what?" Benjamin looked from face to face.
Clearly all of them were in on a secret he'd been denied.

"You fit in so well," said Jean to Mrs. Thorpe. "I
just thought of you as my chaperone."

"Rather than what?" asked Benjamin.

"And I had other things on my mind," Jean said.

"Pleasant things, I hope," said Lord Macklin, glancing at Benjamin.

"Tell me what?" asked Benjamin more emphatically.

Jean turned to him. "Mrs. Thorpe is an actress from London," she said. "A renowned actress. And also a respectable married lady."

The lady in question smiled at this quick addition.

"An actress?" Benjamin digested this surprising bit of information. He turned to his uncle.

"Since she was staying quietly in the village, I asked her to come along and help stave off the Wandrells."

"And none of you thought to mention her background to me?"

"I said I would tell you," Jean replied. "I meant to. Then I was distracted by…other things."

Those seductive other things were plain in her eyes. Benjamin acknowledged that the distraction had been significant. Still, the fact that he'd been left out, in his own house, stung. Particularly where Jean was concerned.

"It was designed as a temporary measure," said his uncle. "A stopgap. I didn't realize we'd have an active… adversary. If I had…" The older man shrugged. "Well, I don't know what I would have done in that case. I thought matters would be settled in a few days."

"Matters?" asked Mrs. Thorpe.

Lord Macklin indicated the younger couple with a sidelong glance. Mrs. Thorpe nodded.

Benjamin couldn't quite sort out what he was feeling. "I ought to have been told," he said, gazing at Jean as he spoke.

"I didn't *not* tell you. I forgot."

She sounded defensive rather than sorry. This bothered Benjamin more than Mrs. Thorpe's profession.

"I was so concerned that the absence of a chaperone

would cause spiteful gossip," said his uncle. "Perhaps I acted too hastily."

"No one in the village knows who I am," said Mrs. Thorpe. "Your neighbor won't easily find out. Though I'm happy to go, naturally, if you like."

Which would only rouse more questions, Benjamin thought, and bring back their original problem. "We'll leave things as they are." He didn't wish to discuss the flaws in his uncle's plan. He hadn't examined it very closely, after all. He, too, had been distracted. By a love that apparently could hurt as well as delight.

Seventeen

In her bedchamber, Jean waited with vast impatience for the house to go quiet. She wanted, *needed*, to be alone with Benjamin, and there had been no opportunity after Mrs. Thorpe's secret came out. People *would* keep on talking, quite uselessly, not going away and leaving them to each other. It might have driven Jean distracted if she hadn't had her own methods in mind. Which were much better anyway, she thought. They would have all the time, and privacy she desired.

After what seemed an eternity, Jean opened her door, listened to silence, and slipped into the corridor. She reached Benjamin's room without incident, knocked, and went in without waiting for a reply.

He stood beside the bed, still dressed in shirt and breeches, about to put on his nightshirt. For a long moment, they simply looked at each other.

"I'm sorry," said Jean. "I didn't say that earlier. I should have."

Benjamin gazed at her. In the flickering candlelight, he looked more than ever like the stained-glass Galahad she'd thought of when she first saw him. His—still unshorn—hair contributed to the impression, she realized. "We've told each other secrets," he said.

"We have." She'd revealed things to him that no one else on Earth knew about her.

"We've shared opinions freely."

"Extremely freely, at times."

This won her a tiny smile. "So I was…startled to find that you'd kept a rather significant fact from me."

Jean didn't say again that she'd simply forgotten. She didn't even argue that the discovery of love had thrust Mrs. Thorpe right out of her mind. Though quite true, these were not the point. "I don't blame you," she replied. "I'd feel the same—or worse, probably—if our positions were reversed. I made a mistake. I'll do my best never to repeat it." She put all her tender feelings for him into the words.

Benjamin's expression shifted. "In the future," he said.

"The future, yes." She drew out that last word.

He blinked, dark lashes obscuring, then revealing those wonderful blue-gray eyes. What Jean saw in them made her heart pound. He took a visible breath. "You shouldn't be here," he said.

"You don't sound positive."

"Because I'm so very glad you are. Though I shouldn't be."

"I'm very tired of *shouldn't*."

"Mustn't," he said.

"Can't," she countered.

"Won't," he replied with a wry smile. "I'm particularly tired of *won't*."

"Ah, but I came to tell you something else as well."

"What?"

Now that the moment was upon her, Jean felt shy. Or worse, she felt as if she was teetering on the edge of a cliff and didn't know whether a hand would reach out to catch her. But she was also determined to move forward into that future they'd mentioned, one way or another. She gathered her courage. "I love you," she said.

He stood still just long enough for her to worry. Then he surged forward and swept her into his arms. "I love you," he said. "Desperately."

The only answer to that was kisses. A flurry, a submergence of kisses.

And then there were garments to shed and bed linens to throw back. They practically leapt into the great bed together, where they indulged in more kisses and caresses and murmured endearments that fired desire. And thus they led each other, step by step, from longing to aching need to a crescendo of release. "My love," exclaimed Benjamin as he held her.

"My love," she agreed breathlessly.

They lay sated and entwined as their heartbeats gradually slowed. The details of the room came back into focus—the candlelight, the cool air, and the scent of potpourri.

"So I accept," Jean said.

"Accept what?" he asked lazily.

"Your offer."

He rose on one elbow to look down at her.

"I assume it's still good."

He thought of teasing her, but he was too distracted by delight. "Absolutely."

"You might say it again. Bits of it were a little... slipshod."

"Shall I kneel?" He would have hung from the canopy and sung the words in verse if she wished it.

They both peered over the edge of the great bed. "It's rather high," Jean said.

"I'm not certain my head would reach the top of the bedding."

"I'd have to bend over to see you. Not the picture of a proposal one wants to remember."

"So I'm all right where I am?"

Jean nestled against him. "Perfectly."

"And will you do me the honor of being my wife?"

"Yes," she said.

He could hardly believe it. But there'd been no trace of doubt in her voice.

"I won't promise to obey you though," Jean added.

"I wouldn't believe you if you did."

She raised her eyebrows at him. "Are you saying I would break my word?"

"I'm saying that you should not be subjected to the dilemma. We will omit the word 'obey' from the ceremony."

"If the parson will let us."

"I'll find one who will."

"You are quite wonderful, aren't you?"

"I'll try to make certain you always think so."

Jean settled more closely in the crook of his arm. "But we mustn't think each other perfection. Mrs. Thorpe says that's infatuation, not love."

Benjamin couldn't resist. "A sage as well as an actress, is she?"

His new fiancée made a face at him.

"Something to watch out for," he went on. "I'm well aware that you're not perfect, however."

"Are you indeed?" Jean pretended indignation, but she was far too happy to be convincing.

Benjamin smiled down at her. "You sometimes make hasty judgments."

"Well, you're stubborn."

"True. Not as stubborn as your hair, however." He ran his fingers through one wild, curling strand.

"My hair is not my fault!"

"Your hair is magnificent."

"You wouldn't say so if you had to keep it in order."

"Yes I would. And will…always."

"You're argumentative," said Jean with a smile.

"I admit it." He smiled back. "It seems we're safe from the perils of infatuation."

"Whatever they may be."

"Disappointment, I imagine."

"Disillusionment."

"A better word."

"Thank you."

He laughed and kissed her, and then there was no more conversation for quite some time.

❧

Benjamin and Jean met at breakfast the following morning as if nothing in particular had happened during the night. They'd agreed that news of their coming alliance must be conveyed to one person first, before any other announcement could be made.

"What if he objects?" asked Jean as they walked up the stairs together after their meal.

"He won't," replied Benjamin.

"You can't be sure. He's unpredictable. If he doesn't want me here——"

"I think he does." Benjamin held up a hand to forestall any further objections. "You've changed his life as much as mine. Geoffrey is uncannily intelligent. He must know this. We will——the three of us——overcome any difficulties."

"Without…oppression."

"Absolutely."

They didn't find Geoffrey in the nursery, however. Lily was alone there, rearranging the clutter of books and toys on a tall shelf.

"Hello, Lily," said Jean.

The girl jumped, dropping a book and putting a hand to her chest. "Beg pardon, I didn't hear you, my lord, miss." She picked up the book and gestured with it. "I'm tidying up. I expect this Miss Warren'll think I'm hopeless. Probably send me off to work in the scullery." Her young face creased with anxiety.

"I'm sure she'll be glad of your help," said Jean. For a moment she worried about Lily's fate. Then she realized, with a flicker of surprise, that it was in her hands as the new mistress of Furness Hall. She hadn't gotten used to that idea yet. "You'll be all right," she said. Lily couldn't know this was a promise, but Jean did.

"Where's Geoffrey?" asked Benjamin.

"He and Tom went down to the stables. Cook let them have some carrots." Lily clutched the book.

"Master Geoffrey said she did. He might have stole them."

"We'll go and find him there," said Benjamin. With a nod, he led Jean out. "I'll be glad to have someone more capable in charge of the nursery," he added when they were out of earshot. "Clearly the post is beyond her."

"Lily stepped in to help when no one else would," Jean replied. "She's eager and hardworking. I shall tell Miss Warren so and ask her to train Lily for larger opportunities."

Benjamin stopped and looked at her. He stood on a lower stair, so their eyes were on a level.

"What?" Her expression was quizzical.

"I suddenly saw that future we spoke of, opening up like a panorama before me. And I felt such… surprise and delight."

She nodded, throat suddenly tight with emotion.

He laughed and embraced her, lifting her to her toes on her step. "Let's get on with it," he said, taking her hand and pulling her along.

In the stables, they found Geoffrey talking to Fergus while Tom groomed Molly nearby. Any carrots, stolen or otherwise, had already been consumed. "Come and take a walk with us," Benjamin said to his son.

Geoffrey gazed up at him. "I didn't do anything."

"Unlikely. But this isn't about you."

"It's about all of us," Jean said.

The boy looked from one of them to the other. "Can Fergus come?"

"Not this time." Benjamin held out his hand. Geoffrey slowly took it and allowed himself to be led outside. They crossed the cobbled yard and entered the garden.

"They were old carrots," said Geoffrey. "From the back of the root cellar. Wi-zened. Tom said they were wi-zened and only fit for horses."

"I expect Fergus enjoyed them," said Jean.

"We gave Molly some, too."

"Good."

Benjamin stopped at a stone bench. He sat and drew Geoffrey to him. "We have some news to tell you," he said. "Miss Saunders and I are getting married."

Jean sat as well. It was better not to loom over a child.

Geoffrey looked at her, then back at his father.

"That means she'll stay here and live with us," Benjamin added.

"She'll be your wife," said the boy. "Like when Wright got married."

"And Jemina came to live in the gamekeeper's cottage," Benjamin agreed.

"Will there be a baby like Tess?"

Jean's cheeks heated, but Benjamin took the question in stride. "There might be, after a while," he said. "We hope there will be. A sister or brother for you. Perhaps more than one."

"But you will always be the eldest and very much attended to and loved," said Jean. "We want you to be happy, Geoffrey."

He considered this. "I'd rather have a brother."

Benjamin smiled. "We'll do our best, but we can't make any guarantee. A sister is a distinct possibility."

The boy's nod was resigned, as if he'd expected no more. Then he brightened. "Can I have the kitten then?"

And with this, it seemed the hurdle was passed. Geoffrey's expression was calculating but untroubled.

"We'll share Tab," said Jean.

"In the nursery," he answered, bargaining.

The cat needed more space, Jean thought. She continually felt guilty shutting the door in his face when she left her bedchamber. And she was going to be busier from now on. Tab would enjoy the nursery. She'd make sure Geoffrey treated him well. "Yes," she said.

Geoffrey grinned.

Benjamin rose. She followed suit. Geoffrey scampered ahead as they walked back toward the stables. "Does he think he traded approval of our marriage for the cat?" Benjamin asked.

"It almost seemed so."

"Cheap at the price," he joked.

She wrinkled her nose at him. "At least he looked pleased."

"He would be stupid not to be, and Geoffrey is anything but stupid."

They found Lord Macklin and Mrs. Thorpe and gave them the good news, with predictably celebratory results. Benjamin announced it to the rest of the household later that day. "Send someone over to the Wandrells and tell them," he instructed the housekeeper after general congratulations.

"So soon?" Jean asked.

"We must share our happiness with our nearest neighbors," Benjamin replied. His uncle and Mrs. Thorpe nodded. "And discourage any more evening visits. Or research projects."

A messenger was dispatched, and wine and ale

broken out to toast the new mistress. Word would be spreading across the estate, Benjamin thought, like ripples in a pond. Most people would be glad, though none as glad as he was. He began calculating how long it would be before he could get Jean all to himself again.

It turned out to be hours. But at last they slipped away to the library, nestling on the settee where they had kissed when barely acquainted. Benjamin kissed his new fiancée now and would kiss her again, he thought, at every opportunity.

"Do you think Anna Wandrell will be made unhappy by our engagement?" Jean asked after a while.

"I never gave her any reason to be," he said.

"That is an evasive answer."

"Mrs. Wandrell will be angry." He repeated the tale Teddy Wandrell had told him. "And so I suppose she'll scold Anna. Even though Anna did nothing wrong."

"We must do something to help her!"

"I don't see what we can do. I imagine they'll settle the matter between themselves."

"You refuse to fight oppression?"

"A strong word."

Jean pulled away from him, spine rigid, eyes flashing. "Not strong enough! When a parent becomes a tyrant, something should be done. Why should they have absolute power over their children? It's a disgrace." She went on in this vein for a while. Gradually her outrage cooled. "You're very quiet," she noted then.

"Letting you have your say."

"You think I'm exaggerating."

"About Anna Wandrell, yes. Her mother may be irascible, but Anna has endured no more than many young ladies whose families are looking to settle their futures. And I suspect her brother will take her side. Her father, too, perhaps."

"She shouldn't need defenders. And she should be able to choose her destiny. And how it is to be achieved."

"That is a rare gift which very few people are granted. And not only young ladies."

Jean drooped a little. "I suppose that's true. But how many even try?"

"Well, they don't have your resolution. Very few could march in here the way you did and capture me."

"I did no such thing!"

"You scooped me up like an expert angler landing a trout."

"Leaving you flopping about and gasping for breath?"

"Certainly gasping," he replied.

His look made her flush. "It wasn't like that."

"Well, I may have helped out here and there. I was certainly happy to…capitulate."

"That's what you call it?"

"Unconditional surrender."

The tender way he said this caused a prolonged pause in the conversation. Some minutes later, Jean surfaced, breathless, pushing back the curls that had fallen over her forehead. "We were talking of over-bearing parents."

"Were we? Surely not." He pulled her closer.

"Well, we began there."

"And moved on to more pleasurable matters," he interrupted, dropping another kiss on her intrepid hair.

"Yes, but… No, you mustn't distract me. I want to talk about Geoffrey."

On the other side of the room, curled up on the cushion of an armchair and hidden by its tall back, a small figure came alert.

"What about him?" asked Benjamin.

"I want to be a good parent to him. Good parents."

"As I haven't been?"

Jean brushed this aside. "I'm not talking about that. The future is the important thing. I will not be an oppressor. Geoffrey must be allowed to be free."

In the armchair, Geoffrey listened hard.

"Certainly. Every boy ought to run wild a bit. But he must also learn responsibility. We want him to be a man of character."

"Encouraged to be," replied Jean. "Shown by your example—"

"Mine?"

"Of course." Her tone suggested this was obvious.

"Thank you." Benjamin was more touched than he would have predicted.

"Geoffrey must have scope and opportunities to shine."

"Along with love," said Benjamin.

"Yes, of course love! By which I mean action and sacrifice, not just an empty phrase repeated with nothing done to demonstrate it."

A tear welled up and ran down Geoffrey's cheek, though he did not make a sound.

"We must constantly be on the lookout," Jean added. "I won't be like my mother, or Mrs. Wandrell."

"You never could be," Benjamin answered. "You're not the least vindictive."

"I hope I'm not. It's a terrible trait."

"Of which you haven't the least trace. Astonishing, really. You might be justified in wishing for a touch of revenge."

Jean shuddered. "No. I've seen what that sort of attitude can do. I only hope that Mrs. Wandrell doesn't—"

"There's nothing she can do to us now."

Geoffrey's small fists closed, and he looked fierce.

Eighteen

"LET'S GO THIS WAY," SAID GEOFFREY WHEN HE AND
Tom set out on their ride the following day.

"We don't want to go down there," the older lad
replied. "That neighbor lady, the one you said has mean
eyes, always drives along that lane in her carriage."

Geoffrey merely urged Fergus in his chosen direction.

"Wait for Bob," called Tom. "He went to fetch a
new bridle."

Geoffrey didn't. He rode faster. Tom was forced to
follow without the groom who usually accompanied
them. "What's the matter with you?" he asked when
he caught up.

"What's 'vin-dic-tive'?" Geoffrey asked.

"Eh, where'd you hear that?"

"What does it mean?"

Tom considered. "I think it's somebody who don't
let things go," he said finally. "Who holds a grudge,
like. Looks for ways to make other people sorry, if
they think they've been done wrong."

"Tries to hurt them?" asked Geoffrey.

"Yes, but not like a fistfight. Sneaky stuff."

"Like when Sam put the beetle in Bob's cider?"

Tom snorted a laugh. "Worse than that. That was a joke, and Bob didn't care. He just pulled it out and drank up."

"What then?"

"Vindictive is a person who waits and schemes. Then when you've forgot all about whatever it was that's bothering them, they do something bad to make you sorry."

"Worse than a beetle."

Tom nodded. "Lots worse than that."

They came out of a stand of trees into a cleared area above the road. Geoffrey stopped on a low rise and watched as a carriage came around a curve and approached them. Tom pulled up beside him, puzzled.

The carriage came nearer. It slowed, then stopped. Mrs. Wandrell leaned out the window and beckoned. Geoffrey went at once. Surprised, Tom scrambled to catch up with him.

"So it seems you're going to have a stepmother, child," said Mrs. Wandrell when the little boy was close.

Geoffrey gazed at her.

"When your father marries again, his new wife is your stepmother. You've heard of those, I'm sure, in fairy tales? The wicked stepmother. They always seem to be wicked, don't they?"

Tom arrived in time to hear this. "Here now," he said.

"They favor their own children over the old ones, don't they?" Mrs. Wandrell continued. "In the stories, stepmothers are always looking for ways to be rid of the first wife's offspring, even kill them."

"Hey, there's no call for that kind of talk," said Tom.

"Your opinion is not wanted," said the woman in freezing accents.

"Well, you got it anyway. And it ain't favorable."

Mrs. Wandrell glared at him. "I won't be spoken to in such a way by a loutish servant."

"I may be loutish, but I ain't stupid. And I know rubbish when I hear it."

"How dare you?"

"It's the circumstances, I expect," replied Tom.

"I shall tell your master that you insulted me and have you dismissed."

"Don't have a master." The lad eyed her sourly. "Nor a stepmother either."

The two locked gazes for a long moment, fuming resentment against solid rejection. Mrs. Wandrell gave up first. "Drive on," she commanded through clenched teeth. The carriage started moving again. The young riders watched it go.

"Talking of fairy tales, she's a right witch, she is," said Tom.

"A wicked witch," Geoffrey replied. "Vin-dic-tive."

"I expect she is. But we don't have to care about her. Or any nonsense she spouts. Which that talk was, Geoffrey. Nonsense, pure and simple. And I hope you know it."

The boy nodded. "We should forget about her. Not tell anyone."

Tom examined him, familiar by now with Geoffrey's devious ways. "Why not?"

"She was mean about stepmothers. Miss Saunders would feel bad."

"I expect she would." Tom considered, then shrugged. "Right. I'll keep mum. Unless that lady goes blabbing to his lordship about me."

Geoffrey frowned. "Do you think she will?"

"No. She won't want me to tell how spiteful she was."

"Spite-ful."

"It's like 'vindictive.'" Tom turned his pony. "Now let's go find Bob before he sends out a search party."

Wordlessly, Geoffrey followed him. Riding ahead, Tom didn't notice the hard glitter in the boy's angelic blue eyes.

◆

"That's strange," said Jean, coming into the library with a shawl she'd gone to fetch on this chilly afternoon.

"What is?" replied Benjamin. At the fireside, with Jean sitting opposite and her chaperone off writing letters, he felt positively steeped in contentment.

"Mrs. McGinnis said a servant came by to inquire about Mrs. Wandrell."

"Here? Why ask our housekeeper? Did they think Mrs. Wandrell had called to berate me about our engagement?"

Jean gave him a half smile, but shook her head. "Apparently she's missing, and they're asking all around the neighborhood."

"Missing?" Benjamin sat up straighter. "Surely she's just out for a drive or some such thing? Though it's hardly the weather for it." He looked out at the sodden landscape.

"It seems not. Her carriage is accounted for, and

all her things. Mrs. McGinnis said it's been several hours, and they're rather worried. They're organizing a search."

He rose. "I should go to see if I can help."

She nodded.

When Benjamin returned several hours later, he paused in the parlor where Jean and Mrs. Thorpe were sitting and told them that he'd joined a group of men riding about the area calling for Mrs. Wandrell, without success. "I only came back to change horses," he said. "Wandrell's putting together a wider search. I must join in."

"Of course you must," said Jean.

"Poor woman," said Mrs. Thorpe. "It's beginning to rain again. If she's lost in this, she's likely to fall ill."

Benjamin agreed. "Her family says she does go walking alone, which I would not have predicted. She's quite fanatical about tramping through the countryside, in fact."

"But not on such a day surely?" asked Mrs. Thorpe.

"It certainly doesn't seem likely."

"I could come with you," said Jean. "Help look."

"No need. We have a large group, all familiar with the neighborhood as you are not. Uncle is joining in, too."

The two men departed soon after. Jean sat on with Mrs. Thorpe in the cozy room, the antithesis of the damp and chill outside. "It's difficult to think of anything but that poor woman lost," said the latter.

"Yes. I wish there was something we could *do*."

The older woman nodded. "We can offer up our prayers that she is soon found, safe and well."

Simultaneously, Jean realized that this was not

the sort of remark she expected from an acclaimed London actress, and that her assumption was insulting. "Yes indeed," she replied, too heartily.

Mrs. Thorpe's eyes glinted as if she understood Jean's thoughts all too well.

"She can hardly be *lost*," said Jean after a while. "She lives here, and if she's so dedicated to walking, she must know the countryside well."

"One can trip and fall in the most familiar sur-roundings," replied Mrs. Thorpe.

"That's true." Jean half rose. "They might not see her if she's on the ground."

"I'm sure the searchers have thought of that."

"Yes." Jean sat back, but she couldn't settle. "I'm going up to the nursery to check on the preparations for Miss Warren's arrival."

Mrs. Thorpe nodded, clearly aware that Jean just wanted to be moving.

Upstairs, Jean found Lily and Tom in the nursery. Tom's coat was damp with rain, and when Jean asked him about it, he said, "I been looking for Geoffrey. I gave him a scold because he took Fergus out early this morning. On his own. He knows he ain't s'posed to do that. I expect he's having a good old sulk someplace or other. But he's not in any of his usual spots. I've looked high and low, inside and out."

Jean immediately thought of the hideaway in the garden thicket. "I might know where he is."

Tom came to attention as if waiting to be dis-patched. Tab blinked at Jean from his new cushion beside the hearth.

She couldn't reveal Geoffrey's secret place without his permission, Jean thought. Even more, she was glad to have some action she could take. Sitting and waiting for others to effect a rescue galled. "I'll go and see if he's there."

"I'm happy to do it, miss," said Tom.

"Never mind. I'll go." Jean went down to her room for a sturdy cloak and shoes, then let herself out into the gray afternoon. It wasn't raining now, but the air was filled with mist. Jean could practically feel her hair trying to escape its pins and curl around her face. She put her hood up as she walked swiftly along the path to the spot where the branches concealed the entrance to Geoffrey's hideaway.

Of course, there was no sign of him near the large, flat rock. That was the point of the place, Jean thought. Its entrance was invisible. She thought of calling, but if he was sulking, he probably wouldn't answer. She pushed aside a branch and stepped past, trying to avoid the spray of droplets it loosed. The hem of her cloak was soon sodden, however.

In the dimness, she followed the faint traces of feet and her memory of the way. She feared she'd gone wrong for a while, but then she saw the outline of the low roof ahead. She moved faster, receiving a face full of wet leaves for her pains, and reached the structure in the next moment.

The ground inside the half hut was dry. Geoffrey sat there, wrapped in a blanket that looked as if it had come from the stables. "I heard you coming all the way," he said. "You can't sneak through the woods like a red Indian."

"No," said Jean. Ignoring the fate of her cloak, she sat down cross-legged, facing him. The place felt even more enclosed on this cloudy day. She pushed aside her nervousness. The cocoon of branches was not closing in on her. "Are you warm enough?"

"It's the same kind of blanket Fergus wears."

"I expect it's good then. But wouldn't you like to go inside?"

Geoffrey looked rebellious. "Tom ripped at me," he replied. "But I had to go out."

"You know you're not allowed to go riding alone."

"I *had* to," the boy insisted.

He sounded so vehement, as if this was more than simple disobedience. "Why?" she asked.

"Papa said, 'An honorable gentleman makes things right,'" Geoffrey replied.

As far as Jean knew, it was the first time he'd ever called Benjamin *Papa*. Her throat tightened at the sound of the word in his high, little voice. "Indeed, that's a good rule."

"That's why I *had* to."

"You had to go out this morning to make something right?"

Geoffrey nodded, seeming pleased that she'd understood at last.

"What thing was it?"

He looked away, not a good sign.

"Was it something you'd done?" Jean asked.

"No! I wouldn't ever be vin-dic-tive."

The words he picked up were a constant amazement, Jean thought. She couldn't imagine where he'd heard this one. And then she remembered a recent conversation and came wholly alert. "Vindictive," she repeated. "People shouldn't be vindictive."

"It's sneaky," said Geoffrey.

"How do you know what it means?"

"Tom told me. They wait till you forget all about them and then do something to hurt you. Before you can even stop them. So I had to make sure she couldn't."

"She?"

The boy looked chagrined at his slip, then fierce. "I won't let her do anything spite-ful," he declared.

"Who, Geoffrey?"

He gazed up at her, his face a pale oval in the low light.

"Do you mean Mrs. Wandrell?" Jean felt a chill that had nothing to do with the looming branches.

"She can't be vin-dic-tive now," the boy added in the tone of one who'd solved a knotty problem.

"Where is she?" Jean struggled to keep her voice even.

"I locked her up. Like a criminal in a jail."

"But she's not a criminal."

He looked uncertain.

"She's an innocent neighbor who has done nothing to hurt us."

"She has mean eyes."

"Geoffrey." Jean waited until he met her gaze. "You can't make things right by doing something wrong."

"Because I went out riding by myself?"

"You know that's not what I mean."

Jean watched his face shift from defiance to concern. "I didn't want her to hurt you or Papa."

"You don't have to worry about that," answered Jean forcefully. "We can take care of ourselves. And you, too. The whole household, in fact. You can trust us to do that. I promise. And you must let us do so."

He stared at her. He blinked and swallowed what looked very much like tears, though she'd never seen him cry. "What should I do?" he whispered.

"You must take me to Mrs. Wandrell right now."

He nodded and stood. Jean got to her feet with a bit more difficulty, hampered by her heavy, damp cloak.

They wove their way through wet leaves out to the garden path. The day had darkened further as the afternoon waned, and the mist was thicker. Geoffrey nearly disappeared into it. She had to call him back to her side more than once.

He led her across the garden to the back corner of the house farthest from the kitchen and stables. The landscape dipped here, putting the ground floor above their heads. The walls were overgrown with vines behind a stand of laurel.

Geoffrey plunged into the bushes. Jean gathered her wet cloak about her and followed. When they'd penetrated the thicket, she became aware of a muffled thumping.

She emerged into a narrow open space right beside the wall. Overarching laurel branches made it dark. In front of her was an ancient, low door closed by a heavy wooden bar. The thumping came from behind it. She looked at Geoffrey. He nodded.

Jean stepped closer, raised the bar, and set it aside. She pulled at a broken hasp, only to have the door slam open so hard that she had to stumble back to avoid being knocked down.

"You little demon!" A disheveled, dusty, furious

Mrs. Wandrell shot out of the opening like a cork from a champagne bottle. She seized Geoffrey's coat collar and tossed him into the dark opening. "See how you like it in there!" She grabbed the folds of Jean's cloak and jerked her forward. "And you! You wretched, wretched woman." Mrs. Wandrell pivoted and, with a surprising surge of strength, shoved Jean after Geoffrey.

Jean, already off balance, staggered through the open doorway. The door banged shut behind her. The bar dropped into place with a resounding *thunk*. Several thumps came next, as if Mrs. Wandrell was pounding her fist on the bar. Then silence descended, leaving Jean enveloped in blackness.

Terror washed over her in a wave. She couldn't see. A musty smell filled her nostrils, threatening to choke her. She was shut away in a dark cupboard-like space, even worse for being unknown. Anything could be in here. She couldn't breathe. She clenched trembling fists and fought for control.

A scrabbling sound made her flinch. "I'm sorry," said a small worried voice.

Geoffrey. Geoffrey was in here with her. She was not alone.

"I didn't know she'd jump out like that," the boy said. "I would've fought her off."

He must be frightened, too, Jean thought. She had to take care of him, even if she felt quite desperate. And with that thought, an iron resolve rose through the suffocating veils of Jean's fear. She wasn't going to be the sort of parent, the sort of *mother*, who took her own struggles out on a child. The past would always be with her—no help for that. But her legacy wouldn't shadow Geoffrey. She *refused*, no matter how difficult that might be. She took a deep breath, and another, reaching for calm.

"I told her you *were* a wicked stepmother, and you were beating me," said Geoffrey out of the darkness. "I told her she could hide in the house and watch you do it. She wanted to tell Papa. So he wouldn't like you anymore."

"A wicked stepmother?" Had they fallen together into a fairy tale?

"She said you'd be one, but I knew you wouldn't."

"Mrs. Wandrell said I would be a wicked stepmother?" Jean's brain was slowed by her fear.

"I knew you wouldn't be," Geoffrey repeated.

"No, I won't." Her voice wanted to tremble, but she didn't let it. "I promise."

"She wanted to scare me. I could tell."

"Could you?"

"Yep. But I don't get scared."

"I do, sometimes." The admission popped out before Jean could catch it. She bit her lip, wishing she could call the words back.

"You don't have to worry. I've been in here lots." His voice was astonishingly cheerful.

He wasn't afraid, shut up in the darkness. He wasn't like her. Jean might have envied or resented his insouciance, but she was only glad. "If we just had a light," she said.

"There's a candle."

"There is?" She was pathetically grateful to hear it.

"Yeah. I didn't tell *her*. But I use it when I come down here."

"Why would you come down here?" Jean couldn't conceive of a reason.

"There's interesting stuff. Wait a minute."

After an interval of scrabbling sounds, Jean heard the welcome scrape of a tinderbox striking. And then there was the miracle of light. She raised her head—and found herself face-to-face with a black-and-scarlet, wild-eyed, fanged creature, glaring at her out of the dark. She screamed.

"It's all right." Geoffrey stepped between her and the horrific vision. He held a stubby candle in a metal holder. "It's all right," he repeated. He reached out and patted her arm. "It's just one of the old lord's devil masks."

Jean leaned against the door, waiting for her pounding heart to ease.

"My mother had some of the scariest things carried down here before I was born. She didn't want me to see them."

"How do you know that?" Jean gasped.

"I heard old Frank say so, before he died. That's how I knew about this storeroom. So I hunted for it."

Jean's pulse was slowing. She took deeper breaths and looked around. They were in a low chamber piled with boxes and bits of things no one wanted. Several masks hung on the side wall. Now that she knew what they were, they were only unsettling. "Mrs. Wandrell will tell somebody where we are," she said. Her voice was still a little choked; she fought the tremor. "Eventually. I suppose she'll take her time." She certainly would. To punish Geoffrey. And Jean wanted out before that.

"We don't need her," replied Geoffrey scornfully.

Jean looked at him—a small boy with golden hair and angelic features who seemed to have the personality of a marauding Viking.

"The door was barred *and* locked when I found it. I got in another way."

"Is there an entrance into the house?" Jean looked around eagerly.

"Well, there is, but there's a pile of barrels in front of it on the other side. I dunno why. Everybody's forgot about this room."

This was not good news.

"Everybody but me." Geoffrey smiled proudly up at her. "I looked all around until I found a drawer full of old keys. I tried 'em all, and one of them worked! But it broke in the lock. So I just use the bar now."

"But you said you got in another way."

He nodded. "Here, hold up the candle."

She took the holder and did so.

Geoffrey climbed a pyramid of cartons in the front corner of the room. When he reached the top, he sat on the uppermost box, feet dangling, and began to tug at a panel. Jean realized there was a tiny window near the ceiling—just a horizontal slit really, covered with an ancient shutter rather than glass. It was barely large enough for Geoffrey to slither through. He looked down from his perch. "It doesn't work very well. I don't want to break it, 'cause then anybody could come in here."

"No one else in the household would fit," Jean pointed out.

"Oh." He thought this over before nodding. "But squirrels or mice might."

Or rats, Jean tried not to think. She banished the idea of spiders as well.

Geoffrey pried and levered with small fingers. The old shutter creaked. Jean didn't tell him to hurry, much as she wanted to. Should she try to climb up and help? She doubted the pile of boxes would hold them both. Minutes passed. The candle flame swooped and danced.

Finally, with a screech of rusted hinges, the shutter came open. Geoffrey bent to wiggle through. "I'll go out and open the door," he said.

"Good."

He squirmed out, and Jean was alone. Only for a minute, she told herself. She held on to the candlestick like a talisman.

One of Geoffrey's hands reappeared, grasping the edge of the shutter. "I have to shut it," he called down.

"You can do that later."

"No, now."

He tugged and coaxed, his new position much more awkward for maneuvering. Seconds plodded by like turtles.

"Leave it for now, Geoffrey."

"I can do it," he insisted.

She wouldn't shout at him, Jean thought, less fearful than she had been at first. Yes, he was in a great deal of trouble over what he'd done to Mrs. Wandrell, and he must face the consequences. Yes, she was desperate to be out of this dark hole. But now was not the time.

After endless minutes, the shutter grated closed. "Got it," the boy cried triumphantly.

More time passed. Not so very much, Jean knew, but it seemed ages before the bar grated against the door panel. Jean put her hand on the door, more than ready to push it open.

There followed a series of thumps and scrapes and finally what sounded like a kick on the lower part of the door.

"She's put it on all crooked," said Geoffrey's muffled voice. "I can't make it move." Another thud suggested that he'd kicked the door again. "I have to get a stick."

She was not trapped in the dark, Jean told her accelerating pulse. She had a light. Geoffrey was out and could tell someone where she was. "Go and find help," she called.

"I can do it," he answered.

"Geoffrey! Fetch Tom." He wouldn't mind telling Tom, and that resourceful lad would have the bar off in no time.

There was no answer. He'd gone looking for a stick, Jean realized.

Silence closed over her. Shadows shifted in the candlelight, making the masks look as if they were laughing and grimacing, mocking her weakness. Geoffrey didn't understand what this felt like to her, Jean thought. He couldn't be blamed if the time seemed short to him as he worked away at solving a problem.

Knowing this didn't help a great deal.

She would get out, Jean told herself. Hadn't she always gotten out? Hadn't she found her own way to a wonderful new life? She need only be calm and patient. Geoffrey was *not* going to run off and forget about her.

At long last, there were sounds outside the door. "Geoffrey?"

"I got a good stick with a pointy end," came the answer. "I'm just going to—" Something scratched on the outside of the door, followed by scraping and skittering like a wild creature clawing at the panels. Then finally a splintering sound.

There was a pause. Geoffrey spoke. Jean couldn't hear him. "What?"

"The stick broke behind the bar," he said louder. "I made it worse." He sounded remorseful.

"That's all right," Jean called back. "Just go and get someone to help you. Get Tom."

There was a short silence. "He'll be cross with me," said Geoffrey in a small voice that Jean could barely hear through the door. "I expect everybody will be cross with me. Won't they?"

She couldn't deny it. But she wasn't sure what to say with him on one side of the door and her on the other.

"*You* think I was wrong to put that lady in there."

If she agreed, would he leave her here? Jean's history told her that he would. He would storm off and abandon her. Her candle would fail; she'd be alone in the dark. Despair rose in her throat. Her breath quickened. The light trembled in her hand.

But this was a little boy, not her erratic mother. A boy she'd vowed to care for. He'd endured a great deal, and he shouldn't be lied to. That was far more important than her lingering fears. "It was a mistake," she said. "Everyone makes mistakes."

The silence that came after this seemed very long.

"I ruined everything," Geoffrey wailed then. "It was all right, and I ruined it. The lord will be angry. He'll stop speaking to me again."

"No, Geoffrey! That isn't true." The door was a maddening obstacle between them. "You made a mistake, and you'll have to make amends. That's true. But I've made mistakes. So has your father. Everything *isn't* ruined."

The reply, when it came, was very low. It sounded as if Geoffrey was leaning up against the door, almost speaking to the panels. "You promise?" he said.

"I promise," Jean replied, filling her voice with conviction. "On my word of honor." The boy said something she couldn't hear. "What?"

"An honorable gentleman makes things right," Geoffrey repeated.

"An honorable person," Jean answered. "We will make things right."

Cloth brushed against the outside of the door. "I'll get Tom."

"Good. Yes, get Tom." Jean heard nothing more, and it felt as if Geoffrey was gone. She took a deep breath and settled herself to wait. Surely it wouldn't be too long.

Nineteen

BENJAMIN HAD LEFT HIS HORSE AT THE STABLES AND was heading wearily toward the house when he saw his son trotting along a path at the back of the building. Geoffrey was streaked with dust, which was not unusual. "What have you been up to?"

Geoffrey winced, stood still, and gazed up at him. "I was going to get Tom," he said.

"Planning some adventure?" Benjamin looked forward to a soft seat and a warm fire. "Mrs. Wandrell is home again," he added. "I just got word. It seems she marched in, covered in dirt, and declared she wanted a bath before she spoke to anyone."

The boy simply stared at him. He seemed more tentative than usual.

"I imagine she'll have quite a story to tell. I can't wait to hear it." Benjamin wanted Jean. She would appreciate the news, and perhaps cosset him a little. He'd enjoy that. "I must go and tell Jean."

"She's…" Geoffrey began, then stopped.

Benjamin waited, but when his son said nothing

more, he moved on. He was nearly to the kitchen door when he heard, "Papa."

The word brought him to a standstill. Geoffrey had never used it in his hearing before, and the simple sound touched something deep inside. Benjamin turned and looked at the small, grimy figure. Was that distress in his expression?

"I want to be an honorable gentleman," Geoffrey said. His voice caught on something remarkably like a sob.

"That's good." Benjamin moved closer to his son. "Is something wrong?"

"I made a mistake. Does everybody really make mistakes?"

"Yes." He drew his son over to a garden bench, lifted him onto it, and sat down next to him. "What was your mistake?"

Geoffrey shifted on the seat. He looked apprehensive. Or perhaps despondent? Benjamin didn't recognize this expression. "Is Miss Saunders going to be my stepmother?" Geoffrey asked.

Benjamin felt a touch of real unease. The boy wasn't acting like himself. "Yes. But that's just a word, you know. Real stepmothers are nothing like in the fairy tales." Most, Benjamin amended to himself. No need to go into that.

"You know about the wicked stepmothers?"

"I do. The old tales seem to be full of them."

"That's what she…" Geoffrey began, then stopped.

Was *she* Jean? Benjamin waited, though he wanted to push. When his son said nothing more, however, he added, "Jean isn't wicked. She'd kind and gentle. You know that, don't you?"

Geoffrey nodded.

"She came here to help you, and she ended up… rescuing both of us. She made us into a family."

The angelic little face creased as if tears were imminent. Geoffrey still looked just like Alice in outline, Benjamin thought. But the specifics were all his own.

"She's stuck in a storeroom," Geoffrey blurted out.

Benjamin stiffened on the bench. "What?"

"I can't get the bar off the door. It's jammed."

"You locked her in?" He stood.

"*I* didn't. It was the lady."

"What lady? Never mind. Take me to her at once!" Benjamin remembered the stories Jean had told him about her childhood. She must be terrified.

Geoffrey raced off along the path. Benjamin ran after him, his boots crunching on the gravel. At the far corner of the house, Geoffrey plunged into a clump of bushes. Mystified, Benjamin went in after him. When he caught up, the boy was pushing at a bar set across a low door. "It's stuck," he said.

"Geoffrey?" called a muffled voice from beyond the panels.

"Jean?" said Benjamin.

"You're here! Thank God. The candle burned out."

Setting his son aside, Benjamin gripped the bottom of the bar and pulled. It resisted, then gave way with a scrape and clatter. He cast it aside and yanked open the door. Jean fell out into his arms. He held her, hands searching for any injury. "Are you all right?"

"Yes," she said. But her arms were very tight around him. And she was trembling. Benjamin looked down at his son. Geoffrey looked back with Alice's celestial-blue eyes and his own wary resignation. "What the deuce—" began Benjamin.

Jean reached out with one arm and pulled Geoffrey into their embrace. The boy was trembling, too, Benjamin noted. He set aside his questions to simply hold them both. And Geoffrey let him.

It felt good. Wonderful, really. Like redemption, and peace, and the hopeful future. Benjamin might never have let go, but a tiny iridescent beetle dropped from one of the branches onto Geoffrey's golden curls. Benjamin brushed it off. Jean pulled back a bit. And the embrace was finished, for now. "Come along inside," he said. "And tell me how this came about." He felt Geoffrey flinch.

Jean gazed at him. Something serious, Benjamin gathered. That was the bad news. They would deal with it together. That was the good.

❧

Geoffrey stood before Mrs. Wandrell in that lady's own parlor, hands behind his back. He was dressed in his best clothes and scrubbed to shining perfection. "I am very sorry for what I did," he said.

Benjamin, posted behind his son, approved the tone. Geoffrey sounded contrite, unforced. He looked sincere. Jean would have been proud. They'd agreed she shouldn't come along, however, because of Mrs. Wandrell's disappointment over their upcoming marriage.

"It was wrong," Geoffrey continued. "I want to make a-mends." He stumbled slightly over the last word, even though it was his choice. "What shall I do?"

Mrs. Wandrell's eyes flicked up to Benjamin's,

then down again. "Are you asking me to set your punishment?"

Geoffrey nodded. Benjamin reserved judgment. They'd see what she said.

"Huh." The lady's frosty demeanor eased slightly. "You told lies. And you shut me up in that dreadful place. For hours!"

Benjamin thought of pointing out that she wouldn't have been locked up if she hadn't been trying to wreck his engagement. Maliciously. *After* trying to frighten a little boy and poison his relationship with his future step-mother. But he waited. Jean would have wanted him to wait. He was surprised that Geoffrey did the same.

Their reward came when Mrs. Wandrell added, "I wasn't...entirely blameless. Still, what you did was very bad indeed."

Geoffrey nodded again.

The boy was using his solemn angelic look, Benjamin noted. It was usually effective.

But Mrs. Wandrell seemed to recognize the expression as well. She did have children of her own. "What is your favorite thing to do?" she asked.

"Ride Fergus. My pony."

She nodded. "All right. No rides for...two weeks then."

Geoffrey started to frown, but stopped himself.

"No visits to the stables, even. Not so much as an apple or a bit of carrot taken out to Fergus."

This clearly hit home. The lady knew her punishments, Benjamin thought.

"He'll forget about me!" said Geoffrey. "Can't I just go and talk to him?"

"No. As far as Fergus is concerned, it will be as if you were locked away in a dark room." Mrs. Wandrell glanced up at Benjamin again, then down. He waited.

The boy gazed at her. He appeared to be working things out in his mind. "Fergus'll miss me," he said finally.

"I expect he will," replied Mrs. Wandrell.

"*He* didn't do anything wrong."

"No. But he is affected by what you decide to do."

"Af-fected?"

"Things happen to Fergus because of what you do, the choices you make."

"That's not fair."

"It's the truth." Mrs. Wandrell paused, then added, "Once you have a creature you love dearly, you're trapped, because it can be taken away from you."

"You can't take Fergus!"

"No, I can't. And I wouldn't, even if I could."

Geoffrey looked confused.

"So, no pony for two weeks," Mrs. Wandrell said. "And of course you must never do anything like that again."

"I wouldn't!"

"Good. I expect your father will have more to say to you about that. I'll leave it to him." Mrs. Wandrell looked up at Benjamin and raised her eyebrows. "You agree to impose this punishment?"

"Yes." It didn't seem unfair. And he would continue their discussions about proper behavior as well.

"Then we're quits on the matter."

Benjamin nodded. He didn't feel like thanking her,

though her judgment wasn't unreasonable. "Let's go, Geoffrey."

His son's small frame relaxed. He scampered toward the door.

"We all have our hostages to fortune, as I think you know quite well now," said Mrs. Wandrell before Benjamin could follow. "My daughter would have made you a fine wife. And she'd have lived next door to me rather than…wherever she ends up. However far away."

Benjamin spread his hands. He had nothing to apologize for on that score, but he understood her better now. Jean would say that was a good thing, and he supposed it was.

Father and son rode back to Furness Hall side by side. Geoffrey dawdled a bit, probably because this was his last ride for a while. "Did I do all right?" he asked.

"You did splendidly."

"It that how an honorable gentleman makes things right?"

"It is. An apology and actions taken to correct the matter. You've redeemed your honor."

"What's re-deemed?"

"Restored, er, gotten it back."

"So she had my honor until I said I was sorry? Until I do my punishment?"

"In a way."

Geoffrey frowned. "I don't like *her* having it."

He hadn't put this well, Benjamin thought. Should conversations with a five-year-old be so complicated? He wished for Jean, to help him explain. "She didn't really have it," he began. "That's not right. Your honor is always your own. It means the way you treat other people. And keep the promises you make. The only person who can take it away is you."

"By making mistakes," said Geoffrey. "But you said everybody makes mistakes." He sounded apprehensive.

"Most everyone does," Benjamin agreed. Hadn't he been mired in a large mistake for most of his son's life? "But we can make up for them, as you did today. Your honor is lost when you do bad things, and you aren't sorry or willing to set them right."

"And you just keep doing them," Geoffrey said.

"Yes." Benjamin was glad to see Furness Hall up ahead. This talk was feeling like hard work. He wanted Jean more than ever. Fortunately, Geoffrey seemed satisfied by his explanation.

"I can give Tom carrots to take to Fergus," the boy said as they rode into the stable yard. "And tell him they came from me." He glanced at Benjamin, testing out this scheme.

"I think that would be all right." At some point, they would have to talk about the letter of the law and the spirit, but not today.

Geoffrey seemed inclined to linger in the stable as long as possible, but Benjamin sent him off to change out of his best clothes. Then he went to find Jean in the library and tell her how the visit had gone.

"Geoffrey is an amazing little person," she said when he'd finished.

"By his own efforts. I did so little these five years." Regret still tinged Benjamin's regard for his son. He hoped that one day it would be gone.

"We're not looking backward. That is agreed."

He put his arm around her and pulled her closer on the sofa. "It is."

"You've done wonders for Geoffrey lately."

"As have you."

She smiled. "I'm almost sorry Miss Warren is coming. But not quite. How will she get along with Tom, do you think?"

"Ah." Benjamin shrugged. "Apparently Tom is going with my uncle when he leaves. I gather he's been promised adventures."

Jean sat straighter. "Oh, Geoffrey will be so unhappy."

"That's what I thought. But it seems Tom has been telling him all along that he wouldn't stay. From the very beginning. So I hope it won't be too bad. I thought I'd give Geoffrey Molly."

"A second pony in exchange for a human companion? Like a kitten in exchange for a marriage?"

"Only my first idea." He gave her a rueful smile. "I'm finding my way."

"He needs other children to play with."

"We'll find him some." Benjamin waggled his eyebrows. "One way or another." And there was the flush on her cheeks that never failed to beguile him. "But I want to talk about you. Are you truly all right after that bout in the storeroom?"

"I am." Jean smiled back at him. "It turns out that rescue comes from the inside, not the outside."

"Ah." He gazed at her, his heart full of admiration and love. "I can't say 'too bad.' But I should have liked to be your knight in shining armor."

"Oh, you're that all right. My own Galahad. It's just that the dragon has…changed his spots."

"Wouldn't that be a leopard, my adorable biologist?"

Jean nodded. "My metaphor, er, metamorphosed in midsentence."

Laughing, he kissed her. And kissed her again. After that, there was no further conversation for quite some time.

"When you kiss me, I just melt," Jean murmured.

"We must get married at once," Benjamin declared. "If we could go down to the church right now—"

"We must post the banns."

"Weeks too long!"

"I need some time to get ready for my one and only wedding day," she told him.

"One and only indeed!"

Benjamin was kissing her again when the library door burst open and Geoffrey scampered in. "They're hanging my picture. Come and see." He danced from foot to foot in front of them. "They're doing it *now*." When they had disentangled themselves and stood up, he ran out again.

"I must check the locks on all the bedchamber doors," said Benjamin as they followed him to the stairs. "Do you suppose he can pick locks?"

"No." Jean considered and added, "And if he can, you must tell him it is a matter of honor not to do so."

"Good idea."

Arm in arm they walked up to the gallery where the ancestral portraits of Furness Hall hung. Tom's portrait of Geoffrey was being placed next to his mother's.

No one, looking at the two, would doubt that they were related, Jean thought as she gazed at the two pictures. The red-gold hair, the celestial-blue eyes, the piquant shape of their faces. "Cousin Alice was so very beautiful," she said quietly. That glowing perfection was a bit intimidating.

"She was, but not quite as beautiful as that," Benjamin murmured near her ear. "The painter improved on nature. I think he was a little in love with her."

"Why is my picture lower down?" Geoffrey asked the crew placing his portrait.

"We want an equal distance at top and bottom," answered Tom, who was overseeing the process. "Looks best that way."

"That lad is a treasure trove of hidden talents," said Benjamin.

"I'm glad your uncle has taken him up."

"Indeed, I'm eager to see what he makes of himself."

"Where is Lord Macklin?"

Benjamin shook his head. "He received an urgent letter. And then he had to speak to Mrs. Thorpe at once. I have no idea why."

"Another benevolent mystery?"

"Very well put."

The picture was hung, adjusted, and approved. Everyone stood back to get the full effect.

Jean felt small fingers curl around hers. She looked down and found Geoffrey holding her hand. "She'll be up here, and you'll be downstairs," he said.

"That's right," she managed, her throat tight with emotion.

"Are you going to sleep in my mother's room?" the boy went on.

"Not if you don't like it."

"I don't mind." He looked at his father. "I took those things away."

"Did you?"

Geoffrey nodded. "To my own room."

"Good."

"Good," Geoffrey repeated, satisfied.

With her free hand, Jean reached for Benjamin's. The three of them stood together, hand in hand, gazing at the past and toward the future.

Twenty

"It's a disgrace!" declared Clayton. "A member of the peerage to be married—before all his people—looking like an unshorn sheep."

"Mr. Clayton!" Sarah was shocked at his outspoken criticism. Especially here and now. They sat in one of the rear pews of the village church near Furness Hall.

"I beg your pardon, Miss Dennison, but I feel the matter deeply," replied Lord Macklin's valet.

"Lord Furness isn't your charge," Jean Saunders's lady's maid pointed out to him.

"In a way he is. Or has been, I'm relieved to say, as we depart tomorrow." Clayton seemed unable to let go of his grievances. "Because he is my lord's nephew, I extended myself to help. It's not a thing I would do for just anyone, you know."

Sarah acknowledged his condescension with a nod.

"If he had been willing to listen to me… But he seemed to take the matter as a joke. Or an irritation, depending on the day." Clayton's lips thinned. "And I have to say, Miss Dennison, that your suggestion about his hair was useless."

"I am sorry, Mr. Clayton. I didn't know then that my young lady thinks Lord Furness looks like a knight of old."

"With his hair straggling down his neck and about his ears?" Clayton sniffed.

"Seems they wore it longer in ancient times."

"It *seems* they were careless in their personal habits."

"Well, they had to wear suits of armor, didn't they? Helmets and all. Perhaps their hair was a kind of padding."

"That would explain it, I suppose," answered Clayton grimly. He shrugged. "It's your problem now. I wash my hands of it."

"We'll find a likely young fellow and train him up to be a decent valet," Sarah answered.

"Train," repeated Clayton. "More like keep him under your thumb."

"Why, Mr. Clayton, I don't know what you mean."

"Don't you just."

Sarah suppressed a smile. "*Shh.* They're starting."

Benjamin took his place at the altar of the village church, waiting for his bride to come to him. Only a few more minutes, and they would be married at last.

"Nanny said I mustn't fidget," declared the small figure at his side. "I don't fidget."

Glancing down at his son and groomsman, Benjamin smiled. In his new coat and breeches, Geoffrey looked like a miniature town beau.

"What's 'fidget'?" Geoffrey added, somewhat spoiling the effect.

"Moving about, making faces, twiddling your fingers."

"Oh." The boy put his hands behind his back. "Nanny said I would do fine."

Miss Warren was settling in well, Benjamin thought, and seemed likely to be a fine addition to the household. "And so you will."

"But I don't really *do* anything, do I? I just stand here."

"You are lending me your support."

Geoffrey gazed up at him with inquiring blue eyes. "Are you going to fall down? Do you feel sick?"

"No. I feel…quite wonderful."

"Because of her."

His son hadn't quite settled on a label for Jean as yet. Benjamin hoped that eventually he would say—as well as feel—*mother*. "Yes."

"She's good."

"She is. But we must be quiet now. The music is starting." And there she was, finally, at the other end of the church. Benjamin's breath caught.

"She looks pretty with flowers in her hair," Geoffrey said in his high, clear voice. Wedding guests in the pews smiled.

Benjamin gazed out over his neighbors and chief tenants and a few friends who had come down to Furness Hall for the celebration. He acknowledged the smiles and nods as his gaze encountered theirs. It was past time to rejoin society, he thought. And because he was the luckiest man in the world, he got to do so with Jean at his side. "Lovely," he whispered wholeheartedly. "Now *shh*."

Holding Lord Macklin's arm, Jean took a deep breath. As she had no close family, Benjamin's uncle was leading her down the aisle. "It's only right that you should be here," she murmured to him. "You set all this in motion."

"No, you did."

"I?"

"Some spark was set alight when I first talked to you and saw that you were a woman of intellect and spirit."

"You're too modest."

"Not I," he murmured. "Are you ready?"

"Completely."

He smiled at her, and they started off down the aisle. Jean had never felt happier in her life.

"Why is she walking so slow?" asked Geoffrey quite audibly.

There was stifled laughter, but Benjamin didn't care. Watching them move toward him, he felt his heart swell with gratitude to his uncle, and to Jean, and to all the beneficent powers that had allowed a brave new love to burst into his life.

If you love Jane Ashford, check out The Survivors
series by Regency star author Shana Galen

An
Affair
with a
Spare

SHANA GALEN

"Poignant and unforgettable."
—Lorraine Heath, *New York Times* and *USA Today*
bestselling author, for *Third Son's a Charm*, Book 1 in
The Survivors series

Collette Fortier took a shaky breath and pasted a
bright smile on her face.

Do not mention hedgehogs. Do not *mention hedgehogs!*

Collette was nervous, and when she was nervous,
her English faltered and she often fell back upon the
books she'd studied when learning the language.
Unfortunately, they had been books on natural history. The volume on hedgehogs, with its charcoal
sketches, had been one of her favorites.

This ball had been a nightmare from the moment

she'd entered. Not only was she squished in the ball-room like a folding fan, but there was also no escape from the harsh sound of English voices. Due to the steady rain outside, the hosts had closed the doors and windows. Collette felt more trapped than usual.

"He's coming this way!" Lady Ravensgate hissed, elbowing her in the side. Collette had to restrain herself from elbowing her chaperone right back. Since Lieutenant Colonel Draven was indeed headed their way, Collette held herself in check. She needed an introduction. After almost a month of insinuating her-self into the inner sphere of Britain's Foreign Office, she was finally closing in on the men who would have knowledge of the codes she needed.

Lady Ravensgate fluttered her fan wildly as the former soldier approached and then let go so the fan fell directly into the Lieutenant Colonel's path. Lady Ravensgate gasped in a bad imitation of horror as Draven bent to retrieve the fan, as any gentleman would.

"I believe you dropped this." He rose and presented the fan to Lady Ravensgate. He was a robust man, still in the prime of his life, with auburn hair and sharp blue eyes. He gave the ladies an easy smile before turning away.

"Lieutenant Colonel Draven, is it not?" Lady Ravensgate asked. The soldier raised his brows politely, his gaze traveling from Lady Ravensgate to Collette. Collette felt her cheeks heat and hated herself for it. She had always been shy and averse to attention, and no matter the steps she took to overcome her bashfulness, she could not rid herself of it completely. Especially not around men she found even remotely attractive.

Draven might have been twenty years her senior, but no one would deny he was a handsome and virile man. "It is," Draven answered. "And you are…?"

"Lady Ravensgate. We met at the theater last Season. You called on Mrs. Fullerton in her box where I was a guest."

"Of course." He bowed graciously, though Collette could tell he had no recollection of meeting her chaperone. "How good to see you again, Mrs…er…"

"Lady Ravensgate." She gestured to Collette. "And this is my cousin Collette Fournay. She is here visiting me from France."

Collette curtsied, making certain not to bend over too far lest she fall out of the green-and-gold-striped silk dress Lady Ravensgate had convinced her to wear. It was one of several Lady Ravensgate had given her. She'd bought them inexpensively from a modiste who had made them for a woman who could then not afford the bill. Whoever the woman was, she had been less endowed in the bosom and hips than Collette.

"Mademoiselle Fournay." Draven bowed to her. "And how are you liking London?" he asked in perfect French.

"I am enjoying it immensely," she answered in English. She wanted people to forget she was French as much as possible and that meant always speaking in English, though the effort gave her an awful headache some evenings. "The dancers look to be having such a wonderful time." The comment was not subtle, nor did she intend it to be.

"You have not had much opportunity to dance tonight, have you?" Lady Ravensgate said sympathetically.

Collette shook her head, eyeing Draven. He knew he was cornered. He took a fortifying breath. "May I have the honor of the next dance, mademoiselle?"

Collette put a hand to her heart, pretending to be shocked. "Oh, but, sir, you needn't feel obligated."

"Nonsense. It would be my pleasure."

She gave a curtsy, and he bowed. "Excuse me."

He would return to collect her at the beginning of the next set. That would allow her a few minutes to think of a strategy.

"Do not mention the codes," Lady Ravensgate said in a hushed voice, though Collette had not asked for advice. "Lead him to the topic, but you should not give any indication you know anything about them."

"Of course." She had danced with dozens of men and initiated dozens of conversations she hoped would lead to the information she needed. Lady Ravensgate's tutelage had been wholly ineffective thus far. She always told Collette not to mention the codes. Her only other piece of advice seemed to be—

"And do not mention your father."

Collette nodded stiffly. That was the other. As though she needed to be told not to mention a known French assassin to a member of Britain's Foreign Office. What might have been more helpful were suggestions for encouraging the man to speak of his service during the recent war with Napoleon. Few of the men she had danced with had wanted to discuss the war or their experiences in it. The few she had managed to pry war stories from did not know anything about how the British had cracked the French secret code. And they seemed to know even less about the code the British used to encrypt their own messages.

But she had learned enough to believe that Draven ranked high enough that he would have access to the codes Britain used to encrypt their missives. It had taken a month, but she would finally speak with the man who had what she needed.

She watched the dancers on the floor turn and walk, link arms and turn again. The ladies' dresses belled as they moved, their gloved wrists sparkling in the light of the chandeliers. They laughed, a tinkling, carefree sound that carried over the strains of violin and cello. Not so long ago, Collette had danced just as blithely. Paris in the time of Napoleon had been the center of French society, and her father had been invited to every fete, every soiree.

He hadn't attended many—after all, he made people nervous—but when he was required to attend, he brought Collette as his escort. She couldn't have known that, a few years later, she would be doing those same dances in an effort to save his life.

The dance ended and Collette admired the fair-skinned English beauties as they promenaded past her. She had olive-toned skin and dark hair, her figure too curvaceous for the current fashions. Then Draven was before her, hand extended. With a quick look at Lady Ravensgate—that snake in the grass—Collette took his hand and allowed herself to be led to the center of the dance floor. The orchestra began to play a quadrille, and she curtsied to the other dancers in their square. She and Draven danced first, passing the couple opposite as they made their way from one side of the square to the other and back again.

Finally, she and Draven stood while the waiting couples danced, and she knew this was her chance. Before she could speak, Draven nodded to her. "How do you like the dance?"

She'd been unprepared for the question, and the only English response she could think of was *Hedgehog mating rituals are prolonged affairs in which the male and female circle one another.* In truth, the dance did seem like a mating ritual of sorts, but unless she wanted to shock the man, she had to find another comparison.

More importantly, she did not have much time to steer the conversation in the direction she needed. She had not answered yet, and he looked at her curiously. Collette cleared her throat.

"The dance does not remind me of hedgehogs."

His eyes widened.

Merde! Imbécile!

"Oh, that is not right," she said quickly. "Sometimes my words are not correct. I meant…what is the word…soldiers? Yes? The dancers remind me of soldiers as they fight in battle."

She blew out a breath. Draven was looking at her as though she were mad, and she did not blame him.

"You fought in the war, no?"

"I did, yes."

"I lived in the countryside with my parents, far from any battles."

"That is most fortunate." His gaze returned to the dancers.

"Did you lead soldiers into battle?" she asked. Most men puffed right up at the opportunity to discuss their own bravery.

"At times. But much of my work was done far from the battle lines."

Just her luck—a modest man.

She knew it was dangerous to press further. A Frenchwoman in England should know better than to bring up the recent war between the two countries, but her father's freedom was at stake. She could not give up yet.

"And what sort of work did you do behind the lines? I imagine you wrote letters and intercepted missives. Oh, but, sir, were you a spy?" Her voice sounded breathless, and it was not an affectation. She was breathless with nerves.

Draven flicked her a glance. "Nothing so exciting, mademoiselle. In fact, were I to tell you of my experiences, you would probably fall asleep. Ah, it is our turn again." They circled each other, and then she met with him only briefly as they came together, separated, and parted again, performing the various forms.

When he led her from the dance floor, escorting her back to Lady Ravensgate, she tried once again to engage him in conversation, but he deftly turned the topic back to the rainy weather they'd had. Lady Ravensgate must have seen the defeat on Collette's face because as soon as they reached her, she began to chatter. "Lieutenant Colonel, do tell me your opinion on Caroline Lamb's book. Is *Glenarvon* too scandalous for my dear cousin?"

Draven bowed stiffly. "I could not say, my lady, as I have not read it. If you will permit me, I see someone I must speak with." And even before he'd been given leave, he was gone.

"I take it things did not go well," Lady Ravensgate muttered.

"No."

The lady sighed in disgust, and not for the first time, Collette wondered whose side her "cousin" was on. She'd claimed to be an old friend of her father's, but might she be more of a friend to Louis XVIII and the Bourbons who had imprisoned Collette's father?

"Poor, poor Monsieur Fortier," Lady Ravensgate said.

Collette turned to her, cheeks burning. "Do not bemoan him yet, madam. I *will* free my father. Mark my words. I will free him, even if it's the last thing I do."

She knew better than anyone that love demanded sacrifice.

❦

Rafe Alexander Frederick Beaumont, youngest of the eight offspring of the Earl and Countess of Haddington, had often been called Rafe the Forgotten in his youth. He'd had such an easygoing, cheerful personality that he was easy to forget. He didn't cry to be fed, didn't fuss at naptime, and was content to be carried around until almost eighteen months of age when he finally took his first steps.

Once, the family went to a park for a picnic, and Rafe, having fallen asleep in the coach on the ride, was forgotten in the carriage for almost two hours. When the frantic nanny returned, she found the toddler happily babbling to himself and playing with his toes. When Rafe was three, he had gone with his older brothers and sisters on a walk at the family's country estate. It wasn't until bedtime, when the nanny came to tuck all the children in for the night, that the family realized Rafe was not in bed. He'd been found in the stables sleeping with a new litter of puppies.

In fact, no one could recall Rafe ever crying or fussing. Except once. And no one wanted to mention the day the countess had run off, leaving four-year-old Rafe alone and bereft.

By the time Rafe was nine, and quite capable of making himself so charming that he could have gotten away with murder (although Rafe was far too civilized to resort to murder), his new stepmother had pointed out to the earl that Rafe did not have a tutor. Apparently, the earl had forgotten to engage a tutor for his youngest. When the first tutor arrived, he pronounced Rafe's reading skills abysmal, his knowledge of history and geography nonexistent, and his mathematical ability laughable.

More tutors followed, each less successful than the last. The earl's hope was that his youngest son might enter the clergy, but by Rafe's fifteenth birthday, it was clear he did not have the temperament for the church. While Rafe's knowledge of theology lacked, his knowledge of the fairer sex was abundant. Too abundant. Girls and women pursued him relentlessly, and no wonder, as he'd inherited the height of his grandfather, a tall, regal man; the violet eyes of his great-aunt, who had often been called the most beautiful woman in England and was an unacknowledged mistress of George II; and the thick, dark, curling hair of his mother, of whom it was said her hair was her only beauty.

Rafe had been born a beautiful child and matured into an arresting male specimen. While academics were never his forte, men and women alike appreciated his wit, his style, and his loyalty. He was no coward and no rake. In fact, it was said Rafe Beaumont had never seduced a woman.

He'd never had to.

Women vied for a position by his side and fought for a place in his bed. Rafe's one flaw, if he had one, was his inability to deny the fairer sex practically anything. In his youth, he might have found himself in bed with a woman whom he'd had no intention of sleeping with only because he thought it bad form to reject her. Eventually, Rafe joined the army, not the navy as two of his brothers had done, primarily for the respite it offered. His time in service did not make it easier for him to rebuff a woman, but he did learn evasive maneuvers. Those maneuvers served him well after he joined Lieutenant Colonel Draven's suicide troop, and his unwritten assignment had been to charm information out of the wives and daughters of Napoleon's generals and advisers.

Back in London, Rafe was busy once again charming his way in and out of bedchambers. One of only twelve survivors from Draven's troop of thirty and an acknowledged war hero, Rafe had little to do but enjoy himself. His father gave him a generous allowance, which Rafe rarely dipped into, as charming war heroes who were also style icons were invited to dine nearly every night, given clothing by all the best tailors, and invited to every event held in London and the surrounding counties.

But even Rafe, who never questioned his good fortune, was not certain what to do about the overwhelming good fortune he'd been blessed with at his friend Lord Phineas's ball. Rafe, bored now that the Season was over, had talked his good friend into hosting the ball for those of their friends and acquaintances staying in London. Too many of Rafe's female acquaintances had attended, and he found himself struggling to (1) keep the ladies separated and therefore from killing one another, and (2) lavish his attentions on all of them equally.

Thus, he found himself hiding in the cloakroom of the assembly hall, hoping one of his gentleman friends might happen by so he could inquire as to whether the coast was clear.

"Oh, Mr. Beaumont?" a feminine voice called in a singsong voice. In the cloakroom, Rafe pushed far back into the damp, heavy cloaks that smelled of cedar and wool.

"Where are you, Mr. Beaumont?"

Rafe tried to place the woman's voice. He thought she might be the wife of Lord Chesterton. She was young, far too young for Chesterton, who was his father's contemporary. Rafe might think Chesterton a fool for marrying a woman young enough to be his daughter, but that didn't mean he wanted to cuckold the man.

"There you are!" she said, just as the light from a candle illuminated the cloakroom.

Rafe squinted and held up a hand, even as he realized the small, crowded room offered no opportunity for escape.

"You found me," he said, giving her a forced smile. "Now it is your turn to hide. I shall count to one hundred."

"Oh, no!" She moved closer, her skirts brushing against his legs. "I found you, and I want to claim my prize."

"Your prize?" he asked in mock surprise. He knew exactly what she wanted for a prize. "What might that be? A waltz at midnight? A kiss on the hand?" He moved closer to her, forcing her backward.

She bumped against the wall of the room, and he put a hand out to brace himself while he gazed down at her.

"I'd like a kiss," she said breathlessly as she looked up at him. "But somewhere far more interesting than my hand."

"More interesting, you say?" He leaned close to her, tracing his free hand along her jaw and down the length of her neck. "Close your eyes, then, and I will kiss you." His fingers traced the swell of her breasts, and with a quick intake of breath, she closed her eyes. Rafe blew out the candle, plunging them both into darkness. He leaned forward, brushed his lips across her cheek, and then bolted.

As he slipped into the servants' stairway, he heard her call after him. "Rafe! Play fair."

"Never," he murmured and climbed the steps with deliberate motions. Perhaps he could use the servants' corridors to find another staircase that would lead him out of the hall. He reached a landing, turned a corner, and Lady Willowridge smiled down at him, the plume in her turban shaking with her excitement.

"Looking for someone?" she asked in her smoky voice.

Rafe took her hand and kissed it. "You, my lady. Always you."

She was the last person he wanted to see. She was a widow and had claws as sharp as any tiger. Once she sank her nails into him, she would not let go.

When he lifted his hand, she yanked him toward her. She was uncommonly strong for a woman, he thought as he attempted not to stomp on her slippered feet. She wrapped her arms around his neck, and tilting her head back so he could feel the diamonds in her coiffure against his hands, she offered her mouth.

Rafe rolled his eyes. He could simply kiss her, but he'd been in this position before, and she'd tasted like tobacco and stale coffee. Why not give her a little thrill and give himself a reprieve?

Rafe slid his arms along hers, lifted her hands over his head, and spun her around. She gave a little squeak when he pressed her against the wall, pushing his own body against hers and leaning down to whisper in her ear, "Do you want to play a little game, my lady?"

She tried to nod, but her cheek was plastered to the wall. "Oh, yes," she said, her breath coming fast.

"Do you feel my hand here?" He touched the small of her back.

"Mmm-hmm."

"Close your eyes and imagine where I will touch you next." His hand slid over her buttocks.

She closed her eyes.

Rafe stepped back. "No peeking."

And he took the rest of the stairs two at a time and

burst into the servants' corridor. A footman carrying a tray of wineglasses raised his brows, but Rafe wasted no time on explanations. "Where is the exit?"

"To the ballroom, sir?"

"Dear God, man. No!" Rafe looked over his shoulder to make sure Lady Willowridge had not come for him yet. "To the street. Preferably a back alley."

"You just came from that exit, sir."

"There must be another."

"No, sir."

"Rafe Beaumont!" He heard Lady Willowridge's footfalls on the staircase. Panicked, he grabbed the servant's coat.

"Ballroom! Quickly!"

"Through there."

Rafe pushed on the panel and stumbled into the assembly rooms, where an orchestra was playing a waltz. Men and women twirled under the lights of the crystal chandeliers while the tinkling of laughter and champagne glasses accompanied the music.

A girl seated against the wall next to the panel gasped. "Mr. Beaumont!"

Rafe looked at the wallflower and then at the door he'd come through. It would not be long before Lady Willowridge deduced where he had gone.

"Dance?" he asked the wallflower.

She blushed prettily, then gave him her hand. He led her onto the floor and proceeded to turn her about in time to the music. After a minute or two, Rafe let out a sigh of relief. Why had he not thought of dancing with wallflowers before? They were unmarried and therefore relatively safe, not to mention he enjoyed dancing. He could dance all night. He could dance with every wallflower in atten—

Rafe's eyes widened and he met the wallflower's gaze directly. "Miss...uh?"

"Vincent," she answered sweetly. "Miss Caroline Vincent."

"Miss Vincent, your hand has apparently wandered to my...er, backside."

She smiled prettily. "I know. It is wonderfully round and firm."

Christ, he was doomed. If her father did not kill him, one of the ladies he'd abandoned—he spotted both Lady Willowridge and Lady Chesterton scowling at him—would. Rafe danced toward Phineas, catching his eye and giving him a pleading look. Phineas merely glared back at him, his expression clear: *You wanted this ball.*

What had he been thinking?

Miss Vincent squeezed his arse, and he nearly yelped.

"Would you prefer to find somewhere more private?" she asked, fluttering her lashes.

Rafe was always surprised at how many women actually fluttered their lashes and thought they looked appealing. To him, it always looked as if they had something stuck in their eyes.

"No," he answered.

Dear God, would this waltz never end?

Just then, he spotted Lieutenant Colonel Draven. Draven never came to these sorts of affairs. He'd probably come tonight because three members of his troop were in attendance. He spotted Rafe and gave a grudging nod of understanding when he spotted

Rafe's predicament. Rafe gave his former command-
ing officer a look of entreaty as he turned Miss
Vincent one last time and separated from her as the
music ended. He bowed, prepared to promenade her
about the room. He might take bets on who would
kill him first—her furious father, the irritated Lady
Willowridge, the abandoned Lady Chesterton, or the
icy Mrs. Howe. He'd forgotten that he'd left her in
the supper room.

"Excuse me, miss. I do not mean to interrupt,
but I must claim Mr. Beaumont for just a moment."
Draven put a hand on Rafe's shoulder and pulled him
away from Miss Vincent. Draven didn't wait for her
response. His word was an order and always had been.

Draven led Rafe away, and Rafe tried to walk
as though he had not a care in the world instead of
running for his life. Draven steered Rafe through the
assembly rooms, past numerous ladies who would
have stopped him if Draven hadn't looked so formidable. The lieutenant colonel led Rafe down the stairs,
past a row of liveried footman, out the door, and into
a waiting hackney.

Once they were under way, Rafe leaned his head
against the back of the seat. "That was too close."

About the Author

Jane Ashford discovered Georgette Heyer in junior high school and was captivated by the glittering world and witty language of Regency England. That delight was part of what led her to study English literature and travel widely in Britain and Europe. Her books have been published all over Europe as well as in the United States. Jane has been nominated for a Career Achievement Award by *RT Book Reviews*. Born in Ohio, she is now somewhat nomadic. Find her on the web at janeashford.com and on Facebook at facebook.com/JaneAshfordWriter, where you can sign up for her monthly newsletter.

Also by Jane Ashford

The Duke's Sons
Heir to the Duke
What the Duke Doesn't Know
Lord Sebastian's Secret
Nothing Like a Duke
The Duke Knows Best

Once Again a Bride
Man of Honour
The Three Graces
The Marriage Wager
The Bride Insists
The Bargain
The Marchington Scandal
The Headstrong Ward
Married to a Perfect Stranger
Charmed and Dangerous
A Radical Arrangement
First Season / Bride to Be
Rivals of Fortune / The Impetuous Heiress
Last Gentleman Standing